Only One Cozy Bed

ELISE KENNEDY

CONTENT WARNINGS

For content warnings about these novellas, please go to **elisekbooks.com**

ALSO BY ELISE KENNEDY

COZY NIGHTS IN VERMONT SERIES

Fall Inn Love

Falling in Vermont

LOVE IN FAIRWICK FALLS SERIES

Accidentally in Bloom

Wallflower in Bloom

Conveniently in Bloom

Unexpectedly Bookish

Falling at the Barre

TABLE OF CONTENTS

Pumpkin Spice

AND

Pour–Overs

Chapter One

BECCA MEETS LEO

And Literally Falls for Him

Becca Habar eyed the strange, hot dude sitting in *her* reserved train car. She sipped her pumpkin spice latte for the courage to confront him. The syrupy coffee was a rare luxury, much like her reserved seat on the train.

Standing in the doorway, she threw her shoulders back and shook her hair out of her face. *Get it, Habar.*

The train slowly rolled forward, restarting its journey through the winding New England countryside. She'd hopped in at Hartford and wanted an photo-worthy train ride through the changing fall leaves until she reached Vermont.

The Dude Sitting in Her Spot turned his head with an expectant look. "Bathroom's that way." He jerked his head to the left then returned to his newspaper, jolting his arms to straighten it out. Why was that movement so sexy? It reminded her of classic movie stars and TV reruns.

Becca took him in. His watch? Made of gears. His glasses? Horn-rimmed. His cardigan? Yep, it had honest-to-god elbow patches. This was all in stark contrast to his age, which had to be around thirty.

Becca bit back a smile. She totally had a thing for nerdy professor types.

"You're in my cabin," she said, smiling politely. She showed him her phone with the train reservation.

He looked up at her, and she caught the total weight of his stare. A firm jaw, kind eyes, clean-cut hair that was just a touch long, and a smoldering smile.

"This is a shared cabin. It says private booking not guaranteed." He held up his physical ticket. He returned to his paper and moved his legs to the side to give her more room. "Make yourself at home."

She zoomed in to look at the fine print on her phone. *Damn.* She wanted the cabin for her social posts. She couldn't film while some hot dude with the soul of a 90-year-old stared at her.

She chewed her lip. Glancing down the corridor, she saw all the other reserved cabins were filled. *Better stay with the devil I know, I guess.* She stepped inside and the door shut behind her. The cabin felt oddly intimate with the train noise blocked out.

She tried to toss her bag on the storage shelf but couldn't reach. The Hot Professor stood instantly and helped her shove her duffel up. He smelled like spice and shaving soap; even his smell was a throwback. What the hell? Was she having the weirdest sex dream ever?

"Thanks. Uh..." Becca worked up the courage to ask for what she wanted. "Could you switch sides?" She pointed to where he'd been sitting.

Hot Professor had taken the best seat in the cabin, facing the oncoming view of red and orange trees. "Since you're reading, I mean. I don't take the train much, and that side has the best view."

"Sorry, finders keepers. I can't read when I'm moving backward. Motion sickness." He smiled at her with a lopsided apologetic grin, pushing his glasses up. A jump of attraction landed in Becca's stomach.

They were standing knee to knee in the limited space of the cabin when the train slammed its brakes for the next stop. They launched forward, grabbing for stable surfaces.

Becca grasped his lapels without thinking, and his arms wrapped around her as she fell backward. A hand came up to the back of her head before it collided with the plastic train bench. A sharp pain shot through her funny bone as it hit the bench's hard surface.

They both landed tangled on the bench, her legs flopped over his, his arms around her with their chests smashed together. Only six more inches and their mouths would have made train-induced contact.

"Ow. Hand," said Hot Professor, squinting with pain. He'd saved her from a concussion or worse, and damn if he didn't smell better up close.

"Oh my god you saved my head. Are you okay?" Becca lifted her head so he could move his hand. The train lurched once more, and his arm tightened against her instinctively. Goose-bumps prickled Becca's arms, and heat ran down her spine.

A hiss of brakes told them they were safe to move and they sat up. Hot Professor rubbed his hand, blushing. Becca realized her legs were still draped over his, and her skirt had ridden up several inches. She swung her legs down quickly and tugged at her skirt.

"I'm okay, I think." He put on a brave face. "You okay? I didn't want you to crack your head open."

"I'm fine. Becca," she said suddenly, pointing to herself.

"You're Fine Becca?" he asked with a delighted smile. "I'm Relatively Unharmed Leo," he said, sticking his uninjured hand out. She gripped it. He looked so handsome and so tempting, sitting almost underneath her.

Maybe I do *have a concussion.* Or perhaps it was his scent causing her belly to flip flop. It was so rare to find an honest-to-god *man* in his twenties. Leo put all the man-children she'd dated to shame.

"What is that aggressively autumnal smell?" Leo asked, sniffing her.

And then she noticed behind Leo that her pumpkin spice latte now doubled as a Jackson Pollock painting on the wall.

"My latte. Pumpkin spice. Cause, you know, festive fall train ride." She gestured to the window and the foliage beyond.

"Ah. I've never had one, actually." Leo took out a cloth handkerchief and dabbed at the drops of latte that had fallen on his jacket.

"You're joking, right? Is this a bit?" Becca pointed at his handkerchief.

Leo stopped dabbing and stared at her. "A bit?"

"Yeah, like you pretend you've never heard of the internet, it's really 1965, etcetera. Oh no, wait. You're a hipster," she drew out the last word with realization. She grabbed napkins from her purse and wiped her latte from the wall.

"I'm not a hipster." He rolled his eyes and moved back to his seat but slid over on the bench. He gestured for her to sit next to him at the window.

Joy streaked through her as she realized he had given up the best seat in the cabin for her.

She settled down with excitement, snuggling in. "Being a hipster is like being a Trekkie. If you deny it, it only makes the force grow stronger."

"You're mixing your franchises." He grabbed his newspaper from the floor.

Becca waved a *whatever* hand at him while she recorded the train leaving the station.

Splashes of burnt umber, cardinal, sunrise orange, and bits

of green covered the trees as they took off from the station. It was drizzling in Massachusetts, and the pitter-patter of drops hit the glass as they gathered speed toward the next stop.

"What brings you on your festive train trip?" Leo asked, his elbow grazing her arm on the snug bench seat.

"Job interview," she sighed wistfully toward the window. She was a book-obsessed, minimally paid publicist at a major publishing house on her way to Benning Falls, Vermont. She couldn't stand living in the city any longer. She dreamed of running Benning Books, a classic New England bookstore she'd been to for several of her authors' book tours. She wanted to hustle for something real, not just flash-in-the-pan publicity runs on the latest children's fantasy series.

She knew there was another candidate in the running for the role, but she hoped to god it was some old-school local she could outgun with energy, ideas, and publishing connections.

"You?" She turned to him. "Are you off to write the Great American Novel on a typewriter you've stashed in that duffel?"

He snorted as he flipped his paper. "Silly Becca, typewriters don't travel well." He peered at her with a mischievous grin before settling into the sports section.

She turned back to the window, smiling with heat sizzling under her skin from that look.

"That's why I brought my quill," he murmured into the paper.

Becca let out a very unattractive boom of laughter at his sly humor and saw him smirking.

"Oh, and thanks. For the seat," Becca said suddenly. She smiled at him with all the gratitude she could muster. She was going for a job interview, but she hadn't had a vacation in years.

He stared back, his gray eyes connecting with hers. "Everyone deserves a special view of New England in the fall." His quiet voice sent reverberations down into her depths.

She felt a quickening in her chest and realized she should tear her eyes from his gaze before she threw herself onto this stranger's lap, ripped his glasses off and landed her mouth on his.

Distraction. She needed one badly.

She turned the Instagram camera to selfie mode and checked to make sure she looked half-way decent after her tumble. She snapped a quick selfie while the trees blew past in the background.

"You're ignoring the view in favor of social media?" he said, quirking an eyebrow at her.

"I'm *celebrating* the view with social media, thank you," she said, waggling her head at him.

"Just saying. Best seat in the house, and you stare at your own face instead of living in the moment."

How dare he? "I am not staring at myself, Leonard—"

"Leopold," he interrupted.

"Like reading a paper is any better. It's like my feed, but it's outdated, boring, and rubs off on your fingers. Plus," she sighed, realizing that she was defending a life she didn't want. "I have to maintain an aspirational social presence for my current job. That's why I want a different one."

"Are you interviewing to be the Social Media Director of Autumnal Trees?" He grinned at her.

She rolled her eyes. "That job sounds fantastic, actually, but no." *Butthead.* "I work in publishing, and I'm interviewing at a bookstore. To run it, actually."

He nodded, impressed. "Running a bookstore sounds pretty amazing. Think you're up to the challenge?"

Just like a man to doubt her. She might only be twenty-seven, probably the same age as him, but she'd made a life for herself that she could only have dreamed of as a kid. Now, she was ready to claim her next dream: a cozy, profitable life in

Vermont surrounded by books, her favorite thing in the world.

"I know I'm up to the challenge." She turned and smiled into the window, enjoying the view on the way to what would hopefully be her forever home.

They passed the remaining hour and a half in easy silence. She made several videos to post on social, and though he grinned at her, he didn't make her feel self-conscious again. He even offered to hold the phone to capture a wistful angle of her staring out the window, but she politely declined.

After he finished his paper, she expected him to bust out a pipe and glass of scotch. Instead, he produced a battered copy of the latest spy thriller and settled in, checking his watch briefly.

After posting her tenth story to social, she heard the train conductor announce Benning Falls. She gathered her things as Leo was doing the same.

She pulled her coat on. "Benning Falls is your stop?"

"Nothing gets past the maple tree's Instagram coordinator," he said as he gathered his coat and bag.

"Oh my gosh, I was on my phone for like, fifteen minutes." She tried to grab her bag from the rack above her.

As the train lurched to a stop, she started to fly backward again, but his hand claimed her waist to steady her. Her eyes met his for a moment before she allowed one split second glance at his mouth.

"Thank you," she said breathlessly as he handed her bag to her. She looked up after checking the cabin one last time, and he was already on the platform. There was a small jump down from the train, and he held out a hand to help her down.

She eyed his hand briefly before taking it.

No big deal. Just a kind, bookish Prince Charming who smells great. No need to start planning the wedding.

Yet.

He held her hand firmly as she made the jump in heels, and Becca was sad to let his hand go.

"Wish me luck on the interview," she said up at him, enjoying the way he smiled down at her. His broad shoulder straightened and his eyes went soft as they met hers.

"I don't think I should. Something tells me the other candidate might just be the best *man* for the job." His eyebrows waggled at her with a sparkle in his eye as he hefted his bag over his shoulder. She angled her head in confusion as he walked confidently across the street.

To Benning Books.

Her Benning Books.

Son of a bitch.

Chapter Two

IN THE BOOKSTORE
Of Becca's Dreams

Becca stood motionless on the train platform with shock as she watched the door of Benning Books swing closed behind Leo.

She'd sat next to the other candidate for her dream job for *two hours* and he hadn't said a word.

Bastard. She felt her cheeks flush with embarrassment.

Nothing was going to prevent her from getting this job. The job she desperately wanted to believe was her destiny. Without looking around at the adorable town, she marched across the street and swung open the door. She saw Leo shaking the hand of George Williams, the owner of Benning Books. They both turned around as she came in and Leo sent her a warm, knowing smile. She ignored the heat pooling in her belly.

"Ms. Habar," George said. "You're early."

"I couldn't wait to see the store in person again and pick up a book or two." She sent him a sparkly smile. A little charm never hurt.

"Well." George clapped his hands together. "Let's get started. Leopold, you're with me. Becca, feel free to make yourself at home. You know where everything is."

Leo sent her a questioning look as he followed George into the back office. *Ha.* Becca triumphed at not having shared that she'd known George for years, and that his bookstore was her favorite stop on her author tours. She always went out of her way to make sure her authors made an appearance in the small town she adored.

Becca took a minute to stare out onto Main Street. It was peak leaf-peeping season, and the town was buzzing with fall tourists. They meandered in the crisp air outside the store and warmed up with hot drinks at Two Dog Coffee next door.

Becca looked around the large bookstore. It was an institution in Benning Falls, and like many things in the town, it hadn't changed much since it opened decades ago.

Better take some time to get a leg up on her competition. She explored the antique, collectible books displayed in the front, and eventually rounded her way to the large, more modern bookcases in the back. A huge fireplace sat in the middle of the back wall, surrounded by staff picks and best-sellers.

She loved the charm of the store, but knew they could double their revenue if they tried online sales and posted to social media. She also had a million connections within the publishing industry, all of whom would love a gorgeous trip upstate for special author events.

She wandered through the tables and overheard a group of girlfriends talking about the latest romance bestseller. She clocked them as millennials who loved Hallmark-style holiday movies. She knew just the series they'd love to cuddle up with.

A blonde woman held up a flowery cover with a bold font.

"Oh, I love this one," she told her friends. "It's come up on my feed like a million times."

Becca couldn't help but insert herself into the conversation. "If you're obsessed with that book, you have to read the author's other series. It's set in a bakery in France." She pointed to the series on the shelf.

"I've heard such good things about that," the customer said, grabbing a few books off the shelf. Becca fell into an easy conversation with the women. After a while, all of them grabbed armfuls of books and wandered to the checkout counter.

"Do you work here? I'd love for you to get commission," the blonde woman said, angling her head toward her friends at the counter.

"Not yet," a thundering voice boomed behind her, "but maybe you can put in a good word with the owner."

Becca turned around and saw Leo and George behind her. Leo was peering at her with that warm, quiet smile. She ripped her eyes away from his. She needed to stay focused. *In it to win it.*

But the memory of his hand gripping her waist flashed through her memory and goosebumps fluttered down her arm. *Go away. I don't need to catch feelings right now.*

"Becca, it's your turn. Would you mind sticking around, Leo? There's going to be a part two." George sent an excited glance to each of them. *He's enjoying hiring his replacement just a little too much.* She fell into step with the spry older man.

"You did great back there." He threw his thumb to the romance section.

"It's my job to sell books," Becca said, shrugging. "I love doing it, and I'm pretty good at it." She sent him a confident smile that she hoped covered her nerves.

"I know you are." George flopped into a groaning leather

desk chair in his office. "Real question is, why the hell are you here? Young person like you really wants to settle in Benning Falls and run a dusty old bookstore when you could be livin' it up in the big city?"

"George, I want to take this store and continue your legacy." He had to know how much she wanted this. That this wasn't some escapist fantasy that she'd tire of in a year or two.

"Did you know I grew up in Burlington?" she asked. George shook his head. "I've loved my time in publishing, getting to work with amazing authors and coming to adorable bookstores like yours on author tours. But it's just not enough anymore. I miss Vermont. I hate the city and love it here." Even now, the longer she was here, the more she felt the anxiety evaporating from her chest. She just wasn't built for a big city full of noise and people, or her long commute from cheaper rent in Connecticut. It was all too much and sent her nervous system into overdrive.

"I want to see someone's face light up when they find the exact story they need to read. Host author events, community events. Create something special as the epicenter of town. You know your bookstore has always been my favorite stop. I've pretty much blackmailed every author I work with to come here just so I can spend time in Benning Falls."

"I know you helped manage one of those big-box bookstores a while back. How would you run this place? I'll be retired but I need to keep the store in the black. It's my retirement money. Unless my husband Maurice finally hits it big with his retirement hobby: French pastries," he said, patting his belly.

Becca saw her opportunity. "I'd keep the physical store pretty much the same. Your layout works. The vibe is warm and welcoming. I'd focus on opening up new lines of business online. Creating a social media presence, allowing people to buy ebooks and swag from you." She pointed at his Benning Books t-shirt.

"That sounds like a lot of work for one person." George eyed her.

"The job would be my focus, one hundred percent. I could set up social channels within a week and I have a great web designer who could set something up fast and cheap."

He squinted at her, sizing her up. "Vermont can get awful lonesome in the winter."

"Then all the better to be at the store where I can see other people," she said, arching an eyebrow. She bit her cheek, trying not to get too excited.

George slapped his legs hard and stood up. "Follow me."

Becca was jolted back to reality. It was over? Her interview had been a lot shorter than Leo's. That could be really good, or really terrible.

Chapter Three

BECCA NAILS THE INTERVIEW
But Not Her Schedule

She hustled after George, her heels clip-clopping on the antique oak floor. They stopped in the main area of the bookstore. Leo walked through the front door with two coffees. George motioned for them to join him in the middle of the room. Leo handed Becca one of the to-go cups.

"Sorry, no pumpkin spice," he said, sipping his own. "But they make a decent pour-over."

Becca stared down at the cup with suspicion. "Thank you," she managed slowly. Why would he go out of his way for her? Shouldn't he be throwing her under the bus any chance he got?

"Sorry for not telling you about the job interview," he said, pushing his glasses up with an embarrassed smile.

Flip flop went her libido. *Stop it. Bad girls,* she scolded her stupid brain and lady parts.

She took a sip. *Blech.* Hardly any sweetener. It was still a nice gesture though. "You are not forgiven," she said, walking to George as Leo rolled his eyes at her.

George gave them an unexpected assignment: spend an hour in the store and pitch him something they'd change.

Becca looked at her watch. She needed to catch the final train through town that night up to her gram's house a few hours away. She'd be cutting it close but she could make it. Even if she missed the train, she'd figure something out. There had to be a million B&Bs around here.

They split up and wandered the store. Becca observed people browsing happily. They tended to wander in and then wander out. *What would make them stop and stay?*

Benning Falls tripled in size during the fall. The tourist season practically paid everyone's annual bills. She noticed that most of the tourists were missing the store's swag – buttons, stickers, mugs, etc. They had been shoved in the back with the Vermont-centric books. George used the front tables to display popular series.

Not bad, but I can do better.

She peered around to find Leo scanning books with his head buried in his phone. How would he connect with customers like that?

An hour later, George called them to the back room. "Let's hear it. How will you make this place even better?" He stared at Becca.

She and Leo stood shoulder to shoulder in the small office. He radiated warmth and she tried to keep her head on straight, rather than picturing what she wanted to do to him, which was becoming more NSFW by the moment.

"I think you're leaving money on the table with your layout. In the fall, your store's swag and the Vermont books need to be front and center. I'd order more local and store-branded items to sell, really playing up the great history you have. Then I'd rearrange the store from September to December so it's best formatted for tourists. Let them sit and settle into the space so they take home an experience, not just a book or two."

George nodded slowly. "That's the one to beat," he said to Leo, jerking his head toward Becca.

Leo shrugged off his cardigan, revealing a button-up and sleeves rolled halfway up his arms. *Oh come on.* It was like he'd been cast straight out of her professor fantasy. His surprisingly muscular forearms were tan and reminded her of a rock climber's physique. She realized he'd been speaking for a full minute and she'd been ogling him, not paying attention.

"Which is why I'd raise the price by one to two dollars on each bestselling hardcover and any tourist-related sales. I'd also suggest putting in a beverage and snack counter to buffer your book sales. Not everyone wants to carry a book with them, but most people could use a bottle of water."

George eyed both of them with skepticism. "What would you both fix about the other's idea?"

Interesting. He was testing them to see if they saw the flaws that he did.

Becca jumped in. "There's a coffee shop next door and a general store around the corner. Why would we want to compete with that? Why not try to offer things they don't have?"

George turned to Leo. "And you?"

Leo shrugged and put his hands in his pockets. "Her plan sounds pretty great. I don't think the locals would like it. But the tourists might."

Uh oh. If there was one thing old-school Vermonters hated, it was new things that didn't originally come from there. Becca refuted his comment with probably more than a little fire and they spent a half hour debating why each strategy was better.

A high-pitched whistle caught Becca's attention and as she glanced out the window, she saw the worst possible thing: her evening train leaving the station.

Fuuuuuck.

George slapped his thighs again as he stood up. "You two are just gangbusters. I've had the most fun talking with you. I need to think about it, but you both know I want to move quickly. Can you come back tomorrow morning? I'd like you to meet the team and tell them your ideas. We have a staff meeting at nine."

Leo and Becca agreed to come back and thanked him for his time. They grabbed their bags and headed out onto Main Street, which was already cloaked in darkness.

"Shit shit shit," Becca said under her breath.

"Everything okay?" Leo said as he shrugged on his coat in the chilly night air.

"I was supposed to catch that train to go to my gram's house. She lives a few hours away and can't drive at night." She furiously tapped on her phone, scrolling, tapping more. "There are like, no hotel rooms. No Airbnbs. Nothing. And the nearest Uber is an hour away. I'd have to pay a month's rent to get them here."

Panic rose in her throat. Should she talk to George? She knew him a little. But what did it say about her as the potential manager of his business if she couldn't even take care of herself?

"I'm sorry you missed your train," Leo said with concern. "Any friends to call? Family?"

Becca shook her head and chewed her lip, staring at her phone screen, willing a room to appear in her search. "I'll be fine. I'll figure something out." She put on a brave smile and glanced up briefly at him.

"I mean, it's 7 p.m. in the middle of nowhere Vermont. It's more likely you'll get eaten by a bear than find a last-minute hotel room during leaf-peeping season." He paused for a second, waiting for her to respond.

He bent down to catch her gaze. "Let's grab some food. The

best place in town closes in an hour and we can't have you unhoused and unfed."

Her head shot up from her phone. "Dinner with you? Aren't we... We're competing for the same job." She shook her head in disbelief. "Why are you being so nice?"

"You're a human who seems pretty great, and it's just a job. I'd hate to think of you sleeping on the street as I lie in my cushy warm room at the Maple Inn."

Maybe if she refreshed her phone again, she'd find more rooms. Panic started to claw through her. Leo shook her shoulder a little. She finally lowered her phone.

"I was only joking, Becca." Her name sounded so nice in his rumbling baritone voice. He had such kind eyes, and they felt like a lifeline right now. "It'll be fine. Come on. Let's grab food and we can figure something out."

Chapter Four

BECCA FINDS A BED

And Makes a Deal

Her stomach rumbled on cue. "I do need to eat at some point." She hadn't had breakfast or lunch because she'd been so nervous. "Okay. Lead the way, Professor."

"Oh I'm the professor since I gave the better pitch today?" They fell into easy step with each other.

"You are obviously the professor due to the abundance of elbow patches you're wearing," she said, finding a smile despite her situation. "How do you know where to go?"

"I grew up about an hour away, but my parents moved a few years ago. This is my favorite burger joint in the area." They walked toward a building that sat along the train line. He opened the door for her, letting her walk in first. She felt this zing of something whenever she got in close proximity with him. She rolled her shoulders and tried to ignore it. She'd been reading too many romance novels lately.

The burger bar had a concrete floor, old neon signs and antique beer bottles in the walls, but had a gleaming large bar in the middle filled with nicely dressed tourists. Becca and Leo grabbed a table and promptly ordered two beers and two burgers.

Becca's face was glued to her phone from the moment they sat down. Her phone only had thirty percent battery left, of course. Damn her luck. She'd tried every house-sharing site she could think of until she finally – *finally* – found an open room. "Aha!" Her fist pumped with victory. "There's one place." She tapped into the photos to see the details and her hopes fell.

Leo peered over her shoulder. "Zero reviews, a shared living space, and that definitely looks like a murder basement."

Becca had to agree it had murder vibes. Poor lighting, old bedding, no windows. "It beats the street. Literal beggars can't be choosers, Professor," she said, sipping the beer that had appeared in front of her.

His brows furrowed. "It doesn't look safe. Look." He turned toward her and leaned in. "I know you don't know me, and I know we both want the job, but why don't you stay in my room tonight? It has to be better than getting murdered. Or sleeping on, I don't know, a literal pile of leaves?"

Becca blinked in shock. "I don't even know you. That's ludicrous."

"I know, I know. But you don't know," he peered over at her screen, "Lester G either. I just don't want you...out there." He gestured to the street.

Becca considered his offer as she took a slow bite of burger. He was probably right. Staying with a dude named Lester could never end well.

He settled in, selling hard. "What do you need to know about me to feel comfortable? I have two older sisters. My mom is a nurse, my dad is an accountant."

"Maybe your last name?" Becca said. Skepticism at his plan warred with her desire to spend more time with him. *And not wanting to sleep on the sidewalk.*

"Schmidt," he said. "Here, we can FaceTime my sister. Her phone is permanently attached to her hand. You'd love her," he muttered with an arched eyebrow as he pulled out a mobile phone and the familiar ring started.

"Hey," Becca whacked his arm. "My phone is not attached to my hand." She threw her phone down as she realized she was still holding it.

His phone kept ringing. "You're homeless for the night, and you've checked your follower count three times since we got here," he said with a dry look.

"Okay fine, maybe I use it as a coping mechanism, but I don't know if you're aware that I'm in a *bit* of a situation right now, *Leopold*." He smiled back at her, and she realized she was almost laughing.

"Butthead!" A tinny voice sounded out of Leo's phone with all the warmth and affection of an older sister. "Is the world ending? I didn't think you knew how to FaceTime." A pretty blonde woman stared at Leo through the screen.

"Hey, Britt. I need a favor."

"Make it quick. I was in the middle of filming that new dance for my channel, and you ruined a take."

Oh god, I would *love her,* Becca thought with chagrin.

"I need you to tell this woman that I'm not a murderer. She needs a place to stay in Vermont for the night and doesn't have a room booked. I'm trying to convince her that a shared hotel room with me is better than a murder room in a house across town."

"In October? Is she brain-dead? Who goes to Vermont without a resy?"

Becca leaned into the camera frame, smiling despite her predicament. "She's mostly bad at time management."

"Oh hi! Shit, sorry," Britt laughed. "Leo is not a murderer. I might be biased as his big sister, but I think he's pretty great and mostly a squishy nerd who needs to get out more. Maybe this could count as your annual date, Leo."

Becca wanted to be Britt's best friend already. "Does he snore?" She was enjoying this, despite her desperate circumstances.

"Hmm, I don't think so, but I do remember him ripping some pretty gnarly farts when he was little—"

"And we're done now. Bye Britt," Leo said quickly. Becca heard raucous laughter on the other side of the call as Leo hung up.

He rubbed his hands over his face. "Please pretend you didn't hear that." He looked at her with flushed cheeks.

God he was cute. All her intuition told her she could trust him. Or was that her libido? He exuded an air of warmth and comfort, and looked perfectly at home in the dive bar. His hair had been neatly combed to the side, and she wondered what it would look like mussed up from sleep.

"Okay," Becca said. "But I sleep on top of the covers, and pay you for half the room."

"You drive a hard bargain, but you've got a deal." Leo stuck out his hand. Becca grabbed it and felt his warm, firm grasp. His fingers were calloused and his thumb rubbed the edge of her hand. He had steel-gray eyes and long lashes behind his glasses. His mouth was sculpted and firm, and she wondered fleetingly what it might be like to kiss it. What it might feel like if she ran her mouth over his. Wondered how a bookish professor type had calloused hands and strong arms that protected her.

"Two originals with onion rings?" a waiter said, staring at

them. Becca dropped her hand quickly. How long had she been staring at Leo? She saw his cheeks go red again.

Holy lord was it going to be hard to keep her hands off of him tonight.

Chapter Five

HOW MANY BEDS ARE THERE?
Hint: Only One

Becca opened the door to their room in the gorgeous Maple Inn, the only hotel in Benning Falls. She'd never stayed here on her author tours, but she'd always wanted to.

They walked into the cozy room, covered in shades of burgundy, dark wood and crisp, cream wallpaper. The queen bed loomed large in the center of the room, and two small side chairs sat across from it. Becca stood in one corner chewing her lip, bag still on her shoulder while Leo sat his stuff down on the small dresser.

He glanced at her as he unpacked his bag. "Is this what you do in your own house? Pick a corner and stand in it?" He smiled at her, trying to put her at ease.

"I don't know the protocol here," she said. "I thought I'd let you get the first pick of everything and then I'll settle in."

Leo laughed. "It's a ten-by-ten-foot space. Make yourself at home in what little space there is."

Becca sat her stuff down and took her boots off. She then realized with panic that she hadn't packed any pajamas. She normally just wore whatever she'd last left at her gram's house, or sometimes nothing at all. She ripped open her bag, searching for anything that could double as sleepwear.

"Everything okay?" Leo asked as she sent clothes flying.

"Uh, yep." She had to stall. This sleepover between acquaintances was about to get a lot more R-rated unless she thought of something. Worst-case scenario, she could just sleep in her clothes. She glanced down at her outfit: pantyhose, a tight plaid skirt, and a button-down shirt. Oof.

"Which side do you prefer?" Leo asked, pointing to the bed.

"Doesn't matter," she lied. She slept on the left side, but she was aware she only had a place to stay out of his good graces.

"I sleep on the right. Want to change first?" he asked, pointing to the bathroom.

Ha. She wished. "Nope, go ahead. Just going to get settled," she said, weakly pointing to her bag.

The bathroom door closed and Becca rummaged through her things again, willing a pair of leggings and a t-shirt to magically appear. She glanced around the room in panic, trying to figure out how to piece together clothes she could sleep in.

The only fabric she spied were the curtains and extra towels. She looked in the closet for a bathrobe, but no such luck.

Leo came out of the bathroom in flannel pajama pants slung low with a soft gray Henley over his white t-shirt. Becca's mouth watered at how much she wanted him.

Fate was so, so unfair.

She darted into the bathroom and brushed her teeth, washed her face. She debated hiding there until he was asleep, but that seemed weirder than sleeping in your interview clothes.

When she came out of the bathroom, the top blankets were folded on her side. Leo sat up under the sheets on his side, reading a book. His broad chest spanned a considerable portion of the bed. She might prefer her books digital, but there was something deliciously alluring about a guy in bed holding a worn copy of what was clearly his favorite book.

She sheepishly sat her stuff down, plugged in her phone on her side and tucked herself under her blankets.

"Is this a new viral trend?" Leo asked. Becca sent him a puzzled look over her shoulder. She tried not to stare at how picture-perfect he looked. His surprisingly sculpted arms and chest in a cuddly-soft shirt with those glasses and that face.

"Wearing business clothes to bed?" He clarified.

Shit. She had to come clean. "I keep basic overnight stuff at my gram's house, and that includes PJs, unfortunately. I'll be fine, though. I sleep like the dead," she said quickly, flailing her hand to distract him from the conversation. "What time do you get up in the morning?"

"Do you want to borrow something?" His brows were drawn together with concern.

Gulp. Sleeping in a Leo-scented cocoon – no, wait, a stranger-scented cocoon – overnight? She didn't really know him, even after meeting his amazing sister, who she was definitely going to look up online later. She'd lose her damn mind if she started thinking of Leo as a friend or possibly even more. He was her competition for her dream job, and she had to keep her game face on.

"Oh no, I don't want to impose. You don't even know me," she said, shaking her head.

"I know you, Becca. You're the girl who was really nice to the waiter even after they messed up your order—"

"Those ordering systems are so confusing," she countered.

He peered at her with kind eyes and a soft lopsided smile. "You went out of your way to help several of George's customers just for the fun of it. I saw you talking to that mom and boy and totally turned around his meltdown."

Becca felt her insides turn to jelly. Who noticed those kinds of things?

"And I'm pretty sure I saw you pick up a piece of litter on the sidewalk even after you figured out you didn't have a place to stay. I'm confident you're not going to abscond with my shirt or identity or liver in the middle of the night," he said, his eyes back on his book.

Abscond. Ugh, why was he so adorable? She chewed her lips to keep them from splitting into an embarrassed, melty smile. He was thorough in his observations, that was for sure. She felt the itch and closeness of her button-down and pantyhose. "A shirt would be nice," she said quietly from under the cover, not wanting to meet his gaze.

"Here," he said, sitting up. "This is the warmest one I packed. It's supposed to get down to twenty-five tonight and these rooms get pretty drafty." He lifted his arms over his head and pulled the back of his Henley long-sleeved shirt, the white shirt underneath riding up to reveal his abs. He handed the warm – lord, it was still warm – shirt to her with a sheepish grin. She tried very, very hard not to stare at his sculpted arms and the tattoos at the top of his left arm.

A tattooed. Hot. Professor. In her bed. Why did he have to be the one guy she couldn't just say *fuck it* to and pounce on?

"Why are you being so nice? You've given me your room, your bed, your shirt. Did I hit the job competition lottery?" She was suspicious a catch was coming.

"Oh, don't mistake my chivalry tonight for weakness tomorrow. I am coming for you, Habar. Know that it's been my long-held dream to move to Benning Falls and run a shop just like George's." He leaned on his side and waggled his eyebrows. "You might want to shower first because maybe I'll use all the hot water tomorrow as a strategic job competition strategy." His smile played on his lips.

"You'll use a strategic strategy on me?" Becca said, laughing. "My boots are officially quaking." He tossed a pillow at her and she dodged it as she hopped up to change.

She changed in the bathroom and realized a small problem. Becca was definitely what you'd call short, but Leo's shirt still only hit her upper thigh. A little high for 'Hi we met on a train can I sleep by you' company, but she was a modern woman and was determined to make it work.

AKA run to the bed really fast and dart under the covers.

She opened the bathroom door and felt a wave of gratitude that the lights were off, except for the glow of her charging phone. Leo had burrowed under the sheets. As she got into bed, they negotiated the bathroom schedule so they could make George's 9 a.m. meeting with time to spare.

Becca was sure to stick to her edge of the bed and she noticed that Leo was also on the edge of his side, with a valley of space in between them. Still, it was only polite to warn him about her alleged sleeping habit.

"I've been told by exes that I tend to ummm," she cleared her throat, "...aggressively snuggle?"

Leo peered over his shoulder at her. "You plan to aggressively snuggle me? Like to death?"

"No, I mean, I've been told I migrate in the middle of the night and snuggle unknowingly. So, if you want to build a pillow wall or something, that's fine. I can get the chair cushions."

"I...think we'll be fine," he said, shaking his head as he settled back down.

She really, really hoped so.

Chapter Six

BECCA'S DREAM

Is Very Realistic

Warm, strong lips grazed Becca's and she felt delicious friction between her legs as she straddled something hard. She smelled something intoxicating that ignited her core and she deepened her dream kiss.

A tongue grazed her lip and she opened for more. She ran her hands through her mystery dream lover's hair, scraping her nails and feeling the thick, smooth strands. A moan escaped him, his large bulge meeting her cleft at the perfect place. Strong arms came around her and pulled her against him and she ground her hips into him. Strong hands moved from her waist and grabbed handfuls of her ass, pulling her hard toward him. She came up for air and saw her dream make-out partner was Leo, glasses off and face flushed, sleepy with wanting. She'd thought about kissing him all day, so she scraped her teeth along his delicious lower lip and bit it, then traced it with her tongue.

"Ow," Dream Leo said suddenly. "Maybe not so hard?"

Huh. This wasn't usually how her sexy dreams went. She felt a jostling, with the hands still on her ass and she opened her eyes...only to find real Leo's face underneath hers.

Oh shit. That hadn't been a dream. She looked down and realized she was actually straddling the real Leo and – whew – his actual hands were still clutching her ass and *something* was pushing against her just right and...holy shit.

"Why are you kissing me," she said, now freaked out. Her eyes went wide and she scrambled off of him.

"You started kissing *me*," Leo said sleepily. He didn't look too mad about it, though.

Becca looked around, getting her surroundings. She was definitely on Leo's side of the bed. In fact, he hadn't moved an inch all night and was still hugging the edge. Becca's hands flew up to her face. She had somehow migrated over to Leo's side, on top of him, and then made out with him while he slept.

"Oh my god, I'm so sorry," she said through muffled hands. "I thought I was dreaming."

"You dreamed about making out with me?" he said, turning on his side to stare at her, a sleepy eyebrow arched. His face loomed over hers and she realized she was still way too close. A traitorous pull started in her and she thought about pulling his head down to pick up from where they had left off.

"No," she lied. "I had a generic make-out dream." She pushed farther away toward her side of the bed.

"Ehhh. I distinctly heard my name as I woke up," he said, smirking at her. He was looking like he'd caught her with her hand in the cookie jar.

Which was so unfair because that was exactly how she felt.

She scooted again. "I'm going to lie on the floor. It's hard to aggressively cuddle from two feet below." She gathered her blanket that had crumpled at the bottom of the bed.

"You can't sleep on the floor. You'll freeze." He got up suddenly and grabbed the chair cushions. "I think a pillow wall will protect my virtue just fine from your marauding mouth."

Who spoke like that, Becca glanced at the clock, *at 3:30 in the morning?* And why did it stoke her fire even hotter?

He put the cushions in a line down the middle of the bed and settled under his sheets. Becca was so embarrassed but also really didn't want to sleep on the floor.

"Fine, but if it happens again, I'll just get ready early," she said, settling down on her side but staring at him.

He had his back to her. "Becca?"

"Yeah?" She hoped he wouldn't tell her to get ready right now. She craved sleep. Anything to forget the last five minutes.

"If I wake up with you on top of me again," he said slowly and quietly, "I won't be the one to stop it."

Becca sucked in a breath. Tension sizzled in the air between them.

Great. She'd have no problem getting back to sleep now. Just a hot guy who wanted her only three feet away. She'd had a bit of a dry spell the last few months and his arms and chest had felt so good. He'd pulled her closer and harder. She shivered thinking about his body under hers and between her legs.

"Cold?" he said from the other side of the bed.

She wished.

"Just settling in. Night." Becca didn't move. Hopefully he'd think she was asleep. Her face flushed at the thought of having to see him in the morning. Maybe even all day, depending on what George had planned for them. She eventually fell asleep, thinking about her strategies for the next day.

BECCA WOKE up to sun streaming through the window and heard the door to the room click shut. She pieced together where she was from the fuzzy details that were starting to come back to her. *In a guy's room. In Vermont. Wearing his clothes.*

She looked over at his side of the bed. He was gone. His stuff was gone. Panic zinged through her and she grabbed her phone. Had she overslept?

No, phew. It was only 7:50. She hopped up and got ready, appreciating the extra privacy. *Leo probably knew that,* she thought as she brushed her teeth. His older sisters had trained him well.

She thanked her lucky stars she had packed extra clothes for her gram's house that could double as business attire. As she left the bathroom, showered and changed for the day, she heard a rap on the door. She opened it slowly and saw a bright-eyed Leo on the other side.

"Brought some sustenance." He held up two coffees and a bag of pastries.

"When you do the white knight in shining armor thing, you go all out," she said, swinging open the door.

He'd changed into a different button-down, and had a corduroy blazer thrown over it.

She felt like a number-one creep as she tried to catch a whiff of his aftershave as he walked by. Goosebumps ran down her arm as she remembered wallowing in his Leo-scented shirt last night.

"I did get an *extra* special turndown service I got last night," he teased, setting everything on the side table.

Becca groaned. She would never live this down. "Leo, I'm so sorry. I feel absolutely terrible. I invaded your space while you were sleeping—"

"I'm just teasing." He handed her a to-go coffee cup. "It was an accident. Not an altogether unpleasant one. Donut?" He offered her the bag.

She grabbed one and took a big bite of a chocolate-glazed piece of heaven. She downed it with a huge sip of coffee and choked, almost spitting it across the room. "Holy cats, this is terrible." She looked at the coffee in her hand.

"Oh, that's probably mine. I drink mine black. Here." He switched cups with her, rubbing the lipstick off the cup she handed him.

She sipped her new coffee tentatively. It was sweet and milky. Much better. "How do you know how I like my coffee?"

"Your grimace yesterday made it pretty obvious that I didn't get your order right, so I tried again today, channeling Becca energy."

A snort ripped through her. "Becca energy?"

"Yeah, you know. Bubbly, high energy, loves all the latest everything. I figured someone like you cares less about a perfect cup of coffee and more about getting juiced up for the day. Hence," he sipped his cup delicately, "the massive amount of sugar you're consuming now."

She finished inhaling her donut and threw the wrapper away. "I think this was a *strategic strategy* to give me a sugar crash in about an hour."

"Both things can be true," he said, smirking at her from behind his cup. "Hey, you have something," he said, pointing to his mouth.

Shit. She was such a neanderthal when it came to donuts. She rubbed at her face.

"May I?" He walked up to her and rubbed his thumb against the side of her mouth.

Becca's breath caught.

"Got it," he said quietly. But his thumb didn't leave. It grazed her lower lip, once.

Twice.

She couldn't rip her eyes away from his. She wondered what he'd do if she caught his thumb with her teeth, if she kissed his palm.

He leaned in closer and Becca thought what an amazing, terrible, perfect idea it would be to kiss him right now.

Chapter Seven

PITCHING A VISION
And Leo's Surprise

A reminder went off on Leo's phone for George's 9 a.m. meeting in a few minutes.

Leo didn't move. His eyes never left hers. He sat his coffee down with his other hand, his thumb still grazing her jaw. Becca didn't care about the consequences; she just knew she needed his mouth one more time.

She pulled his shirt down and he nodded in silent agreement before he captured her mouth in a hot, desperate kiss. A kiss that betrayed how much he'd thought about her since 3 a.m. that morning. His hands came up to frame her face, running through the back of her hair. He tasted like cinnamon and coffee, and she pulled him closer. She needed more of him surrounding her. Filling her senses. She licked his bottom lip and he smiled under her kiss. He pulled away. "For the record, I like that a lot more than your bites."

A second reminder sounded on his phone and they both looked at the clock, 8:50. Their hands fell and Becca forced herself to slowly step back, taking a deep breath to steady herself. She couldn't think of what to say, so she silently gathered her things and avoided eye contact with Leo as he opened the door for her.

They made their way down the inn's long hallway. The silence was killing her. "Why did you leave with your stuff so early this morning?"

"I only booked that room for one night, but I figured George might have something cooked up again that would make us stay late." They made their way down the grand staircase.

Leo jutted his chin toward reception. "You can stow your bag with them. I got us a different room for tonight," he said.

Us? "Oh I can get my own room," she said, rounding the landing. She didn't want him getting the wrong idea.

"You can try, but they only had that one left for tonight. I asked for two, and she said she'd let me know if something opened up. Otherwise, you can room with me if you miss the train again."

She stopped at the reception desk and he sent her a wave as he opened the front door. He headed out and crossed over to Benning Books as Becca dropped her bag off with the front desk for storage.

She stared after him while she waited for her valet ticket. *Why is he being so nice?*

It didn't make any sense.

A WHILE LATER, Becca sat in front of George's small motley crew of staff. She and Leo had observed their weekly staff meeting, and the staff had stayed on to interview them one at a time. Leo's interview was finished and Becca had already fielded several questions. She was trying to make a connection with them, but they were all locals and not exactly excited about having a new, young boss. "I grew up in Vermont, so I know it can be tough during the tourist season," she said. *Try to help them see that you're just like them.*

"But you said you wanted to change everything. Add a bunch of new things," the grizzled stock manager said, stroking his beard.

"Only online. It would hardly change anyone's day-to-day here. I know all of you get a bonus when the store does well. And I want to make that happen even more throughout the year, not just in October."

George sat taking notes in the corner. Becca looked at the clock. Only five more minutes. "This store and town feel magical to me. I've been to over a thousand bookstores during my author tours, but you know why this one is my favorite? Because each of you have had a hand in making it special. I want to continue George's legacy and share this magic with even more people around the world. Don't you think everyone deserves a New England fall in their own home? Even if they can't visit us?"

"How would you do that here? We're just a bookstore," an older lady said with an optimistic curiosity.

"Books are nothing more than stories, and stories have united people for thousands of years. I want to embrace that tradition of storytelling and share our community with the world. Show them that Benning Falls is special twelve months out of the year, not just three."

Becca looked around the room and considerably kinder eyes stared back at her. Maybe she'd made an impact.

George stood up and Becca took the hint. Her time was over. They stepped out into the hallway. "Give me a bit. You and Leo can meet me back here at twelve."

Uh oh. She didn't love the sound of that. Becca had secretly hoped this would be the last part of the interview and she could finally book her ticket to her gram's house. She didn't need a repeat of last night.

"Sure, George. See you in a bit," she said with a bright smile. She wanted this job so badly, even after meeting his old-school staff who didn't think her vision was exactly what the store needed.

After the terrible sleep she'd had last night—no thanks to her sleepwalking mouth—she needed another hit of caffeine. Becca walked out into the bookstore and found herself looking for Leo.

No, Becca. He's a dreamboat but he's still your competition. Don't let him get in your head.

She shook her hair back and stalked out of the bookstore to Two Dog Coffee next door.

She opened the door and saw Leo sitting at the back of the shop, chatting with an older woman in an apron. They both glanced up as she came in, and she sent Leo a small wave. He sent her an unsmiling nod in return, and went back to his conversation.

Right. I'm an acquaintance. If he was chatting with someone special, why would he bother introducing a woman he barely knew?

Becca loved stopping at Two Dog when she was in Benning Falls. It skewed a little hip, and pieces from local artists hung on the walls. The coffee selection was sparse, but she could usually find something that hit the spot. She walked up to the tattooed, pierced, and purple-haired barista decked out in the Vermont-issued flannel shirt.

"What can I get you?" the barista said with a bored voice.

"Do you have anything sweet?" Becca asked.

"Uhh, chocolate milk?" the girl said with a bored sneer.

I cannot drink chocolate milk like a toddler in the middle of the biggest job interview of my life. "Just a coffee with five sugars then. Thanks."

A low buzz of indie tunes hummed through the speakers in the shop. Customers started to file in one after another. Maybe a bus tour had stopped?

Becca heard the scrape of chairs and saw Leo shaking the woman's hand. He ambled up to her, his eyes sparkling and a smile spreading on his lips. "How'd it go this morning?"

Nope. Don't give your competition an edge, even if he looks delicious. "Are you interviewing for two jobs?" She glanced at the woman who had moved behind the counter and was now slinging cider to all the tourists who had filed in.

"Maybe. I've always loved this place and it turns out Betty is looking to sell."

"Sell? As in, you'd buy the whole business?" Becca shook her head. How much did she really know about Leo anyway? She'd made up a story in her head that he was some bookish professor. They hadn't talked much about their actual jobs the night before. He'd just said he was a consultant, which could mean anything.

"Maybe. I think it's a good opportunity. Margins on coffee are pretty good. It's a year-round operation but fall helps even out the bottom line. What do you think of it?" He stepped back to glance around the place.

"I think you'd make an excellent coffee shop owner since you're such a coffee snob," she said, quirking an eyebrow at him. He let out a gasp of feigned hurt.

"Me? A coffee snob? At least the barista can tell my order apart from a seventh-grade girl's."

He had her there. Becca loved living life to the fullest, and that usually meant the more sugar the better. She looked around again and liked the vibe. "I think you should definitely buy it and then when I'm running the store next door, you can bring me free coffee." She peered at him over her drink, chancing a flirty look. She'd kept replaying their kiss that morning over and over in her head. Maybe he was trying to throw her off her game so he'd get the bookstore job.

"I said I'm *thinking* about buying this place, not running it. I could still run the bookstore. Maybe I have an evil grand scheme you know nothing about, Becca," he said through his golden, pure, was-probably-an-Eagle-Scout smile.

She shook her head, sizing him up. "The only evil scheme a cinnamon roll like you has is convincing someone to wait five minutes for a cup of bitter black coffee."

He sent her a side-eye glance. "Did you just call me a breakfast food?"

Becca burst out laughing. No way she was letting him in on the romance trope speak she'd picked up on social media. She needed every advantage she could get for whatever George had in mind next.

Chapter Eight

BECCA HAS DINNER

With a Frustrated Leo

Leo and Becca met George back in his office.

"We're gonna have a little chat," George said, closing the door to his office. "I'll shoot it straight to you. The staff doesn't think either of you is fit for the job."

Becca's mouth fell open in shock. Was this it? Her biggest hope and dream determined by a thirty-minute chat with part-time staff members? Her stomach dropped and her gaze fell to the floor as she ran through what she had said to them.

"I know them, though, and they absolutely hate change. I think they're in denial about me leaving. So," he slapped his hands together, "we're gonna show them. Because you're gonna need their help when I'm not here. It's hard to find good people who will trudge through the depths of February to come in on time."

"Show them?" Leo said, echoing Becca's thoughts.

"By proving we can run the store without you?" Becca guessed.

"Correct, young lady," George said, pointing a finger at her before flopping down in his chair. "Becca, I want you to do a trial run of managing the store today from one until four. Leopold, you'll take from four until we close at seven. We have several bus tours coming in, in addition to the normal weekend fall traffic. I'd like you both to stay close in case we need a final tiebreaker tomorrow. Will that be a problem?"

They looked at each other, heat sizzling under their gazes. Leo bit back a smile.

"Not at all," Becca said, her eyes never leaving Leo's.

BECCA'S SHIFT in running the store had been uneventful. She'd made fast friends with Margie, the septuagenarian who part-timed at the store between teaching piano lessons. They'd bonded while checking out a huge bus tour from South Carolina. Becca had figured out a faster way to organize everyone and had created a shortcut in the point-of-sale system to make everything go quicker.

She enjoyed chatting with the customers and made easy upsells, suggesting new titles and series to people who had originally given her a simple 'just browsing.' She restacked books, righted a jumbled display, and saw the bus tour had made a dent in several Vermont-themed book stacks she'd moved to the front of the store.

More importantly, Becca felt alive. Fucking electric. This was what she was meant to do, always moving around to adjust, perfect, and problem-solve like a book-loving shark. Chatting with a never-ending stream of new customers and starting relationships with regulars.

In her head, Becca already ran Benning Books. She'd allowed her imagination to run wild during the three-hour session, thinking of all the things she'd improve once given the job, and how she'd win the rest of the staff over, come hell or high water. She was sorry to hand over her staff lanyard to Leo.

"I'm going to go to the inn and see if another room has opened up," she said to him quietly.

Leo shrugged at her. "If it hasn't, I'll see you back in the lobby at seven?"

She nodded, half hoping there wouldn't be another room available. His eyes glowed when he looked at her, and she wanted a repeat of that morning.

Of last night.

Of his hands on her waist. Anything to be near him again.

"Wish me luck," he said, sending her a sarcastic wave and walking onto the shop floor.

"You're going to do terribly," she called after him, laughing. He sent her another pretend hurt look, clutching his chest.

"For people after the same job, you're awful friendly," Margie said, a confused look on her face. "Do you know each other?"

"Sort of. Only through this. But I guess it tracks that people who love bookstores and want to relocate to Benning Falls would be friends," Becca said as she gathered her things.

Margie set a motherly hand on her arm. "Sweetie, I think he's after more than friendship," she said, with a warning eyebrow and a solemn face.

God, I hope so.

THAT EVENING, Becca sat in the lobby of the Maple Inn, scrolling Instagram and posting stories from her walk through the town. It had been a crisp evening with dusk falling, and she felt like she was in a Hallmark movie, kicking leaves as she walked along the cobblestone paths. She'd finally had time to visit the shops before they closed. She got an oversized shirt and leggings that could pass as pajamas if Leo demanded his shirt back.

Leo walked through the front door at 7:05, and his eyes eagerly searched the lobby for her. *Adorable.*

"No luck?" he asked, motioning to the front desk.

"No luck. Sorry, you're stuck sharing a bed with me for another night," she said, chewing her lip and having a hard time meeting his gaze.

"Good," he said with finality.

Her eyes shot up to meet his. Did he want her as much as she wanted him?

"You can buy me dinner in return for my excellent hospitality," he said, a heated glow in his eyes.

How excellent was he promising? She fought another shiver of excitement as it tried to run through her.

OVER DINNER, they talked about the books they loved, and what they did when they weren't reading (her: endless pictures of her cat on social; him: rock climbing in an indoor gym in Manhattan, which explained the muscles). They steered clear of interview talk until Becca couldn't help herself anymore.

"What made you want to run the bookstore?" The Chardonnay had loosened her up, and since she would never see him again, there was little to lose.

"Does it surprise you that a consultant would want to run a bookstore?" he said, toying with her.

She snorted into her wine. "I'm surprised that a super hot, nice, dreamy professor/rock climber wants to move to the middle of nowhere and catalog nominal book price increases," Becca said, shoving another fry in her face.

A stunned silence met her on the other side of the table. She looked up and saw him staring at her, eyes hot and teeth clenching.

Oh no, had she been too honest? *Fuck, I always talk too much.*

He bit his lower lip briefly, as though considering something. He downed the rest of his beer, threw two twenties on the table, and reached his hand out to her.

"Let's go," he said, a commanding tone in his voice. Unexpected throbs started somewhere below her belly as she adjusted to this new side of him. Commanding. She held his gaze, and he arched an eyebrow at her with a challenge, his hand still outstretched.

She slowly slid off the bench and grabbed her coat. He took it from her and helped her put it on, pulling her hair out from under her collar. *Phew boy.* Either the wine was hitting her all at once, or she was getting flushed from the feel of his hands on her neck.

She turned around and he put his hand on the small of her back. They wound their way through the packed bar. The cold and quiet hit Becca as she stepped outside, but all her attention was on the gentle pressure on her lower back. The main street was empty. Everyone in Benning Falls was either inside or tucked in at home.

Becca could feel the tension rising with every step they took. Leo ducked around the corner of the building and drew her to him. Her back on the cold brick wall was a stark contrast to the warmth rolling off of him. His hand held hers tightly, and his other hand came up to land beside her head. His nose was inches from hers, and the steel gray of his eyes bore into her. She sucked in a breath at the wall of man in front of her.

"I'm acutely aware of two facts," he said, breathing heavily. "One: you have nowhere to stay tonight except with me. Two: I want nothing more than to kiss that pouty mouth. I've thought about it all fucking day."

Chapter Nine

BECCA STAYS WITH LEO
And Might Commit Murder

Ragged breaths drew through her. She wanted to lick the corner of his mouth. She needed to bury her face against his chest.

He stared at her mouth. "I'm trying to be a gentleman here, but I'm finding I—"

Becca yanked his shirt down until his mouth found hers. He let out a breathy groan, wrapping his arms around her waist. He pulled her close, and she grabbed his jacket with both hands. His mouth sank into hers, and she tasted him again. That mixture of coffee, spice, and cologne. She felt a pull at the center of her forehead, urging her on. She licked his lip that was currently in her mouth. He tightened his arms around her and backed her up against the brick wall. His legs intertwined with hers, and she wanted more of him. He pushed forward, and she felt delicious friction right *there*. She sighed, unable to hold it back.

The door opened around the corner, and a burst of crowd noise and music sounded through the night. Leo pulled away and glanced around the corner. No one had spotted them.

His hand came down to her jaw and he rubbed a thumb across her lips, now swollen from his nips and sucking.

"Guess we should go back to the inn," he said tentatively. His eyes searched hers.

He was saying so many things at once. Could they keep a healthy distance tonight? Did she even want to? He stepped back and held out his hand again. She grasped it and they walked back to the Maple Inn a little faster than their previous pace.

They walked up to the night manager at the counter. "We need to pick up our bags." He held out his ticket.

"Sure thing," the manager said. She looked at Becca. "Oh, hi, you're the one who asked about another room, right?"

"Yeah, any luck?"

Say no, say no, say no.

"Not yet. We have a couple that said they may need to move their reservation to tomorrow. I asked them to let me know by ten, so you could have their room," she said with a helpful smile.

Phew. She didn't really want a valid excuse to leave Leo after experiencing the mind-bending combination of his leg between her thighs and his tongue in her mouth.

"Okay, thanks. I'm just going to stay with my friend unless you have a room available." Becca pointed to Leo. Friend. She guessed they were friends. *Dude I met on the train and made out with a little between interviews for the job we're both vying for* didn't really roll off the tongue.

"Sure, I'll let you know. Hey, didn't I see you both at the bookstore today?" the night manager asked. "George is my uncle, and I came to visit. Are you guys new on staff?"

She and Leo looked at each other. This was a minefield. Did other people know George was planning on retiring? What would he say if it got back to him that she and Leo were staying together?

"Nope, just visiting," Leo said lightly. "Come on, Becca." He grabbed her bag, and they headed upstairs.

Becca threw the night manager a small wave and telepathically tried to say *Please please please help a girl out and don't tell me if there's a room available.*

"You know what I've been thinking about?" Leo asked as they walked side by side down the hallway.

Becca could take a big fat guess, and she was just as guilty.

"We'll never be coworkers," he said in a low voice. "Never have to work with each other."

Becca's breath caught. "No repercussions to our actions," she said, staring up at him.

They arrived at the door and Leo looked at her, breathing harder again. "We're just two people who can do whatever they want," he said as he slid the old-fashioned key into the lock and turned it forcefully. He swung the door open and walked in ahead of her, throwing down their bags. She shut the door behind her as fast as she could.

He grabbed her waist, one hand slipping down to grab her ass. She met his mouth with all the heat that had built up that day. She wrapped her arms tight around his neck as his tongue just...fucked her mouth. He walked her backward against the door. Hard surfaces – this man liked them.

He squeezed her ass hard, his other hand going down to squeeze the other side. He kissed her jaw, her neck. "I've been staring at this for two fucking days," he said, squeezing it again. "You tortured me today." She smiled, thinking of the tight slacks that tugged at her generous curves. He ground against her as he squeezed her to him.

Her hands came up to grip his arms, something she'd been thinking about all day. His biceps and shoulders were defined under his blazer. She needed to feel more of him. She pushed the blazer down his arms and he shrugged it off, his mouth never leaving her. He sucked her bottom lip into his mouth, licking and teasing it. She shivered and raked her nails through his hair. She'd never felt such a strong attraction before.

At her whimper, he pushed them both back against the door and she moaned. She loved this. He wasn't shy about what he liked and what he wanted. She'd never met anyone who was so kind but so ruthless about taking their own pleasure from her. His hand came to her breast and rubbed a thumb over her swell. "I need more," he panted. She nodded at him before meeting his tongue with her own.

His hand deftly slipped up the back of her shirt, flicked open the catch of her bra, and grabbed her breast, eliciting another moan from her. He played with her nipple, and she revved higher and higher. A strange, handsome, fuckable man toying with her nipple in a strange hotel room in the dark. She might come from just this alone.

Her hand left his shoulder and grazed the front of his pants. Whoa. *Leo is working with some significant equipment.* She moaned again as he nipped her neck.

"God, you sound...you sound perfect," he said, his breathing ragged. "Can I show you what I've dreamed of doing since you straddled my cock this morning?"

Becca could only nod dumbly as he kissed her neck and removed his hand from her breast. He turned her around to face the door but kept a firm grasp on her waist. Her arms came up to grasp the back of his neck.

His hand traveled from her nipple down her stomach, past her waistline and cupped her mound from outside her pants. She gasped.

"Did you know you were wet last night when you rode me?" he whispered in her ear.

"No," she whispered back. She felt drunk with lust.

"I could feel you were so wet for me, Becca. You were soaking. My pants were wet."

"S-sorry," she gasped as he found her clit over her pants.

"Sorry? I came in the shower this morning after thinking about it. Are you wet again, Becca?"

"God, yes." It was practically running down her leg. "Yes, more," was all she could get out.

"Do you want more of this, Becca?" he growled in her ear, holding her pussy.

She undid the fly of her trousers, and his hand slid inside slowly. *So* slowly. He found her clit, and she nearly screamed. He circled it, giving her feather-light touches.

"More," she begged, as quietly as she could.

"Spread your legs and you'll get more," he hissed. Heat thrummed through her and she gasped at his words. She felt his foot move hers until she was straddling him, pushing her ass up against him.

"Good girl," he said. A throb between her legs threatened to turn into a full climax at those words alone.

"You're so wet for me, Becca." She heard the liquid sound as he played with her, but she didn't care. She needed more. She'd do anything if he didn't stop moving his hands. He circled her clit in quicker and quicker circles.

"You know what will make me come?" he said in her ear, still pinning her to the door.

"Anything, just keep going," she said as he placed teasing feather-light touches.

"Hearing you scream my name," he whispered.

And Becca decided she'd actually commit murder tonight because someone decided that was the perfect moment to knock on their hotel room door.

Chapter Ten

BECCA GETS WHAT SHE WANTS
And So Does Leo

S hit. Had they been too loud? Becca zipped her pants and grimaced at Leo. She opened the door and peeked out, standing in front of Leo and his very obvious arousal. The perky night manager smiled back at her in the bright hallway.

"Hi. Great news! The couple canceled, so we have a room for you."

C'mon, man.

How could she, without words, tell the perky young manager to come back after she'd finished coming on Leo's hands? Was there a girl code for that?

Vibrations ran through Becca, her nerve endings on high. The woman stared at her expectantly, and Becca shook her head, trying to clear it.

"Oh, right now?" Becca asked.

"Yeah, I just need to get a card and your info on file," the attendant said.

"Sure." Becca picked up her bag and walked out of Leo's room. She sent him a quiet wave. She couldn't make a whole thing out of their goodbye in front of The Woman With the Worst Timing Ever. Not when that woman knew George.

Becca stared at Leo's swollen mouth pouting into a grumpy line. She saw him think for a minute and then gently shut the door behind her.

"Lucky for you, the others canceled, right?" Amanda said. Becca finally saw her name tag as they walked down the hallway to the front desk.

Bullshit. That was the most unexpected, hottest encounter she'd ever had, and she was lucky? Far from it.

"Yep," Becca said through gritted teeth.

They got her squared away, and Becca found her room at the other end of the hallway from Leo.

She changed into her new leggings and eyed her new large t-shirt, but decided against it. She picked up the soft Henley she'd permanently borrowed (okay, stolen) from Leo and threw it on. She lifted the soft fabric to her nose, feeling like a weird goblin huffing it, trying to capture any of Leo's magical scent. She closed her eyes and tried to relive their kiss. Shivers ran down her back, and she had to shake her head to clear the memory of him whispering dirty things in her ear.

Should she go back to his room? No, the attendant might notice. Too weird.

I'll just text him.

Shit, wait.

She didn't have his number. He might leave before she did, and she might never see him again. Only one of them could get the job, and the other may never be back in Benning Falls.

She threw on shoes and hustled out her door, darting quickly down the hallway to Leo's room. She'd just get his number. No pressure.

She knocked on the door lightly and Leo swung it open. Relief flooded his face and a slow, simmering smile appeared.

"I don't have your number," Becca said awkwardly. "I just thought maybe it might come in handy at some point." What she really wanted to say was, *Let's pick up from where we left off,* but maybe the mood had passed?

Leo stepped back and opened the door all the way without saying a word. Becca walked in slowly, suddenly shy. The door closed, and she stood in the darkened entryway.

"You can just type it in." She handed her phone to Leo. She tapped her toe and found an interesting spot on the ceiling as he typed in his number.

How did one communicate, *I would very much like to finish our booty call now if you could be so kind?*

A *ding* come from his phone across the room. "That's me." He held the phone back out to her.

"Thanks," she said, grabbing it.

But he didn't let go.

Her eyes finally met his. What was he doing? She tugged on her phone, and he tugged back, bringing her closer.

Oh.

She was close enough for him to grab her hip and pull her against him.

"Uh, well," she stammered. "I hope you have a good night." His lips were on her neck as waves of goosebumps flew down her back.

"Mmm," he murmured as he rubbed his lips back and forth on the curve of her neck. "I intend to."

"O-okay." God, she hoped he wouldn't stop. That she would be lucky enough to get a repeat performance of earlier. His mouth moved to her earlobe, and her knees embarrassingly buckled before she caught herself. "Night," she whispered into the air.

"Night," he said, his nose drawing a line across her cheek, nuzzling her. She sucked in a breath from the contact, her eyelids heavy and electric need shooting into her core.

He captured her mouth with a long, hard kiss. His hands moved from her waist to frame her face, one coming up to her chin. She met his tongue with hers dancing in a slow, lazy assault on her senses. Her nipples tightened as she felt his chest scrape hers, need vibrating through her. She let out a small moan, and he yanked her hard against him.

Her restraint broke and her hands climbed up his chest to pull him even closer. He angled her head to keep taking what he wanted. His hand came up to her breast over her shirt, and she thanked every deity she could think of that she wasn't wearing a bra. He groaned at that fact and decided to take what he wanted. The buttons of his Henley were open, creating a long V-neck that revealed most of Becca's cleavage. His clever hand ripped away the fabric to expose her breast, his thumb flicking her nipple. A thrill ran through her, and she felt herself go wet again.

"Leo?" she gasped.

"Yeah?" He pulled back, his eyes searching hers.

"Can you, um, do that again?"

His face transformed into a wolfish grin.

"I'll do you one better." He spun her around to face away from him and she found herself in front of a full-length mirror. His hands went to her hips and gathered the fabric of her shirt, raising it slowly to reveal her midriff. He locked eyes with her in the mirror, a silent question. She nodded.

She closed her eyes as he yanked it over her head. She felt his cock at her back, pushing into her. A look of reverence came over him as he stared at her breasts in the mirror. His hands moved up around her ribs to grab her breasts, pulling her hard against him. "Look at you, Becca. You're so fucking beautiful."

His mouth moved to her ear. Licking and sucking along the

edge, never breaking eye contact with her in the mirror. "Tell me," he whispered in her ear. "Are you wet for me again?"

Tell him? Holy fuck, she could only manage to catch her breath.

"Love, I want to hear you say it." He tugged hard on both nipples, arching her back.

"Yes," she sobbed. She shoved one of his hands into her leggings and a hiss of air escaped him.

"Your panties are soaked," he said playfully chastising her. His finger rubbed slow circles around her clit, and she let out another small sob.

"Open your eyes, Becca. Watch me." Her eyes flew open to see him behind her, a dark look in his eyes as one hand massaged her breast and the other moved slowly in her panties. She could feel the pressure building, and she desperately wanted to see him and feel him. She bit her lip, afraid to ask. She stared at her middle. "I…"

"What do you want, love?" he asked. She felt his hardness push into her. She wanted it so bad.

"I want to see you," she managed to get out as he tortured her with long, slow circles on her clit.

She felt him smile against her. He moved her to the side and yanked down his sweatpants, his hand never leaving her pussy.

His length appeared beside her and he stroked himself. She let out a shudder at the sight of the precum on the end of his cock. She licked her lips. Not able to take her eyes off of it.

She moved her hand so she could grasp him.

"No, love," he said, shaking his head. "I want you just like that. Watching me stroke myself."

She felt another rush of wetness as he placed her hand back on his neck. He stared at her breasts moving up and down as she breathed so hard, coming apart from his motions, his hands on her. "I want you just like this."

He stroked himself harder and the sight was too much. She bit her lip hard, muscles clenching, needing more and more. His rhythm turned from teasing to a jackhammer, pressing hard against her clit, ravaging her. She cried out and arched her back, seeking his hand. Electric need shot through her as she came screaming his name, and he thrust hard into himself, coming with her on a whisper.

Chapter Eleven

BECCA GETS A PHONE CALL
That Changes Her Future

Becca opened her eyes to her phone ringing. Leo's arm was tucked around her waist as they slept, and she gently moved it to grab her phone. It had taken very little convincing on his part for her to stay the night, given she'd had aftershocks from her orgasm for a solid two minutes.

She looked at the clock as she darted to her phone. Already 8 a.m. She scrambled for her phone, which was buried under the pile of her clothes in the entryway. The caller ID said 'George Williams.'

She shot a glance over at Leo, who was still sound asleep. *Shit.* Whichever way this went it was going to be awkward as fuck.

She darted into the bathroom and answered the call. "Hi George," she said as brightly as she could with a husky morning voice.

"Hey, hope I didn't wake you," he said with a chipper tone. Maybe this was good news?

"Been up for hours," she lied. "What's up?"

"Job's yours, kiddo," he said with excitement.

She shook her head, not believing her ears. "Mine? I got the job?" She started bouncing up and down while she tried to maintain a professional tone.

"You got it. We can sort out the offer details via email, but I wanted to tell you as soon as I could. You let me know—"

"I accept," she said quickly, then smacked herself at her excitement. "I mean, pending a salary discussion."

"You're a shark, Habar," he said dryly. She laughed in spite of herself.

"I'm just so excited. Can you send everything over via email?"

"Sure, and if you want, you can swing by the shop to sign the paperwork today."

"Ok, I'll be there at ten," she said. Her train back to Connecticut wasn't until the afternoon, so she had most of the day to start her daydreaming and planning.

After hanging up, Becca opened the door quietly and saw a sleepy Leo sitting up, shirtless (yum), in bed. His eyes were a bit sad, but he smiled at her. "Good news?" he asked.

She chewed her top lip and grabbed her shirt – well, his shirt – from the floor. She couldn't be naked for this conversation. "Um, yeah. I mean, it's complicated. But I got the job." She fought a smile, and when he smiled back at her, she felt that warm glow from the previous night.

"I'm happy for you," he said earnestly.

He held out his hand and beckoned her back to the bed, tugging her to him. He pulled her down for a long, slow kiss.

"You're an awfully good sport," she said, gasping a little as his mouth ran along her neck and his hand made its way to her hip to flick her panty line.

"I've never had quite so good a consolation prize," he murmured into her chest as he nipped and sucked his way down.

His phone lit up on the dresser and started ringing. His head lifted and he met her eyes. *George,* she thought.

He hopped out of bed in his boxers, his desire for her on full display, and he sent her an eyebrow waggle as she stared at it. "You're an animal, Habar."

His eyebrows shot up with surprise as he looked at his phone. "Betty, hi," he said, ducking into the bathroom and closing the door.

Becca tried to think where she'd heard that name and realized it was the cafe owner.

After Leo had been in the bathroom talking for fifteen minutes, Becca decided to throw on her leggings and write him a note that she was going to her room to get changed.

After showering, she gathered her things and saw a text from Leo – though he'd put himself in her phone as Hot Professor.

HOT PROFESSOR

Meet you in the lobby in 5? I have news.

BECCA

I can't believe you named yourself hot professor. What am I on your phone?

HOT PROFESSOR

Fine AF Becca.

Becca snorted.

BECCA

😊 Be there in 5!

She walked down the staircase and saw a freshly showered Leo in a mishmash of clothes from the past two days.

"You are looking at the new owner of Two Dog Coffee," he said with a smile.

A thrill of possibility shot through her. "What?" She threw her arms around him. He hugged her back and placed a kiss on her temple.

"So you'll come to Benning Falls sometimes to check on the store?" she asked with what she hoped was cool detachment.

His hands stayed on her waist and his thumbs stroked her sides. "Actually, Betty is fully retiring. I'm going to manage the store as well."

A shout came out of her, and she threw her arms around his neck again. This was the happiest she'd felt in a long time. Leo was so kind, funny, sexy, and just...such a good man. She wanted to make something more out of their weekend than just a sexy fling.

His arms went around her and held her tight. "I start managing the store in a few weeks, but the purchase won't be finalized for a few months. I did have one very important concession in my negotiation, though, before I agreed to take over," he said, taking her hand as she stepped back. They grabbed their bags and walked to the door of the inn.

Becca shot him a quizzical look. "What's that?"

"They have to add pumpkin spice lattes to their menu starting tomorrow," he said, a shy smile flitting over his face.

Becca stopped in her tracks and grabbed his shirt, bringing his face down to meet hers. She planted a firm kiss on his mouth. "Did I ever tell you how glad I am that you sat in my train cabin?"

He responded with an arm wrapped around her waist and another sizzling kiss before they walked out to their future in Benning Falls.

Bonus Epilogue

LEO

Leo Schmidt had many talents.

He was thrifty, great with numbers, fastidious in his appearance and habits, killed at crossword puzzles, and he knew to lock down a good thing when he saw one.

Which was why he'd immediately turned to Becca Habar before she left his sight three weeks ago and asked her on an official first date for the first Saturday she lived in Fairwick Falls.

Now, three weeks later, he anxiously paced in his new cottage before walking the two blocks to pick Becca up at the bookstore.

His heart was beating out of his chest.

I knew the fourth coffee was a mistake.

What if their chemistry was a one-time thing? What if those two days with her were so hot because of the 'no-strings' consequences?

But they'd texted non-stop as they both moved to Benning

Falls in the last two weeks. He'd purchased a cozy cottage, and he'd be lying if he said he didn't imagine living in it with her.

Which is nuts. Don't tell her even a whisper of what you're thinking.

He didn't *really* know this woman, right? What was her favorite color? Did she like sports? Did she dog-ear the pages of her books like a lunatic? Did she like dogs? Did she want kids, maybe with him, maybe in three to five years, pending the state of their combined finances?

Fuck. Stop that.

He'd honestly given up on dating in New York. The hustle culture was real, and the people he met in consulting made his soul weep from boredom. Everyone was interested in the next deal, or comparing the size of their metaphorical consulting dicks to see who billed more hours and who was more tired as a result.

He was happy to be off that hell-bound merry-go-round.

And even happier that a dead-sexy, curvy ball of sunshine had bounced into his life, throwing him for a loop.

Leo jaunted to the bookstore, expecting to see Becca locking up after her first big day. He'd dropped off coffee on her stoop that morning, but hadn't had a chance to say hi in person since he'd hugged her goodbye on the platform three weeks ago.

Breathe. She's just a woman. Who you made come a few times three weeks ago.

Three to be exact, he snorted with pride. *And who you've thought about every night since.*

He entered the bookstore, and Becca stood chatting with a customer far after closing time.

As he took in her bright, picture-perfect smile that still knocked the wind out of him, two thoughts occurred to him.

One. This was not just a three-weeks-ago fling.

He still wanted her. Badly.

Two. He was going to marry that girl.

A montage appeared in his head of him in future years of picking her up from the bookstore after closing, tearing her away from her work, and convincing her to eat food and rest.

He stood back, not wanting to screw up her conversation. Plus, it gave him more time to watch her in her element. She intently listened, *really* listened to the older customer who was telling a long-winded story. Becca wasn't placating her, wasn't bored. Just wanted to connect over their shared love of books.

A shiver ran down his spine at how much he wanted her. That kindness, that goodness.

Becca caught sight of him and her smile widened, if that was possible. She started walking the older lady to the door.

"Sheryl, I hope you come to book club next Thursday. We need your hot takes," Becca said with a smile as she flipped the sign to 'Closed' on the door.

"Won't miss it, young lady," the woman said in a brittle, excited voice as she toddled out.

Becca waved, then slowly turned in place as she met Leo's eyes. "Hi." Her voice was soft and breathless, sounding as nervous as he felt.

Happy warmth ran over him. "Hi," he murmured, walking to her and gathering her in a fierce hug as she wrapped her arms around him.

He breathed in that floral scent he'd missed as his nose nestled in her hair. He lifted her up and just held on, eventually sliding her down his body.

She reached over and flipped off the lights of the store. "I'm so glad it's not weird," she said, staring at his mouth in the dark.

Her lips were this perfect shade of mauve he'd dreamed

about. The same color as her nipples, he'd remembered. Fuck, he needed to taste her again, and he bent down to press his mouth against hers. First a tentative touch, then hungrier.

Then ravenous as her hands fisted in his shirt.

He let his hand wander down along her ass and squeeze as she molded herself against him.

No more of this, otherwise you'll get her fired for having sex in her store the first week on the job.

He pulled away even as every nerve-ending in his body told him to haul her up to her apartment above the store.

"I'm glad it's not weird too," he murmured against her lips, stealing one more kiss. "I think we better stay in town. The other place in Jasper will close soon."

Her head thumped on his chest. "Our first date and I already screwed it up by running late. I'm so sorry." She let out a long sigh. "I've loved every minute of the last few days getting the store the way I want, but I'm honestly running on fumes from the move."

He tilted her chin up. "How about I go grab two burgers from the best restaurant in town—"

"The *only* restaurant in town," she interjected.

"—and I bring it up to your place. A low-key first date." He kissed the tip of her nose because he couldn't help himself.

"You don't mind?" Her big caramel eyes looked grateful.

"We'll have tons of opportunities in the—" *Fuck. No. Stop.*

Becca's eyes went wide as a smile played on her lips, realizing what he was going to say.

"—I mean..." He cleared his throat with a blush. "As long as I'm with you, that's all I need."

An hour later, burgers demolished and several glasses of wine consumed, they cuddled up on her overstuffed brown leather couch. They'd covered their recent moves, their dating history (his: nearly non-existent, hers: tumultuous with several long relationships), favorite TV shows, and the fact that yes, thank god, she did like dogs.

But one question still haunted him. "So." He cleared his throat. "I'm...*aware* this is our first date..." His finger traced the top of his wine glass as he stared into it, not having the courage to look at her. "And I have no right to ask, but..."

He straightened his spine, willing himself to look her in the eye. "You're...not seeing anyone else, right?"

She burst out laughing, hiding her face in a pillow. "Right, Leo. With all my free time, I'm dating half of Benning Falls." She shook her head at him as if to say *silly boy.*

He ran his thumb along her cheek. So soft. He'd never felt such a greedy need to keep one woman to himself. "I only want to date you, Becca. See you. Sleep with you."

She caught his thumb between her teeth with a wicked grin and sucked it into her mouth.

Fuck me. His cock jumped to attention.

He pulled her chin toward him and kissed her, tasting the tart bite of the wine on her lips.

"I'd love nothing more than to date your brains out, Leo Schmidt," she said with an impish smile. "Though it is peak tourist season so I'll basically have a second boyfriend and we're standing on top of him."

Second boyfriend? Meaning he was...

Her eyes widened at the slip. "Shoot, I mean, I didn't mean..." She shrugged as if to laugh it off. "Labels are...you know...whatever."

His hand threaded into her hair as he turned her to face

him. "I'm glad I have first place in the boyfriend department already."

His eyes searched hers as they took that awkward tumble into the dance of '*do you like me as much as I adore you?*'

"How about I make us a fire and we'll see if I can stay in first place?" He kissed her cheek as he got up to start a fire in her fireplace, stepping over half-empty boxes.

She yawned. "Sounds amazing. I'm going to close my eyes. Just keep talking. Tell me about your day."

He worked to build up a fire as he explained how he'd overhauled the pricing structure at Two Dog Coffee and started investigating a new bean source. He was inordinately excited to test out different roasts to make the absolute perfect pour-over. And he'd already started toying with homemade pumpkin spice syrup so he could stop using the mass-produced garbage. Becca, and his customers, deserved better.

"Okay, I think we're..." He turned to see Becca fast asleep on the couch, her mouth open.

...Just going to cuddle tonight. A lopsided grin flitted across Leo's face. It was honestly the perfect ending to a perfectly imperfect first date.

~

ELEVEN MONTHS LATER

GOD, she looked really fucking cute when she snored.

Leo bent down and moved a lock of hair out of Becca's face. Sunlight peeked in through the windows of his bedroom.

Well, our *bedroom now,* he guessed. It was day three of moving Becca's things into his cottage. All fourteen and a half boxes of books, seven boxes of clothes, and a small shoebox of kitchen supplies.

In the last eleven months, he'd learned Becca's kitchen talents were limited to ordering takeout. But oh did she make up for it in every other aspect of their life together. *Lucky I like to cook, though, or we'd be skin and bones.* The takeout options in Benning Falls were limited to burgers and a deli that was open approximately two hours every day.

But never the same two hours in a row.

Leo wafted a mug of steaming coffee underneath Becca's nose, and she fluttered her eyelashes as her eyes slowly opened.

"Hey," she croaked with a smile, her voice thick with sleep.

His thumb caressed her forehead. "I thought you needed to sleep in today, and deserved a special treat this morning."

It was already 10 a.m., but they'd had a long day yesterday. It took all day to move Becca's stuff down two flights of stairs and around the corner to his cottage. Half-empty boxes surrounded their bed.

"Is something on fire?" she said, sniffing, still unmoving in bed, looking at him with a raised brow. The weather had turned chilly suddenly in the last few days, heralding the beginning of autumn. It was the perfect way to start their life together.

"First fire of the season, and I thought you deserved a pumpkin spice latte to go with it."

Becca's eyes lit up as she glanced at the mug in front of her as he crouched down. He'd foamed the milk just like she liked it and had finally perfected his concoction of pumpkin spice syrup because he was such a *'snob'* about it, according to her. He couldn't stomach serving some chemical syrupy overly sweet garbage in his coffee shop.

"The way that you make it?" she said excitedly, sitting up and grabbing the mug. He'd also sprinkled cinnamon on top and grated fresh nutmeg for her.

"Only for you," he said with a smile. "Okay, well, for you

and anyone else who stops into Two Dog. But no one else gets nutmeg. That's just for you."

She took a long sip from the mug and let out a shudder of happiness. "It's really happening," she said, bouncing on the bed. The sleep cleared from her eyes, and she shook her long hair back.

Becca was like a freight train; when she was up and raring to go, she went a thousand miles an hour. When she was asleep, she was dead to the world. He always looked forward every morning to the freight train waking up and barreling him ahead in their life together.

"Eggs?" He asked, standing up.

"Two please." She snuggled back into her nest of blankets.

The scent of wood smoke curled around the cottage, and he tapped her leg, ready to go fix a little bit of breakfast for the both of them.

He'd bought the cottage with her in mind only a few weeks after they'd started dating but had never told her that. It would have terrified Becca, chaos incarnate, to think that he was planning that far ahead in the future with her.

Until yesterday, Becca had lived above the bookshop, renting an apartment from George. She practically never left the building except to come visit him at Two Dog Coffee or to stay over. They'd both built pretty amazing businesses the last eleven months in between building their relationship. He ran the numbers to increase her profits on best sellers, and she upgraded Two Dog Coffee's website.

They made a pretty great team.

And of course, that was all thanks to George ensuring they ended up meeting during the interview process. He swore it wasn't a setup, but Leo had since learned George was a big romantic at heart.

It had been almost too easy the way they'd fallen for each

other, though they'd bumped heads occasionally in the last year. Becca was a workaholic whose nervous system was driven on caffeine and social media likes. He'd finally convinced her that *maybe* she didn't need to sleep with her phone in hand every night. Now, she relished their screen-free nights, just the two of them connecting over books and wine in front of the fire. She'd made him more open to change, teaching him to not always assume that the old ways were better than the new ways.

So while they'd had bumps, mostly things had been so fucking good.

So fucking good, he had a hard time believing that this was all real. That he hadn't been in a coma where this was all just part of his dream life, living in a cozy brick cottage in his dream town of Benning Falls, Vermont at the start of fall with a drop-dead sexy girlfriend who was smarter and kinder than he ever deserved. He adored her spunk, and she breathed life into his world. He'd been suffocating in Manhattan: waking up, going to the gym, spending fifteen hours as a finance consultant, going back home, and rinsing and repeating.

Becca was possibility; Becca was his future; and once he packed her off to the spa with her friend this weekend, he hoped she'd agree to stay with him forever.

Till death do they part.

LEO SCRAMBLED EGGS, and Becca flopped down the cottage steps in her fuzzy slippers and oversized shirt she'd permanently stolen from him since that first night together.

"I think you have something that belongs to me," he said with a smile, referencing their old joke.

She shoved at her mass of curly hair. "Your heart?" Her gorgeous lips were curved into a smirk.

He pulled her by his shirt toward him until her mouth greeted his with a kiss.

"My heart *and* my shirt."

She flopped her head on his shoulder, staring at him pushing the fluffy scrambled eggs around the pan. "You sure you don't mind covering for me while I'm away this weekend? I feel terrible."

He'd made sure Becca 'won' a spa weekend so she'd be out of the house while he prepped for the biggest question of his life.

"Becs, you haven't taken a vacation in almost a year. I think it might actually be illegal to work as hard as you do." He plated her scrambled eggs, putting a dash of hot sauce and guac on it just the way she liked.

"I know, but the tourist season has already started and I can't let anyone—"

"You are not letting anyone down. Joe's really stepped up at the coffee shop and I'm just right next door if he needs anything. Your staff is amazing, and I'm happy to help troubleshoot anything that comes their way." He kissed her head and handed her the steaming plate.

"You think George did this on purpose?" she said through a mouthful of eggs, tucking in with fervor that she never turned off. She practically inhaled her food. She inhaled life, and that was why he loved her so much.

"You mean get two managers for the price of one?" Leo grabbed his pour-over that had gone cold and popped it in the microwave.

"Best of both worlds. He pays one salary and he gets two smart, very sexy people who run his bookstore," she said, squeezing his butt as she walked past, already done with breakfast.

"Given you haven't taken a vacation, his plan is working miserably. I'm going to open the store in a few. You'll text me when you're on the road?"

This would be the first day they'd been apart in a long time. They'd both been practically living at their businesses and spent the rest of their time with each other.

"I'll bring over the last few boxes while you're out," he called behind her, wandering up to the bedroom.

Becca turned to him with bare breasts, having tossed off his shirt that she slept in.

She stared at him with a sly smile as all the thoughts left his head.

Almost a year of seeing her naked and it never gets old.

His breath caught as she stretched, giving him a show. Her breasts were already chilled from the morning air, and her nipples were tight peaks begging his mouth for attention.

"Fuck," he muttered, rounding the bed. "You taunt me even though you *know* I'm supposed to open your store in ten minutes."

She wrapped her arms around him as his hand came to her tit. He squeezed her hard, loving the soft feel of her overflowing in his hand. Becca liked it a little rough. Liked to be teased.

And oh, how he loved to tease her.

His cock was thick and hot with wanting her, and she grazed the outside of it with her hand.

"It's your fault for wearing those gray sweats this morning. They hide nothing and show *alllll* my favorite parts." She squeezed his cock over his pants.

Fuck yes. He wanted to be inside her. Wanted to taste her.

"Damn you," he cursed with a smile, picking her up and tossing her on the bed. She erupted in a fit of giggles but quieted as he tossed his shirt off. She liked his chest almost as much as he liked hers.

He leaned over the bed, crawling toward her.

"You better be quick, Mr. Schmidt. Your boss at the bookstore will dock your pay if you're late." She arched her back as he licked his way down her neck to her breasts and traced along her stomach.

He glanced up as he pulled her leggings down inch by inch. "I think my boss will be pretty fucking happy about why I'm late after I make her come." He yanked the last of her leggings down until they caught around her knees.

"Fuck, you're so hot," she sobbed as her nails ran up his scalp.

He was so, *so* thankful she had a thing for guys with glasses.

He pulled her panties to the side and decided his breakfast would be far better than Becca's had been. A hot lick from her opening all the way to her clit had Becca shrieking.

"Fuck, I love when you scream for me," he murmured into her pussy. They had to be quiet above the bookstore, never knowing who might be there. But at his cottage, she could be as loud as she wanted.

He wanted to take all day, but this would have to be a quickie. He only had eight minutes to make her scream his name.

"You like to be teased, don't you, love?" he said, barely touching her clit with his tongue. A light lick on one side of her clit, then a breath along the other side, barely touching her.

Her hips bucked, seeking friction. Her hands reached for his head.

"Hands above your head; you know the rules," he ordered.

She absolutely loved being told what to do.

She grabbed the headboard behind her head. "Fuck me, Leo. Please."

"You have to spread your legs." Her pants strained on her knees. "*Wider.*"

"Please, fuck me," she panted, splaying her hips wider. She was laid out in front of him, glistening, and already near her peak.

His tongue traced each side with a whisper-soft lick on one side of her clit and then the other. He loved torturing her with pleasure. She threw her head back, arching her back so her tits were high in the air. "Yes," she moaned, building and building. He licked and blew over her clit, again and again.

He tugged his already weeping cock free.

"Please, Leo."

Yes.

He kneeled and crawled up to her. "You want this cock, love?" he asked with a dark grin, knowing she craved it. Nearly coming when he thrust against the ridges of her pussy.

"You know what I want," she moaned.

He rubbed the end of his cock against her clit, getting it glistening and wet. He rubbed his shaft into her. He adored that Becca loved it when he came against her.

"Yes, yes," she panted, nearing climax. Her tits bounced as she ground her hips into his.

"Come on me," she moaned.

"God, you're so wet." His cock was practically coated. "Such a good girl." And with that praise, like clockwork, Becca screamed as she ground against him.

He thrust against her clit one more and came against the cleft of her pussy, obsessed with the sight of his cum covering her.

Fuck, this will never get old.

Becca panted in large heaving sighs, her fantastic tits still taunting him. He licked one as he worked his way back up the bed.

"God, every time. How do you do it?" she whispered.

He placed a slow, lingering kiss on her cheek and winked as he leapt up to get a cloth for her. "And with three minutes to spare."

LEO WALKED the one and a half blocks to Benning Books and Two Dog Coffee. The trees were dotted with golden leaves as the promise of fall came closer. Old school Vermonters still wore t-shirts and shorts, ignoring the sixty degree weather, but he'd already started spotting a few tourists in their Instagram-issued vests, boots, and scarves. Families had arrived over the last two weeks, eager to do fall photo shoots with the pumpkins and gourds that local businesses had set out on their stoops.

Leo adored living in Benning Falls. It was a big adjustment not being able to get Thai food whenever he wanted, but over-all, the change had been positive. It felt like he could reconnect with all the best parts of his childhood. Full seasons. Kind, if a little gruff, people around him. Goats and sheep dotting the fields as he drove around town doing errands.

It would be a perfect place to raise a family.

He and Becca had already started talking about what the future might look for both of them, even going so far as talking about a five-year plan. Okay, *he* talked about a five-year plan and Becca added on ideas, usually sending the plan into a tail-spin but somehow making it better at the same time.

He popped into Two Dog Coffee before opening up the bookstore. It had been a steady cornerstone of the community for over a decade, so all he'd basically had to do was not fuck it up after buying it last year.

He'd updated the menu and modernized the interior, changing the fixtures but keeping the overall grunge-meets-style look the same. He'd also changed the house coffee roast, and he was proud that it had increased sales by fifteen and a half percent.

"Morning, boss," Joe shouted from behind the counter. He fastidiously cleaned the cash register.

This is why I like him. "Morning. I'll be next door if you need anything today."

"Want anything to go?" Joe offered, gesturing with a to-go cup.

"No, nerves are already on high alert today," Leo said, walking over to the counter, lowering his voice

"So it's time, huh?" Joe said, smiling. There hadn't been many men under sixty to befriend when Leo moved to town, and he and Joe had struck up a fast friendship. Joe had introduced him to what was essentially now his entire friend group, including Max, the maple syrup farmer who'd moved back to his hometown only a few months after Leo moved in.

Leo's grin nearly split his face in two. "Yeah, today's the day. Well, the start of the weekend before the day. I have a little while to get everything ready."

Joe chuckled to himself, wiping down the espresso machine. "I can't believe you're taking the plunge. I don't think I could ever do it."

"You never know who you'll find when you least expect it," Leo said, tapping the counter with a warning smile. "I'll be next door. Text if you need anything."

A few short steps later, he slid the lock into the bookstore's front door. He always enjoyed coming over into Becca's book-shop. It'd become warmer, friendlier, and more *Becca* since she'd taken over.

His pride had hurt a little when she'd beat him out for the job, but he'd won so much more than a job in return. He'd found his best friend, an amazing business opportunity, and the life he'd always dreamed of. It would have been hard to convince Becca to stay here if he'd gotten the job.

It was probably time to send George another thank you note. He tried to send one every few months, never wanting to lose gratitude for the perfect life that had been dropped in his lap.

The smell of books surrounded him as he walked to the table. He pulled the folder of secret paperwork out of his bag, and since Becca would be on her way in about an hour and unlikely to come back to the store, he started his project of convincing her to marry him with only slightly stolen information.

Two days later, Leo's heart hadn't stopped beating in his throat since he'd woken up in a sweat that morning.

What if she said no?

What if the chaos-incarnate love of his life thought that marriage was too much to be tied down to?

Yes, she loved the bookstore and planned to be there for a good long while, but she was young. They both were in their late 20s. She could chuck it all away, quit her job, and want to sail the world still.

That would be just like Becca: wanting to do something seemingly impulsive that she'd been thinking of for years and told no one about.

He really hoped that she and her friend, Josie, would be running exactly on time coming back from the spa.

Then Becca would get the surprise of her life, but only if she was on time because they couldn't miss their train.

Becca's car turned the corner and parked in front of the store. She looked refreshed and stunning in her sexy outfit. He'd told her they would go to dinner when she got back. Confusion spread across her face as she clocked him in a suit standing outside of the decorated bookstore. He'd made the executive decision to close thirty minutes early that Sunday evening, and all the staff had only been too happy to help him decorate the inside of the bookstore.

Her friend Josie hopped out of the car and walked over to her boyfriend, Max, who also stood in a suit.

"Did you have a good time?" he asked as she walked up with her overnight bag.

"Hey, hon," she said with slow confusion. "Why are you... what's going on with the store?" She tried to look behind him, like a mother hen checking on her nest. "And why are you so dressed up? I thought we were just going home after I dropped off Josie."

"I thought we'd step inside first. Max and Josie are going to go do their own thing."

"Why don't I run home and change first?" Becca set her bag down and wrapped her arms around him. He kissed her briefly, already aware he was two minutes behind schedule.

"Not on your life," he murmured against her lips, pressing her to him for a brief second of warmth and happiness. "I have a surprise," he said, opening the door for her to the bookstore.

She did a double take as she saw the inside completely decorated with flowers and twinkle lights. He'd gotten her favorite romance quotes written in calligraphy on 8x10 framed canvases and placed them throughout the store.

"I did a little snooping," he admitted. Okay, he'd *stolen* her e-reader and found the highlighted passages of all of her favorite romance novels. Becca liked all types of books: memoirs, thrillers, sci-fi, but she had a special place in her heart for romance novels, and the sappier the quote, the better.

"What are you doing?" she said, turning around in a full

circle, trying to take it all in. He'd surrounded each quote with flowers and twinkle lights throughout the store. That was where they had first met and where he'd first fallen in love with her energy, her positive attitude, her kindness, and the potential of their life together.

"Becca, I love you so much." He heard her gasp as she put two and two together, finally realizing what was happening. "The last year of our life together has been unreal. Building our businesses together, you crowding me every night in bed, snuggling me into a corner."

She burst out laughing even as her eyes still looked around in wonder. "Hey, I gave you fair warning."

His hand interlaced with hers, and he pulled her around the bookstore as she took it all in.

"I wanted to do something special in your favorite place in the world—"

"With my favorite person," she interrupted, squeezing his hand.

"You've made me a better person in the last year—"

"You were already pretty great," she interjected again.

"Any guy who wouldn't share his room with you to avoid Lester should be tarred and feathered."

She giggled as her hand traced the lettering on one piece of calligraphy, her favorite Jane Austen quote from *Pride and Prejudice.*

"Becca, I love the way you live life to the fullest. You changed my life and brought your tornado of happiness into it. My collection of typewriters and I wouldn't be the same without you."

He did *actually* have a collection, he'd admitted, after she'd teased him on the train that first day. "And though I know you're just back from an amazing spa, I was wondering if"—he pulled her toward the front of the store, toward their bags —"if you wouldn't mind taking a train ride with me."

Becca's face fell in confusion. "Oh," she said brightly. "Yeah. Wait, another vacation?"

"Just to Burlington, to see the leaves since they've started to change up there already."

"But the store," she said, turning around, looking at all of her books as though they were a puppy she'd left behind for too long.

"It'll keep for one more day. We'll be back tomorrow afternoon. Promise." An alarm went off on his phone. "We better go. Can't miss the train this time," he said with a twinkle in his eye.

So far, so good. His heart had settled down to somewhere in his chest cavity, rather than in his throat where it had been for the last twenty-four hours.

He hoped to god that Brit had found the right train car. He wasn't sure if he'd be able to pull off what he envisioned for his proposal, given the train's online reservation system was about a decade behind everybody else's technology.

"It's been ages since I took a train up to Burlington," she said as they hurried across the street. A huge commuter train whistled as it pulled into the stop.

As he glanced at his phone, he saw a picture of Brit come through that she texted him with a thumbs up of her in a cabin fully decorated the way he'd asked her to.

Luckily, it was just a quick jaunt across a small main street to go to the platform to board. Leo pulled the two tickets out of his pocket even as he heard a snort of giggling beside him.

"I like physical things, okay?" he said, jostling her hand as he kissed her temple.

"I know, and it's absolutely adorable," she said, leaning her head against his arm. "What sparked the trip?"

He nodded his head back and forth. "I thought we needed to celebrate being in Benning Falls for almost one year."

The shrieking train came to a stop with a loud hiss, and the doors slid open. He grabbed their bags in one hand and Becca's hand in the other. He held her hand as she hopped up onto the steep train steps in her heels. He was very distracted by her ass in her skirt and had to shake himself to focus as he hurried up the steps behind her.

He glanced at the instructions from Brit: *Train car seven.*

"Let's try this way," he said, his head turning as he scanned the commuter train. He'd booked a private cabin for them but knew that they wouldn't be guaranteed to have it to themselves, so he'd bribed Brit to hop on at Union Station and guard a cabin with her life until they got to Benning Falls.

"Is that...your sister?" Becca said with confusion, peering up ahead at the perky blonde woman waving like a maniac.

Real subtle, Brit.

She and Becca had become good friends over the last year, and she'd stayed with them multiple times, getting away from the city. She'd been absolutely begging him to put a ring on Becca's finger for months in case Becca were to, quote-unquote, "wise up and leave his dorky ass so fast."

"Oh my gosh, hi!" Becca said, cooing in that distinctly female pattern of friendship and recognition. "What is your sister doing on a train ride? Oh, is this a whole family thing?" Becca wiggled with excitement. She got along well with his parents, even if she overwhelmed them a little bit.

"Nope, I'm hopping off here." Brit gave him a cheek pinch and Becca a big hug. "Don't fuck it up," Brit whispered as she walked past.

He gulped so loudly, he thought Becca might have heard it.

"What, she's not staying?" Becca said, turning around in

confusion. "What on Earth is going on here?" Leo pulled open the door to the cabin that Brit had just left.

Thank god Brit had followed his instructions perfectly. The calligraphy sign he had shipped to her was perfectly tacked up on the train window. Cozy flannel blankets and pillows with pumpkins and orange-and-cream patterns on them were tucked in and around the cabin. There was a small table off to the side with a bottle of champagne chilling in an ice bucket.

He'd decided to splurge for the sleeper cabin this time. You only proposed to your soulmate once in your life, after all.

Next to the champagne were a piping hot teapot filled with hopefully passable coffee and a couple of mugs at the ready. He wasn't sure what she'd be in the mood for: either the sentimental reminder of their first time together or celebratory champagne if she said yes.

Oh god, he hoped she said yes.

Well fuck, he hadn't said anything, and she'd just been staring around the cabin as the train started to lurch and chug slowly out of the station.

She just spun around and around, looking at the decorations he'd begged Brit to put together. She'd FaceTimed him as he had instructed her on what exactly he wanted earlier in the afternoon.

"Becca, I wanted to ask you the most important question in the place where I met the most important person in my life. You're gorgeous. You're kind. You've made my life an absolute chaotic dream come true. And I'm so very glad you sat in my train car that day."

"I thought you sat in *my* train car." She smiled with tears in her eyes as his hand interlaced with hers.

The door was still open to their cabin, and he figured that now was as good a time as any.

He kneeled down on one knee, his heart beating like a

hummingbird's. It was an out-of-body experience actually seeing himself kneel down. One of the moments he'd remember until he was on his deathbed: seeing this gorgeous, curvy woman in front of him on the perfect train ride surrounded by trees swishing beside them as they rumbled through the center of Vermont.

"Rebecca Habar, will you please marry me?" he said, hoping like hell she'd say yes.

He barely got out the words when she yelled "Yes" and threw her arms around him.

A laugh erupted out of him as he caught her mouth, standing up in the bumbling train. The brakes screeched as they stopped at the next small town, and the two of them went flying against the wall. Leo managed to put himself between her and the wall so at least she didn't get hurt when the door slammed behind them.

An *oof* sounded out of him as his back hit the wall. Their hands found purchase along the edge where the coat rack of the small cabin was. Luckily, Brit had secured the liquids in a special tray that had a high enough lip so they didn't go flying.

The train screeched to a halt.

"You always know just how to protect me," Becca said, staring up at him with a dreamy look in her eyes. "Good thing I'm marrying you."

She patted his chest, and her face went curious as her hand landed on the small box in his breast pocket.

Oh shit, right. He pulled it out and she gasped as he flipped open the box.

He'd decided to go out on a limb when he found the ring a few months ago. An antique cameo ring surrounded by diamonds on a rose gold band. It was funky, and gorgeous, and instantly reminded him of her.

She just nodded and stuck out her hand, gobsmacked.

His face split in two. She'd said *yes*.

She pulled him down for a long, sizzling kiss but the start of the train out of the station pulled them out of it.

"This cabin is amazing," she said, getting her balance as the train got going. "We have this all the way up? And Brit did this?" She turned around.

"Well, I gave her the instructions," Leo said, defensively, pulling out his shirt cuff that had gotten rumpled in all the mayhem.

"I absolutely love it," Becca said with excitement. "And I love you," she added quietly.

"What? No selfies?" he said, smirking as he looked down at her, knowing that she wanted to share with the world when she was happy.

"Maybe in a minute," she murmured. "I just want to take this all in."

Her hand came to his jaw, and she ran a finger over his cheekbone. He leaned into her. She'd given him such comfort in the last year. He'd been nervous for them to jump into a relationship at first, but he'd known that he didn't want to let a good thing go.

"And you know the best part of this cabin?" he said, kissing her wrist.

"Champagne?" she offered.

He pulled down the blind over the cabin door and locked it. "Privacy," he said with a wicked look.

It had been several days since he'd had her, and he'd already missed her body against his.

"Mr. Schmidt, are you seducing me?" she said in a scandalized tone. "I thought you were a proper gentleman on train cars." A hand clasped to her heart in mock outrage.

He walked toward her, moving into her space and walking

her to the back of the cabin where the cold press of windows showed the countryside of the small town they'd stopped at.

"A man is allowed to seduce his soon-to-be wife," he said, pressing her against the row of windows.

"You do love a flat surface," she said as she tugged him down by his tie to meet her mouth.

And as bright orange and yellow leaves swished past outside, Leo thought there had never been a luckier man in all of Vermont.

THE END

Apple Cider

AND

Subterfuge

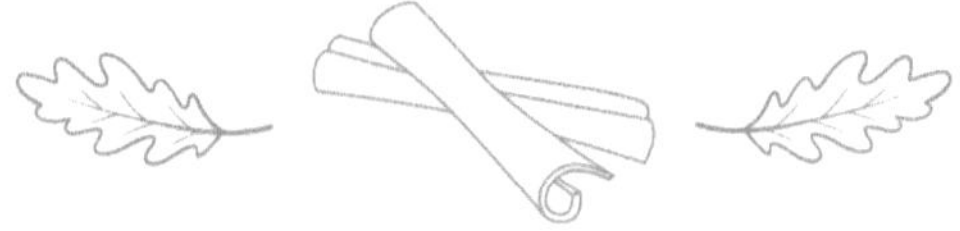

ALEX

A blaring beeping sounded in Alex's ear. He threw a hand on his phone to silence it and looked at the curved figure beside him, still fast asleep in the gray morning light. The sheet had fallen off of her, and her silk nightgown had ridden up to reveal the delicious curve of her ass.

Fuck my life.

Alex took a deep breath and convinced his dick to pay less attention to the sultry, warm, gorgeous woman beside him.

It was Day 157 of sleeping next to the one woman Alex couldn't have: his FBI undercover partner, Brynn.

Inside the house, they were nothing more than coworkers who slept in the same bed. He glanced at the cameras that were always on throughout the house. Fraternization was entirely off limits, despite their cover identities of being newlyweds.

Outside the house? They were lovestruck newlyweds who had just moved to the small town of Wellington, Massachusetts, conveniently living next to an alleged kingpin money launderer.

Goosebumps covered Brynn's arms as she lay fast asleep,

curled up in a ball. Alex grabbed the blankets they shared and covered her, tucking her in so she'd stay warm in the November morning.

He longed to run his fingers along her delicate jaw. Move her long hair out of the way so he could kiss her neck. Run his nose along her shoulder and move his mouth down to her curved, firm breasts. The feel of her tits pressing against his chest haunted his memory from when he'd hugged her goodbye in the driveway as her dutiful (fake) husband.

He tried to find a reason to kiss her when they were outside the house, away from the cameras. Brynn always responded to it, but they'd never talked about it. Never let themselves get caught up in the moment. The stakes were too high, and they couldn't afford to get distracted.

He moved silently out of bed, cat-like, so as not to wake her. She had a hard time falling asleep, and they'd need every ounce of strength for today's mission: getting in good with Peter Petrov, the piece of shit money launderer.

BRYNN

BRYNN WOKE with a stretch and heard the shower shut off.

Good. Maybe I'll get a show this morning. Alex usually woke and showered first, but about half the time, he forgot to bring his clothes into the bathroom.

She wondered if it was her lucky morning.

She snuggled back under the covers, pretending to be asleep. Her favorite way to start the day was seeing his dripping chest, biceps, and abs from under nearly closed eyelids. Imagining what he might feel like, all damp and warm from the shower. She cursed the security cameras hidden throughout their house, preventing them from trying anything physical.

A muffled *'Shit'* came from the bathroom and her eyebrows quirked with awareness.

He didn't usually make a big deal when he forgot to grab his clothes.

The bathroom door opened slowly. Alex peeked his head out and glanced her way. She must have sold the fact that she was sleeping because he walked out with nothing more than a washcloth covering himself.

Brynn took a quick breath at the sight of him and sighed slowly, pretending she was still asleep. He usually came out with a long towel around his waist.

Which is still in the dryer downstairs, she realized.

Oops.

Or not so oops, she thought as he stalked across the room, glistening and naked.

He had powerful, thick thighs burnished in a golden tan like the rest of him. She got a glimpse of his round, perfectly sculpted behind as he breezed by, but she lost him out of the corner of her eye. *Damn.* Maybe if she leaned back on the pillow, he wouldn't notice her staring.

Brynn gently moved onto her back, fully aware she was in pervert mode. *It's been a long six months, okay?* She angled her head and opened her eyes just enough to see him staring at her in the mirror.

Fuck. Caught in the act.

He had the audacity to wink at her, smirk, and carry his underwear to their walk-in closet, shielding all his delicious parts from her eyes. The door handle closed with a cacophonous click.

Fuck, fuck, fuck.

Brynn's hands came up to cover her face as she went beet

red. She'd never hear the end of this. She jumped in the shower to avoid him.

Thirty minutes later she came downstairs, ready for the day.

"Next time I'll charge admission," Alex said as he poured a cup of coffee into his mug, biting back a smile.

"Don't flatter yourself." She grabbed the fridge handle and yanked it open. Heat burned at her cheeks. "I was just waking up and accidentally caught an eyeful."

"I bet that's why the towels are still in the dryer. This was your long con to see me naked before we're done."

"Oh, yes. I'm working the most important job of my life, yet I still find time to strategize how to see the office pretty boy's man butt."

He peered at her with steamy eyes over his mug as he took a sip. "See? Long con."

She rolled her eyes at him and bit back a smile as she threw on her coat. "You're meeting me at the Cider Festival at six, right?"

"Yep. I'll wear my best shirt," Alex said, using their code word for wire. They could never be too careful.

Tonight's operation was an essential part of their mission. First, prove Petrov and the police were working together and then second, become indebted to Petrov. They needed to see his operation from the inside. They'd already established a friendly relationship with him, playing the roles of the hapless neighbors who always needed to borrow a power tool.

Brynn opened the back door of their rental cottage, and western Massachusetts's crisp air invaded her lungs. She made her way down the stairs and saw her car already on and warming up, ice melting from her windshield.

Did Alex do this? Her instincts ran on high alert outside the house. She turned to see him running out of the front door without a coat.

"That was me." He walked toward her with a travel mug of coffee. "Thought you'd want a toasty ride this morning."

God, she loved being fake married to him. She let her genuine smile shine through. She thought of all the other agents she could have been paired with: Sweaty Hands Ben or Al, the guy who microwaved fish. Instead, she got the sweet, jacked agent who could have moonlit as a Hollywood heart-throb stand-in.

He handed her the warm tumbler of coffee, and she accepted it with a smile. "How did I win the best husband?"

His hand came up to her jaw. *Yes.* She loved it when he played up their relationship for everyone else. Loved that he took any opportunity he could to touch her outside of the house.

If he only knew how much she craved it.

"I think you won it with those spectacular, perfect curves I woke up to this morning." His serious eyes locked with hers.

A thrill shot straight through her, and she caught her bottom lip between her teeth. He'd never said anything about her body before. Never acknowledged the building heat between them.

His thumb traced her bottom lip, and her breath hitched. *Fuck it.* The mission would be over in a few days.

Chapter Two

BRYNN

Brynn felt all the want of the past months build up inside her, and decided she needed to taste his mouth more than she needed her next breath.

Her mouth took his, landing quick and hard on him. Her hands traveled up around his neck. He deepened the kiss, angling her head to grab more of her. Her tongue slid against his lip and tasted like coffee and spice, which had her sighing like a horny teenager.

Their tongues warred with each other, and she ran her nails through the buzzed hair on the back of his head. He moaned and tightened his arm around her waist, pressing her painfully close.

He slowly melted his mouth away from hers, their foreheads still touching, their breathing ragged. Their hot breaths puffed into clouds in the chilly morning air.

He still held her close, and as his chin angled back towards her mouth, his eyes questioning hers, a thick Russian accent broke through the quiet morning.

"I thought I was going to have to turn the hose on you," Petrov said with a fatherly smile in the driveway next to them.

"Newlyweds," he smiled with a shake of his head. "How I envy you."

He tugged his gloves on and hopped into his luxury SUV. The Petrovs always kept their cars in the drive despite having an oversized garage.

"Why don't you kiss me like that anymore?" Nadia, Petrov's young wife, whined from the front door of their stately home.

Brynn and Alex broke apart with embarrassed laughs. "Sorry," Alex called back over the driveways. "Don't want to cause a fight. Have a good day, hon." Alex placed a quick kiss on Brynn's temple.

Brynn so desperately wanted to live in the fairytale she let herself fall into during their kisses.

That he really was her husband. That he really did love her and kiss her like that every morning.

Every night.

She winked back at him as he walked to the house. Alex sent her a quiet wave and hustled back inside. His cover was that he worked from home for a tech startup, which provided a great opportunity to watch the Petrov family's every movement.

Brynn called over to the Petrov's driveway. "Want a ride, Nadia?"

"Ohmygawd yes. It'll take friggin' foreva for the ice to thaw on my car," Nadia squawked in her thick Boston accent. The Petrovs had moved to Wellington only a few years before, likely to set up another wing of Petrov's money laundering network. Nadia's accent grated on Brynn's nerves, which was unfortunate because they worked almost every shift together at the local boutique. Brynn tried anything she could to get scraps of info on the Petrov operation.

Nadia slid into the passenger seat. "God, enjoy that shit while it lasts," she said, peering her thickly-lined eyes over at Brynn. "Peter hasn't lifted a finger for me since 2012."

Brynn faked an easy laugh. "Didn't you get married a few years ago?" She put the car in drive and turned toward the village square.

"I nevah said I was smaht," Nadia said, chomping on gum while her nails click-clacked on her phone.

"Are you and Peter going to the Cider Festival tonight?" Brynn said, making easy conversation. She liked Nadia well enough, despite her voice. The FBI assumed that Nadia wasn't involved in any of the Petrov family business. She worked at the boutique to keep herself busy and check out the latest clothes before everyone else. Brynn guessed that being the wife of a Russian mob boss was pretty lonely.

"Ugh, yes. You know he never misses a Friday night at Toni's, and it's right there, so," Nadia waved a hand in the air. "I guess we'll go. I'm not really into all this cutesy shit."

The woman decked out in head-to-toe cheetah print didn't want to go to a cutesy small-town festival? Shocker.

Brynn's eyebrows feigned surprise. "No? Oh, I love it. You know this is just my kind of thing." She pulled into the Main Street parking lot and saw volunteers stringing fairy lights for the festival. Brynn actually did love it in Wellington. Most of her other undercover ops hadn't been quite this adorable or this cushy. "Didn't you know you were moving to a cute town stuffed full of festivals?"

"I mean, I guess. But we moved for Peter's work. He had to be close to his *suppliers*," she said, peering over at Brynn. "If you know what I mean."

Excellent.

"Oh, are they not on the level?" Brynn played dumb. Hopefully, Nadia would finally spill something specific.

"Well," Nadia faced Brynn in the car, ready to dish. "You know how we got that TV for cheap?"

Brynn nodded with what she hoped was wide-eyed earnestness.

"Maybe it fell off a truck. That's all I'm sayin'," Nadia said as she flipped down the visor to check her makeup.

"Wow, that's so cool," Brynn lied. "Could you get us a deal? Our TV is so old and tiny."

"I bet Peter can hook you up. He's got all sorts of connections, and he's gettin' more TVs soon," Nadia said as she hopped out of the car for their shift.

Let's hope he does, Brynn thought, blowing out a breath as she followed Nadia inside.

Chapter Three

ALEX

Alex stood in front of the Apple Cider Festival entrance booth holding two cups of cider and checked his watch one more time.

6:07. It wasn't like Brynn to be late.

He checked his phone again, seeing if the pot dealer had texted yet.

They planned to smoke a joint in the alley where Petrov and the local police chief met each week. Weed was legal in Massachusetts, but it couldn't be publicly consumed. Hopefully, Petrov would talk to the cop and convince him not to write them a ticket. Then, they'd be indebted to Petrov and be able to get a little closer to the operation.

Living next door hadn't netted the FBI much hard proof on the Petrov family business, not that Alex was complaining. He'd gotten to see Brynn every day and kissed her when they were out in public. The town must think they were the handsiest pair of newlyweds that had ever moved in.

"The big one better be mine," a husky voice sounded behind him.

Alex turned around, and there she was. His fake wife,

although he'd had a hard time remembering the *fake* part the last few months.

Brynn was fresh and lovely in her caramel-colored pea coat and plaid scarf. Her long brown hair fell in waves, framing her face.

He loved her face. She had round cheeks that looked almost cartoonishly angelic and long lashes framing light brown eyes. The combination made her look incredibly young and guileless, which couldn't have been further from the truth. He knew she could be as deadly as he was if she needed to be, and wasn't that a hot combination? A deadly angel.

She grabbed the large cup of hot spiced cider in his hand and took a long pull, her eyes smiling at him as she drank. Heat crawled under his collar despite the freezing temperature.

"Hey honey," he said, cupping her chin in his hands. He kissed her soundly, pulling her lip in and licking it a bit with his tongue. He felt her hiss at the contact and opened her mouth to nip his bottom lip. His thumb stroked her cheek as she pulled away.

"Alex, we're in public," she said, playing the part of a blushing newlywed well. She waved to the older ladies at the Cider Festival entrance. Alex leaned over his shoulder and saw the older ladies staring mooney-eyed at them.

He leaned in to whisper as he escorted her into the festival. "If only I could do the things I wanted to do in private."

Her breath stilled, and he placed a slow kiss on her temple and slid an arm around her waist.

She stared at him as he pulled away, and her cheeks were pink. Was that from the cold? Or was she blushing?

He hoped blushing.

After a few months of them playing a couple, he figured out she liked his physical affection. She'd stopped wearing sticky lip gloss, and when he'd asked her about it, she said it made it easier to kiss him when they were out in public. Half the time now, she initiated it, likely feeling the clock ticking down on their operation.

They'd soon move on to other ops and probably wouldn't see each other again for a long time.

Maybe ever.

"We have a few minutes before we meet our friend," Alex said, looking at his watch. "Still no word from him, though."

"Let's take a lap," Brynn said, eyes scanning the horizon for the dealer. "Hey Betty, hey Carol," Brynn sent the two older ladies working the entrance booth a warm smile.

"Go ahead, honey," Betty growled through her smoker's cough.

"Your hunky hubby already paid," Carol said, winking at her.

"I'd recommend the spiked cider next time," Betty said, jutting her chin at Brynn's drink. "Warms ya right up." She lifted her cup and took a long pull.

Alex wondered with a smirk just how many times her cup had been spiked that evening.

"Isn't it time for you both to go inside?" Brynn asked Betty.

That was Brynn. Surprisingly lethal yet unyieldingly kind.

"Nah." Carol waved a mittened hand at her. "It's just the beginning of winter. It'll take more than this to beat us old New England battleaxes down. Go on and have fun, you kids."

Alex sent both ladies a smile and looped Brynn's arm through his.

They walked to the center of the town square, which was covered in twinkle lights and apple-themed decor. The town of Wellington had made its mark in New England as the home of the most award-winning apple cider manufacturer on the east coast. The town held the festival in early November to signal the end of the cider season when everyone could finally relax.

Given the proliferation of cider at every turn in the town, Brynn had taken to drinking a hot mug of it every evening to wind down. She claimed it tasted almost as good as the glass of wine she usually had when she wasn't on an operation. Alex would never be able to smell cider again and not think of her curled up in their living room - shit, their *fake* living room - looking so soft and kissable.

There were carnival games, kids running around, and everyone enjoying a low-key, family-friendly night before the Christmas season kicked off.

"Looks like they've got cider-flavored everything. In case you need some apple cider-flavored fried chicken," he squinted at a food truck's sign, "or fries."

Brynn squinted her nose up at him. *God, she was cute.*

"I love it as much as the next person, but I think I draw the line at fries." She took another sip of her drink.

"Suit yourself, but I'll try anything once," he said, taking a sample of apple cider seasoned fries from a tray. A brown sugar and cinnamon coating offset the fried potatoes. "Shockingly, it's pretty good."

He held one to her mouth, and she opened it. He popped a fry in.

"Not bad. If you want sweet fries." She grimaced. "I'll stick to the liquid form, thanks."

They walked through the town square filled with twinkle lights and apple cider-themed booths. Bundled-up families walked through the festival, sipping hot cider and eating fried donuts and other cozy snacks.

They wound their way through the festival, saying hi to neighbors and the few people they knew. They'd tried to ingrain themselves in the cute little community since they'd moved in six months ago.

"Do you want anything else?" Alex asked as they wound

their way through. He'd heard Brynn's stomach growl as they passed the apple cider donut stand.

"No time to stand in line." Brynn sighed wistfully at the sugar-coated goodness. "Though I'd eat five thousand of them if given a chance on another night."

"You do seem to love cider to an alarming degree," Alex grabbed her hand and brought it to his mouth for a kiss. "I won't be able to smell it and not think of you."

Brynn sent him a steamy smile. "Good."

Chapter Four

A thrill jumped through him at that smile. They'd have something to keep them connected after this was done.

As undercover agents, they'd move on and pretend as if the operation never happened. They could only talk about it with a handful of work colleagues. There wasn't anyone he could really tell how much he craved her, how he loved living with her, even her annoying habits like leaving the cupboard doors open. He smiled, remembering the first time he'd walked into the kitchen after she'd been there. He'd thought a demon haunted the place and had thrown every cupboard door wide open.

Alex had a few serious girlfriends in college, but none since. The job always came first, and he was happy to make the sacrifice. No one else had ever been worth taking desk duty for. Settling down for. As he rubbed his thumb across her fingers, he let himself heave a long sigh, wishing for what could have been if they'd met under different circumstances.

He glanced at his watch. "Want to play me in apple toss? Winner chooses dinner?"

"Nah, it's no fun. You'd have to throw the game. You can't give away what a good aim you are."

Petrov was merciless when double-crossed, so they couldn't risk being found out. They used Smiths for their fake last name, and they both happened to go by their legal middle names, so searching for Alex Smith wouldn't connect anyone to who he was. A couple of wrong moves, and they'd have to abandon the entire operation.

His stomach lurched at the thought of something happening to Brynn. It was part of the job, but he still couldn't stand the thought of it. She was a higher-ranking agent than he was, but he wouldn't forgive himself if he jeopardized her safety. She'd come to mean so much to him in the last five months.

He cleared his throat. "Okay, no apple toss."

"Did you have a good day?" She asked.

The question was simple enough, but it struck him in the gut. He was lucky to be paired with her for this assignment. They only had a precious few days left before the operation ended, and he felt it slipping away. Having her constant companionship highlighted how lonely his existence had been for the last ten years of his career.

"My day was pretty uneventful. I did recon at the local deli to see if Petrov's team had any connections. All I got out of it was a great pastrami sandwich. You?"

Alex considered how he had the cushy stay-at-home job, whereas Brynn had to sit and listen to a whining voice most days for hours at a time.

"Nadia told me that Peter had a lead on stolen TVs." She sent him a knowing glance. "I told her we'd love to have any back-of-the-truck hookups they might have. Any word yet?" Brynn asked without looking at him.

She was surveying the landscape as he was, taking in all the details in case they needed to improvise later.

"Not yet. Imagine that, a flaky pot dealer," Alex said. They could just go to any cannabis store if they were ordinary people. But that required a squeaky-clean background check, which they wouldn't pass as undercover agents with fake identities.

Brynn checked her watch. "It's almost time."

Didn't he know that? "Well, someone was seven minutes late, *honey*," he said, squeezing her side with a teasing grip. "We'll think of something."

Petrov met the local police chief in the back alley of Toni's every Friday night at 6:30, probably for a cash payment for the police to look the other way while Petrov did...whatever Petrov did.

His watch buzzed. 6:20. "Let's go," He tugged her toward Toni's.

Brynn quickened her pace to keep up with him. "What do you want to do to get the chief's attention?"

"Not a clue."

They crossed the street, and Alex flew through the list of options in his head. They couldn't vandalize anything. They were adults, for chrissakes. They needed to do something that a cop would want them to stop, but not bad enough to damage their reputation in town.

They ducked around the corner of the restaurant and into the back alley. They'd be able to see the back door of Toni's from their darkened hideout and let themselves be seen by Petrov.

Alex looked around the alley, hoping for inspiration, when he felt a tug on his waist. Brynn was unbuckling his belt.

"Whoa," Alex said, trying to keep up with her. "Honey, we're in public."

A cat-like smile curled on Brynn's lips, and she raised a suggestive eyebrow. "Exactly."

Chapter Five

ALEX

Wait. This is how they'd get caught. God, she's a genius.
His eyes searched hers for a frantic moment and he saw the hunger in her eyes that said she wanted him too.

He grabbed her face with both hands, pressing his mouth to hers just as he'd dreamt of doing the past *five fucking months*.

It had been torture being next to this woman and not being able to tell her how much he wanted her. She kissed him back, sucking his bottom lip into her mouth, and he angled her head so he could take more of what he wanted. The scent of cinnamon and sweetness imprinted on his memory as her signature taste.

They were playing a dangerous game. They had to keep an eye on Petrov and the cop. He'd have to keep his wits about him, not get too sucked into the dream of actually having her the way he'd wanted to.

He tugged her as close as he could, wrapping his hands around her body. Their tongues danced lazily, and he felt the

106

heat ratchet up with each passing second. He wanted her so badly, had dreamed of this.

Somewhere in his head, he heard a door open, but he couldn't stop thinking about the perfect, firm breasts pushed against him. Brynn ripped her mouth from his, and she urged his mouth to her neck.

"That's them," she whispered in his ear. He nuzzled the curve of her neck, and she gasped. She smelled like lavender and vanilla, but he couldn't lose his senses in her. He had to keep his head in this operation, the consequences mattered too much.

He peered around her neck as he kissed it, whispering what he saw. "Chief, two o'clock. Petrov beside."

"Shh," she said. They needed to listen before they were spotted. Other agents had planted mics along the alleyway by the door, so at least headquarters would get something even if they didn't.

Alex closed his eyes and let himself stay in the curve of her shoulder. She had stilled as well, gently stroking his back but making no sound.

"Evenin'," the police chief said to Petrov outside Toni's back door. "Enjoyin' the festival?"

"Yes, but I think you dropped this," Petrov said, handing him an envelope of what Alex had to assume was cash. Paying the police department to look the other way so he could do whatever he wanted.

"Ah, thanks. Silly me," the police chief said with no inflection of surprise. He tucked the envelope in his jacket pocket. Alex felt a buzz on his watch and an incoming text message that said, "Got it." The other agents had what they needed from the police interaction.

Alex squeezed her waist. "Showtime, honey," he whispered into the curve of her neck.

BRYNN

Brynn felt goosebumps cover her body hearing those two words. She was so, so grateful to the flaky pot dealer for giving her this delicious opportunity to ravage Alex like she'd dreamed of.

His mouth came down on hers with a ferocity that was startling, squeezing the breath out of her. It only took a split second before she pushed back with all the heat built up inside her, unzipping his jacket so she could slip her hands up his chest, feeling all of the hard muscles underneath. Her hands moved to unzip his jeans. They needed to look like they were actually having sex in public, which would cause a police officer to get involved.

She shoved his jeans down just enough so they looked convincing as he continued to nip and suck at her lips. "Christ," he murmured against her mouth. He was wearing a wire, so they were acutely aware of other agents listening in, but she guessed that was for her benefit, not theirs. She brushed his boxers, and judging by his bulge, he was definitely in the moment. She wanted to let her hands linger there, but they had more important business.

His hands came down to her ass and moved under her pea coat. He cupped her bottom, and she took his cue, jumping as he picked her up. His mouth continued to plunder hers, never missing a beat.

She wrapped her legs around him and thought just how much she loved her job. She'd worn a dress that day but hadn't bothered with tights since the shop was blazing hot. In picking her up so quickly, Alex had accidentally - or maybe *not* so accidentally - bunched her skirt, which meant his hands were making equal parts contact with her dress and her underwear.

Lord have mercy in heaven. How did she get so lucky today? She was going to send that pot dealer a dozen cases of beer.

He spun her around so she was sandwiched between him and the brick wall of the alleyway. He came up for air and whispered as he nuzzled her neck. "You ready, honey?"

"Yes," she said as she captured his mouth again. His grip tightened on her ass, and she felt him thrust against her, starting their pretend sex-in-the-alley act. The very not-at-all-pretend bulge met her in just the right spot, and the loud moan she let out was only partially acting.

He thrust again, and she moaned louder, a strangled cry against his mouth. "More, baby," she said a little louder.

He moaned against her neck. "Fucking," *thrust*, "torture," *thrust.*

She knew exactly how he felt. His mouth captured hers again, and he hefted her up. His fingers slipped under her underwear as he held her; this time, her moan as he thrust was only too real.

"Yes, yes," she said, panting loud enough to catch attention.

"Hey!" the police officer called from down the alley. A flashlight shined in her eyes.

Halfway there.

"This is a family event, fella," the police chief said.

Fella? Like I haven't been the one moaning like I'm in a porn? Ugh, dudes.

Alex stilled and sat her down, discreetly disengaging as if they were really having sex. "Sorry," he sent an embarrassed wave.

"Sorry? Not good enough. My kids are around the corner. Come here," the police chief said.

Right, since this guy was a paragon of moral fortitude, Brynn thought, remembering the wad of cash in his jacket.

"Charlie, come now," Petrov said with a gentle smile. "Don't you remember what it was like to be in love?" He angled an eyebrow at the police officer.

Charlie, the Dirty Police Chief, got his ticket pad out of his back pocket. "Sorry, Mr. Petrov, rules are rules. I can't have anything X-rated goin' on in my town."

Brynn bit back a snort. As if this guy should make moral judgments on others.

"I'm so embarrassed," she said, feigning innocence. She widened her eyes, trying for her best baby deer impression. "It won't happen again. I promise, officer." She clutched Alex's bicep and looked embarrassed.

"Please don't write us up. My wife is trying to become a substitute teacher," Alex begged. "Peter, you know us. It won't happen again. We'll do anything." He sent Petrov a pleading look.

Petrov put a hand on Charlie's arm, and he stopped writing. "Charlie, let them go. I can handle them."

Charlie held Petrov's gaze and flipped his book closed. "Okay, but this is your one and only warning," Charlie said to them, a finger in their faces. "This is an upstanding town; we don't appreciate it when some people think they're above the law."

Brynn had to bite down on the inside of her cheek from laughing at the irony.

"Thank you so much," Alex said, fawning over the police officer with what appeared was genuine gratitude.

"Thank Mr. Petrov," Charlie said as he walked back into Toni's without another word.

"Peter, thank you so much. I want to finish my teaching

degree and, well...with a public indecency charge...," Brynn said, making her eyes go misty.

A forbidding smile grew on Petrov's craggy face. His beard and coal eyes glinted in the light of the dim alleyway. "My pleasure. What are neighbors for?" Petrov moved to stand between them and put a fatherly arm around their shoulders.

His fingers gripped Brynn's shoulder with surprising intensity, and he peered down at her. "Now, I need a favor from you."

Chapter Six

BRYNN

Petrov walked them down the alley back toward the festival. "I'm having some packages picked up Sunday evening from my garage. I need you to let them in and make sure they get everything. Nadia and I will be out of town."

Petrov's grip was still straining on Brynn's shoulder. She'd probably have bruises there tomorrow.

He sent her a chilling smile. She swallowed the bile in her throat and smiled back. This piece of shit was exactly where they wanted him.

"Sure thing, buddy," Alex said, all smiles and innocence. "Whatever you need."

"Excellent. Here's the garage key," Petrov handed the key to Alex. "Just keep this between us. It's a few gifts for my Nadia's family, and I don't want her to get suspicious."

"That is so sweet," Brynn said, pulling out of his grasp. She wanted to shudder at the freedom, but she shook her head back instead and sent him a winning smile. "You are such a good husband."

Petrov shook Alex's hand. "What we do for love, right?" He sent them both a knowing glance before he walked away.

Brynn took a big breath and looped her arm through Alex's. They turned and walked in the opposite direction of Petrov.

"You did great back there," Alex said, placing an innocent kiss on her temple. She leaned into it, appreciating the normalcy even though he was her fake husband.

"You, too." She turned her face up for a kiss. A slow smile spread on his lips, and he came down for a chaste, gentle kiss.

"Don't want our friend Charlie to think we're going to try any alley tricks again," he whispered as he pulled away.

Warmth flowed through her as she remembered their simultaneous fake and real make out session that already seemed like a lifetime ago.

Brynn laughed, and he threw his arm around her shoulders, his fingers landing where Petrov's had been. She hissed at the touch. Yep, there were bruises there already.

Alex's brow furrowed immediately and stopped. "What's wrong?"

She shrugged her shoulders, so his arm fell. "Petrov had a titanium grip. Here," She offered her hand. "Don't you owe me some cider donuts?"

He took her hand and tucked it back through his arm. "After your performance in the alley? I'll buy you the whole fucking booth."

A half-hour later, Brynn was stuffed with apple cider donuts and ready to leave the festival. Alex had been true to his word and had jokingly asked what the entire booth would cost him. He'd flirted outrageously with the elderly owner, and Brynn loved him for it. He could charm the pants off of anyone when he wanted to.

They walked back to Brynn's car in the parking lot behind the boutique. The side street was quiet and empty, and they walked hand in hand silently down the old brick street.

Alex cleared his throat and looked away. He always did this when he was about to say something hard.

"Out with it," Brynn ordered. Being his closest partner for five months helped her learn all the shortcuts to get what she needed out of him.

"I uh..." He looked down as they walked. His mouth twisted.

Jesus, what was he going to tell her?

She willed him to look at her, finally giving his hand a tug. "Alex, what?"

He stopped and looked around, ensuring they were alone.

"Was what happened back there okay? I just want to make sure we're okay." He finally met her eyes.

"The...donuts? I mean, I think we should have gotten *two* dozen instead of one."

He smiled at her. "No, you goof. The alley."

"Alex, it was *my* idea."

"I know. But we've never done any of...that. Never gone that far." His eyes glanced down to her mouth.

They were in one of the few places that weren't bugged or under surveillance by their colleagues back at headquarters. They had received confirmation the wire wasn't transmitting any more. They could finally talk.

"It was fine," she lied.

It was amazing, and I want a repeat of it right now.

But no, everything would be over soon. She couldn't get entangled. Couldn't let her crush turn into something more, though she suspected it already had.

What was someone supposed to do with an office crush, but that crush happened to live in your house and kiss you all the time for work?

It royally screwed with her head to the point where she went through a mental checklist every night before bed: *He's not your husband. He doesn't love you. This will be over soon. Don't get used to it.*

"Fine?" His face flashed a look of disbelief. He rubbed a hand over his face, and the look was gone. "Yep, okay." He took a breath and turned around to go to the car.

She grabbed his arm. "Are we not okay?" Maybe he needed to debrief more.

"Brynn, we're fine."

"Alex, talk to me." She wouldn't let go of his hand and wouldn't move. His only option was to wrench away from her or turn around.

He turned toward her, looking like a caged tiger ready to bolt.

"What's going on?" she said, shaking his hand. "You can talk to me—"

"It wasn't fine for me," he said, his eyes landing on her mouth.

"I'm sorry—"

"Stop. Just let me finish. It wasn't fine for me because...it was..." He took a big breath, glancing around briefly, then back to her. "It was *everything*."

Blood thundered in her ears.

His hand came up to her jaw, and she leaned into it, enjoying the warmth of his hand on her.

"Are you the world's best actress?" His quiet smile nearly split her in two.

She slowly shook her head no, her eyes never breaking with his.

"Then, speaking as your non-husband, can I kiss you?"

Chapter Seven

BRYNN

His dark brown eyes searched hers, and Brynn felt adrenaline spike through her.

This was against the rules. And Brynn Hannebaker was a rule follower. She always had been. It's why she was top of her class, the first to be recruited for the FBI's undercover program. Rules had kept her safe for a long, long time.

So what could breaking one little rule hurt?

Just one kiss. It wasn't any different than any other public date night where people had seen them kiss.

She worried at her lip as she slowly nodded, giving in to every desire and sex dream she'd had for the last five months.

Light sparkled in his eyes as he leaned down. He took his time, placing his forehead on hers. She thought her heart would pound out of her chest.

Why did this feel so different? They'd kissed a thousand times, but this carried its own weight of expectations. This was *them.* The real them. This was Alex, an FBI agent and certified hottie wanting to kiss who she actually was.

His nose found the length of hers, drawing a slow line. She leaned into him, rubbing her nose against his and feeling his breath on her lips, still waiting to kiss her. The suspense was killing her in the most delectable way possible.

"We might only get to do this once," his voice was low and breathy. "So I want it to count." One hand slid around her waist, and his hand on her jaw drew her closer until there was a scant space between their mouths.

"Close your eyes," he whispered as his nose nuzzled her cheek.

"I want to see you."

"Just," he chuckled, "let me win this one time."

A smirk threatened her lips, but she complied and closed her eyes.

She felt a soft, lingering kiss at her temple. His warm lips pressed into her skin at her hairline as if he was starved for her. He moved to kiss one eyelid, and Brynn sucked in a breath at the unexpected tenderness. When had he ever been this gentle?

He broke away to place another lingering kiss on the corner of her other eyelid, his five o'clock shadow stubble grazing her cheek. She felt every nerve-ending tingle from that brush of friction.

His mouth moved down to her jaw, landing a kiss just under her ear, and she felt her knees give a little from the contact. His kiss was still soft and lingering, but her breathing had turned ragged, and she clutched at his coat.

"Now this," she said through heated breaths, "is torture."

She felt the low chuckle rumble through his chest that stood as a wall surrounding her. "Good. Payback, honey."

His teeth caught on her earlobe, and she was *this* close to begging him to kiss her. He sucked on her earlobe, and it shot straight down to her panties. She felt herself go wet just from that nibble alone. He was several inches taller than her, and all she wanted to do was to bury her face in his chest. To forget about the job, about the past, about what they'd have to do in the future. Just be with him right now.

Fuck it, she'd beg.

"Please," she whispered into his ear.

He grinned against her skin. He pulled back, keeping his hand on her jaw, and stared at her with open wanting. "I've waited almost six months to hear that."

His delighted smile was short-lived as she pulled him down, and their mouths finally met. His lips captured hers in a smile, and she felt the blissful pause as they savored their combined breaths. He tasted like cinnamon and wood smoke. She thought about how this kiss - this genuine, heart-melting kiss - felt different than all their others in the last six months.

His arms came around her like a vice, pulling her towards him. He took what he wanted from her mouth, no tentative-stage kissing any longer. She wrapped her arms around his neck and met her tongue with his. She ran her hands through his hair and tried not to think about what they could do with a little extra privacy. Where she'd imagined that head when she was alone trying to work out her lust.

He nipped at her lips and caught her mouth in one long kiss as their breaths drew together. His arms loosened, and his forehead rested on hers. They finally came up for air, gasping.

"That felt...different," she said, her eyes questioning his.

"Good different?" His eyes narrowed in a responding question.

"Very good different." She grazed her hand over his stubble and stared into his eyes, now almost a midnight-blue. "Unsatisfying, and frustrating, and very, *very* good."

He wrapped her in a fierce hug, and she nuzzled in, breathing in the scent she knew would be there when she went to sleep and when she woke up. The scent now smelled like home to her.

This would all be over soon, and she had to protect herself. She pulled away, hoping to make it home and beyond the mission with a shred of her heart intact.

"See you at home?" She dug the keys out of her coat pocket.

"You bet," he said, placing a brief kiss on her cheek and walking to his car across the lot from hers.

Ugh, back to acting.

ALEX

As Alex brushed his teeth that night, he decided two things: one, he'd never get the taste of cider out of his mouth after their foray at the festival, and two, he was definitely, stupidly, completely in love with Brynn. He loved her taste, her brains, her body, her gentle kindness. She had a calming air that soothed him; made him less chaotic. She made him better just by being her.

She cared for others in a bone-deep way, and he'd tried to care for her in that same way in return. She always seemed surprised when he did little things for her. It pissed him off that she hadn't been treated like that every day of her life. They only had a few more days of the operation, though Alex had considered throwing the game and screwing up the mission just to have a few more weeks with Brynn.

He padded out to the bed, and Brynn was under the covers reading the latest bestselling mystery. She had on her usual slinky, low-cut silk nightgown that left very little to the imagination. He practically knew the shape of her breasts by heart.

Alex took a deep breath and looked at the ceiling. Anywhere but where he desperately wanted to stare.

"That was a big sigh," she said as she flipped a page nonchalantly.

He loved their bedtime ritual. He hadn't slept next to a person so consistently since...well, never. He loved that he could just sigh, and she knew something was up.

"I don't know about you, but I had an eventful day today." He tossed a decorative pillow on the ground from his side of the bed.

Brynn snorted. "You could say that." She kept her eyes trained on her page, but Alex knew she wanted to glance at the security cameras. It was so weird that people at headquarters were watching them go about their lives, but finally understood why their director had insisted on protocol, keeping cameras everywhere except the closet and bathroom.

It was too easy to fall in love with someone in conditions like these.

Alex settled under the covers, and Brynn turned out her lamp and turned on her nightlight. She always had trouble falling asleep and usually had to read herself to sleep. He didn't usually think about her light, but tonight it only reminded him of her.

He tossed and turned to the other side, but no. That was worse. He could smell her, and goosebumps traveled down his arms as he thought about their kisses. About her moans in the alley. Her legs wrapped around his waist as he grabbed her ass. He shook his head to clear it.

"You ok?" She looked down at him, her hair falling in waves, her face fresh and clean. The thin spaghetti straps on her purple nightgown were begging to be pushed aside. He'd only have to give them a whisper of a tug, and he'd have everything he wanted.

A growl came out of him as he sat up, his head between his hands.

"Oh my god, Alex. What is up with you?"

"You," he bit out. *Shit.* The cameras. "Sorry. Didn't mean to yell. It's not you. I just…," he threw back the covers and grabbed a fresh towel from the stack in the laundry basket.

"You're taking a shower now?"

He looked back, and her head was cocked to one side in utter confusion. How could she be this unaffected? He was practically climbing the walls thinking about their kisses and unable to touch her now.

He walked to her and spoke very softly, towering over her.

"You might be unaffected by today, but I need to work off some tension. Please be asleep before I come back out, so I don't throw off those covers, fuck you senseless, and lose my job."

"Oh." Heat crept up her cheeks. She chewed on her cheek and slid under the covers. "Got it. Night," she said as she turned and stared up at him, her long lashes beckoning him down for just one more kiss.

Another growl ripped out of him as he turned, stalked to the bathroom, and slammed the door, eager to finally have a fucking release after the sexually-charged, torturous day next to the woman he loved.

Chapter Eight

Alex pushed vegetables around the sizzling pan as car headlights shone across the kitchen windows. Brynn worked with Nadia again today and hopefully would have more intel. She'd thankfully been gone before he managed to drag himself out of bed this morning.

The front door lock turned, and a blast of cold air from outside blew across him.

"Smells amazing. My favorite," Brynn said, unwinding her scarf from her neck. She sent him a warm smile that he knew meant more.

"It's a special night," he said, not looking at her. He cracked an egg into the stir fry to add more protein. He couldn't bring himself to say it was maybe their last night. Plus, you never knew who was listening.

The ops team investigating the police now had solid proof that the Petrov family was bribing the entire police force.

Their director at the FBI thought it might run deeper, and they hoped that intercepting the delivery tomorrow night would help them finally understand Petrov's next move.

"How was work?" Alex threw his signature sauce onto the stir fry to finish it off.

"Nadia worked the whole shift with me." Brynn groaned as she massaged her temples.

"Tylenol is there." He jerked his head to the glass of water and pill bottle he'd set out for her. He didn't know how she hadn't bound and gagged Nadia after the first three hours.

"You're an angel." She shuffled over to grab the bottle like a lifeline and chugged the water. "Nadia and Peter are going on a trip," she said, between taking the extra strength pills.

He quirked an eyebrow at her. "Lucky them. Where to?"

"She said it was a surprise. Someplace *'tropical,'*" she whined in an imitation of Nadia's shrieking voice.

"The Cayman Islands are lovely this time of year," Alex said as he went back to stirring.

"They leave tomorrow and won't be back for a few days."

Convenient. Maybe too convenient. They'd need to keep their wits about them.

"Any luck with you today?" Brynn asked as she got the plates down for dinner.

"I interviewed a few folks." That was a nice way of saying he had spied on people he thought might be working with Petrov. "Didn't learn anything meaningful other than Petrov is now on the community board."

He plated their food, and they sat down. Their last dinner together, and didn't she look absolutely perfect?

She bit into the stir fry with fervor. "You have to give me this recipe," she said, her mouth completely full. "How do you get the sauce just right?"

"No way am I giving you my date night recipe." He smiled at her through bites. "I'll just have to keep making it for you."

Her eyes fell to her plate.

The likelihood of them having dinner again was pretty

unlikely. They might cross paths if they were lucky, but this would probably be it. No more late-night talks, no more shared dinners talking over their days.

After dinner, Brynn made her usual hot cup of cider, pouring from the jug of Wellington's finest. "Angela at the boutique said this year's cider tastes weird to her. She said it's usually a lot better, but she couldn't figure out what was different."

She sipped from her mug and padded through the living room and into the bedroom to change.

"Eh, people's tastes change, I guess," Alex called back to her from the living room. "Hey, did you want to watch—"

The house fell into darkness, and Alex grabbed for the gun hidden under the side table.

"Brynn?"

"Power's out on the block. Whole street is dark," she called from the bedroom.

He got his breath under control as he used his phone as a flashlight to find her. "I thought...I don't know what I thought," he said as he peered through the blinds. The entire neighborhood, all house lights, and street lights were pitch black. "Just a little jumpy."

"The power company estimates it'll be back on in an hour," Brynn said, looking at her phone. "Must be the wind tonight."

Alex made a non-committal sound as he peered out the window.

Brynn walked over to their dresser and lit a candle. The flash of it set the room into an ambient glow. She lit a few more candles on the bedside table that she kept for decor.

"No wonder people had a lot of kids in the 1800s. It's pretty romantic in all this candlelight," he said, trying to lighten the mood.

He couldn't take his eyes off her as she walked back to him, hands in her back pockets. What he wouldn't give to have her alone, surrounded by candlelight, and nowhere to be. No bad guys to chase.

"Yep, nothing more romantic than a candlelit bedroom," she said as she bit her lip. That bite went straight to his crotch.

He saw a flash of an idea light in her eyes.

"Alex, look in the corner." She nodded to the fake plant that held their surveillance camera.

No light shone back.

He grabbed his phone, and a text message came from their director, Jose.

Cameras are down. Stand by until power is back on.

His eyes found Brynn's, and he felt himself go breathless as he put two and two together.

Her breathing grew ragged as he stared into her eyes. He thought of her face in his hands yesterday. The feel of her lips against his. Her breasts against him.

"That means..." He couldn't finish the sentence.

Her cheeks flushed, and she nodded her head slowly at him. "Do you still feel like you did last night?" She asked, her breathing heavy and her voice barely above a whisper. She looked almost nervous.

"Worse," he admitted. "I'd take you right here if given an inch of a chance."

Chapter Nine

ALEX

"You get the shower," she called as she walked into their closet, the only other place in their house without a camera, just in case the power came on.

Alex bolted into the bathroom and shut the door. If the power came back on suddenly, the shower would buy them a few minutes of cover story. He turned on the shower full blast and walked through the adjoining door to their walk-in closet, where Brynn was waiting. Her cell phone was perched on a shelf, casting the entire closet in a soft glow.

He stopped dead in his tracks when he saw her.

She'd already taken her shirt off and was unbuttoning her pants. She stood in a maroon lacy bra and teal panties peeking out of her unzipped jeans.

"No time for seduction." She wiggled out of her jeans.

"You're seducing me just fine right now, Hannebaker," Alex said as he stalked toward her and gripped the back of his shirt, pulling it over his head.

He needed to feel every inch of her skin for the one and only time they could be together. He ripped his pants off, throwing his belt across the closet. The closet wasn't quite long enough for him to lie down. He spotted a chair in the corner and swiped the stack of clothes off of it.

He turned around, and she was already there. His mouth crashed down on hers with all the desperation he felt. He gripped her in a vise against him, feeling her velvet tongue already moving with his. He wanted her in every way imaginable. In every position imaginable, but they'd only have this one shot. He had to make it perfect for her. To tell her, without words, what she meant to him.

"Hey, slow down," he panted as she clawed at his boxer briefs. "We have a few minutes." He sat down on the chair.

"No time," she said as she reached back to unhook her bra.

"Brynn, wait."

She paused in midair.

"You're doing my favorite part." He smiled at her and sent her a smoldering look. "Come here."

She walked to him, and he grabbed her hips, his thumbs running against her hip bones. It felt like velvet, this smooth, soft patch of skin. He wanted to savor this time between them.

He placed a kiss along her belly and bit into her hip along her hipbone. She hissed out a breath.

"This okay?" His eyes met hers through the dark light. Her eyes were molten, and she bit her lip. It was driving him fucking wild.

"More than okay."

He stared into her eyes as his thumb moved under her panty line at her hip, stroking her on her hip. "How about this?"

She nodded. She stepped between his legs, and her nails raked through his hair. He grabbed her ass with the other hand, loving the firm sculpting of it. He fought an urge to dig his fingers into her to appreciate just how firm.

He slid his thumb along the underside of her silk panties all the way down until he reached her apex. The fabric was already dark and wet. He kissed her belly and stroked her on the outside of her panties.

She let out a soft moan.

He kissed each breast, still in her bra, licking as he went. God, he'd dreamed of this a thousand times. Burying his face right fucking here. He leaned his head in between her tits, nuzzling her. His thumb moved against her clit on the outside of her panties.

"Brynn."

"Hmmm?" she said through her soft moans.

He stopped circling his thumb. "Brynn, look at me."

She gazed down at him with a lusty, hungry look. Her hand came up to frame his face.

"I want you to know that you are so special to me. That I've dreamed of this for months. Of kissing you here..." he pushed a bra strap to the side and pulled down her bra, revealing one breast. Her nipple pebbled under his gaze.

He kissed the top of her breast, finally breaking her eye contact to take her nipple into his mouth, sucking on it and rolling it around with his tongue as she whimpered. His cock was so hard that he was going out of his mind.

His other hand brushed her other strap aside, and he reached around and unhooked her bra.

"And here..." He placed another kiss on her other breast, licking along the underside of it as he'd dreamed of doing. She had perfect, handful, tear-drop breasts, and he'd never forget the sight of them in front of his eyes until the day he died. He inhaled her vanilla and cinnamon scent as he licked along her breast. Her hand came under his jaw and urged his mouth to hers. Despite their languid pace, he could feel her pulse racing as fast as his.

He pulled back, finally releasing his wicked grin. "Now, I think it's time you sat on my lap."

Chapter Ten

BRYNN

B rynn didn't think she'd ever heard a sexier phrase uttered. She grazed her hand down Alex's jaw and felt his stubble along her fingertips. His fingers pulled at her panties, and he was practically licking his lips as he tugged them down.

"Condom?" he asked as he slowly pulled her underwear over her curves. He knew she was on birth control, and they both had been through strenuous physical exams before beginning the mission, including an STD test.

She leaned down to whisper. "No," she said quietly and nibbled on his ear.

He sucked in a breath at that combination, and she felt victorious.

He grabbed her hips, and she settled herself on his lap, now fully naked. She straddled him and felt his bulge underneath her. His hands pulled at her, and she moved her hips, rubbing against him. Curls of need shot through her.

"God," he whispered into her hair. "You are perfection." His hands gripped her breasts and rolled her nipples between his fingers. Pleasure engulfed her.

"More," she cried, unable to hold it back anymore. She rocked her hips against him, making his boxer briefs wet but not wanting to stop at the perfect friction she felt.

"That's it, take what you want, honey," he said, pulling on her nipples harder.

A sob escaped her. She was so close to coming from this alone. "More."

He chuckled low, and she felt it vibrate against her breasts. "You're greedy, Brynn. I like that. How's this?" He placed a thumb on her clit as she continued to ride his cock, making his boxer briefs absolutely soaked.

His thumb rolled one time around her clit, and she felt an orgasm rip through her, pleasure shooting through her, followed by a tingling shower of goosebumps.

She slowly came back to herself, taking a breath. "Holy fuck."

His hand came up to her cheekbone, pressing her mouth to his. She ran her hands up and down his biceps, finally taking advantage of feeling him as she'd wanted to do for so long. His body was hard and muscular, but she hadn't anticipated how soft his skin would be. She grasped his biceps, and a new ignition of need smoldered within her. His tongue danced with hers, and he sucked on her lower lip. She rolled her hips again, wanting him even more.

"I need you," she murmured into his neck as he made his way down, kissing her neck and running his hands over her curves.

"You've got me, honey." He drew back to stare at her. "You've got all of me."

Her heart cracked down the middle, knowing she was in love with the one man she couldn't have.

She needed him on a primal level. Wanted him more than anything she'd ever had.

She stood up and yanked his boxers down. He lifted up to help her, and she straddled him again, grabbing him and wrapping her fingers around his base. *Good lord, he is the perfect size*, she thought as she squeezed him. She kissed him as his hands settled on her hips.

He pulled back as she gazed at him. His hair was mussed and absolutely perfect in the low light. God, she loved him. She fucking loved him. How cruel was her life?

"You ready?" he asked tentatively. She nodded as she lifted up and guided him into her slowly, so slowly. It had been a while since she'd been with a man, and he was larger than she was used to. He hissed out a curse.

"So, so tight," he threw his head on her shoulder. She was still crouched, not fully encasing him yet.

The fullness of him felt so good, and she inched down until she finally sat down on his lap. He threw his head back, hitting the jackets behind him.

"Holy hell." He bit his lip, and his hands held onto her hips. "Don't move," he commanded. "Don't move for a minute." He gathered his breath. "Or this will all be over." He closed his eyes and pushed out long breaths. She wanted to run her tongue along his throat, feel him under her as she rode him.

"What will you do if I move?" she asked, feigning innocence.

"I'll come right here," he said, opening one eye to stare at her.

"Prove it," she said, breathing heavily. She was so close to finishing again, just from rocking against him as she'd slowly lowered herself down.

He pounced on her quick as lightning, his mouth on hers, and he pulled her hips into his, grinding her against him at a punishing speed. She felt herself rock higher and higher, wanting to wring every bit of lust and need out of him.

She matched his frantic pace, riding him harder and harder until they both sobbed their cries into each other's mouths and came against each other.

Chapter Eleven

ALEX

Alex's heart was thundering in his ears as his hands skimmed Brynn's back.

Her head was resting against his shoulder, and he couldn't remember when he was happier. His heart might burst. Was it from adrenaline? Or bliss? He wasn't sure.

"You're trying to kill me, aren't you?" He leaned his head against hers, placed a kiss in her hair, and heard her chuckle.

He closed his eyes and tried to memorize her scent. He was ashamed to admit he'd already thought about buying a bottle of her shampoo after the operation so that he could have something that smelled like her again.

She dragged her head up and ran a soft, delicate hand down his cheek. He never wanted her to leave where she was right now. On his lap, arms around her, she was safe. A sudden urge reminded him that this would all be ripped away in minutes. He crushed her to him.

"I know we don't have long, but I need to tell you..." he petered out. Was he brave enough? Could he put himself out there even though he knew it couldn't go anywhere?

He could handle hand-to-hand combat, getting shot at,

drug dealers no problem. But telling the woman he loved, who he could never be with, that she meant everything in the world to him?

Who could be brave enough for that?

"You okay?" She rubbed a hand on his shoulders. She pulled back to look at him. She had those devastating, big, round eyes trained up at him, full of worry.

"I wanted to tell you..." he started again. "That was mind-blowing. Best of my life." It wasn't a lie, but it wasn't the whole truth, either. *I am such a chicken shit.*

A cocky corner of her mouth tilted up. "Yeah? How about round two?" she said as she nibbled on his throat, running her lips along it until she hit his ear.

"I notice you didn't return the compliment, Hannebaker," he said as he squeezed her ass. He'd never get tired of doing that if he was given half a chance.

"Mmmm did I ever tell you that your cologne has driven me crazy for months," she murmured into his skin.

He chuckled but heard an important word in that sentence: months. She'd felt the same way he did.

"Months, huh? Guess you got it bad for me?" He pulled back and locked eyes with her.

She chewed on her lip, debating how to respond. And it only enticed him to actually think about going for round two. How he wanted to steal that frown on her face and replace it with his kiss.

So he did.

He pulled her closer until they were a fraction apart.

"Unless," he whispered, "you're completely unmoved by me. So you wouldn't mind if I didn't kiss you right now." His lips trailed to her jaw. "If I pulled my cock out of you." He heard her hiss with an intake of air. "If I didn't squeeze you anymore."

He moved one hand to her breast and kept the other on her ass, squeezing hard.

"No," she said, almost whimpering.

"No, you don't have it bad for me?" He tugged on her nipple.

"Yes," she sobbed, rocking against him again slowly.

Maybe he *was* ready for round two as he started to harden inside her. He'd dreamed of this for so long, and they had one chance. Why not see if they got lucky twice?

He crushed her to him just as a FaceTime call sounded on Brynn's phone.

They both froze.

"Shit. It could be Jose," she said, climbing off of him.

He felt like his winning ticket to a happy ever after had just been ripped from his hands.

"It's him," she hissed as she grabbed a t-shirt and flung it over her head.

He leaped up and bolted into the bathroom no time to grab clothes.

"Hey, Jose," Brynn answered the video call breezily.

Alex listened to Jose update her on the case and what they'd learned about the police involvement. It was deeper than they'd initially thought. Petrov had a significant source of money coming from somewhere.

Alex shook his head, trying to clear his racing thoughts. Maybe they'd have to extend their mission? They had estimated they'd be done this week, but he might get to stay if this was a more extensive operation.

The call with Jose took longer than anticipated, and Brynn was still in the closet. He wouldn't be able to sleep tonight if he still smelled like her. He decided to hop in the shower.

～

BRYNN

AFTER SHE HUNG up with Jose, Brynn peered out the window. Something was moving in the darkness near the Petrov's garage.

"Alex?" She called out in the darkness.

He appeared looking criminally delicious. She couldn't risk another round of getting caught up in his arms, with the power coming back on at any moment.

Brynn picked up her binoculars and looked through the window into Petrov's backyard. "There's movement happening in the garage."

"What kind?" he asked as he threw on fresh clothes.

"Three men, dolly, medium-sized truck."

"Big coincidence that the power just happens to be off, along with any security systems that might capture what they're doing."

Brynn sent him an arched eyebrow.

"Let's go," he said.

They waited to head over until the men in the truck left, but they still wore dark clothing and ski masks as a precaution.

The power was still off, and who knows how long they'd have until it suddenly came back on.

"Did you tell Jose we were heading over?" Alex asked.

"Yeah, he couldn't guarantee to keep the lights off even if they came back on. So, we're on our own."

"Well, Petrov's not home, but their security system is state of the art, from what I could tell when we were over for dinner last week."

They crawled back through their backyard bushes and cut through a neighbor's side yard. They entered the Petrov property from an alley, slinking through the shadows to the garage.

Alex peeked his head up into the window. "No security

cameras visible." They tugged their masks on. They'd look like burglars if anyone caught them.

He jimmied open the lock on the door leading into the garage. A quiet click sounded, and they slid through the door, taking up as little space as possible.

"What's that smell?" Brynn sniffed the air.

"A spice, maybe?"

Alex checked the garage perimeter as Brynn lifted a lid on a carton. She shined a flashlight and saw several smaller boxes within the large carton.

"It's written in some script language I can't read," she said. "Maybe Hindi or Thai. The box also looks," she paused, "international. What the hell is that smell?" It was driving her nuts. The packaging was unlike anything she'd seen in the U.S.

"Hold on. Here's one word. *Ceylon*." She tried to figure out where she'd heard that before. "Maybe it's some sort of food."

Alex's head shot up. "Ceylon cinnamon. It's the purest type. Most of the stuff you see at the grocery store is imitation cinnamon and cheap. This stuff is what the pros use, and it's super expensive. They must be masking the smell of something else with cinnamon to throw people off."

Brynn opened up one of the boxes to root around. Sure enough, vast packets of brown powder were in each box. Alex opened a few others to double-check.

"Shocking there's no coke in here, what with the disguised smell," Brynn said. "Why would he hide thousands of pounds of fancy cinnamon in his garage? Also, how do you know about this?"

"What? A guy can't bake when he's stressed? All the other cartons match that one. C'mon, we should go." He put the lids back on the cartons and wiped any cinnamon dust away, erasing any trace they'd been there.

"You haven't baked once since we got here," Brynn said, packing her carton.

"Well, maybe I haven't been very stressed in the last five months."

She caught his eyes in the darkness, and heat sizzled between them again.

Somewhere in the garage, they heard a whir start-up, and a security light flickered to life outside.

The power was back on.

Chapter Twelve

BRYNN

"Shit," Alex ground out.

They slipped out the door, and as they clicked it shut, they heard loud footsteps enter the garage with voices.

"No time, let's go," she whispered to Alex. They crept along the back of the garage and disappeared into the bushes, coming out into someone else's backyard. They ripped off their ski masks, turned their coats inside out, and crept along the edge until they ended up on the sidewalk on the street behind theirs.

They zipped their coats and stuffed the masks inside, easing their pace into a walk.

"Why on earth would anyone want five thousand pounds of cinnamon?" Brynn asked as she took Alex's hand. They were simply a couple out for a late-night stroll.

"Let's think about this. Who is the largest consumer of cinnamon in the regional area?" Alex leveled a gaze at her.

"Oh my god. He's in cahoots with the Wellington cider people." Brynn hit his arm in excitement.

"Or intercepting it and stealing from them."

"Okay, so he intercepts it, then what? And if you and I are

supposed to let people into their garage tomorrow, where will it go? There wasn't an extra square foot of room in that garage."

Alex shrugged. "Maybe they're gonna switch it."

"What would the markup be if they put shitty store-bought cinnamon in the Ceylon boxes and then sold the original Ceylon at a markup on the side?"

"I don't know. Maybe a hundred grand per shipment?"

Brynn typed on her phone and showed the screen to Alex. "On the Wellington Cider website, they claim they only use free trade, Sri Lankan Ceylon, the highest quality, which is why their cider is so delicious." She angled an eyebrow.

"Who would have thought people might go to jail over cider?"

"I mean, it's pretty good cider," she said, smiling at him.

Alex burst out laughing. She'd miss his face and his good humor when they were done.

He brought her gloved hand to his mouth to kiss it. They were still around the block from their house, and it was late. No one to perform for, but no one watching either. She tugged him closer and settled her arms around him.

"Today has been one of my favorite days," she said, debating how much honesty to give him.

She leaned her head on his chest. She couldn't tell him how she felt. That wasn't fair to either of them.

To tell him she loved him and then never see each other again? No way. Better to keep the secret to herself.

He placed his head on top of hers, and they stood on the dark sidewalk in the freezing cold. "Me too." He let out a long sigh. "It's a luxury having a partner who you can bed and then go on recon trips with."

She felt warmth travel down her spine as he stroked her hair.

"Alex, you are..." *Say it.* "Special to me." *Gulp.*

He pulled back and kissed her gently, slowly. She lingered on his taste, wanting to memorize it, trying to remember the feel of his lips on her, the feeling of absolute safety. She'd always had a hard time trusting anyone she'd dated. Tears threatened her eyelids. *Dammit. Don't think about how you won't be able to kiss him again soon. Just appreciate what you have.*

He pulled back and immediately saw the unshed tears in her eyes.

"Hey," he said quietly. He stroked her cheek. "I feel lucky every day that I get to be your partner. You are beyond special."

A shiver overtook her, despite her flaming cheeks and her racing pulse.

"C'mon. Let's get you home," he said as he put an arm around her. "Big day tomorrow."

And potentially the worst day if it was their last day together.

THE NEXT MORNING was quiet as they went about their morning routine. Brynn walked downstairs and found Alex with a to-go mug of coffee for her, per usual.

"Looks like the Petrovs are moving whatever is in their garage," Alex said, nodding to the back window. Three men wheeled large cartons back into a truck quickly and quietly.

"Interesting," Brynn said, holding his gaze. "Have you talked to your boss this morning?" It was a challenge speaking in code within the house, but it was worth it if it protected their lives. They didn't have the resources to do bug sweeps regularly.

"Yep. He said the goods being shipped today will be picked up later this week," he said, jutting his chin in the direction of the truck.

"Good." There was definitely something up with whatever was in the garage and the entire Petrov operation.

Brynn grabbed her coat and purse, ready to head for a shift at the boutique. She grabbed her travel mug, and Alex cleared his throat. He gave an imperceptible head shake, maintaining eye contact with her.

Ooookay.

She sat it back down on the counter and grabbed her keys. "I'll see you tonight at the Petrov's for the delivery?"

"Maybe I should just take it. You stay here in case anything happens," he said with a worried look.

Brynn burst out laughing, and then she realized he was serious. "Sweetie," she said, forgetting that they were inside. She cleared her throat, mad at herself for her slip. "I mean, you are sweet, but no, I'll go along with you. I'm happy to help the Petrovs."

In another life, she would have found his offer patronizing or political within their office division. Plenty of dudes she worked with would love a major win on their record by themselves. But after last night, she knew that he just cared for her. He wanted to keep her safe, just as she wanted to keep him safe.

She both hoped and feared that today would be their last day on the mission. She took a good look at him before she left. Fresh from his morning shower, in bare feet, a sweater that hugged toned arms and shoulders, and jeans that hung just right on him. He'd worn his glasses this morning because he'd had a hard time falling asleep last night. She loved him in his glasses. She sent him a quick wink before she left through the front door.

She walked outside and grabbed her keys, preparing herself for the day ahead. She waved to a neighbor as she was herding her kids into the family minivan. She'd miss this cozy town with its picket fences and nearly-continuous festivals.

She heard her name being called and saw Alex jogging toward her. He'd run outside in his sweater and thrown on tennis shoes, holding the travel mug of coffee.

"Forgot something again, honey," he said as he walked to her, catching her gaze. He waved to the neighbor as the minivan pulled out into the street.

Aha. Clever man. He'd orchestrated one more send-off. One more chance to touch him, to kiss that mouth she'd dreamed of every night for the past few months.

"This is why I love you," she said, willing herself to maintain eye contact.

Chapter Thirteen

BRYNN

She'd kept her comment light and airy. There was no risk in that sentence, but ultimately it was true. She loved him so much it hurt. It maybe hurt more to tell him to his face right now, under the guise of pretend.

He took a big breath as he reached her. "I can promise you," he kissed her soundly, "I love you more, honey." He held her chin in his hands, and her eyes filled up. She chewed her lip to keep from crying.

"Always the lovebirds in the mornings," Petrov boomed from the front door. He smiled down at them from his front porch above. "Oh no, what's this, my little cheese puff," he cooed. "Why the crying?"

Damn. A tear had escaped her notice. She wiped it away. "Oh, you know, newlyweds. Fighting and making up every other day," she said as she wrapped her arms around Alex. She squeezed him more for herself than to sell it to Petrov.

"Ah, yes. My Nadia cried every other day when we were first married," he said as he made his way down the stairs to his car.

I bet she did.

"Women, right?" Alex shook her a little and winked at her.

"Women," Petrov walked towards them. "We are better for them, no?"

Alex chuckled with him.

"Now, you will both be here to receive the delivery from my company this evening? Remember, it's secret," he said, looking over his shoulder. "No one can know, not even my Nadia. I whisk her away later today."

"Sure thing, happy to help," Alex said.

"Oh, Brynn, wait for me," Nadia yelled from the front door. "I want to fill you in on all the hot goss I learned last night. Apparently, Becky's pregnant—"

"No way!" Brynn played along.

"And Jim's *not* the father." Nadia clocked a look at her.

"Oh man, get in and dish." Brynn nodded her head toward the car. She held Alex's gaze. Their own secret language between them with just their eyes.

I love you. I'll miss you. She willed him to know that she meant it.

"I love you, sweetie. I'll miss you," she said, keeping it light and breezy again with a quick peck.

"Love you," he whispered back, seemingly only for her.

Her heart thundered as she walked back to her car. He had to mean more with the way he'd said it.

That would have to be good enough for now. Maybe forever.

ALEX

ALEX HEARD the door open that evening and looked at the clock. "Hey, Brynn, look who's here," he said, calling her from the kitchen.

A shocked look on Brynn's face was quickly replaced with a smile. "Jose, I didn't know you were stopping by."

Alex felt like his balls were in a vice since their director had arrived a few minutes before. He'd dropped by unexpectedly, which usually wasn't a good sign. Did they figure out he and Brynn had developed feelings? Or that they'd had sex? Surely that could wait until after the end of the mission. They were almost through the thick of it.

"I've had some exciting times at work in the last few days," he said, staring at them. "One of my staff members..." he paused in thought.

Shit, shit, shit. They knew about what had happened in the closet.

"Found some interesting things on their drive. Accidentally crashed into a cinnamon truck, of all things."

They'd intercepted the truck, like Alex had asked Jose this morning, to see if anything had changed. He hadn't been given an update yet.

Jose typed on his phone and showed the text to both of them.

Cinnamon had been changed out. Selling the Ceylon to other distributors. Backup is around the corner if needed.

They both nodded, and Brynn sat her things down. "Cinnamon? That's so weird. Do you want to stay for dinner?"

"Nope, just wanted to come by and see two of my favorite people. I'll be around," he said, throwing a wave behind him as he walked toward the door.

They heard the lock click in place as the door shut, and they both let out a breath.

"How was our friend Nadia?" Alex looked at the clock. Only twenty minutes until they were to head over to the Petrov's garage to receive this mysterious shipment.

"Excited about her trip. She wasn't sure where they were

going." Brynn reached automatically for the Tylenol Alex had sat out for her.

Interesting. "No details? Nothing?"

Brynn shook her head as she swallowed the pills. "Nope. She left this afternoon, so the headache isn't too bad."

That matched up with the timeline Jose had told him. Nadia and Petrov would already be out of the state by now while this new shipment was coming in.

"Want something to eat?" Alex asked her as she rubbed her temples.

"Nah, I'll eat after we go to the Petrov's."

He knew how she felt. His stomach was masquerading as a truckload of butterflies, trying to piece together why a Russian mob boss would bother with overpriced cinnamon for a cider company. It didn't make any sense.

He rubbed at his temples. What would a large cider company have to offer an organized crime syndicate? Unlimited apple cider access?

"Speaking of which, I think it's about time we head over," he said.

Brynn checked her watch and nodded her head. "Let's get our coats out of the armoire. It's a little chilly tonight."

The FBI had put a large gun safe disguised as a decorative armoire in their bedroom. They usually carried concealed weapons, but Brynn was smart to suggest getting backup weapons just in case.

They walked to the bedroom, and Alex pressed his finger to the thumbprint reader on the backside of the armoire. The hiss of the lock clicked, and the door opened to reveal a backlit repository of any weapon they'd need. He grabbed Brynn's go-to gun, handed it to her, and then grabbed his own.

He thought about grabbing one more, just in case. He felt a

desperate need to keep her safe. "Think we should grab a scarf too?" He nodded at the knives on display in the armoire.

Brynn frowned at him and shook her head. "Nah, we won't be there that long." She held his eyes and sent him a questioning, silent look.

He nodded in response and tucked his weapon in to hide it from plain sight. As far as Petrov's people knew, they were just everyday citizens who had never even fired a gun. This was just a precaution. He hoped they'd learn something about Petrov's operation, but it wouldn't escalate beyond that. The most successful mission was one where they acquired intel, and no one got hurt.

They locked their back door a few minutes later and walked to Petrov's garage. They'd sent Jose a message that they were on their way, and he'd confirmed that backup was on standby. No one knew exactly what to expect.

Alex slid the key into the lock, and Brynn was at his back, watching to make sure no one surprised them from behind. He opened the door into the pitch-black darkness and reached for a light switch. He couldn't find one and stepped inside the garage.

"Do you remember seeing a light?" he asked Brynn.

She stepped in behind him, and the door slammed shut after her.

Alex felt a gun at his back.

"Don't make a sound," a familiar voice warned.

Chapter Fourteen

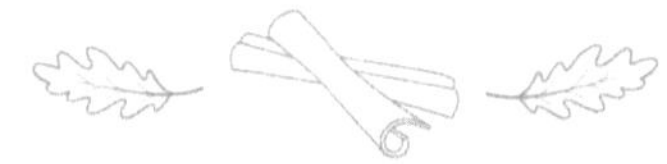

ALEX

uck. Petrov.

Alex sucked in a breath and bit back his desire to call for Brynn. How many guys were here? Did she also have a gun at her back?

The lights flipped on overhead, and Alex's eyes shot toward Brynn. She had a gun to her back and gave him a subtle head nod that she was okay. Her lip started to tremble, and she widened her eyes.

Ah, that's how she wanted to play this. They were just two friendly neighbors who got caught up in a bad situation.

"Peter, what's going on?" she said in a wavering voice. "We thought you were out of town?"

The henchman shoved them around to face Petrov.

"Hands in the air, FBI Agent Hannebaker," he said, punctuating her name.

Son of a bitch. How had they been caught?

"What?" Alex said in disbelief. "Peter, you know us. C'mon. Put down the guns. We're your neighbors, the Smiths."

"Hands in the air," Petrov warned. His henchman made a

149

threatening move toward Brynn. *No. No, no, no.* Not her. He had to do something.

"Hey," Alex barked out. "Let her go. She doesn't know anything about my job in the FBI."

A smile spread like oil on Petrov's face. "So, you're why my operation has been found out?" His low voice etched through the silence like a threat. "You son of a bitch. My Nadia is in handcuffs."

He had to draw the henchman's gun away from Brynn. "Why aren't you in handcuffs, you bastard?" Alex spit out.

The henchman's gun ticked over to his chest, muscles flexing to pull the trigger.

A guttural scream ripped through Brynn's throat, and she leaped in front of him while she grabbed her gun from behind her back. Alex shoved her aside as he heard a shot fire. He felt a hot slice of lightning go through him. Pain radiated from everywhere all at once, and he couldn't see through the shock.

Several more shots were fired, and Alex heard the blessed sound of sirens in the distance. Footsteps thundered outside the garage. The light was getting dimmer, and he couldn't keep his eyes open. He called for Brynn, screamed her name, but no response rang back that he could hear. Blackness swallowed him as he thought of her face one last time.

BRYNN

BRYNN PACED the floor of the hospital hallway. She'd visited every day for the last three days, staying as long as the staff would allow. There were FBI guards positioned outside Alex's room, so the nursing staff knew something was up, but she'd never corrected them when they assumed she was his wife.

An image of Alex covered in blood flashed through her mind again. She shook her head to clear it.

She'd landed two clean shots on Petrov and the henchman as she dove for Alex. She'd killed the henchman, but Petrov was now recovering at a prison hospital. She thought of her hands covered in blood as she staunched Alex's wound until backup arrived a few seconds after he'd been shot. He'd been hit in the chest just beside his bulletproof plate. He'd whispered her name repeatedly until he fell unconscious, and the memory of his raspy voice haunted her. What she'd give for him to be awake.

A nurse waved to her as she came out of Alex's room. "He's awake and asking for you, but he's groggy."

Brynn realized she was running by the time she got to the door. She cracked it open and peered in. A disheveled Alex lay in the bed where she had left him yesterday, but his eyes were open.

"Honey, you're home," he said groggily, with a goofy grin.

She smiled and closed the door. "Hey, partner. You scared me." She couldn't stop her feet from rushing toward him. The sight of him was too good to be true.

He'd been in surgery for hours and then in an induced coma to ensure everything was okay for a few days.

She sat on the edge of his bed and grabbed his hand, placing one of hers on his stubbled cheek. He gave her a weak smile through half-open eyelids. "Sorry," he said, rasping out each syllable.

"Shh, you just woke up. You've been out for a few days," she said, stroking her thumb on his cheek. She'd sat and held his hand every minute she could be there, talking to him, confessing everything she couldn't say a few days ago about her feelings—things she'd never said to anyone else.

"You were in my dreams," he said as he closed his eyes

again. "And you wouldn't stop talking." A smirk curled on his lips as he settled back down to sleep.

Maybe her confessions had made their way into his subconscious? She tucked his sheet and blanket tighter over him as he snuggled in. "What did I say?" She both hoped and feared he'd heard her.

"You said you couldn't live without me," he snorted with sleepy laughter.

She stroked his cheek one more time, happy to see his smile.

"What did you say back?" she whispered, half hoping he'd fallen asleep.

"I said," he took a deep breath. "I'd never leave the woman I love." He nuzzled her hand and promptly fell asleep.

She bit her lip to stop it from trembling, but a few stray tears fell down her cheeks. She squeezed his hand and pulled up a chair. She'd wait in the room until he woke up. She could finally get some sleep now that he was okay.

BRYNN HEARD gentle voices around her. She opened her eyes to see Alex sitting up and talking with a doctor Brynn hadn't seen before. She rubbed the sleep from her eyes and sat up, willing herself to alertness.

"She's awake," Alex said as he leaned over with his good arm and squeezed her knee.

"Are you the wife?" the doctor asked.

"Yes," Brynn said automatically. *Wait, the mission was over.* "Oh, wait—"

"She's my wife," Alex said with a gentle smile, looking straight into Brynn's eyes.

Chapter Fifteen

BRYNN

Brynn's heart plummeted into her stomach at hearing those words one last time. She tried to savor them. She looked down at her hand. She hadn't taken off her fake wedding ring, even though the mission had been over for days. She tried to take it off a few times but couldn't go through with it until Alex was okay.

"Doctor Achebe was just explaining my recovery plan, honey."

"I'll let you catch up. A nurse will be back to check your vital signs." The doctor flipped her clipboard closed and walked out.

"You look good," Brynn croaked, her voice groggy with sleep.

"You look better." Alex reached out a hand to her, and she took it as an invitation to sit on the bed. She situated herself at his hip on his uninjured side. He'd grasped her hand tightly and pulled it to his chest. His left arm and chest were bandaged under his gown, and Brynn saw the IV drip of pain meds going into his arm.

"How do you feel?" Brynn asked.

"Like I got shot with a bullet." His smile belied his words, though. He looked much more refreshed than he had a few hours ago. "What's the situation with the case?"

"Petrov's in jail, still in the prison hospital. They were selling the Ceylon cinnamon in exchange for using the Wellington Cider company's interstate distribution network for drug and black-market goods delivery."

Alex threw his head back on the bed. "Of course, their trucks that go everywhere along the eastern seaboard. You never suspect the hometown cider company." He shook his head back and forth in disbelief.

"Our breakthrough helped the rest of the team know where to look. Everything was solved about an hour after you were shot," she said, willing him to understand how vital their work had been.

"Just wish we'd been the ones to solve it," he said, looking back at her from the bed. "This has been a hell of an operation."

"How long will you be out for?" She stroked a thumb over his fingers. How much longer would he be somewhere where she could see him? Maybe a few weeks?

"The doctor said I have a long time before I can even hold a gun. I could maybe be back out in the field in six months."

Hope rose in her chest. She could take some vacation time, maybe spend it with him before he went out on another operation.

He cleared his throat. "But I've decided to take desk duty for the next year, at least."

Brynn shook her head in disbelief. "You've always been out on operations. You hate staying in the office."

"I recently found someone worth staying for."

A smile escaped her lips. "Are you sure that's not just the morphine talking?"

"Brynn. I recently survived the most painful experience of my life, and I don't intend on repeating it."

"I can't imagine how much it hurts," she said, staring at the bandages.

"Not that." His face was serious, tinging toward anger. "I'd take bullets any day over spending another six months next to the woman I love and not being able to touch her. Not being able to tell her that her smile was my reason for waking up in the morning." He tugged her hand, so she bent toward him and nestled into the curve of his uninjured shoulder.

She thought her heart might burst.

"Not being able to bring her into my arms at night as she tosses in bed for thirty minutes trying to find the perfect spot. Not being able to kiss her whenever I wanted." He placed a long kiss on her temple, on her cheek. "But the worst part is, I'm not sure if she ever loved me back."

Brynn buried her face in the curve of his neck, glad to feel his warm skin on hers. Her heart beat like clanging bell, heavy and echoing in her ears. Could she do it? Could she tell him how she really felt?

She forced herself to meet his eyes. Why was telling your best friend that you loved them the scariest thing you could ever do? Admit that you loved them, not just for themselves, but their entire person? She knew this man in and out. His quirks, his faults, his strengths, and she loved him for all of it.

"I bet," she started, moving her lips along his throat. "She loved you more. I bet she'd try to take a bullet for you."

He pulled back to stare at her, serious as a heart attack. "I'm so mad at you for that."

Her eyes narrowed. "He was going to shoot you."

"So it would be better if he shot you?"

"Yes," she said, getting ready to sit up, but he tugged her back to the bed. She smiled despite herself.

"Honey, that is the wrong answer." He kissed her hair and smoothed it down.

She loved that he used the same nickname as before. "When did it become real for you?" She stared at their interlaced hands.

He pulled back to look at her. "Some part of it was always real. I loved being fake married to you. But I figured it out on the day of the festival. Any woman who can outthink me, eat that many apple cider donuts, and look that good doing it all has my heart forever."

"I'm going to miss being fake married to you in a small town with an endless supply of fairy lights," she said, thinking of their mostly happy days gathering intel in the cute little town.

"I'm going to miss being fake married to you, too." He settled her into his arm, stroking her hip with his thumb. "Now that you know I'd take a bullet for you, I was wondering if I could take you to dinner as your not-fake husband." He pulled back to look at her with a smile.

"Now that you know I'd take a bullet for *you*, the answer is a resounding yes." She placed a slow kiss on his cheek. She thought she might expire from happiness.

"I only have one rule if we date," he said, giving her a stern look.

Brynn arched an eyebrow at him. "No more bullets?"

"Absolutely," he squeezed her tight, "no more apple cider."

"Deal." She captured her fake husband slash real boyfriend's mouth with an eager, grateful kiss.

Bonus Epilogue

BRYNN

Brynn nervously fussed with her hair in the hallway mirror beside her front door.

He should have been here by now.

He only lived two blocks away, for chrissakes. She looked at her phone again—no text. Looked out the peephole—no one in front.

Time to pace. She glanced at her makeup in the microwave reflection.

Was this too much? Was this too weird? They'd been living as man and wife, 24/7, for six months. After spending only two weeks apart, she worried maybe she didn't even know Alex.

Maybe everything would be changed now that they weren't fake-married. Now that they were going on their first *real* date. Maybe all of this was a bad idea and it would ruin whatever they'd built the last six months.

A strong knock interrupted her thoughts, and she fought between running to the door and trying to play it cool.

Fuck it. Run.

She dashed to the door and swung it open without first looking out the peephole, and a sheet-white Alex stood with a bouquet of flowers and a grimace that he tried to turn into a smile.

"Oh my god, what happened?" She ushered him inside, looking in the hallway of her apartment building to make sure he hadn't been followed.

They'd moved across the country, but you could never be too careful.

"I'm fine. I just need a…" He clutched the countertop that led into her apartment kitchen, beads of sweat along his brow.

"I knew I should have picked you up."

"Can't. You're my"—he took a deep breath, gritting through the pain—"girlfriend. First date…IthinkIneedtositdown," he said all in a rush at last.

Brynn grabbed his waist and looped his good arm over her shoulder as she moved him ten feet to the couch. "This was too much. You've only been out of the hospital a week."

"I'm fine," he said in a weak voice as he gripped her shoulder.

"You were nearly dead a week ago."

"Two weeks. You forgot the joy-filled week-long hospital stay after I regained consciousness. I'm never eating orange jello again."

He was so stubborn. He'd insisted she focus on her move and not nanny him at his apartment when they got to Pine Creek, a small town outside of Seattle.

She should have trusted her instincts. "We can do this another night. Why don't I drive you home?"

"Why don't I lie on your couch and put my head in your lap and stare at your pretty pretty face?" he said, falling onto the couch. "I don't need you to nanny me. Just give me like, thirty, forty, a hundred minutes tops, and then I will sweep you off your feet." He clutched a hand on his head as he regained equilibrium.

She pushed his hair back from his face. At least he probably had the sense to get a cab or rideshare here. "You didn't drive here, did you?"

"No," he said, scoffing, as if that was the dumbest thing anyone could think. "I walked."

"You *walked*," she yelled.

"It's only two blocks."

"*Up. Hill,*" she scolded. If he wasn't nearly dead from the exertion, she would have killed him.

Brynn had subleased an apartment two blocks away from Alex in a particularly hilly neighborhood. The kind of hills where you could touch your nose to the sidewalk, they were so steep.

She'd genuinely liked Wellington, but for obvious reasons, they could never go back. Petrov's crime unit still had tendrils tucked along the East Coast, so it would be a long time before either of them worked or lived within throwing distance of the Eastern Seaboard.

She kissed his head and walked to her kitchen.

"Where are you going? I'm supposed to stare at your pretty face," he mumbled, his eyes closed, his breathing gradually steadying.

"I'm heating up the oven for frozen pizza."

"But I need to sweep you off your feet," he grumbled, "and this is fucking it all up."

"Our date has very little to do with the food," she said, entering in the oven temperature, "and very much to do with the company."

She poured herself a glass of wine from her favorite bottle. She liked being out in the field, but she definitely missed having a glass of wine or bourbon when she felt like it at home. "Can I get you something? Water, ginger ale?"

"Two shots of adrenaline, if you have it," he said, his eyes rolling over to her.

"We'll just let you rest, and there will be no more walking."

"If you're having a drink, that must mean I get to stay over," he said with a coy smile.

"That's the plan," she whispered back with a wink.

Happiness blossomed inside of her, seeing him plopped into her real life.

This didn't feel weird at all.

It felt like it always had been between them. Friendly. Flirty.

Fun.

"You could teach me how to make that stir fry sauce," she said, handing him a glass of water as she sat next to him.

"But then you wouldn't have a reason to have me back."

She put her hand over his and squeezed it. "You figured me out. That's all I've been keeping you around for: a mediocre stir fry sauce."

"Mediocre?" he said incredulously, getting life back in his eyes. "Agent Hannebaker, you shoot to kill with your words."

She snorted with laughter. "There's the Alex I missed."

"You missed me, huh?" he said, bringing the back of her hand to his lips.

"It's weird living without you," she admitted, putting her wine glass down and snuggling in beside him.

They'd flown home together on a small government plane, but she hadn't seen him since they'd hugged at the tarmac. They'd texted constantly in the last week as she'd gotten settled into her new place. Alex had been under strict orders to barely leave his couch.

"I don't like being away from you," she said, her hand smoothing his shirt over his chest.

"Yeah?" He smiled, getting a little color back in his cheeks. His strong jaw had a dusting of stubble along it, and he looked so good.

There was that feeling again. The buzzing sensation of *I need him* that fizzled through her whole body.

"Yeah," she whispered, leaning in to brush her lips against his. It was their first kiss in over two weeks, and it felt strange, like she was out of practice.

She pulled back with a small panic, and his brows furrowed in thought.

"Bad?" she asked.

He thought for a second, and he looked like he was trying to figure out his feelings.

"Weird. Though..." He held her chin and brought her close with a smile. "I'm willing to work on it if you are."

He pulled her down but held her, running his nose along the length of hers. "I can't count the number of times I wanted to kiss you on our couch."

Our couch.

The drowsy feeling of wanting him hit her eyelids. She held her breath, not wanting to miss a moment. She *missed* living with him. Having an excuse to touch him. To be near him.

He kissed the side of her mouth, and hunger clawed at her for more. She slowly moved to take his mouth, sinking into the feeling of him.

Yes.

His good arm wrapped around her, and his tongue moved against her lips, licking his way into an open-mouthed kiss that was hot and needy. Fire stoked and hissed and popped between them as their tongues met with a burning need.

In the background, Brynn registered an alarm going off.

Later.

She'd feast on Alex instead. Her hand ran under his shirt, finding warm, taut skin covered with a dusting of hair.

"Mmm. I think your buzzer's beeping," he murmured against her lips.

Brynn let herself wallow in his scent. "Food is overrated." She deepened the kiss and pulled him toward her.

"I am more than willing to go on a hunger strike." He placed kisses down the side of her neck, nipping as he went. "But you need sustenance if you're going back to work in a few weeks."

She pulled away reluctantly. "Ugh, fine. Killjoy." She walked over to the oven to insert a mediocre pizza for their first real date. Though Brynn would eat hot dogs off Costco's floor as long as she got to taste Alex again.

"I was wondering"—she sank down next to him—"if you wanted to stay over for a night or two, or three. Or four." She burst out laughing at how eager she sounded.

"Sounds like a fun adult sleepover," he said, tugging her into his lap on his uninjured side. "Lonely without me?"

"Christmas is coming up, and I don't like to be alone for the holidays." She'd lost her parents as a teenager and always dreaded spending the holiday all by herself. "I actually really love Christmas," she said, twining her fingers with his, "but it's been hard ever since I was in high school. I was hoping for a six-foot-two distraction."

"I *knew* you just wanted me for my body." He nuzzled her head, kissing her temple as she snuggled in. "Good thing for you I also bake a mean Christmas cookie. I'm very particular on sprinkle usage."

She snorted at the thought of Alex covered in red and green frosting. "I could think of all sorts of fun activities for sprinkles and frosting," she said with a sly smile.

"Naughty girl." He squeezed her to him. "I like it."

This was such a different dynamic between the two of them, not being under constant threat. She could just be a person who liked a man and wanted to kiss him every waking moment of the day.

She toyed with the hair at the back of his neck, and her eye caught on a chain. "Do you normally wear jewelry?" He'd never worn anything when they'd lived together, but maybe it was something special that he kept tucked away when he was out on missions?

"Oh, you don't have to," he said, putting a hand over it suddenly.

"Oh, come on. You can tell me. Is it a locket of your first dog's fur?" she said, giggling and tickling his uninjured side.

"Not exactly," he said, laughing and letting go. She pulled out the chain, and her breath caught.

It was his wedding ring.

The wedding ring that had been fake but had felt oh-so-real.

Her throat felt thick with emotion. "You kept this?" she whispered.

"Honey," he said, his voice low and serious. "Of course I kept it."

She ran the metal around her fingers. It was warm from the heat of his chest.

From the heat of his heart.

The finish was burnished. It was really just a cheap little ring meant for show for a six-month stunt. *Probably wasn't even real gold, given the FBI had zero budget for costumes.*

But he'd kept it close to him.

"It felt as real as anything else that happened there between us," he said, his eyes searching hers. "And while this is a first date…"

"…It's not a first date," she finished for him. It was their thirtieth. Hundredth. And somehow still only officially their first.

"And I want you to know that I'm as serious as a gunshot wound to the chest about you," he said slowly with a smile.

She felt a little less creepy for keeping her wedding ring tucked away for safekeeping in a box in her lingerie drawer. She'd pulled it out and looked at it over the last week or so. Her hand felt naked without it, but she didn't want to freak him out with how hard she'd fallen for him.

"I really liked being fake married to you," she said, tucking it safely underneath his shirt one more time, but placing her hand on his heart over it.

"All it took was a little subterfuge for me to find the love of my life," he said, his hand grasping hers. Her breath hitched.

Love. It echoed in her heart.

"Love," she whispered back with her stomach full of butter-flies. They'd said it in the hospital, but not since. She'd hoped it wasn't some sort of fluke. She'd fought bad guys; she'd shot guns; she'd even been behind enemy lines; and somehow, falling in love was the scariest thing that had ever happened to her.

"Love," he said with finality, squeezing her hand.

Very carefully, she straddled his lap, careful not to put pressure on his shoulder.

Placing her hands on either side of his head, she leaned over him. He looked at her breasts in front of his face with hunger. She'd worn a low-cut top that evening that showed her modest cleavage, but she delighted in the fact that he clearly *wanted* her.

"I don't think I've properly thanked you for taking a bullet for me," she whispered, leaning over him to kiss his temple. He pressed his face against her breasts as his good hand moved to grip her ass.

"I'm all ears," he murmured, kissing along the swell of her breast.

She pulled back and took off her top, revealing a lacy see-through bra, and leaned down to lick his neck. "Thank you," she whispered and bit his earlobe, feeling him suck in a loud breath. His hand cupped her breast as she leaned into it.

"Pretty sure I've dreamt about your tits every night since I last saw them," he admitted, squeezing her as she moved her hips against his.

She could feel the hard rod of his cock under her already. Pleasure pulled at her as she ground against him, moving to his other cheek. She leaned over him with a whisper-soft kiss and nip accompanied by a breathy "Thank you."

Leaning back, Brynn locked eyes with him and reached behind her to take her bra off. His eyes were black flames of lust, devouring her. She loved that he watched her, like she was performing for him. Enjoying every movement.

Her bra fell down her arms and a guttural moan ripped out of Alex as he brought her to him. He sucked a nipple into his mouth, and the electric need tugged at her. She ground her pussy against him hard. "Fuck that feels so good," she moaned.

He toyed with her nipple, using his tongue to move it back and forth in his mouth. *Jesus Christ, he might finish the job right here.*

Stay on task, Hannabaker. She pulled away and gently pushed him back against the couch on his good shoulder. Holding his jaw, he looked up at her, chest heaving with panting breaths. "Thank you," she said and placed a hot, quick kiss on his lips as she climbed off of him.

"Where…" He reached for her as she knelt down in front of him.

A wicked smile colored his face with understanding as she

reached for his zipper. Placing a kiss on his muscular abs, she whispered, "Thank you," as she locked eyes with him.

His cock was hard and thick and mouth-watering, and as she took it out she clenched her pussy, desperate for it. *Later.* The doctor had said six weeks until more active sex.

She ran her tongue slowly from his base to the leaking tip of his cock and felt herself go wet at the taste.

Brynn Hannabaker was a good-girl rule-follower. Always had been, always would be.

But fortunately for Alex, Brynn also really, *really* loved sucking cocks.

Feeling so bad while making someone feel so good.

It was a cheat, really, thanking him with something she enjoyed. But as she sucked the tip into her mouth, never breaking eye contact with him, she saw his eyes roll back in his head with pleasure.

"You'll never top this," he muttered. "Never in a million years."

She smiled to herself and sank her mouth slowly onto his cock until the salty taste hit the back of her tongue and sucked.

"Fuck, never mind," he cursed. "Just topped it."

She slowly slid his cock out of her mouth, stroking him as she went. She'd pegged him for wanting it a little sloppy, and she was curious if she was right.

God, she hoped so.

"I want you to fuck my mouth," she murmured against his tip.

"Jesus, did Petrov send you? Are you here to finish the job? You're killing me," he said, thrusting in between her lips and throwing his head back.

She chuckled as she licked around the head, lapping up more pre-cum.

Knew it.

She unbuttoned her jeans to slide a hand into her panties. *Just a little relief,* she thought, rubbing her clit.

"Fuck yes. That. More," he said, staring at her hand in her panties. "I always wanted to see you get yourself off. I thought about what you did while we were in the house. How you did it. Where," he panted.

She sucked his cock into her mouth again to get it dripping.

Time for some truth. "Every day," she whispered, still looking at him as she rubbed him with one hand, the other still in her panties.

He groaned and thrust into her hand.

"I'd lock the door to the closet," she whispered, licking along his cock while she rubbed up and down. "Take my vibrator and find one of your shirts that smelled like you." She sucked his tip, exploring the slit with her tongue.

His chest heaved up and down as he waited.

"Then I'd come thinking about you fucking me from behind in the closet, shoving me against the shelves."

She sank back onto his cock, rubbing her clit that was now nearly dripping.

"Such a bad girl, Brynn." He gathered her long hair and looped it around his fist.

Fuck yes.

"Do you like it rough, love?" he ground out, yanking her hair so she'd look at him.

A moan escaped her as she sucked him. "Yes," she sobbed around the tip of his cock. She circled her clit faster.

"Good," he said and shoved her head back down. She greedily took him in again and again as he fucked her mouth. Spit and pre-cum dribbled down her chin, but Brynn fucking loved it.

"Such a good girl for me," Alex cooed as he fucked her

mouth harder. "I want to see you come while sucking my cock. Scream for it."

She rubbed harder, loved being taken and fucked. As she inhaled, nearly choking on him, the rip of her climax throbbed through her, and she screamed around his cock.

"Need to see you suck it all down," he said, thrusting deep. She looked up with watering eyes as she chased the trails of her pleasure.

"Fuck," he screamed, coming down her throat. Her pussy clenched at the salty taste of him.

His chest heaved up and down as she slowly slid him out of her mouth. She licked the end of his cock, catching the last drop.

Smiling, with tears running down her cheeks, she whispered, "Thank you."

A FEW WEEKS LATER, they sat eating a Christmas dinner made entirely of frosted Christmas cookies and exchanged presents in Alex's apartment.

"I feel like I've been waiting my whole life to buy a Christmas tree." Brynn looked up at the twinkle lights they'd strung around the fresh-cut pine tree. "Maybe I'll leave the twinkle lights up all year long in my apartment."

"I distinctly remember that being a big part of the appeal of Wellington." He chuckled. "Here, open your present." He handed her a small box that was flat and rectangular.

It's way too soon for any sort of major jewelry purchase, she thought with relief. She'd barely had any relationships in her adult life and wanted to savor the journey of falling more in love with him every day.

She shook it hard next to her ear.

"Using those FBI deduction techniques?" He smirked.

"I'm a guesser, okay? I think it's... metal. Bullets for my work weapon?"

"Try again, Sherlock."

She ripped open the package, and when she lifted the small lid, she saw a small metal key tucked into cotton.

"It's been torture being away from you for three weeks," he said, taking her hand. "Move in with me, please. Pretty please. However many pleases it's going to take to get you to move in, that's how many pleases I'm going to ask with."

Her eyes filled. This was real, what they had. They had moved past the hot and heavy forbidden relationship of the mission, and the last three weeks had been bliss.

They had all of the closeness of the mission together, but Brynn got to be even more herself now. Less serious, less focused on being a perfect little rule-follower. And Alex had been excellent at tempting her to be very, very bad.

She bit her lip to tamp down the emotion overwhelming her. It had been so long since she'd felt like she had a home with someone who really loved her. She liked her apartment, but she loved being surrounded by Alex's things. By Alex.

"Is tomorrow too soon?" she asked, carefully moving over to kiss him, pressing her mouth against his and trying to imprint this moment in her mind forever.

"For my fake wife and very real girlfriend? Never." He pulled her on top of him, and Brynn lost herself in the possibility of a future under the twinkle lights.

THE END

Hot Cocoa

AND

Mistletoe

Chapter One

Subject: Impenetrable Spaghetti Splatter
From: B.McWilliams@mcwpartners.com
September 1, 7:48 A.M

Ms. Bell,

Please be advised that it took me five hours to clean up the aftermath from the arm wrestle you lost to a gallon of spaghetti sauce in the cabin. The splatter above the cabin stove looked like an active crime scene.

As your fellow co-owner of the cabin, I need not remind you that in Article 4, Section 5 of our Co-Ownership Contract, all shared surfaces must be returned to their *original* state before your time at the cabin is over.

Please keep this in mind as you begin your fall stay in the cabin.

Sincerely,
Bennett McWilliams, Esquire
McWilliams & Partners Law, Chicago IL

Re: Impenetrable Spaghetti Splatter
From: PeriPlansAParty@pbparties.com
September 5th, 11:32 P.M.

Bennett -

Oh, what a *delight* it is to hear from you, as always. I saw your name and thought, "What fresh hell does BenBen have for me now?" And you really outdid yourself.

Five hours for a few drops of spaghetti?
Please.

You know what I just found in the cabin tub? A dark, terrier-sized hairball in the drain. As I have blonde hair, I'm guessing you have the longest hair of any corporate lawyer in Chicago and an unsettling degree of hair loss. De-shed and de-clog before you leave, k?

Also, I've attached paint samples for the cabin living room. I'm thinking Merry Berry Pink or Millennial Hangover Peach. Do you have a preference? The living room could use a pop of fun.

Note: If you're unfamiliar with this term, 'fun' is when you do things to experience joy, resulting in a smile or laugh. Smiling might hurt your face at first, but you'll get used to it.

Tootles,
Peri
Peri Bell Party Planning

Re: Re: Impenetrable Spaghetti Splatter
From: B.McWillliams@mcwpartners.com
September 6th, 8:32 A.M.

Ms. Bell,

Do not—I repeat, do *not*—paint the interior of the cabin any shade of anything. Cabins do not need 'pops of fun.'

Cabins are meant to be enjoyed for their rustic purity, which is why I purchased the half-time ownership of the cabin as is.

See Article 7, Paragraph 2 of the Contract. *No permanent changes to any surface shall be made without signed approval from all parties.* And I do not approve.

And I hate pink.

I do not admit causation of any dog-sized hairball, but I will inform you my girlfriend (now ex) will no longer join me at the cabin. Therefore, any future remaining long hair will obviously be yours.

I've made sure to leave ample new sponges and dish soap in the kitchen.

Please use them.

BMW

Re: Re: Re: Impenetrable Spaghetti Splatter

From: PeriPlansAParty@pbparties.com
September 9, 1:02 A.M.

OMG did you sign your email with BMW?? Hahahaha who even are you?? Is typing 'Bennett' really that much harder?

Does your penis get bigger with every letter you save when typing an email?? Does your confidence skyrocket and your opposition cower knowing you are known by three letters alone???

Genuinely curious,
Periwinkle M. Bell
P. S. - It took me 4 extra seconds to type my name 🫠

Re: Re: Re: Re: Impenetrable Spaghetti Splatter
From: B.McWillliams@mcwpartners.com
September 10, 8:15 A.M.

Ms. Bell,

I implore you to leave my nether regions out of future communications.

Sincerely,
Bennett
(Happy now?)

The smell of vanilla sugar cookies wafted under Peri's nose as she tapped her foot to Ella's rendition of *White Christmas* (the best one, thank you). Only six more garlands to hang before she'd be finished decorating her upstate cabin.

Sugar plum pink, mistletoe green, and clouds of white fake snow were her theme for her first-ever holiday party at the cabin she co-owned. As a professional party planner, she could whip up an informal holiday get-together in hours, but this was no ordinary spur-of-the-moment party.

Peri planned to host her framily (friends who she liked better than her family) this year. They were a motley crew of friends she'd collected over the years who either were too cash-strapped to visit their family during the holidays or who weren't accepted by their families anymore. They'd rock out their own Christmas in Peri's upstate cabin, situated in the middle of the Wisconsin forest. It was a long drive from Chicago, but she knew she could make the experience worth it for them.

This also happened to be her first Christmas at the cabin without her dad, the spirit of Christmas embodied. He'd had a short, cruel bout with cancer several years ago, and they hadn't even realized their last Christmas in the upstate family cabin would be their last. For the last few years, she'd packed her holidays full of work so she didn't miss him so much.

This would be the first year in a while that she'd spend Christmas here. The centerpiece of so many happy memories.

She looked around with pride. Her two-story A-frame cabin, complete with huge log walls and a second-floor balcony overlooking the kitchen, dining, and living area, practically burst with holiday cheer.

Peri had managed to get everything decorated and hung up herself but had saved the garland for last. She'd wrap it around the enormous beam that ran the length of the cabin for maximum visual impact.

She wanted to create something fun, sparkly, and special for her friends. She switched out her normal throws for large fuzzy white ones that acted as metaphorical snowdrifts in the cabin. Several glittery candles and shiny tinsel created a sparkly effect she hoped was disco-meets-Christmas-level festive. The seven-foot tree was up and decorated, matching her new theme naturally, but she'd kept several sentimental ornaments she'd made with her dad over the years.

Peri stared at the sparkling pink, sage-green, and white handmade garland currently lying in a huge pile on the floor. She'd need to figure out some way to hang it from the rafters, but she couldn't quite reach it even when standing on a step stool.

Why the hell couldn't I be four inches taller?

She hopped up on the stool and reached one more time, stretching to hook the sparkling garland along the edge of the beam. She eyed the counter in front of her.

Maybe if I stand on the counter, I can reach it.

Hopping down from the stool, she hoisted herself up onto the counter with all the grace of a drunken sea cow.

Flawless, as always, Peri.

She hung one side with no problem, and she decided to try her luck by leaning over the stove and seeing if she could launch the garland over the rafter, creating a drapey effect.

As she prepared to toss the garland, a rattling sounded at the door.

The doorknob started twisting, and all of Peri's worst fears of being alone in the woods came true.

She'd be murdered here in the middle of the remote forest where no one could hear her scream. Her friends would find her body after this murderer did...well, whatever murderers did to her.

She dropped the garland and picked up the first weapon she could find to defend herself on the counter: a frying pan.

No one murders me on Christmas, damn it!

Pan raised and ready to strike, she crept to the edge of the counter where the door opened. Maybe the element of surprise would give her an opportunity to leap out the door and run away.

The lock twisted down, the door opened confidently, and in charged a huge, energetic wet dog, followed by the scraping of a suitcase and a man she'd recognized from hours of online profile creeping.

Bennett McWilliams.

Fuuuuuck.

Chapter Two

"What the hell are you doing here?" Peri said, still holding her frying pan in the air.

She may have looked at photos of this guy online once or seven hundred times, but she still didn't *know* know him.

Maybe he *was* a murderer. Maybe chopping people up and sautéing them over a campfire wasn't a hobby he'd listed on his LinkedIn profile.

In person, Bennett McWilliams looked like a Highlander who decided to become a corporate lawyer in Chicago. His broad shoulders filled the doorway, and Peri thought he'd look more at home as a defensive lineman for the Bears than as a very fancy-pants attorney who shared her upstate cabin half of the year.

"What the hell are you doing up *there*?" Bennett stared at her very logical place on top of the counter.

"Clearly, I'm defending myself," she said, waving the frying pan.

"The knife block is right there." He shut the door.

She looked at a knife block beside her foot. *Damn*. She hated it when he was right.

They'd never officially met, and she shouldn't technically know what he looked like even though they'd exchanged passive-aggressive and eventually aggressive-aggressive notes about the upkeep of the cabin for a few years.

"And who are you?" She shoved back the wisps of hair that had escaped her ponytail and crossed her arms. She pretended as if she hadn't stared at his stupidly handsome face more than a couple of times over a glass of wine when she was particularly annoyed at him.

"Bennett." He held out a hand for her to shake, and she reluctantly bent down and took it. "I'm guessing you're Peri."

"Bingo." She withdrew her hand and tried not to think about the warmth of his fingers and how his dumb enormous hands had enveloped hers. "It's winter. Are you aware of this?" AKA her half of the year.

Why had he come up to the cabin without asking her?

When her father died, her dad's will stated the cabin ownership would be split between her mom and herself. After only one year, her mom had opted to sell her half-time use of the cabin (something that still bothered Peri to this day).

He angled a glance up at her. "Are you aware it's Christmas? I always come here at Christmas since you never have."

A bolt of memory sailed through Peri. *Shit.*

Her idea for a Friends-mas had seemed so spur of the moment she'd completely forgotten he'd spent Christmas at the cabin the last three years.

She could never bring herself to spend Christmas week by herself here, and her mom refused to come to the cabin because it brought back too many memories of Peri's dad.

"Ummm...I just remembered?" Peri chewed her lip, feeling extra stupid standing on the counter with a frying pan still in hand. She'd even confirmed it in August when he emailed to double-check.

"So, you'll leave." He said it as a command rather than a question. "Also, please get down. You're in slippery socks, and that's granite. You'll crack your head open."

Peri looked down at the piles of decorations on the counter and the chair in the middle of the room that had scooted away from her earlier.

"I'm good," she said with an unconvincing shrug and head nod.

She'd sleep up here before looking completely stupid, flailing, and rolling herself off the counter in front of McBeefcake, Esquire.

He stared at her with bored eyes and finally walked over to her, shaking his head. "Bend down," he said, reaching up to her waist and standing in front of the counter.

"I can get down just fine. I just prefer it up here."

"Peri, get down," his voice firm and louder than before.

Peri had what you might call a *problem* with authority, but her body had conflicting feelings about being told what to do by a broad-shouldered domineering man. A flush hit her cheeks.

"BenBen, I will do as I please. At least half of this counter is mine." To prove it, she swung the pan around to show him her side and, in doing so, lost her footing on the slick marble counter, careening toward him.

Her life *should* have flashed before her eyes as she fell six feet downward, but all she could think was how mad she was that Bennett was right.

She flailed her arms for purchase, grabbing at nothing like a demonic windmill set for destruction. Bennett grabbed her hips as she fell, and they tumbled in a tangled heap to the floor. His thick barrel chest cushioned her fall as he grabbed her and he'd somehow landed under and *around* her.

The frying pan clanged loud enough on the wood floor to be

heard in Chicago, and the large dog ran for its life to the bedroom.

"Am I dead?" Peri muttered from underneath his arm as the last clang of the pan rang out.

"You ought to be," Bennett said as he rolled out from under her. "I'm adding a no-standing-on-slippery-surfaces addendum to the contract. You okay?"

His tone made it clear he was asking as a polite, perfunctory request.

She rolled her wrist and felt a pang but said nothing. "Yep, never better." She gripped her way to standing, still rubbing her wrist.

Bennett marched back to the bathroom as if he owned the place. *And I guess he kind of does.*

He came back a few seconds later holding a bandage. "Wrist," he commanded, holding out his hand.

"So you're a doctor *and* a lawyer?"

"I'm certified in first aid, and you're clearly in pain from having twisted it. Wrist," he said more forcefully.

"I'm fine," she sent him a half smile. "So, are you planning to leave now, or..."

"Peri, for the love of god, stop rubbing your wrist and hold it. It'll feel better if it's stabilized."

Heat flushed her cheeks against her will at him saying her name in his stern, deep voice. "I do not consent to be serviced by your dubious medical training," she spat back, even as pain throbbed in her wrist if she didn't hold it just right. *Distract him.* "What's your dog's name."

"Jax. Here boy," Bennett called, and a blinding flash of black fur flew at Peri.

Jax was a very good boy and, therefore, immediately put his huge paws on Peri's stomach and shoved his head into her hands, causing an equal mixture of delight and pain to shoot through her.

She yelped in pain and Jax sat down, afraid. *Shit.* Okay, maybe she did need an ace bandage.

Bennett sent her an arched eyebrow. "Now?"

Peri closed her eyes to prevent herself from rolling them and nodded, trying not to tear up at the throbbing in her wrist that was making its way up to her elbow.

A surprisingly gentle hand grabbed her injured one, and Peri's eyes shot open.

This guy was the subject of so many of her text rants to her friends that they'd nicknamed him BenBen McTightass, Fucksquire. She assumed he showered in a three-piece suit, ate plain toast for every meal, and sat dutifully in a blank white room while not at work, charging on his battery station.

That image didn't match the hand that currently held hers in a shockingly close distance. His fingers were warm but rough, and she stared at his hand holding the bandage in place on her forearm. Heat radiated off his skin, and she realized he was still wearing his coat. The trendy, expensive all-weather jacket strained across his broad shoulders, and she wasn't sure what to do with her eyes other than stare at the sculpted chest being featured in a tight black shirt under his open jacket. She'd seen pictures of him online, but she was surprised at just how enormous and cut he was up close and personal.

She needed him out of here ASAP, or she'd have to finally admit that she had a raging, secret crush on her number one enemy.

Chapter Three

"So..."

Peri wasn't sure how to broach the tinsel-covered elephant in the room. "Is your heart set on spending Christmas here?" She chewed her lip and grimaced, expecting a lawyer-laden lecture about to wash over her.

He rolled the bandage around her wrist in an X-shaped pattern and blew out a sigh. "Well, it is my holiday tradition, and you *did* agree to my use of the cabin. I think we both know who should spend Christmas here."

She narrowed her eyes in challenge. "I'm so glad you agree it should be *me* who stays."

He peered up at her with annoyed eyebrows, head bent over her wrist. "We agreed to my staying four months ago."

"I have guests coming for a four-day Festive-stravaganza. I have all my party supplies here. I can't host five people in my one-bedroom apartment in the city."

He wrapped the last of the bandage against her wrist, now firmly stabilized. "Those all sound like problems that aren't mine." He shrugged and started rolling his bag to the staircase.

Peri crossed her arms and fumed. "Yes, it is your problem because we had an unofficial agreement. That's all it was. *Unofficial.* I'm now making it official that I get Christmas cabin use from now until hell freezes over. I'll even send you a singing telegram so you can shove it up your beloved contract."

Bennett clicked the handle on his bag down and picked it up, hefting the full-sized suitcase as if it were a rag doll. He started up the steep spiral staircase to the second floor.

"I have a paper trail to prove your consent, and I'm not leaving. I expect you to be gone in the morning," he said, eyes straight ahead.

Peri followed him up the steep spiral stairs waving her arms as if landing a plane. "No, no, no. There is no walking up the stairs. There is no unpacking. You need to go the opposite way. To your car."

"No one is leaving tonight. It was sleeting all the way up here, and the driveway is an ice rink. You can leave in the morning."

Peri followed him up the staircase and across the hall. "You might be a lawyer, but I'm annoying as hell. I'll chain myself to the oven before I leave willingly."

Bennett turned around in the doorway of the upstairs bedroom, facing her suddenly. Her nose practically hit his chest. "You'll chain yourself to something? Promise?" A wicked grin spread on his face, and a flush hit Peri's cheeks as she realized what he was insinuating.

"Ew, creeper," she smacked his chest. *Whoa.* Did lawyers bill their time at the gym? Her flush grew deeper, and she could feel it spreading to her chest. "Not chained like that."

He brushed past her and went back down the steep stairs. "Jax, c'mon." He motioned at the big black dog who was currently lounging on Peri's feathery blanket on the couch.

Jax looked up with a bored, sleepy expression and snuggled back into the blanket.

"He's fine. Just leave him," Peri said.

"No. He'll be a big baby in the middle of the night and will try to climb this death trap of a staircase. Jax, come," he commanded.

Peri knew she'd found her soulmate because Jax got up, huffed at Bennett, and trotted back to the master bedroom where Peri was staying, giving Bennett the dog middle finger.

Peri and Bennett looked down the hallway and saw Jax roll on the ultra-soft blanket on the master bed.

Peri heard a low growl and was surprised it came from Bennett, not the dog.

Bennett stalked back to Peri's bedroom. She followed him back to say hello to her hopeful, four-legged roommate.

"Jax, come," he said from the doorway. Peri sat down on the bed next to Jax.

"Hi roomie, I'm Peri. Do you prefer being the big or little spoon?" Peri cooed as she pet Jax. He lolled his tongue out of his mouth and looked up at her with grateful eyes, rolling onto his back.

Bennett's dark blonde hair, dark eyebrows, dark eyes, and five o'clock shadow gave him an ominous air as he glowered at her from the doorway. His arms were crossed, and she tried not to stare at his broad chest in the tight shirt that hugged every muscle in his thick arms.

"He's used to this room since it's my room," Bennett said.

"Well, technically, it's *our* room." Peri instantly regretted her words.

Visions of a certain hot lawyer in her bed danced through her head, and she wished she could take back the 'our' in that sentence. She tried not to think too much of what went on in this bed when she wasn't here, but it sometimes popped into her mind that she shared a bed with the hot half-owner.

Bennett's jaw clenched, and he bit his cheek as he continued to glower at her. He turned on his heel. "Shut the bedroom door, so he doesn't get out."

She might have stuck her tongue out at him as he turned away, but Jax would never tell on her.

Bennett's thundering steps made the spiral staircase creak as he went to bed. Peri looked over at Jax, who seemed too happy for words. She heard the sleet pelting the windows and decided she'd lucked out at having a big, warm, snuggly companion for the night who wouldn't lecture her on how to do anything properly.

PERI GOT ready for bed in the en suite bathroom and ignored the visions flashing through her head of Bennet's chiseled jaw as he scorned her with disappointment.

She figured he would be a *by-the-rules* guy, but she hadn't expected the sternness.

Shivers went down her arms. *Oof.* She hated that she had a thing for stern, serious guys.

Why couldn't she love the easygoing guy or the goofy guy? No, she loved it when they glowered. Even better if they frowned while doing it.

She thought back to the wide expanse of his back and the feel of his hands on her when she'd tumbled off the kitchen counter. Peri wasn't small, and he'd handled her well enough. A little shiver of memory made her want to dance in her place.

Her phone dinged with a new message.

JESSIE

Hey girl. PUMPED for tomorrow. Bringing the champagne and the vibe as always xoxo

Her best friend Jessie hadn't spoken to their parents since coming out last year. Peri was determined to host an amazing Friends-mas to make sure Jessie had the best holiday of their adult lives. There would be activities, a hot cocoa station, games, and about a billion cheesy holiday movies to watch. They'd get white girl wasted, make crafts, and then get up the next day for a big breakfast of mimosas and pancakes.

This was going to be great.

Peri didn't even have to think about the fact that her mom had moved on to a new life without her. She'd just focus on making the perfect holiday party for her friends.

PERI

Can't. Freaking. Wait. Drive safe and watch for deer!!

Peri had typed that last phrase without thinking, but it punched her in the gut as she read it back. It always reminded her of her dad. He never failed to say it whenever she was driving somewhere. He'd called it the midwestern version of "I love you." She shoved the thought away before she could get lost in her memories.

She threw on pajamas and dove under the covers as the wind kicked up outside. A howling gale sounded through the trees, and the man-size dog next to her whined.

"Oh, it's okay, buddy." She rubbed his ears. "Want under the covers?" Peri lifted up a blanket, and Jax scrambled under it.

Was she sleeping with a stranger's dog? Yes.

Did she also watch that dog grow up on Instagram because she was a stone-cold weirdo who looked at his owner's profile every six months?

Also yes.

Jax snuggled closer to her, and Peri scratched under his velvet ears, as much to soothe herself as him. He let out a long-suffering sigh and almost immediately started snoring.

Come tomorrow, both the handsome guy next to her and his very hot owner were going home, come hell or high water.

Chapter Four

Peri woke up from a blinding brightness shining through the curtains.

She looked at the clock - only 7:30 A.M.

It shouldn't be this bright yet. Was it unusually sunny in Wisconsin today? Had she time traveled and it was really summer?

And then a sinking realization hit her.

Oh no.

Peri threw back the blankets so quickly that Jax barked. Peri peeked through the curtains and saw the worst possible thing: a blindingly white landscape that had been forest green last night.

They were snowed in.

No, no, no, no.

She threw open the door and hustled to the living room to find Bennett already there in pajama pants and a layered Henley shirt.

He took a sip from his coffee mug. "Looks like neither of us is going anywhere for a while."

Dread sank into the pit of Peri's stomach. She ran to the window looking out onto the driveway. There were at least four to five feet of snow on the ground. *Damn lake effect.* The sleet must have turned into snow unexpectedly overnight. It was so rare for them to get lake-effect snow she hadn't even worried about it.

"But you can shovel. I'll help," Peri said, her voice sounding panicky. "I have people coming this evening."

"That's not possible," Bennett said, gentler this time. "Three huge trees fell down from all the wind last night and are blocking the driveway up the hill to the cabin. I've called our normal guys to deal with it, but they said they have about fifteen people in front of us. Some are first responders and doctors who have to get out. I told them we could wait."

"You what?" Peri railed at him, shooting daggers with her eyes. "You should have woken me up. I'm a co-owner. You don't know my life and what's important to it."

"Are you a first responder? Do you have a life-threatening emergency to deal with?"

Peri willed back the tears forming on the edges of her eyes; she wouldn't do it. She wouldn't cry in front of this soulless piece of stone.

"You had no right. From now on, all decisions and communications are shared. My friends have nowhere else to go for Christmas."

"Do they have homes?" Bennett asked, and Peri couldn't tell if he was being sarcastic.

"Of course they do, you jackass, but that doesn't mean they want to be there for Christmas. A house isn't the same thing as a *home*."

"I can agree with you on that," Bennett said quietly into his mug. "Look, I made an executive decision. The guy said they'd get to us as fast as they could."

Peri thought about whether her ten-year-old sedan could go off-roading through the woods. *Ugh, probably not.*

The light was so blinding, as the sun reflected off the

snow, and everything seemed like it was just too much. Peri bit back tears, thinking of what she'd tell Jessie and everyone else.

Plus, she couldn't stomach the idea of spending Christmas alone with some dude who passed the Illinois state bar but somehow lacked the word 'sorry' in his vocabulary.

Peri threw her coat on, shoved her feet into tennis shoes, and ran out into the snow-covered driveway. She got four steps out the door before she was waist-deep in snow. She could barely see the end of the curved drive around the trees but saw a hulking mound of branches where an entryway to a road should be.

This was it. Her chance to make Christmas fun and memorable and give someone what her dad gave her, and it was all ruined.

Everything was ruined. She'd have to hole up in the cabin for the next three days and be reminded of what she didn't have: her parents. She talked to her mom once a month or so, but it hadn't been the same since her dad died. Not really. And she'd be surrounded by mental pictures of her former favorite time of year.

In a word: torture.

The cold of the snow started to sting her legs, and she turned to go inside. She shook off the snow in the entryway, took off her coat, and bit her lip to keep from crying.

She'd be alone on Christmas. In the saddest place of her life.

A rogue tear escaped and fell down her cheek. Bennett rounded the corner. "See? I told you, snowed in," he said with a smug smile.

Peri burst into angry tears. "Why are you so happy about this? My holiday is ruined. My friend's family stopped talking to them. I wanted to make Christmas special for them. Special for me," Peri admitted, as her spittle flew through the air at the passion in her words. She was sobbing now and saw the color drain from Bennett's face.

"Hey, hey." He walked toward her as if she was a spooked horse. "What's going on?"

She shook her head, unable to get a breath from her sobs. "I'm trapped here with *you*."

"This is all because you have to cancel on your friends?" He was looking at her like she was crazy. Maybe she looked crazy, but he didn't know why she hadn't been able to be here for the last three years at Christmas.

She shook her head *no* and used her sleeve to wipe her tears away. "You don't understand. You don't even like it here. You want to sell to that developer." He'd tried to convince her several times over the last year to consider a local real estate developer's offer.

The cabin was the only connection Peri had to her dad anymore. Her mom had tossed out everything of his right before she'd married her new husband. She'd said it was too painful to sort through everything, but Peri knew she just wanted to move on. Forget all the pain. The cabin was the only physical thing left to remind Peri of the happiest times of her childhood. She couldn't lose it. She really would chain herself to the stove before she let anyone take it away from her.

"You could buy an even better cabin if you'd just think about the offer. No more rickety doors, no wind blowing through the windows that need to be replaced. And you'd never have to see me again." Bennett crossed his arms, a confused look on his face.

"Maybe I like everything the way it is. Not everything is about money, Bennett." Peri grabbed her phone to text Jessie and the others. It was only December 23rd. Maybe there would be a Christmas miracle heatwave, and they could just hop over the trees blocking the driveway.

PERI

Bad news. 😢 Four feet of snow and several trees down mean you might not be able to access me.

JESSIE

Worse news. We have even more snow herreeee. 😭 Angela said she'd borrow her mom's SUV if we can figure a way out of the city. We'll try our best. Kisses!

The fight's not over yet, kiddo. Her dad's words came back to her. Peri's lip quivered again. They'd figure something out.

Surely she couldn't be trapped with Bennett for all of Christmas, right?

Chapter Five

After a semi-calming cup of tea, she was feeling a little better. Peri sighed and looked at her garland that still wasn't hung. It was the last thing she needed to do to decorate the rustic cabin.

The tree had been up for weeks, stockings were hung with some level of care, but she'd wanted the cabin to feel magical, and thought hanging fairy lights and garland on the huge rafters would finally add that "wow" factor.

Jessie had responded that they'd try to be here. Peri still had to hope.

She let out a huff and wiped her nose on her sleeve. Yes, she knew, so attractive. She had more important things to worry about than what Bennett McButtface thought.

"For the record, I don't think everything is about money. I just know a good investment when I see it," he boomed from across the living room as Peri stood looking at the garland.

"My life isn't an investment you asshat," she spat, turning on him. "This is my home. The last—" she stopped herself.

He didn't need to know her business. Didn't deserve to know this was the last place she was truly happy. Before everything changed.

"Last what?"

"Nothing." She turned around and grabbed a chair to see if she could reach another beam to start on the next garland. If she was going to be trapped here, she'd at least use her time wisely and decorate for when Jessie would be here. Because they *would* be here.

"Peri, that doesn't look safe."

"Good thing I don't really care what you think," she said as she tossed a garland over the large beam that started at one end of the living room. It swished over the beam easily and landed on the other side. Peri looked down to find Bennett glowering up at her from under the beam.

She hopped off the chair and pulled it forward until she was nose-to-nose with Bennett.

He didn't budge.

He was a solid head taller than her and looked like he benched logs for fun. She wouldn't get caught up in his simmering dark eyes. She would make the best of this holiday and hope like hell her friends could get out of the city.

"Scoot," she poked at his chest. She ignored how solid his muscles felt underneath the flannel.

"Let me help you."

"No, thank you." She hoisted herself up onto the tall chair, scrambling and almost tipping it over but righting herself at the last minute.

"Fine. Break your neck. Then I won't have to worry about coming back to a pink cabin." He grabbed his coffee cup and stomped up the spiral staircase to his room.

Peri let out her pent-up frustration on the garland, swinging it so hard that it came back and *thwacked* her in the face. She let out a scream of frustration so loud that Jax trotted back to the master bedroom, his ears tucked down.

"Aw, I'm sorry buddy," she called, and he trotted faster away from her. She couldn't have her one ally in the cabin scared of her. She grabbed a treat from the bag Bennett had left out and followed Jax back to the room.

"Hey," she said softly, offering a treat to the dog who was curled up on the bed. "Can't have you mad at me." She scratched Jax's ears, and he gobbled up the treat, licking her hand as if to say *We all have bad days, it's okay.*

She sat on the bed and scratched his ears, finding therapy in a dog's non-judgmental friendship.

Her pajama pants felt wet and heavy against her ankles, and she realized she was cold. The shock of the morning had sent her brain into overdrive, and she hadn't even bothered to change when she came in from the snow.

She closed the door to the bedroom, and the echo of her saying "our bedroom" to Bennett had her cheeks flushing. This had been one hell of a twenty-four hours, that's for sure.

She rummaged through her drawers to find her snuggliest fleece pants, complete with little holly and snowmen. She threw them on and crawled under the covers. Maybe if she went back to sleep and woke up later, everything would be better. Tears threatened her eyes as she laid her head on the pillow, but she pushed them away for later.

Images of Bennett from this morning, in his tight-fitting shirt, danced in her head, and then more images of his broad shoulders filling the bedroom doorway last night popped through her head. She didn't want to think about him like that. He was the bane of her existence. He threatened her ability to even stay at the cabin she loved.

But, maybe she could have one little fantasy, right?

She let her imagination run wild, thinking of him cornering her in the kitchen and letting his hands run all over her. The scent of his designer cologne danced under her nose as she imagined his head bending down for a nip and lick along her throat. About what it might feel like for his wide hands to grab her waist and yank her toward him. She felt his stubble graze along her skin as she wound her hands through his hair, encouraging him on.

In her dreams, he turned into Dream Bennett, who did what she wanted him to, including, but not limited to, ignoring his desire to sell the cabin and touching her in just the right places. Moving his hand along her side until he came to her breast, toying with her nipple. Dream Bennett's tongue licked along her throat until he took her mouth.

Peri fell into a fitful, light sleep, dreaming of all the things she wanted Bennett McWilliams to do to her.

A few hours later, she woke up with a groggy yawn. She checked the bedside clock. It was a little after noon. *Must have been more tired than I thought.*

Jax was nowhere to be found.

Bennett must have come in for him. Maybe by some miracle, the roads were clear?

She jumped out of bed and ran to the living room, and her mouth dropped open in shock.

Holy shit. Bennett has a heart.

Chapter Six

Peri looked up at the perfectly spaced hanging garland wrapped around the beams of the cabin in shock and, yes, awe.

He'd even rehung her lumpy, initial attempts.

Peri smiled with pride at how perfect the garland looked on the beam. It really did elevate her Sugar Plum Fairy theme.

She spotted a note on the table beside the boxes of fairy lights she'd bought for the garland.

> Gone on a hike with Jax. Try the remote. –
> Bennett
> P. S. – You're welcome.

Peri rolled her eyes. She could practically hear his smug satisfaction.

She picked up the tiny remote that had come with the battery-operated fairy lights. She aimed it at the beams above. They were artfully wound through the garland, almost as well as if she'd done it herself.

Apparently, Bennett had layers.

It looked so magical it nearly took the sting out of being trapped here.

Peri went to check her phone to see if there was any update on the weather or a message from Jessie. The cabin's satellite internet moved at a turtle's pace on the best of days, and Peri fixed herself a cup of coffee while she waited for the weather report to load.

Panic swirled in her imagination. *Maybe we'll be trapped here forever. Maybe we'll have to gnaw on each other's bones for food and invent a new shared language because we've been secluded from the rest of humanity for ten years.*

She tried to reel back her imagination and closed her eyes hard to manifest her friends barging in her door in a few days for Friends-mas.

She sipped the hot hazelnut goodness and cataloged what provisions they had. They were lucky she'd made a huge grocery store run yesterday for the house party. The fridge was stuffed to the gills with snacks, meats and cheeses, veggies, and most importantly, all the ingredients she'd need for the hot cocoa station she'd planned. She'd wanted to go all out for her first Christmas back in the cabin. She'd told herself it was for Jessie, but the more she contemplated Jessie not being there, she realized it might have just been for herself, too.

Peri loved planning parties so much that she'd made a career out of it, trying to figure out what combo of food, vibe, drinks, and music would deliver on her client's needs. She'd designed baby showers, wedding showers, a "Thank Cod I'm Finally Divorced" fish fry, tastefully bland corporate holiday parties, and everything in between. The first Christmas back in the family cabin was going to be her hardest. She needed to think about the future, not the past. Think about how to make new traditions with her friends.

Peri saw the weather report loaded, and her stomach fell.

Another fucking snowstorm? She was going to write a strongly worded letter to someone. This willy-nilly snow business was ridiculous.

She glanced out the window and saw the sky darkening with the incoming snowstorm. She spared a thought for Bennett and Jax but knew better than to worry about Mr. *I Have It All Together All of the Time and Peri I Said No Standing On the Counter.* He probably had an MBA in Outdoorsiness, concentration in *'I told you so.'*

Peri decided to make a pot of soup and play a record of swingin' sixties Christmas hits to while away the time. After popping on a record, she chopped and diced away her worries for a long while, only looking up when the record clicked off. The sky was noticeably darker, and the wind whipped the tree branches back and forth.

She walked to the record player and saw something black and shivering at the sliding glass doors. *Oh my god, Jax.*

She sprinted to the door and let in a nearly frozen Jax covered in snow.

He ran inside and shook himself off, shivering from his floppy ears to his paws.

"Oh my god, buddy. I'm so sorry. I didn't know you were out there." She slammed the sliding glass door shut to prevent a snowdrift from blowing inside.

She grabbed a blanket and started wiping snow off Jax. She needed to get him dry and warm immediately. Who knows how long he'd been outside? Peri glanced over her shoulder at the glass door, waiting for Bennett to come marching through.

"Where's your dad, huh?" she said to Jax. She sat the sopping blanket down and wrapped him in a thick, snuggly, dry one. Luckily he was right in front of the heating vent, so she made him a nest.

Peri looked at the door for about the twentieth time in two

minutes, expecting Bennett to come stomping through, but nothing outside moved. "Am I actually worried about my worst enemy, Jax?" She scratched Jax's ears, and he burrowed his nose under the covers, letting out a contented sigh.

Ok, he's not my worst enemy. He's not even quite so bad once you get to know him a little.

Did he even know the forest around the cabin? She'd grown up wandering the peaks and valleys through every season, but he had barely been up here in the winter and had probably never seen it snow here. Maybe he'd gotten turned around?

She looked back at Jax, currently sleeping, and walked back to the stove to turn off the burner.

Time to rescue Buttface McEsquire.

She tossed off her pajama pants and found her thermal underwear, the ancient snow-pant overalls that had been her dad's, the thickest jacket she'd brought, two scarves, a balaclava, gloves, and warming packets she could break when she found Bennett. She glanced out the window one more time as she was getting her layers on. It was getting even darker and heading toward dusk, even though it was barely 2 p.m.

The snow howled through the trees. It would be easy for her to get turned around if she wasn't careful. She looked around to see what she could use to improvise as a tracking device. She didn't have any flares, and they'd probably go out in the snow anyway.

She spotted the silly party favors she'd brought. Her friends loved a photo moment, so Peri had made sure to get goofy props they could use for holiday selfies, including blinking light-up reindeer ears and Rudolph-inspired noses. She clicked them all on, and thank god, they worked. She grabbed the extra fairy lights and turned them on to blinking red and green, and waddled out into the snow like the abominable party-planning rescuer she was.

Chapter Seven

"Bennett!" she screamed out into the forest. She thought back to his note and headed for the hiking path behind the house.

Once she got far enough away from the house, she wrapped a tree branch in blinking red and green lights in case she got turned around in the white-out.

Another few hundred feet and she could still see the blinking lights, but she put down a blinking nose just to be safe. The lights of her house weren't visible now through the conditions.

Her fingers and face were almost already numb from the wind. She tried not to think of the worst-case scenario. What might happen if she never found him?

The wind died down for a minute and she heard a faint call in the distance, yelling Jax's name.

She screamed Bennett's name again and walked toward the sound of his voice, tying a light-up reindeer ear to a hanging branch.

Bennett's calls for Jax got louder, and Peri finally made out a hulking, hobbling shadow in the snow.

"What the hell are you doing out here?" he called as she approached.

"Jax is in the house," Peri yelled back, still making her way through the snow. At the news, Bennett collapsed or fell. Peri wasn't sure which. She waded through the snow to him.

"He's safe?" Bennett asked with a waver in his voice.

"Yes, all dried off and napping. Let's go." She watched him struggle to get up and went to grab his elbow.

"I've got it," he said with a snap.

"You're limping. Let me help you."

"I'm fine. Lead the way." Bennett favored his left foot and hobbled slowly.

"Oh my god." Peri forcefully grabbed his waist and shoved his arm around her shoulders. "Let's go, or I'll be a Peri Popsicle by the time we get home." He didn't pull his arm away as they walk-hobbled their way to each blinking party favor.

"Clever," Bennett said finally, through chattering teeth, as they passed the blinking Rudolph nose.

She remembered the heating packets and stopped, taking one out and activating it. "Here," she said, handing it to him. "Hold this so you can get some feeling back in your fingers."

"You're an angel," he said, hiss teeth chattering with gratitude as the warming packet worked its magic.

"See? Now I know you needed saving because you're delirious." The faint flow of blinking red and green came into view, and behind it, the outline of their cabin.

A weak laugh came out of him as they made their way down the hill toward the cabin.

Peri pulled on the sliding glass door, and a warm and happy Jax greeted them with cries. Bennett fell onto the floor of the cabin and grabbed Jax.

"Hey buddy," he said through a choked voice. "I thought I'd lost you." Jax licked Bennett's face in a mixture of anxiety and happiness. Peri even got one lick on her hand once she'd degloved.

"No more off-leash walks for you ever, buddy. I thought…" Bennett hugged him and Jax, being a perfect angel baby, sat his head on Bennett's shoulder.

Peri decided to give them a minute and took her snowy things off in the laundry room. She was so glad she'd gone after Bennett. She pushed visions of the worst possible scenario that could have happened out of her head. He would never have found his way back through the white-out conditions, and who can blame him for staying out in the storm? He thought his best friend was lost and freezing.

Peri walked back to the living room to find that Bennett had shed all his outer clothes and was hobbling to the staircase.

"I can grab some dry clothes for you from upstairs if you want?" Peri offered.

"It's fine. I can do it." He slowly hopped toward the staircase.

"Oh my god," Peri said with frustration building. "Bennett—wait, what's your middle name?"

A long suffering sigh escaped him as he stood on one foot in the middle of the living room. "Graham."

"Bennett Graham McWilliams. Learn to ask for and accept help, 'kay?" She stomped up the steep spiral staircase to the top bedroom. Why wouldn't he ever just let her do what she thought was best?

"I have some sweatpants and—"

"You will get what I give you," she called back down the stairs.

After she came back down, he glared at her from the couch where Jax was now surgically attached to him.

She tossed him the clothes. To her surprise, he started disrobing right in front of her, pulling his wet, long-sleeved shirt over his head and stopped when he grasped the waistband of his sweatpants.

He met her wide eyes with a wicked grin. "You staying for the show, Ms. Bell?"

Chapter Eight

The use of such a formal name coming out of a half-naked man was too much for her, and she turned her back to him like an old-timey schoolmarm.

"What happened with Jax?" She called over her shoulder and, okay, maybe glimpsed a peek in the window's reflection behind her. He was built like a linebacker, and she wasn't going to miss the one time she was in such close proximity to this much half-naked hotness.

"A hunter shot something in the distance before the snow kicked up and he got spooked." The couch groaned as Bennett levered himself up to pull on his sweatpants. "It was my fault. I should have leashed him. It's just...he's a black dog in the snow. I didn't think it would be easy to lose him. Right, buddy? I'm sorry." Bennett flopped back down on the sofa and took Jax's face in his hands.

So he could *say sorry when he wanted to*, Peri thought with chagrin. "How's the ankle?"

"It's twisted but should be fine in a few days. Could you grab some ice?"

"Look at you asking for help."

He sent her an angled smirk. "I'm a very fast learner."

Peri grabbed an ice pack from the freezer and tossed it to him. She sat on the edge of the couch facing him.

As Bennett iced his ankle, he chewed his lip. "Hey, I'm... sorry. For being an ass earlier."

Peri clutched her chest in mock horror. "Bennett? Is that you? Did you get body-snatched by a snow ghost? Quick, what's my nickname for you?"

He snorted as he moved the ice around. "McFucksquire, I believe."

Peri's jaw dropped. That wasn't the one she meant. "How did you know that? I mean," she cleared her throat. "What a terrible name to call someone. I would never." She batted her eyelashes at him sarcastically.

"You drunk emailed me. Instead of forwarding it to your friend Angela, you replied to me with a scathing commentary on the size of my manhood, how much of a tight-ass I am, and incidentally, how incredibly sexy you found my recent profile picture." He sent her a slow, knowing smile.

Shit.

Peri threw herself down onto the couch to avoid looking at him. She called up to him through a mouthful of pillow. "You must be thinking of someone else. I, a professional, would never do something so ludicrous."

A warm laugh rumbled out of him, and she very much tried to ignore what that did to all her lady bits.

"You would *definitely* do something so ludicrous. You're always an adventure, Periwinkle M. Bell. Maybe I should invent a nickname for you. How about...Winky?"

Her head shot up with horror, and she saw his teasing smile. "That's the absolute worst nickname in all of humanity. I should have done us all a favor and let you freeze."

He finally let out a genuine laugh, and Peri was transfixed.

This Scrooge-meets-bean-counter lawyer transformed into a warm, sparkling human right in front of her. Did she have some sort of frostbite-induced hallucination?

"Winky it is," he said. "Did you make soup?" he asked, sniffing the air suddenly.

"I started to, but I had to go on a rescue mission. Want some?"

They could be friends, right? Maybe they'd be friends now that she'd rescued him and he said the *S* word to her.

Maybe the weather would turn around, and he'd leave because she saved his life. Things could change.

Maybe.

She hopped up to put the veggie soup back on and check to see if she had a message from Jessie. Maybe they could get here through the snow before the next snowstorm hit.

A zing of possibility shot through her as she saw an unopened text.

JESSIE

Positive developments: I found an amazing Ski Bunny-inspired outfit and Angela got her mom's SUV. We're planning to make it up to your place tomorrow morning first thing. Still ok?

Peri:

Yaaaas. Better bring your best party dresses, the best booze, and get here safely

A fluttering started in her chest, and she let herself hope for a few seconds that everything would be alright. Maybe Christmas would be special this year. Maybe it would be her best Christmas yet. The tree, as if on cue, blinked on from the timer she'd set.

Peri scooped up bowls of veggie soup and carried them over to the couch.

"This smells amazing. On a day like today, my mom would always make a huge pot of stew and then make fresh cinnamon rolls in the morning," Bennett said.

"Are your parents coming up to the cabin too?" Peri was curious why he'd insisted on having the cabin for Christmas.

"No, they love doing tropical vacations during the cold. Usually, I'd host Jamie's family here. My ex," he said, clarifying. "Somehow, I thought it would be just as good if I came by myself this year, but on the drive up, I started to reconsider."

"And you were still going to double down and make me leave?" She sent him side-eye. *Ugh. This guy.*

"I was trying to avoid spending the holiday with a crazy stranger," he said, eating a spoonful of her stew.

"The crazy stranger who saved you and is now feeding you." She waved her spoon in his direction.

"I didn't say my first impression was right." He sent her an unapologetic shrug and finished his bowl off. He sat it down and wiped his hands over his face. "This was a weird, exhausting day. C'mon Jax, let's go to bed early."

Bennett half-hopped, half-hobbled his way from the couch to the staircase. Jax followed closely behind, never wanting to be more than a few inches away from him. Bennett stood at the bottom of the staircase, considering how to get up. The staircase was a spiral with shallow steps.

He tried picking up Jax, but couldn't handle it on one foot. Bennett looked over at Peri with frustration. "I can't make it up the stairs with him. I'm not even sure I can make it up the stairs myself on one foot."

"He can just stay with me," Peri said, but on cue, Jax whined and pushed his head toward Bennett's leg.

Bennett hobbled back over to the couch and grabbed one of

Peri's blankets and a throw pillow. "This will do for tonight. C'mon Jax." Jax launched himself onto the couch and managed to step on Bennet's bad ankle. He sat bolt upright and winced in pain. "This isn't going to work."

He wiped his hand over his face, and Peri enjoyed seeing his hair flail up in dishevelment.

Bennett looked exasperated as he met her eyes. "Could we trade?"

"Beds?" Peri laughed. "I'd freeze out here. And that bed upstairs is a torture device. I wouldn't be able to walk tomorrow."

"How about if we share?" Bennett stood up and hobbled over to her where she stood, arms crossed. A ghost of a smile passed his lips. "You did say it was *our* bedroom after all."

Peri felt herself flush under his gaze. She'd never get a wink of sleep if she was in his bed.

"I'd be a perfect gentleman. Jax would see to that. Plus, it's a king. It'll be like I'm in another zip code."

Peri chewed her lip. She didn't want to give up her bed. Every ounce of sleep was hard-won for her, but she also didn't know about sharing a bed with the man who haunted her sexiest dreams. He was trustworthy, for sure. But could she trust herself?

"Fine, but the minute the roads are even halfway clear, I get the cabin, and you high tail it out. Okay?" She stuck out her hand, and he grabbed it.

She looked up to make eye contact with him and realized they were under a sprig of mistletoe she'd hung from the balcony.

Whoops.

His eyes followed hers, and his head tilted back, his hand still holding hers. "Is that...?"

She'd placed it there for decorative effect, not actually

considering someone would stop under it. "Uh, yeah technically, it is." She tried to ease her hand away, but he held it firm. She met his eyes and saw an equal mixture of challenge and humor in them.

"Are you scared of a little kiss, Peri?"

Chapter Nine

Yes. She was very much scared of what might happen if she broke the seal on the secret crush she'd been harboring.

She needed to keep him firmly in the big, bad lawyer category and not in the hulking, smell-good, hot guy category. The hot guy who was going to share her bed in a minute if he'd ever let go of her damn hand and make an agreement.

"I'm never scared," she said.

He tugged her closer.

I am such a liar.

"Great. Prove it. This was your mistletoe. I expect you to deliver on the implied obligation you created when hanging said mistletoe."

"Did anyone ever tell you it's supremely unattractive when you speak like a law book?" she lied, sticking her chin out with defiance.

"You *don't* find me attractive? Noted." He sent her an angled, chagrined smile.

Right. Not attractive. He just looked like a fourteenth-century Scottish clan leader who had decided he should claim a bride, and she desperately wished it would be her.

"Nope. Not attractive in," she took a shaky breath, "the least."

He still held her hand tight in his. *Just get it over with.* She leaned up on her tiptoes and gave him a quick, chaste peck on the cheek. Her lips barely made contact with his stubbled skin, and she met his eyes with defiance.

The cheeky bastard still held her hand.

He looked impressed. "I applaud your use of a loophole. That was, by definition, but not in spirit, a kiss."

He let go of her hand. It stupidly felt like it had been abandoned. Did she *like* the feeling of his hand holding hers?

Ridiculous.

He was still standing far too close to her.

"Well," she took a breath. "Night roomie." She started for the bedroom.

"Peri, wait."

She turned around, and his eyes locked with hers. There was a challenge in them, but also something else she couldn't figure out.

"Come back." He was still standing under the mistletoe. She stopped about a foot away. "Don't be a weirdo. I don't bite."

She took a few steps toward him until she was almost under the mistletoe. It was hard for her to draw in a full breath. Her insides felt jittery like she might take flight if she met his eyes. She found a very interesting spot on the ceiling to inspect.

Don't be weird. Maybe he wanted to talk about their schedule tomorrow, like who would take a shower or if she'd help shovel the driveway so he could leave—

"I'm pretty shit at things like apologies and thank yous, so I might fuck this up." He took a deep breath and caught her eyes.

Innnteresting. A smirk crossed her face, waiting for the high and mighty Bennett McWillams *I-know-everything*, Esquire to admit she did something right.

"You saved my life today and my best friend. I owe you everything." His voice cracked, and he rubbed a hand over his face, trying to keep it together. "It's not easy for me to admit that I was so turned around that I'm not sure I could have gotten home. Jax is my everything. I would never have forgiven myself if—" his voice fizzled out. He chewed his lip and nodded, gulping down any more emotion.

He looked up at her with an expression of open gratitude. "I'm really glad you were here. Thank you for saving us."

Her smirk melted away, and she felt like she saw the real Bennett for the first time in their four-year co-ownership. This was a man baring his soul to her, and she, unfortunately, found that vulnerability very, very attractive. He toyed with his watch strap as he waited for her response.

"You're both very much worth saving." She pressed her lips together, not sure what else to say.

"Peri…" He chewed his lip, looking like he was debating with himself.

Lord, he was pretty cute when he didn't act like he had every-thing all figured out.

"Yeah," she said more breathlessly than she'd like.

"Can I uh," he faltered as his eyes met hers, "…hug you?"

Chapter Ten

Can an enormous, muscly man who smells great hug me in thanks?

Jackpot? Party of one?

"Sure," she said, trying to play it cool. *Be cool, Peri. Cooler than cool. The coolest—*

Her thoughts took a screeching halt as he wrapped his eagle-sized wingspan around her and squeezed her tight, lifting her feet off the ground.

She fired enough brain cells to wrap her five-foot-four-sized arms around him in return and bury her face in his chest. He pulled her hard against him, and she squeezed him back.

She loved a hugger who meant business.

She thought about pulling away, but he still squeezed her tight. She let herself nuzzle in, loosening her hold but not moving her arms.

The softness of his shirt cushioned her cheek against the pillow of muscles under it. This man was why the word "beefcake" was invented. He smelled like cedar and expensive cologne, and Peri closed her eyes, trying to memorize it.

How on earth was this the same man who emailed her a forty-point cleaning checklist and instituted a *"No Glitter and Yes I'll Know If You Bring It In"* policy? He was an asshat sometimes, but apparently, pretty sweet and squishy when he wanted to be.

Bennett loosened his hold but didn't pull away. The weight of his head rested on hers. She was in a cocoon of his arms, surrounded by his scent and the safety of a wall of man. Peri considered how lonely and scared she might feel if she was here by herself in the biggest snowstorm Wisconsin had seen in decades.

"I'm glad you're here, Bennett," she murmured against his chest.

He pulled back just enough to look down at her. "But you have your Friends-mas planned."

She kept her arms around him because he hadn't moved his either.

Was this awkward? Maybe, but she didn't want to let go.

"I'd be here by myself in a snowstorm. No one to tease," she smiled, trying to deflect the building tension she felt. His thumb stroked her back, and she sucked in a breath.

Damnit, Peri. We said we'd keep it cool.

Bennett stared at her mouth, a happy glint in his eyes. "Oh, so I'm just someone to tease. That's it."

"Well, and eye candy." She slammed her mouth closed at her slip and shut her eyes, so she didn't have to look at him.

She felt the laugh run through him as he held her. She opened one eye to chance it, and she felt the bright red flames of embarrassment burn through her entire face. "I mean, for people who like your kind of thing."

He lifted an amused eyebrow up. "My kind of thing?"

"You know," she pulled away so she could gesture. "Tall, the muscles and the hair," she pointed to his thick, light brown hair that fell into perfect waves even after their rescue mission. "And the stubble that I'm sure you spend too much time perfecting. Anyway," she took two steps back.

Run Peri. Your stupid mouth revealed too much, and you can't stop talking, so just get out of there.

"The look works, congratulations." *Run, run, run.* "Uh, guess I'll see ya in there...tiger."

She started walking faster and faster to the bedroom they'd be sharing tonight. She didn't stop gaining speed until she shut the door to the bathroom and laid her forehead against the door.

Oh my god. You are the weirdest weirdo to ever weird. 'Tiger'? You called a hot dude hot to his face and then cataloged his hotness to him, and then acted like his little league coach.

She turned to face herself in the mirror, gripping the countertop. "What is wrong with me?"

"Too many things to list," Bennett yelled back from the bedroom. She heard the bed creak under his weight and the jingle of Jax's collar.

Aaaaaaaagh. That was it, the final straw. She'd just have to pull up the tiles in the bathroom, dig a tunnel with her hands and go live a new life in Canada. That was the only logical option for her situation right now.

She brushed her teeth for the full dentist-prescribed length of time, took extra care with washing and moisturizing her face, and even flossed for the first time in forever. Anything to extend her time in the bathroom, so she wouldn't have to face Bennett still being awake in her bed.

Their bed? Oh lord. Their bed.

After twenty minutes, she peeked her head out of the bathroom, and the light was off. Through the pitch black, she snuck to the far side of the bed. She'd crawl in, all stealth-like, and by morning, they'd forget any of this ever happened.

She lifted the cover and sat down on a giant lump of human who was definitely not wearing a shirt.

"What are you doing?" Bennett's voice was already thick with sleep.

Peri leaped up, but a sturdy hand reached out and grabbed her waist, preventing her from moving, and yanked her back down. His hand rested heavy on her hip, and she sucked in a breath, every hair on her arm on end. Heat pooled in her middle, and she tried not to think about what he looked like—what he *felt* like—without a shirt on.

"Stay," he mumbled.

Tingles ran down her middle and flamed the fire building inside her.

"I can move over if it's your side," he said. He took his hand away, leaving her feeling like she lost something that she never even had.

The mattress creaked as Bennett shifted his weight to the far end of the king-size mattress, and she felt Jax move to sleep between them.

She wrapped herself under the cover and, like the goblin she was, reveled in the warmth of the sheets where Bennett had been. Her pillow now smelled like an intoxicating combination of his cologne and his scent. She couldn't remove her nose from it even if she tried.

After a few minutes, all three of them settled down under the covers, but Bennett's voice broke through the silence.

"Night tiger."

Peri willed herself to melt through the bed and disappear so she wouldn't have to face the half-naked hot man in the morning.

Chapter Eleven

Peri woke up the next morning to an empty bed. Apparently, Bennett and Jax were early risers. She glanced at her phone and saw two missed calls and a text from Jessie.

Oh no, no, no. She opened the text.

JESSIE

Girl. Answer your dayum phone.

Peri hit the call shortcut, and Jessie picked up in one ring.

"You're alive." Jessie's voice felt like a hug to Peri's ears.

"I'm alive, but boy oh boy, do I have news. McHotPants is here."

A screech sounded from the phone that was either a falcon or her best friend having a heart attack.

"BRB, just gonna charter a helicopter to the cabin real fast so I can sit on his lap and tell him how bad I've been this year." Jessie giggled on the other end of the line from sheer delight. They had a secret hate-to-love crush on Bennett, too.

"I know. I can't even tell you how much of an ass I've made of myself already. You need to get here immediately so he'll leave, and I don't have to look at his stupid, chiseled face anymore."

A small pause on the other end of the line had her stomach dropping. "The roads are terrible here, P. We got another, like, two fucking feet of snow. We are trapped here forever. Like, buy a headstone and bury me under the pile of fucking snow in the backyard in sixty years. I made it to Angela's parent's house, but we are for sure trapped here. The entire region is shut down."

Peri bit her cheek to keep from crying. It was Christmas Eve. Jessie and Angela had to be back at work on the 27th, so if they didn't get to the cabin the next day, there wasn't any point in coming. Their other friends, Steve and Gabe, lived downtown and would be just as stuck as Jessie and Angela.

"It's fine," Peri said, barely above a whisper. "I'll be fine. I don't want you to be unsafe." A rogue tear escaped down her cheek. "Just stay put and let me know if anything changes, okay?"

"I'm so sorry, babe," Jessie sounded as heartbroken as Peri felt. "I feel terrible you're up there all alone."

"Hey, being trapped with McHotPants is better than the frosty McMansion of Angela's parents. Call me when things change with the conditions, okay?"

"K girl. Love you byeeee."

"Love you more byeee." Peri echoed.

The reality that she'd spend Christmas by herself sank in, and Peri padded to the kitchen. She glanced out the window to the blinding snow and noticed it was even higher than before. She poured herself a coffee, grabbed a Christmas cookie, and shuffled to the couch. *Breakfast of champions.*

It was more insult to injury that Christmas Eve was her favorite day of the year. Not Christmas Day, with all its glitz and expectations, but the unassuming, quiet Christmas Eve. There was so much hope and happiness in the air, the anticipation of so many good things yet to come. It was the day she most missed her dad. Every year, she packed her schedule full, so she didn't have to feel the gaping wound still trying to heal from his sudden loss.

This year, she'd made a list of activities to do on Christmas Eve and had planned to distract herself by playing the perfect party hostess.

Her lip wobbled as she tried not to feel sorry for herself. She was lucky to be in a warm, happy cabin with a ton of supplies and access to her friends only a phone call away.

But it's still not the same. She let herself break, and tears flooded out. *It's not the same as being surrounded by love.*

She wiped her eyes with her sleeves right as Jax bounded in from the snow, and Bennett followed him. Cold, snowy paws launched themselves onto her legs, and she screeched with laughter through her tears.

"Jax, you naughty boy, get down." She got a lick in the face. And he shoved his head in her hands. Dogs always knew when something was up. She let him lick a few more tears away.

Bennett's face fell when he walked into the living room.

"What's wrong now?"

"I thought my friends could come, but since the snow's worse, they pretty much canceled on me." Her mouth twisted as she bit back another sob. He didn't deserve Super Messy Peri. The one whose emotions spewed out like a confetti cannon. She needed to keep it together.

"That really sucks," Bennett said, sitting on the couch next to her. "It looks like we got at least another foot overnight, maybe more. I don't think you're going to be rid of Jax and me any time soon. Sorry to break our handshake." He wiped the snow off of Jax onto the rug.

"I don't want you to leave. It would be too lonely without both of you here. Right Jax?" Jax's tail *thwapped* against the coffee table as he beamed up at her. "Jax, I wish you were human and could do all the fun things I'd planned."

"What am I? Chopped Christmas cookies?" Bennett looked at her with scorn.

Peri snorted. "I mean, yes, you're human, but I'm pretty sure you're allergic to this kind of fun. It involves making a mess, silly games, and a whole bunch of things you don't want to do." She got up to refill her coffee and seriously considered adding Bailey's to it to ease the pain of the day but settled for a peppermint stick instead.

"Excuse me. I'm a ton of fun." Bennett followed her into the kitchen. "I love a well-structured activity. Let's see your agenda."

Peri snorted so hard that the coffee she was drinking came out of her nose. *So attractive.* "Agenda? This is a house party, not a shareholder meeting. There is a loose assortment of activities I have for when the vibe is right."

Bennett rolled his eyes and looked like he was trying to stave off a headache. "Well, I'm declaring the 'vibe'" He used air quotes, *god why did she love nerds so much?* "Officially right. C'mon. Give me the activities."

He crossed his arms across his considerable chest, and Peri surveyed the stern, serious man glaring in front of her. "You don't have to."

"Oh, I have to because it is of utmost importance I beat you at every game." He sent her an arched eyebrow. "Little known fact: lawyers are incredibly competitive."

"Fine." He'd see just how ridiculous this plan was, and then he'd tuck tail and run. "First, gingerbread house decorating, followed by a hot cocoa bar, followed by the Saran Wrap ball game—"

"The who what now?"

"—Followed by building a snowman, and finally adult drinks to warm us up, paired with Christmas karaoke."

He walked to the kitchen sink and rolled up his sleeves,

washed his hands, dried them, and turned around with a steely glare and a smirk. "Be prepared to lose, Bell. I intend to win Christmas."

She glimpsed his forearms and tried very hard not to stare. Why did she have such a weird thing for sexy, sculpted forearms? She shook her head to snap out of it. "You don't have to. It's fine. I'll just curl up with a book—"

"And I'll find you quietly sobbing again in twenty minutes. Answer me this: did you or did you not save my life yesterday?"

She swallowed a smile at how fucking cute he was being. "Technically, yes," she said slowly.

"Excellent. That means I owe you exactly one day of festive activity to repay my debt."

"Your life is only worth one day?"

He grabbed an apple from the bowl on the counter and took a big bite as he walked past her. "I am a lawyer. A day might be too generous." He sent her a wink that had her feeling very confused until she realized she'd said something like that to Angela. Or, well, him, in the email that she'd sent him.

"Let's go, tiger," he called back to her as he unboxed the gingerbread house.

Chapter Twelve

"I'm never going to live that down, am I?"

"Not as long as I have a working memory." He fiddled with his phone as she got out the ingredients for her famous hot cocoa recipe. As notes of *White Christmas* filled the air, Peri's head flew up in surprise.

Bennett smiled back at her as he made his way back to the kitchen. "You can't beat Ella at Christmas. Plus, it goes with your retro garland thingies."

"Maybe you are a judge of vibes, McWilliams." She nodded in surprising approval as she measured the ingredients to make the hot cocoa.

"What are you making?" he asked, a skeptical look around at the counter suddenly covered with ingredients.

"I told you. Hot cocoa bar."

He frowned at her as he glanced around. "Where are the packets?"

Peri shook her head, unable to compute. "I'm sorry, have you only had terrible powdered hot cocoa?"

He shrugged. "I think so. I've never been a fan of hot chocolate."

She gasped, jaw nearly on the ground. "Are you a secret ax

murderer? Do you hate rainbows and kittens? Tell me this, BenBen—who hurt you?"

"I don't get the appeal of drinking warm chocolate milk." He sent her a confused shrug.

"Buddy, I'm going to rock your world today. Start making the gingerbread house, and I'll have my internationally famous hot cocoa for you soon."

They worked quietly for thirty minutes in companionable silence. Snowflakes fell outside, and Peri almost forgot she was trapped here against her will.

Almost.

She stole a glance over her shoulder, and Bennett was lost in his work of measuring, sanding, and re-measuring each gingerbread house piece to ensure it was perfect. By the time he had it all pieced together, Peri was done with the hot cocoa base.

"Ready for toppings and booze," she called, perhaps too loudly, because Jax barked in surprise and ran into the kitchen. His long tail caught the gingerbread house and knocked it across the room, shattering it into pieces.

Peri's hands flew to her mouth. As Bennett's head fell. She tensed, not sure which way he'd take his hard work being thrown all over the dining area. But he surprised her by throwing his head back and laughing. "Jax has decided my baked goods construction is shit. Sorry, Peri." He rubbed his eyes.

Laughter. An unprompted 'sorry.'

Maybe this Bennett guy wasn't so bad after all.

"It's fine. I'm terrible at gingerbread houses anyway."

Bennett grabbed the broom. "So I have to ask, why haven't you done Christmas here before? You seem to love it."

He swept all the gingerbread pieces out of the corner of the golden-hued wood floor.

"I'm excellent at planning a party; there's a difference." But she did love Christmas. Or used to, before it was too painful. "This place always reminds me of my dad."

Bennett nodded slowly, catching the unsaid parts of what Peri meant. "And that makes this time of year hard?"

"I hoped my friends could distract me and ease me back into spending Christmas in the cabin."

"Your mom?"

"Happy with her new husband and his family. We chat, but she doesn't make a big deal out of the day. The tree is put away by dinner on Christmas Day at her house."

Bennett threw the cookie debris in the trash can. "And how exactly did she end up with a daughter who makes a custom garland that matches her specific color scheme for an informal Friends-mas, complete with a personalized stocking for each guest." Bennett looked over at the stockings she'd made.

Peri threw an embarrassed shoulder shrug at him. "My dad always made everything over the top for the holidays. Wanted everyone to feel special on a special day." She stirred the chocolate mixture so it wouldn't burn.

"He sounds like you," Bennett said.

"How would you know?" She sent him a skeptical look.

"I..." He rubbed the back of his neck and chewed his lip, considering how to proceed.

"Out with it, McLawyerFace."

He chuckled at her. "I might have looked you up when I first bought the cabin timeshare. You know," he quickly followed, "just to make sure you weren't crazy and wouldn't try to kill me in my sleep in the middle of a forest in Wisconsin."

"And?"

"Well, you're definitely crazy." He dodged a punch on the arm, catching her hand with his and squeezing it before he dropped it.

Why did that give her butterflies?

"And I found pictures of your events, and they are amazing. Honestly, Peri."

She stopped stirring for a split second to meet his eyes, the shock of his genuinely kind words throwing her for a loop. "Wow, thanks. I uh," she went back to stirring. "Not sure what to say."

"Say you're done stirring." He picked up a mug and held it out to her.

She ladled the creamy, chocolatey heaven into his cup. When he tried to take it back, she held his mug tight. "No, the toppings are crucial. Don't break my heart and say you don't like whipped cream."

"I would never break your heart, Peri."

Her eyes flitted to his but she thought better than to get lost in him.

She perused her toppings station. "Are we in a peppermint mood? A spicy mood?" She shimmied her shoulders for effect.

"Chef's choice."

"Brave man, impressive." She put a shot of peppermint schnapps in his mug, followed by a large dollop of whipped cream sprinkled with chocolate shavings and a candy cane to stir. She handed him the perfect mug of hot cocoa and waited with bated breath.

He took a tentative sip and jerked back as if he'd been bitten. "Holy fuck."

He took another larger sip and shook his head. He stared with an equal mixture of surprise, horror, and want. "I'd marry this hot chocolate. Buy it a nice house, picket fence, dog, everything." He took several sips, savoring the flavor as he closed his eyes.

Peri tried to ignore how much happiness his praise gave her. "Upstate cabin, too?"

"Obviously. It's where we met." His smile sent a pang of want straight down into her core.

Peri snorted as she fixed herself a mug. She chose a coffee liqueur for hers and extra whipped cream and put the rest of the mixture off to the side.

"Okay, now that you're beyond the initial shock. I'll show you how to drink it properly, the way my grandma taught me. First, two hands."

He obeyed and wrapped both hands around the mug.

"Now, bring it close so you can smell it," she ordered.

He sent her a skeptical smirk. "I'd rather just drink it."

"BenBen. This is part of the activity." She sent him a scolding look.

He closed his eyes and smelled, giving her a 'fine' head shake.

"Now, the most important part. Close your eyes." She closed her eyes but lifted one open just as he did the same thing to her. She bumped his foot with hers. "No cheating. Both eyes closed and think of your Christmas wish."

She breathed in the scent of vanilla and chocolate and wished for the impossible: her dad to walk through the door, holding holly he'd found in the forest to use for decoration. A tear formed at the edge of her eyelashes as she took a sip.

She opened her eyes, and Bennett's dark, furrowed brows showed his worry.

"Hey," his hand came up to her cheek as a tear made its way down. His thumb wiped it away before it could get too far. His hand felt warm and perfect.

She felt another stroke of his thumb along her cheek, then another.

And another.

Peri didn't know what was happening between them, but she definitely knew she never wanted it to stop.

Chapter Thirteen

She could barely breathe beyond looking at him. His intense eyes stared down at her, and she felt caught in time, unwilling to move for fear of breaking whatever was happening between them.

She faintly heard the clink of a mug on the counter as she registered him coming toward her slowly. She tried not to stare at his mouth, but she'd thought about what it would feel like against hers about a thousand times.

His eyes searched her face, and each stroke of his thumb revved her higher and higher. She was breathing in time to his movement. He stopped a scant half-inch from her, bent down, eyes locked on her mouth. His thumb traced her bottom lip, and his mouth angled towards her.

She grabbed his shirt, unable to take any more waiting, and suddenly, both of his hands were in her hair, and his mouth was on hers.

She breathed in the taste of peppermint, chocolate, and the taste she'd fantasized about for too long: him. His hands moved through her hair to cradle her head. It felt like he'd grabbed her by her heart as she savored his kiss. He moved her mouth and angled her head to take more of what he wanted.

He deepened the kiss to suck in her top lip. As he licked it, all the air rushed out of her. She felt a wave of want run through her, pooling in her middle. She tugged his shirt closer as she opened her mouth for him to take what he wanted.

He moved an arm around her to squeeze her to him. In the process, her arm bumped his and she spilled steaming hot cocoa all over them.

They both yanked back instantly as the hot cocoa sloshed to the floor.

"I'm so sorry." Peri grabbed a towel and furiously dabbed his shirt, but he grabbed her arm, stopping her mid-dab. He grabbed the mug out of her other hand and sat it down.

"It's fine. It's just a shirt." He chewed his lip, unable to stop staring at hers.

Peri always got panicky when she really liked someone. She felt the need to run, to do anything but make eye contact with them.

He ducked down to catch her gaze. "Was that okay?"

Ah, so he'd noticed her freak-out.

She willed herself to look up at him, feeling like a deer about to bolt. She nodded slightly.

"Good," he growled, "because I *really* want to kiss you again."

"Wait," she threw up a hand. "We have activities. I mean," she took a step back. She had to regain control of the situation. "You promised, and I just don't want you to break your promise."

A delighted slow smile appeared on his face. "Did you not like kissing me, Peri?" He took a step toward her, and she felt panic rise inside her.

Yes, oh yes, I did, she admitted to herself. *I want more against that counter, and maybe on the couch, and definitely in the bed.*

"Sure, it was fine," she said, you know, like a dummy.

"Fine?" His eyes popped, and he bent over with a laugh.

"Yikes. I'm out of practice." He scratched the back of his head, embarrassed.

"More than fine," she backtracked. "I mean, I just. I'm not great at this."

"Kissing?"

She gulped. "Banter. Flirting. Chemistry."

His hand reached out to tug her back to him. "I assure you, you're better than you realize."

She stared into his eyes for either an eternity or three seconds; she wasn't sure which. She wanted to run her hands all over his chest, his arms, and plaster herself against him. Instead, she stood stock-still, not sure what to do next.

He placed a slow kiss on her cheek, his stubble tickling her skin, and she felt a pull in her middle that made her want to straddle him, but he pulled away as she was working up the nerve to drag him to a flat surface.

"What's next on our list?" He sipped his hot chocolate with a hint of a smile as he leaned back on the counter.

Her chest rose and fell, and her mind scrambled, trying to keep up with him. "Umm, the Saran Wrap ball game."

She explained the rules of the family-friendly game that she'd stuffed with not-so-family-friendly gifts. Bottles of alcohol, one-dollar bills, condoms, and other silly holiday candy and treats. She thought it would be a fun, drunken game during a boring lull. Instead, it was her panicked *'I don't know what to do now that you kissed all the brains out of my head'* game.

He held up the pair of dice. "So, I just try to roll doubles while you have mittens on?"

Peri had the soccer ball-sized ball of plastic wrap between her thighs as she sat on the ground. Past experience had told her the floor was the best option for this game. "Yeah, and I'm trying to unwrap the Saran Wrap from the ball and get whatever comes out as it unravels. When you get doubles, then you get the ball and unwrap whatever you can. Whoever gets to the center wins."

He looked at her skeptically as he pulled on his mittens. "And I'm wearing mittens because?"

"Because it's harder to unwrap the plastic that way. Oh!" She hustled to the kitchen and returned with two large shots of peppermint schnapps. "The adult version includes shots at the beginning."

They clicked glasses, and Peri felt the welcome burn down her throat as she shot the schnapps and chased it with hot cocoa.

"Okay, come on, big money. Or at least some tiny bottles of bourbon." He looked up at her. "Ready?"

"Go!" she yelled and started furiously searching for the beginning of the plastic. She finally found it and started tugging, causing a mini bottle of vodka to fly out of the wrapped surface.

Bennett yelled that he'd rolled fives and yanked the ball away from her.

Peri grabbed the dice, trying to roll doubles. Maybe it was silly to play since there were only two of them, but Bennett seemed into it. He viciously examined the ball to find the start of the plastic wrap he'd lost.

"Come here, you commie bastard," Bennett muttered to the ball. "Aha." He proceeded to unwrap about a third of the ball while Peri desperately tried to roll doubles. Finally, she got the ball, and they unwrapped it in frenetic turns back and forth—dollar bills, alcohol, condoms, and candies all flying.

They'd finally made it down to the tiny center of the ball.

"What's in the middle?" Bennett asked as he was desperately and hilariously trying to pull apart two melded pieces of plastic with his woolen mittens.

"A hundred-dollar bill and a promise from me to do whatever the person asks." Peri rolled the dice again and again as if her life depended on it

He met her eyes, and a glint of fire shot through them. He tore into the plastic with his teeth, and a piece of paper peeked out of it.

Chapter Fourteen

"Hey!" she yelled. "No way!" She tried to wrestle the plastic away from him, but he wrenched it away from her, grabbing her to keep himself steady until they both toppled onto the rug, her on the ground and him hulking over her.

"No teeth allowed," she said, huffing as his lower body held hers in place against the floor.

"I don't remember a rule that said I couldn't. My mittens are still on," he said between breaths. He had one hand holding her arm down, and one hand held the plastic as he tore the rest off with his teeth. After two tears, Bennett emerged victorious with the one hundred-dollar bill and a slip of paper. "Got it, fair and square."

"I don't know about fair. I'm currently pinned to the ground."

He let his other forearm rest on the other side of her head. Peri looked up at him, the glint of victory in his eyes and a wide smile on his face.

The game was technically over, but Peri didn't dare mention it. That meant he'd move. Bennett was a large man, maybe 6'2, with broad shoulders, and she loved feeling the weight of him on top of her. *It has been too long*, she thought. Too long since she'd felt the press of someone against all of her.

"I'll happily get up. Just say the word," he said between breaths as he stared down at her.

Peri bit her lip and couldn't pull her eyes away from his lips. She didn't dare say a word.

His eyes roamed over her hair, her face, her shoulders, and her breasts, and she felt exposed, which only made her want him more.

He slowly leaned down and placed a kiss under her ear, and heat pooled in her middle. He ran his nose along her jawline, and she considered if there was somehow a secret link between her chin and her pussy, because she was currently *squirming* with want. Her breaths came in shallow gulps, not wanting to break whatever magic was keeping him on top of her.

His mouth found hers with a punishing kiss, and she kissed him back with everything she had.

Her hands were pinned to the ground with his, and she arched against him, creating a swirling vortex of want that wound its way to her core. His tongue slipped inside her mouth, and she met it with hers, warring with his, relishing all of the tension that had built up between them.

That's it. That's all this was, just a way to get their frustrations out, she told herself. She sucked his tongue, and a moan ground out of him.

He released her hands from above her head and moved an arm around her waist, rolling them over until she was on top of him. His mouth never broke from hers.

He kissed her like a man on fire, and she met him move for move. A yank on her thigh pulled her over him, so she was straddling him. He pressed her closer to him, her breasts squeezing deliciously against his chest. He tasted like peppermint and chocolate, and she thought she might be the luckiest woman in Wisconsin today for being trapped here with his mouth.

His hands moved to her ass, and he rocked her against him as he grabbed it. Pleasure bloomed as her clit found just the right spot against him. She could already feel him hard under her, and she let out a moan she couldn't contain any longer. He kissed his way down her neck, to the top of her breasts peaking out from her low-cut pajama top. He tugged her forward, licking his way down to her cleavage.

They both stopped in midair at a whine from Jax, who was by the back door. They looked over at him, and he was turning circles, tapping his feet.

"Shit," Bennett muttered as he laid his head down on the ground. "He needs to go out."

Peri loved Jax, but she sent him a mental death glare at having the worst timing ever. She looked down at the Viking under her and sighed. It was great while it lasted. "Sure." She moved to roll off of the most delicious body she'd ever been in contact with. His hands grabbed her waist, stopping her.

"This is only intermission," he said, searching her eyes.

She sucked in a breath and nodded, licking her lips so she could taste him one more time.

They got up, and Peri noticed his arousal as he stood.

Holy Christmas cookies.

She averted her eyes for fear of staring and shook her head to clear all the X-rated pictures forming in them.

"I'll join you. You owe me a snowman or two," she said as she grabbed her coat and tugged on boots.

"Prepared to lose again?" He tugged his scarf around his neck. He clipped a leash to Jax's collar and, throwing on a jacket, went outside.

"Uh, I maintain you cheated, like a lying cheating cheater." Peri closed the door behind her.

"That argument would never hold up in court." He sent her a simmering smile.

Peri breathed in the fresh air, smelling of pine and the crisp bite of snow in the air. She usually loved it when it snowed in the forest. Each branch looked perfectly and expertly iced with frosting. Huge pine trees surrounded the cabin, keeping it safe and snug from most of the wind and weather. Bits of green in the trees peeked through the white landscape.

Jax quickly did his business and went immediately to the back door to be let inside. Peri saw her opening and took it. As Bennett closed the door for Jax and turned back around, his face was hit with an ice-cold ball of snow.

A cackle burst out of Peri, and her arms shot into the air with victory. "That's for cheating."

His ankle was still sore, so Bennett walked with slow purpose toward the nearest pile of snow and balled it up to throw at her. He nailed her shoulder, and she lobbed another one at him. He tried to dodge the next one she threw, but he yelled out in pain and fell into the snow bank.

"Shit, I'm sorry!" Peri yelled as she climbed through the snow to him. She'd feel so guilty if he hurt his ankle more because of her.

She leaned over him in the snowbank, seeing if he was okay when he grabbed her and threw her down into the snowbank.

She screamed at the immediate frigid temperature soaking into her skin. Peri landed hard, and snow immediately made its way down her jacket.

"Got ya," he grinned over at her beside him. He held a snowball up in the air for insurance.

Peri faked a gasp and looked behind him, and like a sucker, he glanced over his shoulder. She took a handful of snow and shoved it in his face, and leaped up, racing to the back door. She felt a snowball hit her butt as she neared the door. She sent him a cheeky wiggle in defiance. She yanked open the back door, and they shook off the snow on their clothes.

"Wasn't the light on in here?" Bennett asked.

Peri glanced over to the washer and saw the display was off.

"Power must be out," Peri said. "That happens sometimes in big snows here. The lines get twisted or downed when big piles of snow fall from the trees."

Bennett shed his coat and boots. "It's supposed to get below zero tonight."

Peri thought about how she'd keep warm. Maybe she could convince Bennett to stay in their bedroom one more night.

They walked into the living room, which was already chilly from the lack of heat. Bennett turned around and headed back to the laundry room.

"Where are you going?" Peri asked.

"We need the firewood that's outside. It's already fifty degrees in here and only going to get colder."

Peri spotted Jax cuddled up in a blanket on the couch. She went over to tuck him in. They were lucky that they had a pot belly stove in the living room and a fireplace in the downstairs bedroom.

The back door closed, and a snowy Bennett came in wearing a frown as he carried the wood to the stacking area. "We don't have much dry wood."

Peri pushed away all the dirty innuendos on the tip of her tongue and focused on the task at hand. She couldn't remember if they even had an ax on the property. She usually bought her wood from the store.

"I guess we should ration it."

"Yeah, I don't think it makes sense to heat the living room. Too big of a space. I think we need to sleep together, Or—" a pained look crossed his face. "I mean, we should both sleep in our bedroom—the downstairs bedroom, I mean." He wiped a hand down his face. "Use that fireplace and just heat that room."

Peri tamped her excitement down as far as it would go, trying to play it completely cool. *Our bedroom.* "Yeah, of course. Makes sense."

He nodded, avoiding her eyes. "Great, I'll bring it in and put it in the bedroom."

Peri fixed them cold-cut sandwiches as Bennett made a fire. She tried not to think too much about how quickly they'd become easy roommates.

Roommates who made out a little.

Roommates who made out a little and who would sleep next to each other tonight. A shiver passed down her shoulders, remembering him between her legs as she straddled him earlier in the day.

Chapter Fifteen

Peri considered whether she had any pajamas that could possibly be both very warm and very sexy. Given the sub-zero temperatures, she'd decided to settle for being very warm tonight.

Bennett walked into the kitchen. "Man, it's freezing in here already. Oh, thanks." He grabbed a sandwich that she'd shoved toward him. "It's like, twenty degrees warmer in the bedroom. I'll be right back."

She grabbed snacks and drinks to take back with them to the bedroom.

Bennett returned a few minutes later with a dog bed from upstairs and grabbed extra blankets from the couch. "Jax, c'mon." Jax trotted to the back bedroom.

Peri smiled as she came into their bedroom. It was significantly warmer, and she was a little excited about making a nest for themselves for the night. "This is probably the weirdest Christmas Eve I've ever had."

They settled down in front of the fireplace that was beside the bed. Jax settled in his bed and promptly fell asleep.

Bennett popped the wine open. "This is probably the best Christmas Eve I've ever had."

Peri's jaw fell open. "How is that possible? You're trapped

with me, got lost in a snowstorm, are injured, and most embarrassingly, you lost our snowball fight." She smiled at him over her wine and dodged a cheesy poof he tossed at her.

He moved to sit next to her on the floor. Their backs rested against the bed frame with their legs out in front of them, so their feet faced the fire. "Those are all true, except for the last part," he said as his foot hit hers. "But you put a lot of care into how you celebrate. Being with you is half the fun."

He sipped his wine, and they both stared into the fire.

"Can I ask you a personal question?" he said, swirling his wine.

"Only if I get to ask a more personal one."

He sent her a sly smile. "Sure." He wiggled his foot, thinking about what to say next. "Why didn't your mom just give you her part of the cabin? She never even mentioned you when we spoke." He sent her a concerned smile.

Oh boy.

"You're gonna need a very large trunk for all the family baggage I have," she said, trying to lighten the mood. "But the short answer is my dad's death was unexpected and expensive. Cancer. This was always our place more than hers," she said before she downed her glass of wine. "I don't blame her for selling. I just wish she'd given me a chance to buy it first, you know? We don't communicate well."

He nodded and stared at the fire. "I get that. Still seems kind of unfair. It's clear how much you love it here. I'm sorry I brought up the developer thing and selling before. I didn't know you had..." He cleared his throat. "That it meant so much."

She'd been with this guy for what? Forty-eight hours? How did he already get her more than her own mom and so many other people she'd dated in the past? She started feeling her crush slip into something more dangerous and gooey. She needed to reel herself back in. See what he was about.

"Thanks. That means a lot," she said as she bumped his shoulder with hers. "My turn." She moved to face him. "What happened with your ex?"

He choked on his wine. "Wow, okay." He wiped his hands on his sweatpants. "You get points for being direct, Bell."

"I warned you." She grabbed a carrot and waited for the hot goss that she and Jessie had speculated on so many times. Jessie strongly believed Bennett's 'girlfriend' was really a robot that he accidentally broke with his huge, amazing penis.

"The boring answer is..." he licked his lips, "our life was boring. Our future was going to be more boring. She's a lawyer. Different firm, thank god. She wanted to get married and 'get serious about life.' Her words," he said, as he used air quotes. "She had every single piece of our future picked out for the next five years: the perfect neighborhood, the perfect wedding venue, the perfect preschool. Everything had to be perfect, or it wasn't good enough. I tried to end things before we got any more serious. Turns out trying to be perfect is pretty boring."

"Really? I mean, don't all long-term relationships feel a bit stale over time?" Peri was confused. It's not like Bennett was normally a barrel of laughs when she emailed him.

"Maybe, but I found myself looking forward to anything that would break up the monotony of our lives. My parents have been happily married for decades, and their lives don't seem boring in the least."

"Probably because they smartly avoid snow in December."

He nodded. "I have you to thank, actually."

It was Peri's turn to choke on her wine. "Why me?"

"I realized I looked forward to your ridiculous emails more than I did texts from Jamie. I figured if that was the bar, I needed to re-evaluate some things." His eyes met hers tentatively. He looked like he just told her his biggest, darkest secret.

I'm the reason they broke up? What did that mean about this tension building between them?

"My emails aren't ridiculous," she whispered with little feeling as she stared at his lips. She realized how close they were. Their shoulders and arms touched down to their elbows, and his lips were only a few inches from hers. She felt the weight of wanting him on her chest. The magnetic pull toward him that she needed to fight.

His eyes roamed her face as he leaned toward her slowly. "Your emails are perfectly ridiculous." His mouth kissed the side of hers, and she felt it burn into her. "*You're* ridiculously perfect, Peri," he whispered.

His mouth landed on hers, soft at first, and he pulled her toward him.

Yes. She wanted this so badly. She kissed him back, sucking in a breath and feeling desire travel down until it pooled deep inside her.

He broke away. "I want to use my ball prize."

Peri came out of the fog of his kiss. "That's a weird name for your penis, Bennett."

He rolled his eyes, even as he smirked at her. "No, the thing with the hundred-dollar bill. I can ask anything of you."

She bit her lip. She really, really hoped he'd use it for sex. Because then it was like she won, too. "What did you have in mind?"

Please be sexy. Please be sexy.

A smile melted onto his face. He turned to her, grabbed her hips, and swung her legs over his, bringing her onto his lap. "Okay?"

She nodded in shock. How did he know exactly what she secretly wanted?

He held her tight against him, and Peri thought about how warm the room suddenly seemed. How flushed she was starting to feel.

He leaned in and whispered in her ear as a finger trailed down her neck, playing with the wisps of hair.

"I want you to describe, in detail, what exactly you'd like me to do to you tonight. In perfect, ridiculous honesty. Because Peri," he took a breath and, lord have mercy, his lip brushed her ear lobe with a hot puff, "Whatever it is, I bet I've thought about doing it to you."

Chapter Sixteen

She sucked in a breath as his mouth landed on the corner of her jaw. His cock hardened under her legs, and she felt herself go wet at everything he was asking of her. His thumb brushed her hip as he held her, and she started to close her eyes in pleasure.

"Now, Peri," he growled at her.

Goosebumps formed on her arms.

"Anything?" she asked breathlessly.

"Anything." He kissed her neck. "I've thought about this too many times. I'm hard just thinking about what you might want."

Wasn't there a line about being honest at Christmas? Peri decided to set aside her fears and, for once in her life, just be honest about what she wanted. She took a shaky breath to describe the dream fantasy she'd imagined so many times before.

Her breath came out as a whisper. "You start with playing with my nipples." His mouth moved to her throat. His hand had already moved under her shirt to her breast, caressing the side.

She thanked her lucky stars she hadn't worn a bra that day. He swiped a thumb over her hard nipple, and she lost the power of thought. She sucked in a hard breath as she felt tingling pleasure spread through her.

"And then?" He asked, his voice a low growl.

"Then you," her breath hitched. Could she say it?

"Peri, be a good girl."

Oh fuck. She hadn't even mentioned that part. "Then you... spank me, and finally," she paused her breath, unable to utter the last phrase out loud. She moaned as he pinched her nipple.

"What do I do after I spank you?" His voice was a low rumble in her ear, and his cock was rock hard under her.

"You spread my legs and bury your face in me." She sobbed the last phrase. Her skin was crimson, flushed with desire.

"Good girl," he whispered.

Quick as lightning, he grasped her hips and flipped her over so she was face down on the carpet. "Hands above your head, Peri."

Her ass was in the air, centered on his lap. He grabbed her wrists that she held outstretched on the ground. "Comfortable?"

She nodded, unable to form sentences.

"Tell me to stop, and I will."

"Don't stop," she sobbed.

She felt him tug her leggings down, so they were on her upper thighs. The cool air of the room touched what wasn't covered by her panties.

"These are pretty," he said as he traced a finger along the scalloped edge of her cheeky panties. He then yanked them down forcefully until they were on her thighs.

She was so wet at how completely exposed and naughty she felt. The panties cut into her thighs, and the cool air kissed her skin. Need shot through her as Bennett's hand slowly caressed her.

"This is one of the first things I noticed about you. Your perfect, grab-worthy ass."

All of Peri's attention was on the moving caresses Bennett gave to her skin, side to side. Back and forth.

"Do you want to be spanked now, Peri?" His voice was firm and low.

"Yes," she sobbed. The vibrations of his voice against her were enough to make her come.

A smack hit her ass, and the brief pain and ensuing pleasure were too wonderful. Bennett rubbed where he had smacked her, then brushed the lips of her exposed pussy.

"More," she whispered.

He spanked her again and again. He'd brush his fingers in and out of her pussy between spanks until he had two fingers buried deep in her. She was so close to coming already. She ground against him, needing more.

Needing him.

"Peri, you're so wet. I need to taste you." He yanked her pants down until her legs were free. She turned over, and she finally met his eyes. The wild hunger in them left her breathless. He looked like he really would eat her up.

"No. Up here," he said, pointing to his mouth.

Peri took a shaky breath. "Are you sure?" She worried at her lip. Wouldn't she be too heavy? Too much?

He pulled her up to sit and kissed her deeply with a raw hunger. He pulled back, eyes dark. "Please," he whispered. He looked at her as though she could grant every wish he'd ever had.

He pulled her up to the bed, so she was on all fours. She felt one more spank on her ass and sucked in a breath of pleasure.

The bed creaked as he laid down, and Bennett pulled her thighs apart even wider.

A snaking of pleasure wrapped around her at feeling so

exposed. A brush of hair against her thighs told her he was under her and his hands moved over her thighs.

"Peri, you're so beautiful." He kissed her inner thigh, and she felt his tongue give her a tentative swipe on her clit.

A gasp escaped her at how good it felt. He lapped her shamelessly and she moved against him, holding the bedpost for balance. She moaned at having her deepest darkest fantasies fulfilled by Bennett. At having his head between her thighs.

He tugged her backward so she was fully seated, and his tongue was lapping her, firm strokes and nibbles on her clit, harder and harder. She gripped the bedpost, working against him to take what she wanted.

He moaned as she sat back, and one of his hands grasped her breast. Toying with her nipple, tweaking it and her body pulsed with need. She gave herself over to him, taking what he gave her as desire and lust took over.

She felt herself about to come and managed to look behind her as she threw her head back. She saw him stroking his cock as he ate her, and the sight was too much for her. She came hard, rocking against him with a shriek. He buried his face into as he came with her, moaning her name.

PERI WOKE up bright and early to happily find the power back on. She and Bennett had fallen asleep spooning, nearly naked.

It was Christmas Day, and she was naked with her former enemy wrapped around her. This was the most scandalous she'd ever felt in her life. The most *alive* she'd ever felt in her life. She thought back to how the day could have been and placed a quiet kiss on Bennett's sizable bicep under her cheek. She considered going back to sleep or waking him up for round two but decided on a surprise instead.

She threw on clothes and padded out to the kitchen.

An hour later, she pulled out a pan of cinnamon rolls as Bennett walked into the kitchen. He had the decency to be shirtless so she could enjoy the view.

"Morning," he said, placing a kiss on her temple and a squeeze on her ass. "What's all this?"

"You said your mom made cinnamon rolls for special occasions, so I thought I'd surprise you. This is your Christmas present, by the way."

His arms wrapped around her, and she thought about how she could get used to this exact situation. A sexy man, with a sexy smell, in her cabin, with warm cinnamon rolls waiting.

He nuzzled the curve of her neck. "You are the absolute best. I didn't think you were paying attention when I said that." He was clearly happy and surprised. "I also have a present for you. Let's sit."

They both grabbed coffee and a cinnamon roll, and he brought out his phone.

"I'll send the official version to you later, but...Merry Christmas," he said as he handed his phone to her. He squeezed her side as she looked down to read the small, official-looking writing.

Her mouth fell open. Peri gasped as she read and re-read the sentences. "Bennett, this is a purchase agreement. For the entire cabin."

Chapter Seventeen

er eyes scanned and rescanned the typed legal letter
on his phone. *I could buy the cabin a little at a time
from him. For no interest. For as long as it takes. What?
What?*

She blinked rapidly to see if it would clear her thoughts.
What?

"So *this* is what it takes to make you quiet. Noted," he said
with a smile.

"Bennett, I can't. I mean. It might be a really long time." Peri
couldn't take her eyes off the phone. Didn't want to hope for the
possibility this could be real.

"I know. We'll use the price I paid your mom. Chip away at
it. You deserve to own this place and spend as much time as you
want in it for the rest of your life. However long it takes is fine
by me."

"This isn't because we…" Peri pointed to the bedroom.

Bennett laughed. "You think I'm a man-ho and that's all it
takes to win my assets from me? Some excellent action?"

Peri shrugged a sassy shoulder at him. "I mean, maybe I'm
that good."

He pulled her in for a kiss that started to heat her up again. "You'll think about it?" he asked.

"Yes," she said. "I mean, yes I want to do it. Thank you." She threw her arms around him and let herself dream of what could be. What she could do with the cabin once it was finally hers.

"Peri, can we stay together for the rest of Christmas, even when the roads clear?" he asked into her hair.

She pulled back and felt sunshine beam from every corner of her heart. "And maybe sometimes other weekends?" she asked as she stared at his mouth.

"And in Chicago?" he asked as he brought her down for a kiss.

He pulled her onto him, and she straddled his lap, eager to show just how thankful she was. She kissed him, sucking his bottom lip into her mouth. His hands moved up her ass, riding up the short pajama bottoms she was wearing. She wanted a repeat of last night, and she wouldn't be ashamed to beg for it this time.

As she lifted up to say something, an odd sound caught her ear. She looked down at him. "Is that..."

"Sleigh bells?" Bennett said, looking at her with the same confusion she felt.

Their front door burst open and in spilled five chattering jingle bell-hat-wearing people who all stopped in mid-stride to stare at a shirtless Bennett with his hands on Peri's exposed ass cheeks.

Screams ripped through the air as Peri launched herself at Jessie. All of them mashed in a group hug, and everyone talked at once.

"Thought you couldn't—"

"Who is that—"

"*That's* McFucksquire?"

"You should have—"

The party wheeled their things in and took off their coats.

"P, did we just clam-jam you?" Jessie nodded their head in the direction of Bennett, who was walking to the bedroom, ostensibly to put a shirt on.

"I have so, so, so much to tell you," Peri said, shaking Jessie. "Come in. Give me two seconds, though." Peri ran to the back bedroom to find Bennett.

She shut the bedroom door, so they could have some privacy. "Come out and meet everyone," she said to Bennett, who was putting on a second layer.

"Sure," he said, his face falling a little.

"You okay?" Peri said.

He gave her a quick kiss. "Yeah, I just don't want to get in the way. Jax and I can head out once I get my stuff."

He started to walk toward the door, and Peri yanked him back. "What? No, stay. You said you wanted more things that were perfectly ridiculous. Stay and have a silly, fun, ridiculous Christmas with us."

He considered. "But don't they hate me?"

Peri grimaced at just how honest she was going to need to be. "Actually...they all have crushes on you. Like I did. Like I do. We may have looked up your profiles and made several naughty-themed names for you."

Bennett laughed in embarrassment. "Okay. I'd love to stay and experience the most ridiculous Christmas ever. Man, that Grandma trick with the hot cocoa really works."

Peri pulled on her pants and changed out of her pajama top. "Why? Because you're getting a crazy Christmas full of glitter—sorry, we ignore your silly rule—and show tunes?"

He pulled open the bedroom door. "No, because my wish came true. Your friends made it." He sent her a lopsided smile, and Peri thought she might turn into a cocoa-flavored puddle right there.

She tugged his hand toward the living room. "I can tell you two things with certainty, Bennett: one, you're going to get a pretty amazing bonus Christmas present tonight, courtesy of my vagina, and two, we'll make this the least boring, most fun, over-the-top, ridiculous Christmas Day of your life."

He yanked her back for a kiss as they passed under the mistletoe, dipping her low. They started the Best Christmas Day Ever with hoots and catcalls and couldn't wait for future Christmases in the cabin.

Epilogue

Peri closed the door with a soft click as she walked into *their* bedroom many hours later.

It had been the busiest, most perfect Christmas day with all her friends and Bennett by her side.

Bennett was already in bed with a sleepy smile and put down his novel. He stretched his arms behind his head, looking too perfect for words. Jax was curled up by the fire, and Peri couldn't believe how lucky she was to have the most perfect Christmas ever. Best friends to giggle with and a hot man in her bed.

"Everyone all tucked in?" Bennett rumbled. It had been several hours since he'd excused himself to go to bed.

She was impressed he'd lasted through all the games that night, all the activities, even singing karaoke with her after a few cocktails to *I'll Have a Blue Christmas,* doing his best Elvis impersonation. He was a natural with her group of quirky friends.

"Everyone's all tucked in. It's a good thing you and I are sleeping together," she said, winking. "Otherwise we'd be full up to the gills in this place." She sat on the bed next to him.

"I like your friends," he said with a sleepy smile and squeezed her hip.

"They like you. Well, the real you, not the grumpy you that has emailed me every two to three months chastising me about something."

He pulled her down on top of him.

"I have a sneaking suspicion you liked being chastised," he said, rumbling as her mouth met his.

"I liked having an excuse to tease you." She wrapped her arms around him and settled onto the chest that she'd grown so fond of in the last few days.

It felt like they'd just *clicked*. Since they knew each other's worst faults anyway, everything else was just gravy. All of the best parts of Bennett were her very favorite kinds of things: a man obsessed with his dog, muscles she needed to lick, stern and grumpy but obsessed with doing the right thing, and always caring for the people in his life.

The scent of cedar and warmth and man clouded her thinking, considering how they'd been interrupted earlier that day. "What cologne do you wear?" she said, out of the blue. She rubbed her face back and forth on the fabric of his soft cotton shirt.

"What?" he asked, chuckling. "I don't wear cologne."

"No way." She took a deep inhale, shamelessly taking in his scent, sniffing all around his neck. "That is not just you."

"What else would it be?" He laughed, pulling her all the way on top of him.

"Come on, it has to be aftershave, body wash?"

"I mean, yes. I do bathe."

Maybe this Bennett was magical. Maybe he was a figment of her imagination. After falling down on the ice somewhere outside, she was in the throes of frostbite imagining one last perfect Christmas at her cabin with a hot-as-hell man under her.

"Hmmm. I don't know what it is, but I like your smell," Peri said, huffing his neck and chest. "You *sure* it's not aftershave?"

Bennett laughed and flipped her so he was on top of her, pinning her down.

"You calling me a liar, Bell?"

"That's Periwinkle M. Bell to you," she said, erupting into a fit of giggles, thinking of their email exchange months ago.

"Did you have a good Christmas?" he said suddenly, his eyes searching hers with happy longing.

"Best I've had in ages." She sighed, loving the weight of him on her.

"You're quite the party hostess." His hands moved her hair away from her face.

"It's a labor of love. Though I'm sad that everyone has to head back tomorrow afternoon."

"But then we get three days of just us. Too much sugar, silly movies, and this." Bennett leaned down over her, tracing his thumbs along her cheekbones.

Peri thought her heart might burst from happiness. The sight of this Viking on top of her was too much to handle.

Holy moly, she wanted him so badly. Their molten hot session last night had given her one of her best orgasms ever. She tried not to get her hopes up, but she'd give pretty much anything—even willingly follow his no glitter rule—if he blew her mind again tonight.

His stubble glinted in the firelight, and a slow, sexy smile took her breath away as he leaned down to kiss her.

A throbbing had already started in her core when he'd pinned her. He teased light, nipping kisses along her lips.

But something nagged at her in the back of her head.

"You said you'd thought of me?" she said in between kisses.

He lifted his head and stared at her through a confused, lusty haze. "Come again?"

God, I hope to later. "Last night, you said you thought about me. Did you mean just this weekend?"

A look that was a mixture of shame and humor passed over his face. "Really? You want me to confess all my most embarrassing moments right before we..." He gestured between them.

"I can't help that my mind is great at multitasking." Peri ran her hand across his chest and up across his back. She loved the weight of him. Like her own personal weighted blanket of hotness.

"So," he started slowly, worrying his lip. "I looked you up." He winced as he said it.

Peri smiled. She kind of loved that he was a weirdo like her. "You told me that."

"But then I looked *you* up." He repeated himself, looking directly at her. "Someone tagged your personal account on a photo on your business page and I just glanced through your recent pictures," he said, defensively. "Just once. Honest."

Well, he'd been better than she'd been.

"Oh I full on creeper-trolled your accounts." She laughed, finally fessing up.

Relief washed over his face. "You were just so gorgeous and full of life. I kept telling myself it was so I could be aware of your business, given we share this place. But then I spotted you in person. You planned the Annual Law for Good charity gala last year and I saw you. You were moving through the crowd like a shark. A gorgeous shark, always behind the scenes, always leaving someone with a kind word or helping someone. I noticed you. You might have wanted to blend in, but I couldn't stop staring. That off-the-shoulder number you had on didn't help either."

Had she forgotten to keep breathing? He'd noticed her across a crowded room filled with accomplished women. And he'd thought about her.

He kissed her neck, lingering. "I think your curves were permanently imprinted in my brain that night."

"And yet you still chastised me for a few spaghetti stains." She giggled.

He huffed a laugh against her jawline. "A contract is a contract, and I stand by my assessment. But I enjoyed having an excuse to email you."

Goosebumps ran down her arms. As his mouth moved to her cleavage, he pulled her low-cut shirt down, exposing more of her breast. Kissing it reverently. "I noticed you, Peri. And I haven't stopped thinking of you since."

Fuck. Wasn't that all she'd ever wanted?

He moved to push her shirt up over her head. He licked between her cleavage and moaned. "I've definitely thought of doing this. Multiple times."

She pulled at his shirt, needing to see his chest.

He slipped it off as he sat back on his heels, straddling her. Thick ridges of muscles covered in a healthy layer of comfort and a dusting of hair took her breath away.

He looked at her like she was a steak dinner and he hadn't eaten for days. She leaned up and pressed kisses against his chest, wanting to imprint the memory of this. His scent. The feel of his chest hair against her cheek. He tipped her head up and unclipped her hair. Ran his fingers up through the back of it.

Then, slowly, he leaned down and kissed her.

A kiss that promised love *and* fucking.

A kiss that said *I've wanted you for so fucking long and I finally get my way*. She gave into him, pliant and happy for him to show her what he wanted. To give her pleasure that she'd never dared to ask for before.

"Now," he said with a smile as he pulled back. "Can I

continue?' His thumb stroked the hollow of her cheek. She nodded, smiling.

He'd noticed me.

Without breaking eye contact, he leaned around and unhooked her bra. "Lie down," he commanded.

It sounded like as much of a threat as it was a promise. His eyes were molten as he leaned over her, taking one nipple into his mouth and sucking, looking industrious and wicked. Wanting to wallow in the moment, Peri arched her back into him and closed her eyes.

"Eyes on me," he said, his voice husky and forceful. "I want you to watch me make you come."

Fuck yes.

She loved being told what to do. Loved being dominated. His hand slipped into her leggings, and he pulled them down so he could see her panties.

"God, you're so wet already." He leaned down to lick her other nipple and take it into his mouth.

She fought to keep her eyes open, staring back at his eyes that had locked on her as he sucked and teased her.

"Good girl."

A rush of need and wanting throbbed at her clit.

"More," she said, thrusting against him.

"Well, it is Christmas," he murmured against her breast.

She ran her hands through his hair as he yanked down her legging and panties just far enough to get to her clit.

His eyes still locked with hers, he ran his tongue around her clit. He circled it once, twice, and moved it up and down between the exposed lips of her pussy, barely grazing her.

Fuck, why was it so much hotter when he teased her? She grabbed the headboard behind her to keep from losing her mind.

The sight of Bennett McWilliams taking his pleasure in her pussy was too much.

"I'm gonna come," she moaned, throwing her head back as she thrust against his tongue.

"Shhhh." He chuckled, crawling up over her. He kissed her and flipped them over so she was on top of him. "What if your friends hear?" he whispered, pulling her down for a kiss.

"We tested," Peri panted as he kissed her jaw, "the sound-proofing earlier."

Bennett paused, a sly smile on his face. "For sex purposes?"

Peri nodded, focused on those fucking lips of his. The kind that Italian sculptors would use for inspiration. "For sex purposes."

He shoved her pants off, and she straddled him, now naked. But he froze. "Oh fuck. Wait, I don't have a condom."

Her hopes fell, until she remembered their game yesterday. "Got it," she exclaimed and ran over to Bennett's Saran Wrap ball stash, naked as a flasher at a football game.

He chuckled. "It's a good thing I claimed my spoils."

She jumped back into bed, waving it victoriously. "*And* it's Christmas-themed."

"I'd expect nothing less from the best party planner in the city."

Her pussy clenched. Goddamnit, why did she have to have such a praise kink?

She tore the condom open with her teeth and shimmied his sweatpants down. He had on black boxer briefs. *Ha, Jessie owes me five dollars.* They swore Bennett would be a tighty-whitey guy.

He tugged his boxers down so the top of his hard cock peeked out.

Whoa.

Merry Christmas to me.

He was thick and hard, with a reddened glow that made Peri want to lick him up and down, taste him and memorize the feeling of him in her hands.

He shoved off the rest of his clothes, and she happily sat straddling his thighs with a condom in hand.

She locked eyes with him, and the lust and hunger in them hit her in the chest.

His teeth ground together as he took her in. "You're a wet dream, Peri. Just like this. Tits out, wet for me, and curves for days." His hands squeezed her thick thighs, digging in.

She rolled the condom slowly over his cock, taking him in hand.

"Fuck," he moaned as she stroked him. "I want you on me." He growled, pulling her up by one arm and seating her so her pussy met his tip.

Holy lord. It had been so long since she'd been here. Hovering over a man who was feral for her. Feeling him press at her entrance, wanting to claim her.

"Eyes on me, baby," he murmured.

She opened her eyes as she pressed down onto him, biting her lip. Fuck, he was too big. She breathed through her nose, slowly inching down as she went.

"You're doing so good. Slide on that cock for me a little more." His voice was soothing, firm. His fingers wandered to her clit to tease it.

"I don't know," he panted, trying to catch his breath, "how long I....you feel too good."

She slid further, and further, gasping as she went. He was going to split her in two, but it felt so good.

She finally stopped, fully seated.

He bit his lip. "Jesus, you're gorgeous. Sitting on my cock like the best Christmas present I've ever unwrapped."

She clenched around him and had the satisfaction of

ripping a groan out of him. She lifted herself off and then slowly slid down, down, down onto his cock again.

"Your curves. Your ass. This." He gripped her thigh meat. "I want to see it shake. See all of you bounce on my cock."

Peri leaned forward, pushing her breasts into him as she moved up and down, feeling the scrape of his hair against her clit. He pulled her down onto him harder and shoved her away. Only to yank her back hard.

"Yes," she moaned.

He trailed kisses along her neck. "Did you check the sound-proofing of the room for spanking?" he murmured against her.

"Yes," she lied. She just wanted it so bad.

He popped her ass cheek with a quick slap. "Such a good girl."

A rush of pleasure fizzled through her, and she thrust against him. "More," she begged. The sizzle felt perfect as it turned into pleasure.

"Earn it, baby."

She sat up, pressing her breasts together, and rode his cock, slamming her hips again and again into him.

"Good girl." He rubbed his thumb against her clit. And as Peri threw her head back, a curl of climax building inside, she got another slap on her ass. "You look so good grinding on my cock."

He felt amazing under her. *Looked* amazing. And the tip of his cock hit *just* the right spot to make her leg shake.

She bounced for him and stretched her arms behind her head, letting him take her in.

"Holy fuck," he gasped. He leaned up and grabbed one breast and slapped her ass one more time. "Fucking dream girl."

He flopped back down and used both hands to move her against his cock.

She was going to have bruises tomorrow from how much he'd squeezed her, but she only wanted it harder.

"I'm coming," she sobbed. Bennett let his eyes drift from her eyes down to her ass, watching her riding him, thrusting and thrusting.

"Too good," he ground out and thrust against her. Spiraling pleasure and driving need shot through Peri as she came around his cock and heard his strangled groan as he came.

She collapsed on his heaving chest as his hand came to hold her head against him.

Peri heard the thundering heartbeat under her ear and smiled. It somehow sounded stern and grumpy too. But she'd just made love—well, made love with *and* fucked Bennett McWilliams. AKA BenBen McFucksquire. AKA her very real crush, former enemy, and now something else entirely.

A happy glow surrounded him as he looked down at her lying on his chest. He pressed her to him, holding her like she was the most precious thing. "Merry Christmas, Peri."

She kissed his smiling lips, unwilling to believe her luck.

"Merry Christmas, Bennett."

Bonus Epilogue

BENNETT

The cozy cabin came into view as Bennett parked his SUV in the loop driveway in front of the cabin. Jax whined in the backseat, buckled into his seatbelt with his tail already swishing. It had been a long car ride, and Jax was eager to see Peri when they hopped out.

They both were.

The last six weeks had gone by in a happy blur. He'd had more spontaneous snowball fights, consumed more holiday-themed sugar, and had fallen hard for Periwinkle M. Bell.

He'd almost slipped and said "I love you" when he'd hung up with her that morning, but he'd have to be careful to keep his feelings under wraps this weekend.

Six weeks was too soon for the L word, right? *And* on Valentine's Day? It was too much pressure and might freak her out. He couldn't spook the best thing that had happened to him in years.

Her laughter, the brightness that she brought to even the most mundane tasks made his life light up at the seams. He felt lighter, happier, younger than he had in months. They'd almost been kicked out of the Shop and Save last Sunday when they'd erupted into raucous laughter in the produce section when Peri did a dead-on impression of his boss using an eggplant.

Never a dull moment with the woman he loved.

Bennett opened the door of the cabin as Jax thundered in behind him, only to be met by a jaw-dropping sight.

Peri was wrapped around a new love of her life and was currently showering them with kisses.

"And who are you?" Bennett said with an authoritative thunder. A floppy-eared golden mix turned his head beside Peri with his tongue hanging out and jumped off the couch to sniff at Jax.

"Didn't you get my text?" Peri said, jumping up from the couch.

"I got fifty-seven texts, but I was driving, Ms. Bell." Bennet rolled his eyes at his zephyr of a girlfriend. Of course there was a strange dog in their cabin that she'd probably already gotten attached to.

"I got excited, okay? This is Val."

Bingo. Knew it.

"Val?" Bennet wrapped his arms around Peri and pulled her up so her feet dangled as she hugged him back.

A sigh of contentment sank its way back into his soul at being near her again.

He loved how she fit in his arms. Peri was curvy, short, and basically his dream girl. He'd gotten used to feeling her under his hands as she rode him or squeezing her butt as she walked past when she stayed over at his place. She was perfect for him, and he'd already missed her after being away from her for only a few days.

Peri slid down his chest, but her eyes were bright with excitement. "She was wandering outside, no collar. And I called around to the neighbors, but no one recognized her."

The two dogs sniffed each other in a circle, feeling each other out.

Jax let out a quick bark and dipped into a playful bow, clearly saying, *"Let's ditch these dumb humans and wrestle."* Val snorted and bowed in return, her tail up high, her front paws down low, her tongue panting with a happy smile. They rounded each other and took off through the cabin, paws thundering on the old plank flooring.

"Val seems right at home," Bennett said, shaking his head. You never knew what you were in store for with Peri. "And here I thought *this* would be your Valentine's Day present." He pulled a bouquet of three dozen pink carnations out from his bag on the ground.

"Ooh!" Peri clapped her hands together with excitement, biting her bottom lip as if he'd given her the world.

"Do you know how many dirty looks I got from the flower shop owner for giving my girlfriend *carnations* for Valentine's Day?"

But he knew they were her favorite. She said they always looked lonely in the store and she wanted to give them a good home.

"Well, you gussied them up with all this other fun stuff." Bright green leaves encased the large bouquet, and bright purple violets and white roses were tucked inside.

She grabbed the bouquet and dashed for the kitchen when he grabbed her hand and tugged her back. He'd learned that Peri was permanently in a scramble.

"I've missed you, baby," he murmured as his mouth caught hers. His hands ran up into her hair, tugging through the loose strands all around her face. She melted against him, and it was his favorite thing: a calm, quiet Peri pliant with need and lust. Though busy, tornado-Peri was his second favorite thing.

She pulled back and stared at him starry eyed. "I missed you. Hard to believe it's only been a week."

They practically lived together in Chicago now, but she'd spent regular breaks in the cabin, making time away from her business to plan for the future.

She tugged away and started rummaging in the cabinets, probably for a vase. "Are your parents on track to be here tonight?"

"Their flight's been delayed." He bent down to scratch Val as she lumbered up to him with a happy, dopey grin. "And there's a snow front coming through."

"Oh no, maybe we'll be snowed in," Peri said in mock sadness, shimmying her shoulders with a look over her shoulder at him.

"There's always hope," he said, scratching Val behind her ears. "What's Val short for?"

"Valentine's, of course."

He could hear the *duh* in her voice and snorted. "Valentine Bell, I don't think you know what you've gotten yourself into." He got a large lick on the cheek from Val as she nuzzled into his shoulder. "Will you keep her?"

"Of course I'm going to keep her," Peri said with shock. "Unless she has another home to go to, but she was pretty scroungy when I found her out wandering in the cold earlier today. I think she's been holed up in a little burrow, keeping warm. Whoever had her wasn't taking very good care of her."

He looked at the perfectly clean and happy dog with a round tummy, already fed after a day of spoiling from Peri.

"Do I even *want* to know what the bathroom looks like?"

"Uhh..." Peri's face scrunched up in a grimace.

Oh my god. He could only imagine the soap probably still lodged on the walls and drops of mud along the tub.

It was never a boring moment with Periwinkle M. Bell.

Bennett glanced to the sidewall and sucked in a breath. He hadn't noticed the chaos until just now.

Peri stirred soup on the stove. "Did Val do something adorable again? She caught her tail earlier. Such a smart girl," she cooed as Val plodded over.

Bennett stared at the bright paint streaks over the interior wall of the cabin and tried to breathe through his surprise. *It'll eventually be her cabin; she can do what she wants. Even if it gives me a heart attack.*

"I see you tried some paint samples." Bennett said through a forced smile. The cabin would be Peri's as soon as she paid it off, however long that took her. She'd already made hefty deposits, paying a few thousand after each major party she planned.

"I figured I'd paid off enough to test out paint samples." She stared happily at her handiwork with her hands on her hips. Stripes of many colors were zigzagged across a sidewall. Bright magenta, cream peach, a moody navy, and a sage green all stood side by side as if she was trying out different moods.

He gulped. *This was her cabin. This was her cabin. This was her cabin.*

"Which one's your favorite?" he said, slowly, hoping for anything other than peach.

"I think...Calm AF Green."

He let out a whoosh of grateful air. "Great. That's my favorite, too." He kissed her temple. It was her cabin, but he hoped they'd be coming back to it for years, maybe even decades to come.

She cocked her head, staring at the wall in thought. "Or the magenta. I don't know, we'll see. It'll be a game-time decision."

"You will make a *game-time* decision while painting a whole wall?" He laughed, grabbing her around the waist and nuzzling into her neck with kisses. "I think you'll be the death of me, but I'm going to have a hell of a fun time along the way." His hands dug in on her hips, and he grabbed both sides with a growl. It had been over a week since he'd last seen her, since he'd last felt her underneath him, over him.

And he wanted the woman he loved.

"Oh, I see you're opening your Valentine's Day present early." She snorted, turning around in his arms and wrapping her hands behind his neck.

"What's that?" he said, enchanted with her.

"Me." She flung her arms out wide and dashed to the stove. "Close your eyes. I can't wait any longer to show you your present. And turn around. I know you peek."

He shook his head with a sigh and smiled. Crossing his arms, he turned around and closed his eyes. Who knew what she had planned. In the last six weeks, he'd gone on scavenger hunts, competed in karaoke competitions, and had drag queens serenade him for his birthday. All amazing; all things he would have never thought he'd do in a million years. But he lived to see the happy glow in Peri's eyes when he went along with her schemes.

A scuffle sounded over at the table, and a small *oof* with the sound of a table scooting echoed in the room.

Oh lord. She's moving furniture. Never a good sign of a quiet night.

"Okay, you can open your eyes."

Bennett turned around to find a stark naked Peri sitting on the kitchen table with her wrap dress under her. She held a painter's brush in one hand and a small bowl in the other and had already painted white, creamy hearts all over her tits and stomach. Errant brush strokes were around her neck, and she'd swirled loops on her thighs. The early evening light hit her from the side, and she looked like an actual picture. A crazed, white chocolate-covered picture.

Her face fell. "You don't like it?" A pouty lip extended.

Fuck. He moved to her. "No, honey. You just melted my brain, that's all." His cock was already jumpy when he was near her, and now it was a rock-hard bar in his pants.

He grabbed her waist, stepping between her legs, and licked under her ear to catch a drip of chocolate. "I love you—it," He said quickly, correcting himself.

Fuck fuck fuck. "I love it," he clarified as he pulled back.

Goddamn melted brain.

Her eyes went wide as she processed his words. *Well, fuck.* This was going to be a whole thing. "You don't have to say it back. Honestly. Sorry, I'm sorry I slipped." He ran a hand over his chin. "Let's just forget about it and get back to business."

He dipped his head to the other side of her neck and ran his tongue along a strip of melted white chocolate but stopped. Peri had gone very still.

Never a good sign.

He pulled back to look at her.

Her manicured brows were furrowed in confusion. "You said—"

"We don't have to—"

"But—"

He dipped down to catch her mouth, stealing her words. *Coward. Distracting your girlfriend with sex.*

Maybe this would be enough. Just saying it once and showing her how much he loved her. He grabbed her ass, pulling her toward him so her cleft slid against the zipper of his jeans. She moaned as she tilted her hips against him. He was so hard already, and his cock twitched thinking of being inside her again.

The lure of licking the chocolate off her tits was too great, and he finally broke away, now that he had her panting for him. *Maybe she'll forget about what I said.*

His tongue lapped up the hardening chocolate against her skin. He scraped his teeth against her, loving the feeling of nibbling on her.

"Bennett," she panted. "We should…"

He kissed his way down to her nipple that she'd covered with a healthy coating and sucked it into his mouth. Peri threw her head back and moaned. He toyed with her nipple, biting it, licking it, and she thrust against him.

"I know what," she gasped, "you're doing…and it's—"

His finger found her clit, and a sexy-as-sin, porny guttural moan ripped from her. "I want to hear that again," he murmured. He sucked her other nipple into his mouth, getting rewarded with chocolate, and as he bit down on her, another moan slipped out of her, needy and hungry. He dug his fingers into her cushy ass. "Good girl."

Fuck, he wanted her. His cock was moving of its own accord, jumping every time she moaned. Fast as lightning, he caught her mouth, unzipped his pants, and found her entrance. They'd stopped using condoms weeks ago, thank Christ. She felt so good to slide into. He was going to get white chocolate all over his sweater, but it was a fair trade for the hot, wet heaven of her pussy.

He scooted her hips forward so she met his cock, and her mouth broke away. A pretty flush ran over her breasts.

"You're gorgeous, baby." He slid the tip into her as he palmed her breast, sticky with chocolate. He didn't care. He wanted all of her.

"Wait," she panted.

He froze, barely inside her.

She yanked his head up so he'd look her in the eyes. "I love you. You can't *not* let me love you when I'm about to burst from it." Her voice was urgent and a little angry and fuck if that didn't make him harder.

She loves me back. His heart thudded in his chest, and it matched her fast-talking mouth. He captured her mouth again, craving her taste, but she pulled away again, her brows furrowed.

"Stop distracting me with your sex mouth, counselor." She narrowed her eyes at him.

This was exquisite torture. The best dominatrix in the world couldn't top the luscious torment of having your cock in your slick, wet, willing girlfriend who loved you but wouldn't stop glaring while she chastised you.

"I love you so much," he murmured, moving to lick the chocolate off her neck. "And I will expound on that expeditiously in our post-coital closing arguments. But I will give literally anything to fuck you right now, woman."

A lusty chuckle rumbled out of her. "Goddamn, I love it when you lawyer at me." She pulled his hips closer and wrapped her legs around him. He kissed the smile that formed on her lips as he slowly, slowly slid into home. Her. Perfection.

He held her head against his chest as unexpected emotion clutched his throat. She clung to him, and he felt a sniffle against his chest.

"I love you, Peri." His voice was hoarse. "You are my light. Pure goodness in my life."

She tilted her head back to stare at him, and a tear ran down her cheek. "I love you. All the best and the grumpy parts of you all twined up together."

He kissed the tear away and nuzzled her cheek. "I've never been grumpy a day in my life," he whispered, knowing exactly the reaction he'd get.

She gasped and her hands dove for his ticklish spots until he wrestled her arms behind her hips.

And thrust.

Suddenly, his love's running mouth was quiet. She bit her lip with wanting, and lust took over. "I love when you press your tits into me," he murmured against her mouth, hovering there as he slowly moved them. Her legs were wrapped around him, and he thrust harder, loving the sight of all of her moving under him.

"If you really want my tits against you, you know what you'll have to do," she said, smirking.

He raised an eyebrow in question.

She caught his chin. "Earn it, baby."

Oh, this woman. His heart might burst from wanting her. He bent down quickly and, thanks to his rugby training, had her over his shoulder in a flash.

"Bennett!" she shrieked, giggling upside down. Her ass was in the air on his shoulder, and he gave it a hearty smack.

"That's the idea, love. But maybe try it with more of a moan next time." He walked into their bedroom as she smacked his ass back.

"Out," he commanded, and both dogs scuttled to the living room.

He tossed his beloved onto their bed, and she let out a small *oof* again. He tore his sweater and pants off in a flash while her lust-hazed face stared at him in appreciation.

He climbed between her legs as his cock thrust against her clit. Their fingers interlaced as he reached over her, and he took a moment to appreciate the warm, sexy woman under him. Whom he loved. Who loved him back.

He needed to see her—all of her—come around his cock. But she was right. It was his turn to earn it. So he slid beside her, moving so her back was pressed to his front. He hooked her leg over his, spreading her, and teased her clit. "Did I ever tell you about how I had to pull over when I first drove back to Chicago after Christmas? I sat on an off-ramp side-road, stroking my cock. Picturing you riding it again. And again. Every position I could think of."

Her nails raked against his scalp, and he selfishly enjoyed the view of her tits bouncing as he rubbed her. He thrust into her from behind, grinding his molars at how good she felt. "This was my favorite. Feeling your ass against my cock. Getting to watch all of you as you came, screaming my name."

He rubbed her clit harder and harder and loved watching her face as she took him. Craved what he gave her. "You want this cock so badly, don't you, baby?"

"Yes," she gasped, and she tightened more and more around him.

Fuck. How was he supposed to concentrate with her feeling so good?

"Spank me," she moaned.

A wicked grin curled his lips as he spread her legs wider. His fingers found her clit. "Right here, love? You want it so badly right here?"

A ripping moan of *yes* streamed out of her.

He was only too happy to earn it. He slapped her pussy on her clit with a pop and felt her clench around him like a vise as she cried out. His vision went white as he got his bearings.

"More," she begged.

He thrust and spanked her, hitting her from either side until he heard her cries go higher, higher, higher. She grabbed both of her tits as she shrieked his name and her walls rippled around him.

He finally let himself rut into her, thrusting like an animal hard and fast until finally his balls tightened and the rocketing pleasure covered his body as he came into her.

After several minutes and ensuring his soul was back safely in his body, Bennett leaned over the side of the bed and grabbed his pants pocket. He'd seen a necklace in the jewelry store and knew it would look perfect on her.

"So I know you had your heart set on carnations, but I saw this and I wanted you to have it."

Peri took the box with wide eyes, and she stilled as she opened the jewelry box.

"Crap, I thought that was an engagement ring," she said, clutching her heart. "I mean, that would have been great"—she spoke quickly—"but you know, it's been like a day and a half that we've been dating. That would be nuts, right?" She laughed, but he caught the question in her eyes.

"Yeah," he chuckled, holding her eyes. Nuts to imagine her not in his life.

Goddamnit, why *wasn't* it an engagement ring?

They had plenty of time, he figured. They'd have a full summer at the cabin or in the city, whenever they could spend time together. It didn't really matter if they were in his downtown loft or her quirky studio or surrounded by trees in a Wisconsin forest.

Peri stared at the necklace as she reverently ran a finger over it. It was a delicate filigree snowflake laced with tiny diamonds along the edging.

"I know winter is almost over," he said apologetically, chewing on his lip, now feeling a little embarrassed about the whole thing.

"No, I love it. Because of..." She waved a finger around them in the cabin. "If it hadn't been for all that snow, I'd probably still be calling you McFucksquire." She snorted, leaning down and grabbing his chin for a kiss with a giggle.

"To be fair, I'm pretty sure I heard you call me that on the phone with Jessie last weekend."

"Hmm." She harrumphed. "You were being a buttface," she said, wiggling as she took her necklace out of the jewelry box.

"Here, let me," he said, grabbing the necklace from her. She was still naked, and he thought that that was exactly how the necklace was supposed to be worn. Just her complemented by diamonds. He clasped the necklace around her and kissed the nape of her neck. "It looks perfect."

He tugged her back into the crook of his arm as they settled down to sleep for the evening.

His mind whirled a thousand miles an hour. How soon was *too* soon? He'd had money saved up, but did she want something traditional? Non-traditional? Maybe she was just joking and he misread the situation. Six weeks was way too early to propose. Right?

"I can *hear* you overthinking," she said as she nuzzled into the nook of his chest.

"I'm not overthinking," he lied, squeezing her, loving the feel of her ass under his fingertips as he held on and gave it another squeeze.

"I said the thing and then you thought the thing, and then I ruined the moment and then—"

"—Oh hush," he interrupted. "Or your mouth will have to do some extra credit work."

A giant snore by the fire had them both leaning up. The dim glow of the embers in the fireplace showed Jax and Val already at home with one another, side by side in their dog beds. Bennett thought a family of four or five, or however many Peri would whirl into his life, sounded pretty great.

"Big day tomorrow. My parents should land around eleven," he said, murmuring into her hair as they fell asleep.

"Excited to meet them. Think they'll like me?"

He chuckled. His parents were the embodiment of boring

beige. A far cry from the magenta cream and navy streaked whirl of Peri. "You're going to knock their fucking socks off."

Peri wiggled with excitement, burrowing down into sleep. She let out a contented little sigh, and he was so glad he'd had the stupid idea to spend Christmas by himself this year only for fate to intervene and to tell him what he really needed: the chaos snow bunny that brought color and life into his world.

"Hey, Peri," he whispered.

"Hmm?"

He smiled against her hair, feeling grateful and already planning his next jewelry purchase. "Night, tiger."

THE END

Snowed In
AND
Snuggle Weather

Chapter One

JOSIE

"Here's your demon spawn pizza." Josie shoved a plate piled with pineapple and bacon-topped pizza at her best friend, Max.

"See if I share my breadsticks with you." He snatched the plate from her. "Did you get the cheesy sauce?"

Josie flopped down on Max's well-worn, plaid oversized couch. "Best friend movie night wouldn't be complete without some chemical-based cheese-like substance."

Josie settled back into the over-stuffed piece of heaven and took a bite of her cheesy, not-weird pizza. In front of her, an enormous cobblestone fireplace ran the length of two stories, and a fire crackled in the oversized hearth. Their movie marathon had become a weekly tradition for the last six months, and the cozy living room in Max's log cabin was half the appeal of Friday movie night.

Snow fell outside, creating small drifts on the windowpane. She thought for the thousandth time how happy she was to have him back in their hometown. They'd been best friends since that fateful day in fourth grade, and Max had only recently returned to Benning Falls, Vermont, after breaking off his engagement.

Max flopped down next to her. "Ready for the three best movies you'll ever see?" He smiled with eager excitement, looking like one of those cartoon princes. She could even imagine a sparkly gleam on his teeth.

Josie sighed as she bit into her slice of pizza, trying to will away her attraction to him.

He was her best friend and he knew her better than anybody.

There was no way they could ever date.

She wasn't willing to risk her friendship with the person she loved most in the world by bringing sex into the equation. Plus, his six foot two, broad-shouldered frame with naturally tan skin and a Hemsworth-like jawline meant that Max had his pick of the litter when it came to girls. Josie could amp herself up to cute if given the right amount of time, but she looked nothing like any of Max's stick-thin ex-girlfriends.

She pushed her thoughts away and answered with a mouth full of pizza (so charming). "You can't top last week. *Star Trek: The Wrath of Khan* is the definitive story by which all other stories are measured." Josie pointed at the shirt she wore with the franchise's famous logo. "What are we watching?"

"Since this week is finally my turn after you hogged all of January, we're watching my favorite romantic comedies."

Josie rolled her eyes even as she smiled at his mushy romantic heart. "Love is an illusion."

"What?" Max jerked his head back in shock. "You've had a million boyfriends. You've never been in love with any of them?"

The pizza scratched Josie's throat as she swallowed it.

Nope, not the time. Can't talk about this now. Panic rose in her but she tamped it down with a mental boot stomp.

She could never, ever admit two very secret things to her best friend.

One: She'd never been in love with any of her boyfriends. She'd had short flings with the bottom dwellers she tended to date, but never felt anything resembling love.

Two: She'd actually been in love with Max, the all-star baseball-playing, trust fund parent-having, gorgeous heir to the maple syrup dynasty sitting in front of her.

"I *thought* I was in love. But love is just a fairy tale or actually," she paused, "probably a ghost story. C'mon, hit play, you sappy man. Get it? Sappy?" she said, nudging his shoulder at her pun-tastic wordplay about maple syrup.

He groaned as he smiled at her and nudged her back. "You're hilarious, Thornfield."

Max started the first movie and craned his head to look out the window. "Do you need to stay here tonight?" he asked. "It's coming down in sheets right now."

It was February in Vermont, and Josie was only too familiar with the regular onslaught of snow. The flakes outside looked like they were being dumped from a bucket somewhere above the roofline as thousands of chunky flakes flew down to the ground.

"I have a four-wheel drive, and I've been in Vermont longer than you have." She stuck her tongue out, therefore definitively proving her point.

Plus, your sleepy morning PJ look melts my heart into a pool of butter, and I can't risk falling any farther in love with you.

"You can't keep holding it against me that I lived out of state for six years." Max had lived in Manhattan after college, working as a business consultant.

"I'll be fine. How much snow could we possibly get? Now shush. You're interrupting my ogling." She pointed to a smoldering leading man onscreen.

She grabbed a fuzzy, thick blanket from the couch and spread it over their legs without thinking.

A few hours later, snuggled into the couch, Josie's eyes felt like they were being held down with fifty pound weights.

Max got up to grab another drink, and Josie let herself appreciate the view as he walked away. She let out a loud yawn.

"Early mornings catching up with you?"

"It's not easy getting up at the buttcrack of pitch black every morning," Josie moaned from the couch.

"You think I sleep in? Tapping an acre of maple trees waits for no man." He threw her a shrug. "Plus, second graders can't be that hard to wrangle, right?" He smiled at her, knowing exactly what her answer would be.

"Imagine wrangling thirty pure, sweet golden retriever puppies smart enough to get into serious trouble." She stole one of his breadsticks and dipped it in what was left of the nacho cheese. "They are adorable and amazing and perfect but exhausting. We might have to save the rest of our movie night."

"We were just getting to the good one." He settled back down on the couch beside her.

She noticed how his thigh brushed up against hers and desperately wanted it to mean something, but it was probably just the romcom messing with her head.

"Subjecting me to a 1950s classic romcom right now would be like giving me seven quaaludes. I'd fall into a coma that would make Sleeping Beauty weep from jealousy." Josie rubbed her hands over her face to wake the sleep from her eyes.

"Ugh, you're the worst," Max said, snuggling next to her.

She looked at his long legs splayed out in front of him and wished she could rest her head on his lap. He wore old cozy sweatpants and a faded, torn sweatshirt from college. She thought of the broad chest underneath and dreamed about nuzzling her head on his shoulder, but she didn't want to make it weird. Plus, he smelled so fucking good—that indescribable boy smell that tugged at something primal in her—and she didn't trust herself not to do something stupid.

She sighed and tried to get her head back in the game.

He's your best friend. He doesn't want to make out with you. He smells like pine-soaked sexiness and emotional safety but he is your friend.

"I should go," she said, "before it gets any worse."

Did she mean the weather or her all-consuming crush on him?

"If you feel even a little sleepy on your ten-minute drive home, give me a call." He looked up at her with concern as she levered herself out of the cushy, warm couch of her dreams.

She stretched, feeling several bones creak and wished she was already back on the couch, snuggled under the covers next to him. She let out a shudder as she put on her shoes.

He stood up and stretched, giving her a tantalizing glimpse of his lower abs for a brief second and the deep V that was cut into each hip. Her brain almost blue-screened from the view.

"You sure you don't want to stay?" He sent her a sleepy half-smile.

Max had moved back into his childhood home, an enormous two-story log cabin, last year when he took over his family's maple syrup business. The house had an enormous vaulted ceiling, and original local logs lined the walls. The giant fireplace created a warm, cozy focal point, and the kitchen was a luxury masterpiece.

Every nerve ending in her body screamed, *Yes, I would like to stay and snuggle in your bed and smell all of your smells and eat your fresh maple syrup for breakfast, and never leave because this place is fucking amazing.*

But instead, like a dummy, Josie sighed in response to his question and declined.

"No, I'll be fine..." —She almost called him dear but stopped her mouth before it betrayed her—"...bro," she finished awkwardly.

"Bro?" He laughed with a rich, booming echo that sent butterflies through her stomach. "Your kids teaching you the coolest new slang?" He stared at her over his beer with a mischievous smile.

"I am *so* cool," she said, pointing a finger at him. There, that would show him.

"That unicorn onesie you have says otherwise," he snorted.

"Hey!" Fire pumped through her system and woke her up. "I look freaking adorable in that."

"Yeah, you do look pretty adorable in it," he chuckled. His cheeks turned pink, and he looked away suddenly.

Shit. Her cheeks started to burn, too.

It's cool. Best friends can call each other cute. If a girl BFF called her cute, she'd be like, "Omg thanks, bestie," and not turn into a blushing weirdo, right?

Shit was so confusing when you were in love with your best friend.

Chapter Two

JOSIE

Josie waved awkwardly and headed for the door.

Max walked to the entryway to see her out.

Because he's a swoony gentleman. She cursed herself. *No, stop. Bad girl.*

"Be careful on the steps."

His unnecessary concern secretly thrilled her, but she had to play it cool. She absolutely loved that he worried about her. "Oh my gosh, I've been here more than my grandma's house. I'll be fine, Max."

"Okay, but text me when you get home." He held the door open and stood over her as she walked past. Josie was tall, but she could still look up into Max's face as she stopped in front of him. He had stubble coming in, and she knew he had to shave every morning, or he'd look like a mountain man within two days.

"I'll make sure to text, Grandma Max," she said, throwing an eye roll over her shoulder to chill whatever heat she was feeling between them.

She needed to keep him safely over the fuck there in Best Friend land.

She glanced over his farm as she made her way down the treacherous, slippery steps. The bare trees were frosted in a thick, gleaming layer of ice. The lazy drifting flakes had turned into more of a persistent downfall since she'd last looked outside, and thick snowflakes clung to her hair and eyelashes.

It was the end of February, and Max would soon be busy for sixteen hours each day harvesting the maple syrup from trees surrounding the cabin.

Rolling hills of maple trees sprawled out before her and she heard the whistling wind whipping the snow. She wished she was tucked back in the warm, dreamy cabin.

As she gingerly picked her way down the ice-covered sidewalk, Josie regretted wearing slippery tennis shoes.

"Be careful," Max called.

"Worrywart!" To prove her point, she threw a wave over her shoulder, but her stupid tennis shoes picked that moment to slide on a stupid piece of ice.

Had she lived in Vermont for almost thirty years?

Yep.

Was that going to help as she flailed like an inflatable dealership mascot onto the ice-covered sidewalk?

Unfortunately not.

She did her best baby deer impression, swishing her feet back and forth, trying to regain her balance—*Goddamnit, why is my core so weak?*—and fell in slow motion as Max watched.

She hit her back on the decorative edging along the sidewalk and let out a very lady-like, very loud "Fuck!"

"Oh shit! Hold on." He ran back inside, leaving the door open.

She winced as she sat up. "Um, I'm fine." A hot, electric twinge clawed its way through her lower back from landing on the concrete scalloped edging.

Max walked out in work boots and a coat a few seconds later. "You okay?"

She bit her lip as pain radiated through her. "My back. I just need help getting up. Then I'll be fine."

"Are you sure you should drive home?" Worry etched into his face as he climbed down the steps to her.

"Oh my gosh, if you want to have a sleepover, just say so, Max," she grumbled as she rolled herself over to get up.

Nothing sexier than looking like a beached tortoise in front of your life-long crush.

She let out a low moan as she tried to haul herself up. Not only was she bruised, but her back spasms were firing up in full force. They felt like the devil's hands driving a stick shift with her spine.

"Hold still. Why don't you ever let me help you?" He leaned down to grasp her arms.

"Because I don't need your help." She shot a murderous look up at him from her position on all fours.

"I'll remember that the next time you try ice skating on my sidewalk." He crouched down so they were face to face.

She loved that they could bicker like an old married couple, but he still had her back. Literally.

"Your back spasming again?" he said in a low voice. His eyes caught hers with concern.

God, the intimacy of it all—his voice beside her ear, the feel of him next to her—was a great distraction. Anything to keep the shooting pain from overtaking her sanity.

She nodded, biting her lip to keep her tears at bay.

"Okay, hold on." He got into a squat and put his hands on her waist under her coat. They felt so solid and warm, she almost wished this would take longer. "Up in one, two, three."

Before Josie knew it, Max had lifted her onto her feet.

"You okay?" His hands stayed on her waist to steady her.

'Okay' was a relative term. Could she use her legs to move toward her car without screaming like a dying cow?

They'd find out soon enough.

She blew out a breath. "Yeah, I'll be fine. Just go inside. It'll be harder to hear my screams that way."

"Josie, come back in. We'll ice your back, you'll stay the night, and you won't have to drive home on an ice skating rink."

She locked eyes with him and debated. She wanted nothing more than to sink into his arms, wail at her unfortunate coordination, and have him sweep her up into his bed.

But that was for other girls, not for girls like her.

Girls like Josie lived in the friend zone so long she could run for mayor. Hell, she probably *was* the mayor. She was the sturdy girl who was just someone to have fun with, while the short pilates-and-salad gazelles got guys like Max.

But, she reconsidered, *maybe just this once, I could say yes.* Even the mayor of Friendzone-ville needed help once in a while.

"Ugh, fine. Thank you." Her chin slumped to her chest. "You're, like, very nice, and I appreciate you." She rolled her head at him and pulled a 'why are you always right' face.

His eyes crinkled, and his mouth twisted into a smirk at her fake thank you. "Can you walk?" He stood a few steps in front of her and held out his hand.

"Yep." She let out a shaky breath. She pushed one foot forward and felt like she might crack in two from the pain.

He stood, eyebrows raised in expectation while snow piled onto his shoulders. "Any day now, Aunt Ethel."

"I'll get there. Just, you know, distract me. Tell me about the terrible other movies I have to watch tonight."

"We will literally freeze if I explain the plot of *The Quiet Man* to you out here. Here, let me carry you."

Josie was a curvy, tall girl. She loved her curves, but she was self-conscious about her weight. Her heart clutched, and embarrassment flooded her face. "I don't think you can lift me."

"Come on, put your arms around my neck." He tapped his shoulders and bent down.

This was somehow the best and the worst thing to happen to her in a really long time.

Chapter Three

JOSIE

His arms wrapped around her as he pulled her close. One hand came underneath her knees, and he looked directly into her eyes, his face only a few inches from hers. Snowflakes had caught on his eyebrows which only highlighted the depths of his brown eyes.

"Ready?"

She gulped. She wondered how their obituaries would read. Maybe "Man and Woman Dead After Falling from Icy Backsteps Because Woman Was Too Stubborn to Buy Proper Footwear. Send all donations to the local Teachers' Wardrobe Fund."

She sent him a skeptical glare. "Yep, totally ready. This is totally gonna work, and I have no concerns. Unrelated question: Do you have a will and a burial plot ready?" She stared at him with stubborn uncertainty.

"Such a smartass." He squatted down, and she felt her legs leave the ground in a very odd sensation. She gripped his neck and tried not to think about how good he felt against her.

The heat from his chest bore into her. She closed her eyes, overwhelmed at the sensation of being so close to him all over.

She was thankful for the back pain shooting through her, or she'd swoon from the sheer romance of it all.

To Max's credit, he didn't grunt when he picked her up and made his way across the ice with relative ease.

She wouldn't try to think about how romantic this looked, how romantic this *felt*, how much she wanted to stay right here, and how much she really hoped he wouldn't let her go.

MAX

SHE FIT SO FUCKING PERFECTLY in his arms.

Max shoved away the thoughts invading his head about how good Josie felt against him. His hand grasped her upper waist, and he couldn't stop thinking how close her amazing breasts were as they pushed into his side.

Just focus, Bard.

Max gently sat her down halfway up the stairs. His hands stayed on her waist, and he spun her around, so they were nose-to-nose.

"The steps are too icy. I don't want to risk killing us both."

Her waist felt so good on his hands that he didn't drop them. *For safety reasons,* he told himself.

Her navy-blue eyes connected with his, and that familiar punch in his gut hit him again. It would be so easy to lean in and brush his lips against hers, to see what she tasted like. Play it off as a joke, but no. Not the time.

This was normal best-friend stuff, right?

"Sit on the top step, and I'll pick you back up." He held her hands as she fell back onto the porch's top step and swung her legs around. He gingerly climbed up the stairs.

A low groan escaped out of her as he pulled her up. He hated causing her any pain.

"I can make it," she said through gritted teeth. "You don't have to pick me up."

"Bullshit. Don't be such a baby."

"A baby? What do you mean, a baby?" she said, getting a fire back in her.

Maybe he'd just tease her into distraction.

He grinned at her good-naturedly. "You're such a baby whenever you don't ask for help. Just a little petulant two-year-old trying to muscle through all your pain."

"I am not a two-year-old." Wisps of hair danced around her face in the night breeze, and a cute little line formed neatly in the middle of her forehead as she glared at him. The snowflakes that had caught on her hair were crystallized like a crown around her perfect face.

He thought this would be an excellent chance to, quite literally, sweep her off her feet.

He put his arm underneath her knees again, and her arms came up around his neck. "Great. Then you won't mind accepting some help."

The curves of her thighs pressed against him, and he made a point to ignore the press of her breasts against him.

Again.

She huffed back at him, and he tried not to get caught in her stare and long lashes as he sent a challenging eye back at her.

He trudged into the living room with her pressed against him. She felt so fucking warm and perfect.

"You're going back on the couch, where you will stay. Syrup makers' orders." He lowered her slowly onto the couch and went to search for an ice pack.

"Got any pain meds?" She rubbed her lower back.

"I've got tequila." After putting some ice into a bag, he

headed back toward the couch, grabbing a bottle of tequila and two shot glasses.

She ran her hands over her sleepy face. "That works. I'm about half out of my mind from sleep anyway."

He looked down at her jeans. "Do you want some clothes to sleep in?"

"I have a bag of clean laundry in my trunk." She sent him a 'Please, please help me' smile and batted her eyelashes at him.

"If I die from icy stairs, it's your fault."

A few minutes later, he deposited her laundry bag on her lap, and she fished out a pair of sweatpants with a pained grimace.

If she had trouble leaning, would she be able to bend over? "Can you change by yourself?"

Her face went pale. "Usually I ace putting on pants, Max —" she took a breath, and he had to smile. Even when hurt, she was a sarcastic pain in the ass. "—but I don't know, honestly."

She looked up at him with a vulnerability he rarely saw.

This was going to take their relationship from complicated to really fucking awkward pretty quickly.

Max had danced around his feelings for Josie for a long time. Sometimes it felt like they were just old friends; sometimes, it felt like they could be more, and lately, it felt like they already *were* more.

She shifted the ice pack as her face went beet red from embarrassment. "You know what? It's fine. I'll just lay here forever until I die or this pain goes away. Whichever happens first."

We're adults. We've gone swimming. It's just like seeing somebody in their bathing suit.

Except...the few times he'd let himself think about what it would feel like if something happened between them, it had turned his cock hard in an instant. This would only add fuel to the fire he kept at bay.

"Don't be silly. What you're going to do," Max told her in what he hoped was an authoritative voice, "you'll just...Uhm...." Could he say *take off your pants* to his best friend? That felt weird, right? "...re-remove wh-what you have on," he stuttered.

Chapter Four

Max stared at the ceiling. "I'll close my eyes and pull up the sweatpants until you can grab them." He finally met her gaze.

She grimaced. "This is so weird."

"It's not weird," he said more to himself than her. "Getting into position."

He knelt in front of her and tried not to think how this position played a starring role in his fantasies of her.

Her hands flew to her face. "I need three more tequila shots for this."

That would be a terrible idea. What might happen after a few more tequila shots between them?

He closed his eyes and hoped for the best. "My eyes are closed."

He heard her huff and move on the couch. "Fine, but we never speak of this again."

His mind centered on the metallic roll of her zipper being pulled down, and he tried to stop thinking of what her curves might look like up close and personal.

"I, um..."

"Yeah?" He squeezed his eyes shut to keep them closed, just in case his will won out to see her naked.

Her voice went soft with embarrassment. "I can't push them down any further. Can you grab them?"

He cleared his throat. His chest was just inches from her knees. "Uh, sure."

He grabbed for her pants, and his hand landed on her bare thighs instead. He yanked his hands away quickly as the heat burned on his face. "Oh god, sorry."

She rarely showed her legs, which he thought was a damn shame. Her skin had felt like warm silk, and holy shit, he couldn't keep thinking about that, or he'd never be able to stand up again.

Let's try a different approach. His hands found her calves and grazed up until he met the bunching of her jeans at her knees. "This okay?" he said in a low voice, eyes still closed.

"Mhm." Her voice came out as a whisper, and the gentle beats of her rapid breath etched into him.

His hands lingered on the backs of her knees, thumbs stroking the sides of her calves. Had he ever touched her like this? It took every ounce of willpower to keep his eyes closed. *I wonder what kind of panties she has on?*

Fuck. No, she's your best friend, you creep. Just get this over with as quickly as possible.

He yanked down the jeans to the floor, moving briskly. He grabbed the sweatpants, and he was pretty sure he got each foot into a leg as he pulled up the oversized fuzzy PJ pants.

He got them up to her knees, where she took over. The intimacy of her fingers brushing his as she grabbed the pants from him wasn't lost on him.

"You got it from here?" he asked, hoping she'd say no so he could feel her legs again.

"Yeah, I'm fine."

He started to stand up but thought better of it, given the enormous hard-on he was now sporting under his thin sweatpants.

He turned away and seated himself on the floor, knees bent, so he could just calm the fuck down.

"Okay." She let out a big breath. "All clothed."

He opened his eyes and peeked over her shoulder.

"I will assassinate you if you tell anyone about this." She pointed a finger at him. He grabbed it and batted it away.

"And I need more tequila." She looked at the bottom of her shot glass.

"Same." He grabbed the bottle and poured them both a shot. He needed to drown the sexual tension he felt, or he'd start questioning everything.

"To the secrets we take to our graves," she said, clinking her shot glass to his.

He settled down on the couch next to her. "Want to pick up from where we left off? The movies, I mean," he clarified after her eyebrows raised.

"If you'd like me to be asleep in three minutes, then sure." She smiled with sarcastic sweetness back at him.

"Oh, come on, it's Friday night. We're young. We're hot—"

"—*You* are hot." She snorted and held her shot glass out for a refill.

He poured them another round. "Josie, come on, you've *always* had a boyfriend. You have to know you're hot," he said as his cheeks burned.

It was the alcohol, right? It was definitely the alcohol that made his cheeks feel like they were being roasted over an open fire. He threw back the shot and felt a deafening, awkward silence from her side of the couch.

Shit. Maybe he was too honest. But she needed to know that she was hot, that men found her mind-wanderingly attractive.

Josie was like an embodiment of those 'curves ahead' signs. She had a thick, round ass, curvy thighs, and full breasts he tried not to think about too often, or he'd get lost in thought.

Thinking of her in that way haunted him enough already.

Maybe it was officially time to slow down on the tequila shots.

MAX

"It's fine," Josie said quietly. "You don't have to say that." She circled the rim of her shot glass with her finger, tracing a pattern that sent a surge of lust to his dick for some reason.

"Jos, what's the matter?" He tried to catch her eye.

She shook her head, and he elbowed her playfully.

She bit her full lower lip—*I wonder what it would taste like?*—and her eyes looked away from him. "It's just something Jason said."

Anger rose like bile in his throat. "What did the Assistant Manager of Dirtbags say to you?"

He'd rarely ever liked Josie's boyfriends. Some of them had been okay dudes, but none had been good enough for her. No one was. She was a sarcastic pain in the ass, but she was loyal, funny, smart, and sexy as hell.

"He insinuated that I was too...that I wasn't pretty enough for him," she said as her lips twisted together. "And you know what Jason looked like? A guy with a *neckbeard* thinks I'm not good enough?" She snorted as she put her arm out for another round.

"Maybe we should slow down."

"I am a grown-up, Maximillion. Pour me a fucking shot."

He reluctantly poured her a half shot. "Jason was a gross, wrong asshat. You always deserved better than him." He met her gaze for a fleeting moment before she plastered on a smile.

"Correct!" she said, jabbing her finger up in the air in a victory salute. She waved her hand out in front of her as she swallowed the burning liquid. "No more talk about ex-boyfriends. If we're doing tequila shots, you know what that means?" Her jazz hands shook with excitement.

Max shook his head. *This was dangerous.* "I think we've run out of things to say 'never have we ever' done before."

"Never have I ever..." She ignored him and settled in, adjusting her ice pack.

"And no hyper-specific nevers in order to get me wasted." She could be a little shit when she wanted to be.

She rolled her eyes so hard he could *hear* it. "Oh, you're no fun."

One of them had tossed the heavy blanket over their legs to stave off the chill of the room, and their legs brushed against each other. The fireplace serenaded them with gentle pops and crackles, and Max thought how fucking lucky he was to be next to her while the snow drifted down outside.

The tequila coursed through his veins, and he knew it would loosen his lips. The fire cast a warm glow over Josie's face, highlighting the shine in her honey-golden hair, and Max thought this might be a recipe for an actual disaster.

He'd started developing serious feelings for Josie in the last few months. Maybe they'd always been there underneath the solid two decades of friendship. He had to keep his shit together until he could figure everything out and what it might mean between them.

"What don't I know about you?" she asked, slowly tapping

her chin. She had short nails painted a navy color with little sparkles all over them.

God, she was cute.

She raised her eyebrows in challenge, looking victorious. "Never have I ever had sex in a public place."

Well shit.

As a rule, they didn't talk about their sex lives. It just felt too weird, even if they were best friends.

He could lie and pretend he'd never done that, especially given the chaos it caused him six months ago.

But to see her eyes light up with wicked delight? For her to know a little of what he was like in bed, so different from what she might expect? He debated and decided it would be more fun to thrill her.

Max sighed, glanced over at her, and took a shot.

"What?" she screamed. "I require details." She leaned forward in excitement and her face turned into a grimace. "Ow, fuck." She leaned back, readjusting the ice pack.

"It was Mara. She wanted to spice things up. It was a bathroom in a bar in New York." He rubbed his hands over his face, trying to forget the whole thing and the ensuing fight. How that fight had fragmented his life and led him back to Benning Falls.

"Was it like a sexy bathroom, at least?"

"What the hell is a sexy bathroom?" He couldn't hide the smile that overtook his face.

"You know, it's dark, and there's, like, nice wallpaper and maybe a plant? Oh! Or a lit candle?" Her eyebrows raised up together in eager excitement.

"It was disgusting. More like lighting from a prison cell, no hand soap, and there were piles of dead spiders in the corners."

"Piles? As in, more than one pile?" She shuddered. "If it were a sexy bathroom, that'd be one thing."

"All right, my turn." He thought he should maybe steer

them off the topic of sex since there was tequila, snow was falling dreamily outside, and they were snuggling on a couch in front of a fire.

Josie's back suddenly started to cramp, and her face twisted with a grimace.

"Here. Give me your legs so you can stretch out." He held his arms out toward her.

She lifted her legs in the baggy sweatpants and fuzzy socks and stretched them out in front of her. Her calves landed on his lap. "Ah, much better," she said, cuddling into the corner of the couch.

His hands settled over her legs, and he tried to ignore how much he loved the feeling of her near him.

"Never have I ever chickened out of opening an Etsy shop."

"Hey," she threw a pointed finger at him again. "We said no hyper-specific things."

"If you'd opened up your shop by now, you wouldn't have to take a shot."

"Knitting takes time, and I don't have enough time to open an Etsy shop."

"Oh, bullshit. If we didn't make a 'no knitting during movie night' rule—"

"—I can't help that the needles clack—" Her face was full of laughing indignation.

"—you would have finished seven mittens tonight. Come on, take a shot." He filled her shot glass halfway.

He could see the booze was starting to get to her, but he didn't want the game to end yet.

"Oh, fine, but then you're gonna get a super specific one. Never have I ever inherited a maple syrup farm. That's the most ridiculous sentence I've ever said," she giggled at herself.

He rolled his eyes and took half a shot. "I didn't inherit. My dad retired, and I decided to take over as CEO."

"Yeah, you inherited. Do you know what I inherited from my dad? These eyes. The end. I don't even remember the last time I saw him."

"Well, they're really nice eyes," he said, squeezing her ankles. Her cheeks got a little pinker, and she rolled her eyes. "Even when they do that."

He realized with a start what a very unfair question he had for his next turn. Every cell in his body begged him out of morbid curiosity to ask it.

She lifted a foot up and playfully kicked his leg. "Your turn." She placed the backs of her hands over her eyelids, which already looked heavy with sleep.

"Maybe we should call it a night."

She lifted her hands up and gave him a pouting lower lip. "Just one more."

Fuck it, might as well try. Maybe it was time to talk about whatever was changing between them.

"Never have I ever..." he paused, thinking he couldn't unsay the words once they were said.

He couldn't unknow the information if she decided to tell him.

"...have I been in love with a friend."

Chapter Six

JOSIE

What the fuck did he just say?

Josie clenched her stomach through a tequila haze and felt panic sieze every nerve ending.

It's fine. She wasn't on trial. Also, technically, he said friend, not a *best* friend, so she wouldn't be lying, right? She just didn't take a shot.

She rolled her lips between her teeth. She needed to buy herself some time.

"Have I ever loved a friend? Of course, I love my friends! You don't feel loved as my friend?" She lifted her hands from her eyes, meeting his gaze briefly before putting them back down. She turned them over, so the cool side of her hand rested against her eyelids as her mind scrambled.

"Yes, your constant teasing and refusal to play me in Scrabble make me feel so loved," he said, jostling her legs. He lifted them and resituated them closer to him, her knees now arched over his legs. Sparks of want shot through her as his hands rested on her.

Yep, this was normal. This was normal, best friend stuff. Toooootally normal.

"I, uh...nope. Never been in love with a friend." She shrugged. Her hands were over her eyes, so she didn't have to look at him. She could lie a little easier.

Technically, she *wasn't* lying.

She was in love with her *best* friend.

Him.

"Not even one little crush? In college, a work husband...?"

"You know my work wife is Karrie."

"Maybe you love Karrie."

"I *do* love Karrie, platonically, because she is an excellent work spouse. She laminates all my worksheets without me asking."

She smirked to herself. So far, the lie was going great. She distracted him, and maybe they wouldn't talk about it anymore.

A beat hung in the air between them.

She forced her eyes to look up finally. She knew her cheeks were bright pink, but he would think it was the tequila.

He held her eyes an uncomfortably long time as his thumbs stroked her legs.

She saw the rise and fall of his chest and wondered how many lucky women had fallen asleep there. How many tall, leggy, model-like girls had he dated when he lived in Manhattan?

She thought with a snort. *I bet they've never even had nacho cheese.*

"What did you just say about nacho cheese?" He peered at her, cocking his head to the side.

Oh fuck. That was supposed to be an internal monologue. Change the subject, change the subject. "Okay, well, it's getting late. We should go to bed. Night!" she said, throwing a pillow over her face.

He gently lifted her legs and started to get up. "Two blankets going to be enough?"

"It's supposed to get below zero tonight." She flipped the pillow up and pouted at him.

"I thought you were Vermont-strong. Remember, you've been here longer than me," he said as he went to the closet where he kept his extra blankets.

He was such an adorable smart-ass.

"Being used to driving in the snow and being warm-blooded are two different things."

Max tossed an extra pillow onto her stomach, rolled out two more blankets, and draped them over her. She loved the heavy weight of the familiar blankets she remembered from childhood sleepovers. She could get used to being tucked in every night as she felt his hands shove the blanket down around her legs.

She cuddled into the deep cushions of the worn couch. She let her face nuzzle into the pillow. It smelled like Max and the house where she had so many good memories.

Her childhood had been full of yelling, fights, and a musty, smoke-filled trailer two doors down from the gorgeous farm that had been in Max's family for generations. He was a fourth-generation sugar maker, the head of a maple syrup farm. Josie remembered his grandpa running the farm even before Max had moved there.

She was forever grateful for the day in fourth grade when Max and his parents had moved in. A cute, tall boy (one that was *finally* taller than her) showed up at school, and she was thrilled to see him get off the bus with her. Since Josie's mouth had a mind of its own, they became fast friends as she showed him around the countryside surrounding their houses.

Josie prayed every night of fourth grade that another girl

wouldn't move into their neighborhood and steal her best friend and very first crush's heart.

She felt her shoulder shake.

"Josie, did you hear me?"

She snorted a little as she woke up. "What?"

"Just thought you were dead," he said, chuckling as he walked to the stairs to go up to his bedroom. "Night."

Max flipped off the lights, and the living room fell into darkness, except for tiny embers dying in the fireplace.

Josie sighed with envy, thinking about the lucky person that would eventually stay here every night with Max so long as they both shall live.

How many shots of tequila she had, five? She hadn't done that since college. She tossed and turned, waiting for the blessed blackness that would finally lull her into sleep, but stubborn flashes of Max kept popping into her head.

His grin, his arms, the feeling of him fucking *carrying* her, of all things. She stifled a laugh by leaning into the pillow.

Max had carried her like an old-fashioned bridegroom across his front yard and then across the threshold of his house.

She did not have that on her bingo card for best friend movie night.

She felt the pull of wanting low in her belly as she remembered the feel of his hands on her waist, steadying her. The smell of his aftershave as she put her head on his shoulder when he lifted her.

She let herself picture what it would be like if they had kissed. If his mouth had met hers with the ferocity she felt right now. The taste of his kiss and the pull in her belly as he pulled her closer. She felt herself grow wet at the thought of his hands on her breasts and nipples.

She felt her heart beating rapidly and fought the urge but

finally gave in, sliding her hand down to her panties to imagine a night with Max.

Chapter Seven

JOSIE

Josie felt how wet she was at the thought of Max's mouth on her nape. How he'd lick his way down to her breast, tear apart her shirt and suck one of her nipples. She imagined running her fingers through his tousled, smooth hair as he sucked her and played with her other breast.

She stroked herself at the thought of his hands fucking everywhere. Grabbing her ass, in her hair, kissing her deeply while his thighs spread her legs like he owned every inch of her pleasure.

Would Max be a passive lover? Or would he order her around? She really, really hoped he was a *cinnamon roll in the streets, alpha in the sheets* kind of guy.

It was her fantasy. She would fucking picture what she wanted. Her fingers moved in a lazy circle around her clit.

He would strip off her pants, tearing them off as he forcefully spread her legs outward. He'd pull her pussy up to his mouth as he ordered Josie to stay put. She would grab her nipples as he feasted on her, licking and licking. His tongue would trace her clit in mischievous strokes and stare at her the entire time, daring her to stop him. To tell him it was too much.

But it would never be too much.

Max, she would moan. *Max, more. Yes, more.* He'd shove two fingers in her and lick her while she screamed.

Yes, Max. Fuck me, she'd cry.

MAX

MAX SAT up in bed with a start. He'd fallen into a light sleep but woke when he heard his name waft up from downstairs. He slept with his door cracked open as a habit, and the sound carried easily from the vaulted ceiling and open floor plan that his bedroom overlooked.

Maybe Josie's back was worse? Or had he dreamed it?

He heard gentle movement from downstairs and strained his ear to ensure he hadn't imagined it.

"Max, yes," a breathy voice sounded downstairs. "More, Max," Josie moaned.

Oh.

Fuck.

His heartbeat thundered in his ears. *Was she...?* She must be.

"Fuck me, Max," she whispered loud enough to carry up to him. He heard a familiar, repeated rhythm of movement and felt his cock go instantly hard.

She wasn't just dreaming.

His cock pulsed with want as he heard the brushing of her arm against the couch, faster and faster.

He would lose his mind if he didn't do something soon. He couldn't go down there. It would be too risky for their relationship.

His hand had made its way to the outside of his boxer briefs, stroking his cock. He hadn't been this hard in so long.

And Josie had felt so fucking good when he'd touched her earlier.

He had *tried* to keep her out of his one-handed fantasies. He really had.

He didn't want to cross that boundary too often, or he'd lose his mind trying to keep his hands to himself when they were together.

Plus, there was the incident with Mara.

"Harder, Max," he heard her whisper.

Fuck yes.

One more time won't hurt.

He let himself bring up the image that was always somehow in the perimeter of his mind. Josie in a skin-tight, revealing strappy swimsuit from last summer. Her curves, every inch of her, looked so fucking hot in that suit.

He stroked the precum on the end of his cock as he thought of her huge tits, perfectly cupped in the deep V-cut suit, the curve of her soft stomach, her long legs arched on the pool chair, and the curve of her ass as it peeked out from the tight cut of her suit bottoms. He'd had the craziest, most powerful urge to run his tongue along the underside of her breast that day.

Her nipples had gone hard with the wind blowing, and they poked through her suit in firm points he'd wanted to pinch, lick, cradle, anything. Lust had run through him hard enough to knock him sideways.

"Yes, yes, yes," she chanted in the living room.

He imagined her riding him as he gripped his shaft and rubbed the tip of his cock, matching her rhythm downstairs. He'd rip each swimsuit strap down as she rode him, exposing her breasts and watching them bounce as he fucked her senseless.

"Max, yes!" she cried, finishing below.

He came hard with her, imagining catching her mouth with his as he came into his hand.

Several hours later, a screwdriver ground its way into Max's forehead.

He shoved a pillow over his face, trying to drown out whatever torture device had just been turned on.

His sleep-addled brain combed through the possibilities.

Option one: Josie had poured a bucket of screws into a blender and was grinding away.

Option two: He was the most hungover he'd been in ten years.

He glanced over at the clock; it was barely six am. He groaned and rolled over, thinking about what he'd done last night. He rubbed his face back and forth on the pillow, trying to forget his slip. Of the sound of her voice wafting up to his room. Of the memory he'd conjured up...

No. Get your head on straight, Bard.

It was Saturday, but he had a full day of work planned. It was warm enough now for the sap to drain out of his maple trees.

The awful grinding started again, and though his mouth felt like the Sahara, he managed to get out a half-human groan.

A heaven-sent, earthy smell wafted up to his nose from the floor below. He finally put two and two together; there wasn't a madman in his kitchen trying to torture him. It was just Josie, used to teacher's hours, already up and making coffee.

When he was up, he was up, and if he laid in bed any longer, he'd start thinking about Josie again and couldn't do that. He needed to keep her squarely in the best friend category so he wouldn't fuck up the best, most solid relationship in his life. He threw on his pajama pants, tugged a worn hoodie over his head, and stumbled out of the room.

"It is six in the morning," he said loudly.

She shushed him over her shoulder. "My head is throbbing from your awful coffee grinder. Did you buy it from a Bulgarian torture chamber?"

He padded over to the cabinet and blindly grabbed two mugs. "No one made you turn on the loudest thing in this house before fucking dawn." He laid his forehead down on the island.

"My body's used to getting up at five. I thought drinking coffee would make the tiny men pounding hammers in my head happier."

She looked cute all rumpled up from sleep in her oversized pajama pants and cuddly sweater she kept tucked around her for warmth. Her hair was piled on top of her head and zigged-zagged each way. He thought about all the boyfriends who'd had a chance to wake up to her and had missed out on an adorable, perfect nerd.

She started the coffee maker and laid her forehead down on the marble counter in front of her.

Max knew what he had to do. He'd have to take charge of the situation because she wasn't brave enough to do it.

He flung his body over to the cupboard where he kept bottles of alcohol and grabbed a bottle of his most recent maple syrup batch from the fridge. While he was at it, he pulled out a slab of bacon and frozen waffles from the freezer.

Usually, he'd prefer to make buttermilk pancakes because he was rather particular about how his product was served. Max had only been in the maple syrup game for a year, but it was in his blood. He'd spent so many years living in the city, trying to ignore his destiny. But when his dad got sick and wanted to retire, Max knew that he would only truly be happy living out his days on the farm.

"Oh my god, don't you dare," Josie said as she peered up from the counter.

"You know it works," he said as he cracked open the bottle of rum and poured two helpings. He poured maple syrup in after the shots, tossed some bacon on the pan on the stove, and lit the gas fire underneath. "Maple syrup shots. My family's syrup and all the bacon you can stomach. It's the surefire Bard way to get rid of a hangover."

"I don't have a hangover, Max. I'm still drunk." The coffee was finally ready, and she stumbled over to pour two cups. "Why did we do this to ourselves? We're thirty. We can't have multiple shots of tequila anymore."

He noticed she rubbed her lower back with one hand. "How's the back feeling?"

"Your couch did wonders. Still a little bruised courtesy of your bougie landscaping, but much better."

"You can sleep here anytime," he said, smiling at her. "Though you'd miss the smell of the fish Brittany cooks in your microwave." Josie's roommate was sweet but had some quirky habits.

"Ugh, don't talk about fish," Josie said, putting a hand over her mouth.

They sat in companionable silence, and he realized that was one of his favorite parts of their friendship; they could just be together without it being a whole thing.

"I think the bacon's done," Josie said, staring at him.

He'd been staring off into the distance and had lost track. "All right. Well, two extra crispy pieces for me, the rest for you."

"Ugh, I don't know if I can do it," she grimaced. She was looking a little green.

He plated the bacon and shoved some waffles into the toaster. "Are you ready?" he said, looking her dead in the eye.

She grimaced. "You are very mean."

"I dunno. Maybe you're too weak to do it?" He bit back a smile, loving that he could press her buttons whenever he wanted.

She sent him a steely glare. "Your mind games don't work on me," she said as she took the shot glass from him.

They tossed back their shot glasses with a combination of rum and maple syrup and chased it with two pieces of bacon each.

"For the record, I'm pretty sure the grease and protein in the bacon get rid of the hangover, not the syrup." Josie dangled a piece of bacon before her and nibbled on it.

"I think this is our first sleepover since we were ten," Max said, smiling at her. "I begged my parents every night for a month to let you stay over so we could finish a game of *Super Smash Brothers.*"

"I bet you didn't even like girls then," she said, smiling over her coffee. The color had returned to her face, and she finally looked like she belonged among the living.

He shrugged, "I liked girls then."

Her eyes shot up. "Who?"

Ah, shit.

Chapter Eight

MAX

He stared at her, thinking about how much to betray of his past, how much he could tell her without it influencing their relationship. A long bit of silence hung between them in the air, and, unlike before, it felt heavy with expectation.

The waffles popped out of the toaster, causing them both to jump.

"I don't remember her name. It was before I moved here," he lied. He tossed the waffles on plates, and they both doused them with maple syrup.

He bit into the sub-par waffle and was rewarded with the vanilla, caramel taste of his childhood. The flavor that was forever linked with his land, his destiny, and his joy. He looked at Josie, and her eyes were closed in reverence of the maple goodness.

A drop of syrup had landed on her cheek and he fought an insane urge to lick it off.

He shook his head to clear his thoughts and realized his phone was ringing upstairs.

He jogged to grab it and saw several texts from the guys on his crew. "Sorry, man," was the preview on one. "Can't come" was another. He scrolled through frantically, and it looked like his crew had begged off for the day.

It was still dark outside, and as Max scanned his messages, anxiety clutched his heart in a vice. He'd been so out of it last night, so distracted with Josie and tequila, that he hadn't even bothered to look out the window. He peered into the pitch-black darkness and saw mounds of white snow piled everywhere.

They'd planned to start the first batch of sugar processing today, and he had to make sure none of the sap overflowed on the buckets posted throughout his acreage.

He wandered back downstairs, panic rising. He'd have to work all day and still might not make it.

"You look like somebody just shit in your cereal," Josie said, pouring a second cup of coffee.

"Apparently, we got eighteen inches last night."

She peered out the window into the blackness surrounding the farm and craned her neck to see the driveway. "My car is completely buried," she said, looking back at him in horror.

"Looks like you're snowed in with me. You said your back was feeling better?"

She shrugged. "As good as any permanently hunched-over second-grade teacher in her thirties feels."

"My guys just canceled on me, and I had a full day planned today. I can't wait another day, but I also can't do everything myself."

"Ooh, I finally get to lend my hands at sugar making," she said, shimmying her shoulders. "I didn't think I was trustworthy enough for your precious, precious gold."

"You'll do in a pinch," he said, knocking her shoulder with his as he walked to refill his coffee. "I want to wait until late morning to see how the taps are running, but it would be a big help if you could come with me."

She shrugged, and it looked like she was trying to hide a smile. "I'd consider it my final rite of passage into your family."

His parents had basically adopted her because she had spent so much time at their house growing up. "Yep, then you'll just be one of us forever." Max shoved his thoughts away from what it would mean to have her as part of his family; to have her there in thirty, forty, fifty years.

"Consider me your sous chef. Sous sugar maker?" she said, thinking about it.

He burst out laughing. "You are many, many steps away from a sous sugar maker, but I'll go see if I can find a snowsuit for you. Six hours outside can feel brutal."

She fished out a handful of papers with bright coloring and a pile of stickers. "I have some grading to do while you go find my snowsuit. You might actually be interested in these very special reports." She settled down on the couch with her cup of coffee.

He leaned his head down, almost on her shoulder. "*My Awsum Trip to a Farm*. Does that tree have a penis?" He pointed at a scraggly drawing.

She burst out laughing. "That is obviously a tap on a tree pouring into a bucket, and also, Braxton is not very good at drawing." She sent him a yikes face.

A month ago, Max had suggested she bring her second-grade class on a field trip to his farm before sugar season started. Maple Syrup was Vermont's biggest export, and he took pride in using the old hand-proven methods on their farm. Max had considered moving to a tube system that was far more efficient, but he hadn't been able to break with tradition yet.

Just another thing he'd have to think about as he moved the farm into the twenty-first century. Their family had done very well producing high-end products using the old methods, but he wasn't sure if that would cut it moving forward.

The yoke of anxiety that usually sat on his neck returned, and he felt a sudden need to get going on the day since they were already behind schedule and understaffed.

Chapter Nine

JOSIE

I don't think I'm in good enough shape for syrup-making.

Josie hustled across the crunching snow, trying to catch up with Max. He took off in long strides across the field.

"Wait up! Jesus Christ, is something on fire?" She jogged behind him, picking her way through the snow drifts and trying not to break an ankle.

"Just have a lot to do today, and appreciate the help, but you're not exactly my normal staff."

Ah, his *I'm stressed as fuck* voice; she knew it well. "Hey," she said, grabbing his arm. "We'll get it all done. Okay?" She willed him to look at her, catching his eyes.

He chewed his lip. "Yeah, we'll get it done. Sorry."

She still noticed the underlying panic in his eyes that hadn't been there a few minutes ago. They both took off for the shop that housed all of the supplies. They needed to change out the buckets that were already full of sap. "I'm just frustrated that my dad kept the farm in the dark ages."

"Isn't it nice not to have rubber hoses everywhere?" She

"

almost lost her balance but caught herself on a tree as she picked her way over another snowdrift.

"It certainly looks nicer for field trips," he said, sending her half of a smile.

Josie looked at her watch. It was only 9:30. They still had a long time before it was warm enough for tree sap to run. "Max, is there a reason we're out here so early?"

"We have to walk across the property. If we used the snowmobile, we couldn't protect the sap on the way back, so get ready for some walking." A scowl that Josie wasn't used to seeing appeared on his face as he trudged forward.

Pails in hand, they marched off searching for the furthest reaches of trees in Max's field.

"Wait up. These legs aren't as long as yours."

"We have a lot to do today," he said curtly.

"I know. That's why I'm helping you," she said, kicking some snow at him.

"Josie, this is not a joke. We can't do anything that would jeopardize any of the syrup."

Is this what it was like to work with him? He didn't pay his people enough.

She bit her tongue, knowing that the best way to support him was to let him work out his frustrations on the walk.

They plodded onward until they finally reached the farthest tree on his property. Puffs of white breaths blew out in front of Josie as she caught up with Max, who stood at the tree and sat his pails down.

"Happy now?" she said. "We're here, like, an hour early. The sap isn't running yet."

He glanced up at the sun. "We can always switch out the buckets. Doesn't mean the trees have to be running."

Josie sat her buckets down next to his. She pulled off her beanie and fluffed her hair. Beads of sweat ran down her temples and she felt like a slow roasting tenderloin in a Swedish sauna from his military march.

"Do you do this every day?" she said, putting her hands on her hips, trying to catch her breath.

"It's the best part of the job." He looked around the still, crystalized forest of maple and pine trees.

The wind whistled over the rolling hills, and Josie thought she heard squirrels chirping a few trees away. Last night's snow still sat on branches, and it looked like antique lace had come to life.

It was pretty idyllic once you stopped sweating like livestock.

"You ready to go?" he said, staring at her.

"And do what?"

"We walk all the way back, changing out the pails that need it." The worry lines on his forehead creased as he looked at his watch.

"Max, everything will be fine. We'll get it done today, okay? Every second doesn't have to be accounted for."

"I know, I'm just...this is the first big one I'm doing by myself. I was hoping to get a jump on production today."

"Answer me this," she said, standing squarely in front of him. "Will five minutes make or break your day?"

Max sighed. "Josie..."

"Max..." She said, angling her head at him with raised eyebrows. She could pull out her teacher face when she needed to.

"No, five minutes will not make or break my day."

"Great. I need to pee, so I'm going to walk over there."

He rolled his eyes. "Didn't you go before we left?"

"It's been, like, forty-five minutes." She sent him an exaggerated eyebrow waggle.

"Girls," he sighed.

She walked about twenty feet away. "Turn around, creeper," she said, angling an eyebrow at him.

He turned around, shaking his head. "This okay?"

"Perfect," she said as she scooped down a handful of snow, forming it into a hard ball. On her slog through the ice-covered forest, she'd noticed last night's storm had given them perfect packing snow.

A younger Josie would have put a couple of branches or rocks in the snowball, but she'd *matured* since then.

Just a regular, surprise snowball attack would do.

She packed a couple tightly together for security when he inevitably fired back at her.

"You done yet?" he called over his shoulder.

"Almost." She took a snowball, thanked her lucky stars she'd played pee-wee league softball, and pitched a thick snowball aimed directly at his head. When her target hit its mark, he screamed and turned around, and then she hit him immediately with another one in the face.

"Traitor!" he cried as he immediately scooped up a handful of snow, barreling toward her. "You cheat!" he exclaimed, throwing a snowball at her while she threw her last pre-made one at him. She was pleased to see it hit him squarely in the jaw. He charged at her, and she squealed, running away.

She craved any reason for him to touch her. It had been many moons since they'd had a winter snow fight, but one of her favorite parts was that she almost always lost, which meant she'd get tossed into the nearest snowbank.

A smile blazed onto his face as he caught the side of her shoulder with a giant snowball. As she ran away, she realized she'd been scooped up and tossed into the snow.

The cold, icy crush hit her face, and she screamed as he knelt over her and tossed more snow onto her face and inside her snowsuit.

"*That* is what you get for playing on the job," he said as she grabbed his hands, trying to stop them and screaming with laughter.

She was pleased that her idea had its intended effect; his carefree smile was back. The lines of worry she hated to see were gone, and even better yet, his legs bracketed her thighs as he knelt over her. His hands intertwined with hers, pinning her to the snowbank.

Their deep breaths puffed out like clouds of smoke in front of them.

Neither moved.

The heat from his thighs on either side of hers sent warmth into her core. Josie stared at his perfectly sculpted lips that were parted and wondered, for the thousandth time, what it would feel like if he just leaned down and kissed her.

The moment froze in time and crystallized between them as his gaze drifted down to her lips.

Chapter Ten

JOSIE

Josie felt Max push her hands further back into the snow as he leaned toward her. The cloud of his breath grew closer, and she froze as his chest brushed hers.

She could smell the scent that was so clearly him. It was ingrained in her, the scent that smelled like home.

The molten caramel of Max's eyes sparkled in the sunlight glinting off the snow drift. Their breaths were shallow and the moment crystallized between them, each considering the other.

Would this be it? The moment everything shifted forever between them?

He leaned forward until he was an inch from her. His nose traced the length of hers, grazing it softly as her eyes fluttered closed at the sheer pleasure of that tiny bit of contact. She pushed gently against him, drawing out the friction as he pulled back. Their mouths hadn't even touched yet, but it was the most intimate thing they'd ever done.

She blinked slowly at him, not wanting to break the spell with a question or a request. He licked his lips and stared at her mouth. She knew that look; he was debating with himself on what to do next.

Don't do anything. Don't breathe. Don't say you want this so badly that you'd give your left kidney to be with him, to finally stop all the wondering on what it would feel like to kiss him, to have him hold you, to ride him.

He blinked suddenly and pulled back, sitting back on his haunches. "So, would you say that I won that snowball fight?"

The tension broke between them, and he smiled at her like the best friend she'd known for so many years. He stood up, dusting the snow off his snowsuit and holding a hand out to her.

Nope, I definitely didn't win today.

They walked back through the trees, swapping out the buckets that were already full of sap with empty ones. Josie's arms were screaming by the time they slogged toward the sugar shack, an affectionate name for the gigantic building full of very official equipment Max used to boil the sap into a thick, buttery syrup.

"So *this* is how you never work out and yet look like a runway model." She rolled her shoulders as she sat down. The gallons upon gallons of syrup she trudged half a mile back to the sugar shack sat beside her, and she was completely exhausted.

"It's a perk," he said, sending her a smile. "Go inside and warm up. I'll need to get this into the processing vat ASAP and can take it from here. I'll be done in a few hours."

Josie looked at her car, still piled under a mountain of snow. There was no way she could go home right now, her body half frozen and exhausted. She'd feel better after she warmed up and ate something.

A few minutes later, Josie was underneath a warm stream of deliciously hot water in Max's bathroom. She stood under the scalding water to ward off the chill that invaded her bones.

She closed her eyes and replayed that moment again and again from the snowball fight, the feeling of his skin on hers.

Had she imagined it? Had she imagined what it felt like between them? Maybe it was only on her side.

It wouldn't be the first time she let her imagination run away with her sanity.

But no. His nose had touched hers; she was sure of it. She was sure it wasn't some frozen-in-the-ice fever dream.

She knew they'd never talk about it. They both had an unspoken agreement, AKA cowardice, for when things got close to that line.

They just tiptoed away from it and never talked about it ever again.

Max was truly one of her only close friends left in the area, and though Josie had a full life without him, he was her rock. She wasn't close to her mom. Her dad had left long ago, and so many of her friends had moved away. She couldn't risk the most precious person in her life if it got weird between them.

Regretfully, she hopped out of the shower and dove for the warmest, fluffiest towel she could find in his bathroom. She threw on a mismatched sweatshirt and pants from the pile of clothes she'd brought. She thought about going through Max's closet to find one of his, but that felt like too much after what had happened in the snow.

As she combed her hair, the house phone rang. Max still hadn't disconnected the landline from when his parents lived there.

She grabbed the receiver. "Hi, Bard residence."

A pause hit the line. *Maybe it was a telemarketer?*

Suddenly, a sultry, low voice sounded on the other side. "Oh, it's you. I guess I shouldn't be surprised."

"Hey, Mara," Josie said slowly. *Why would his ex call the house phone?* "Max is out in the sugar shack."

"Moved in already?" the cutting reply came.

"Moved in? No," Josie said, confused.

Mara and Max had broken up six months ago. Max had been devastated, but it had also been the perfect opportunity for him to take over his dad's farm.

"I don't have his address," Mara said. "I found some things at the summer house that are his."

Josie rolled her eyes. Of course, Mara had a summer house in the Hamptons. If Max looked for qualities in women, it was money, high class, and taste. She looked down at her rubber duck-themed fuzzy pajama pants and her old, ripped high school theater department hoodie.

She couldn't be further off from his type if she tried.

"I can give you the address," Josie said.

They exchanged information, but before she hung up, Mara asked, "I just have to know: when did you guys become an item?"

Chapter Eleven

JOSIE

An item? "We're...we're not," Josie stumbled.

Mara laughed. "So he didn't tell you, then?" There was a cloying holier-than-thou tone in Mara's voice that Josie did not love.

"What my best friend tells me is none of your fucking business. Bye, Mara." Slamming the phone on the hook relieved some built-up frustration.

What didn't he tell me? Was she the reason they'd broken up?

She shoved thoughts of Max's ex out of her head and lit a fire in the potbelly stove in the kitchen. Josie loved the homey feeling of a fire crackling in the kitchen as she cooked. *Speaking of cooking, today calls for hearty food,* she thought as she pulled out ingredients for grilled cheese sandwiches. She was starving after her trek through the snowy backwoods and imagined Max would be too.

Josie peeked around to see her car. It would finally be easy enough to scrape her car out from the snow bank that had formed around it. She should probably head out after she finished making Max's lunch.

Max walked in as she ate her last bite of the creamy tomato soup she'd heated up to go with their sandwiches.

"Did you make grilled cheese?" He sniffed the air.

"It seemed like the day for it." She shoved the gooey cheese sandwich toward him.

"I could get used to this," he said, smiling at her as he stripped off his snowsuit in the entryway.

She should tell him about Mara's call. Instead, her mouth decided on a strategy of its own. "Did you break off your engagement because of me?"

The question landed like a thud between them.

Shit.

"Mara called," she added as if that would clarify things.

Max stared at the ground as he hung his suit in the entryway to drip dry. "Did she tell you that?" He walked toward the island where the triangle-cut grilled cheese sandwich waited for him.

"It's clever how you don't answer questions I ask you," Josie said, leaning forward on the island.

Max stuck his tongue in his cheek, weighing his words as he dove into his food. "Mara got jealous of my close friends who were women."

Josie burst out laughing. "Jealous of this paragon of beauty and class in front of you?" she said, twirling around and pointing to her old sweatshirt for effect.

"Hey, you were amazing in that musical," he said, sending her a smirk.

"So were you." She smiled at their shared joke. They both knew that Josie had played the very important role of behind-the-scenes munchkin herder while he played the Scarecrow in *The Wizard of Oz.*

He ate in silence, and she looked around the kitchen. She'd made herself at home, taking a shower here, fixing lunch, and hadn't thought twice about it. Of course, a girlfriend or a fiancée would feel threatened by her.

Shit, maybe she'd been in the way this whole time. He'd had other girlfriends, but they'd never worked out.

Benning Falls was a small town, and there weren't many opportunities to meet people in their thirties who were unattached. She was in love with him but loved him too much to get in the way of his happiness. She'd need to practice setting a better best-friend boundary if he was ever going to date anyone in Benning Falls.

"I'm gonna go," Josie said suddenly, putting away all the cooking supplies. "You're good for the rest of the day?" She peeked over her shoulder as she put things away.

"You don't have to go. It's still crazy snowy out there."

"I mean, this is Vermont. You think I haven't driven on a foot of packed snow in a 2003 Camry?"

"You don't have to go just because of what she said," he said suddenly, standing up. "The wind's picking up. It's threatening to storm again." They both looked outside, and it had turned dark with foreboding clouds. The lights flickered from a gust of wind outside as if on cue.

"I'll just go get my stuff, pack up, and I'll be home before the next round of the storm hits."

"Jos—"

"Don't be a weirdo," she said, shoving him playfully as she walked past.

She went around the kitchen trying to clean up after herself. She picked up her clothes in the bathroom and shoved them into her duffel bag. She tried putting everything away that she'd gotten out, which was much more than she'd originally intended, with multiple blankets, pillows, and towels she used.

By the time she wrapped her jacket around her and got ready to leave, snow was coming down in sheets. "Max?" she called out through the house. He must have gone to the sugar shack to check on the progress of the boil. The lights flickered again. The backdoor opened, and Max looked like an abominable snowman in the entryway.

"Whoa," Josie said in surprise.

"Yeah, the wind kicked up. I don't think you should drive in that. Just stay one more night. I don't want you—"

"I know, I know. You don't want me driving. You are not my caretaker, worrywart." She sent him a cheerful smile. She'd already felt she'd overstayed her welcome, even before the Mara call. She'd just be super careful on her drive home and hole up in her apartment until the storm passed.

"Josie, just stay," he said, blocking her from the doorway. "I'm going to worry about you all the way home." They both peered out the back door window and saw the white sheet of falling snow. Josie could barely make out her car from here.

"I'm okay with you worrying about me for ten minutes." She opened the door and braced herself against the cold wind that shot through her.

Fuck. This was not going to be any fun. She carefully made her way down the sidewalk that had been her demise last night. She tried to keep pictures of Max carrying her fireman-style back into the house out of her head.

She scraped off enough snow on her windshield so she could drive and hopped into the tundra-like interior of her car.

Her phone rang with her roommate's ringtone. Her fingers were already nearly frozen and she swiped two times to get the call button to answer. "Brittany?"

"Hey, um...Josie? So our pipes froze?" Brittany said slowly. Brittany was, at best, a little loopy and, at worst, a complete and total space cadet.

"Is that a question, or do you know they froze?"

"Oh, they're definitely frozen? I'm staying at my mom's?

The super said he'd try to fix it tomorrow, but there's no water, so...don't come here. Just stay at your boyfriend's house?"

Josie laid her forehead on her steering wheel. "Crap. Okay, thank you." Josie didn't even bother to correct her and hung up the call. She let out a big sigh.

God, she hated it when Max was right.

Chapter Twelve

MAX

Max watched with interest as Josie got out of the car, grabbed her bag, and walked back inside. A smirk threatened his lips.

Josie hated when he was right.

He opened the door right as she raised her hand to knock. He stood staring at her, and his arms crossed with a smile. "Yes?" he said slowly.

She blew out a breath. "May I please stay, my very smart and kind best friend?"

He stepped back and swept his hand to invite her in.

"Pipes are frozen, which means no water. Indoor plumbing is essential to my lifestyle." She stamped off the snow in the entryway.

The kitchen lights flickered one more time and went out with a blink.

"Well, we'll have water, at least," Max said, looking around at the house.

He threw on his jacket. "I need to make sure the backup generators are on for the sugar house. Make—"

"—myself at home. I know, I know," Josie finished.

Max chuckled as he carefully walked down his front steps across the backyard to the sugar shack.

He tried to ignore how happy he was that Josie would stay for another night. It had been a long time since they'd spent days back to back to back together. They would go to the movies, hang out, grab dinner, and lounge about his house on lazy snowy days. But essentially, living together for multiple days? He didn't know if they'd ever spent that much time together, plus half the time, she had a boyfriend, or he had a girlfriend.

He let himself into the building and verified that the generators were on. He needed to keep the building above freezing so the product he'd packaged earlier that day wouldn't freeze and ruin.

With a start, he realized this was the first time in a long time that they were both single.

He shook his head, trying to clear the picture from earlier in the day when he almost let his guard down and took her mouth in the snow. The curve of her mouth looked so perfect and tempting right underneath him, but she was his best friend. He couldn't risk it.

No one knew him as well as she did, and he selfishly protected their relationship. Since returning to Benning Falls, he had tried to rekindle friendships with other high school friends, but everyone was already settled in their ways. He'd thought about trying to date the handful of single women he knew, but it was always more fun to just hang out with Josie.

As he closed and locked the building, he wondered absent-mindedly if Mara had said anything about their breakup. *Probably not*, he decided. *It would be embarrassing for her too.*

He opened the back door of his house, and the delicious smell of pancakes hit him.

"I'm still starving from earlier. How do you do that every day and not eat your left hand?" Josie called.

The power was still out, and the house was dark. A warm glow shone from the kitchen. Josie was making buttermilk pancakes on top of the pot belly stove. He realized how easily she fit into his life, like she was the last puzzle piece clicked into place.

He saw her in her tousled hair, warm fuzzy pajamas, and no makeup. He'd seen her glammed up, and she could definitely wow when she showed off her curves, but he realized he also liked her just like this: His best friend. Someone to come home to who was already two steps ahead of him with even better ideas.

"Sounds great," he said. "I'm still pretty hungry."

He couldn't decide if a cocktail would be a fantastic or terrible idea to keep his hands off her, but he would suggest it anyway.

"Want a drink?"

"It's barely five."

"Yes, but the powers out, and there's nothing else to do."

She shrugged. "When in Vermont."

He made a round of rum and cokes, knowing it was Josie's favorite.

Max spotted the stack of school papers she'd grabbed from her bag. It looked like the remnants of the *We Went to a Maple Syrup Farm* reports. "Is there anything about me in those?"

"They said there was a nice man. That's all the mention you got." She sent him a sparkling smile that shot straight into his gut. He loved it when she was truly happy and knew teaching was her passion.

"What did Jason think of you teaching?"

"He was a big fan of my paycheck." She flipped a couple of

pancakes over. "He loved mooching dinner off of me, given he didn't have a job."

"I mean, did he like kids?"

She let out a laugh. "He *was* a child. Emotionally. So, no. I don't think he wanted kids. That was the biggest disagreement we had, obviously. You know I want them."

He nodded at her. She craved a family. Kids were her passion. She volunteered any way she could at the Benning Falls Elementary School in addition to her position as the sole second-grade teacher.

He handed her a drink, and they both took healthy gulps.

"Maybe we should make a pact." His heartbeat sped up a little, but he'd play it cool.

"A pact?" She plated a couple of pancakes and tossed some bacon and pecans on top.

"You know, if we don't each have kids by a certain time, then you and I will have kids." He shrugged to give himself an out just in case she laughed in his face.

She threw her head back and cackled with surprised laughter.

Annnd there it was.

"How would you suppose we make these kids?" She sent him a shy look that didn't meet his eyes as she poured more batter onto the pan.

"I mean, there's always a turkey baster or," he paused, "the old-fashioned way." He handed her another drink since hers was empty. Her cheeks flushed.

Probably from the stove.

"How badly do you want kids?" she said, ignoring the elephant that had popped into the room.

"I've always wanted to leave this place to somebody, and you know Kelsey isn't going to have any."

"Yeah, your sister's not exactly the kid type," Josie said as she held her glass and clinked the ice around the rim of it. "And our supposed turkey baster children would live half the time here and half the time at my very chic shared apartment with Brittany?" She sent him a slow smile.

"No, we'd all live here," he said, enjoying the fun of planning a pretend future. "When I go on dates, you'd watch the kids, and when you go on dates, I'd watch the kids."

"Oh, multiple kids. We have multiple now," she said, taking the frying pan off and setting it to the side.

He grabbed a piece of bacon and chomped on it quickly so his fingers wouldn't burn. "I mean, one would be so lonely. That's why you were over at our house, right?"

Josie let out a little laugh. "Yeah, it was always more fun here with you guys." She came back and chewed on a pancake as they stood in front of the fire, warming their hands. "All right, so potentially multiple children if we're not married by... what, seventy-five?"

"I think it'll be a little too late to have kids. How about thirty-five?"

"All right, so in five years. Turkey baster or the old-fashioned way," she said, taking a step toward him, and he mirrored her. "I guess we'd better shake on it." She stuck her hand out.

Max reached out and grabbed the hand that Josie offered. They were standing only a few inches apart, and he was distracted by her wide, sparkling smile at their silly pact.

Her skin felt so soft as his hand gripped hers, and it reminded him of the silky skin on her thighs.

He thought about earlier that day when she'd been underneath him, and he'd had to stop himself. He didn't want to force himself on her. Plus, she was his best friend; there was a lot to lose. If he made a move and she wasn't interested, it could put a foundational crack in their relationship.

She'd seen him at his worst, and she was still here. She

helped scrape him off the floor after he and Mara ended things. As he looked down into her heart-shaped face surrounded by flyaway curls, he finally let himself fall into the depths of her ocean-blue eyes. The kind of blue that you'd see in tropical photos, the type that beckoned you toward comfort and safety.

He had inched forward without realizing it, holding tightly onto her hand. He had dropped his arm, so they were just holding hands, and her face went shy. There was a flush in her cheeks from the heat of the fire.

She'd never looked prettier, and he thought what a terribly amazing idea it would be to finally, finally fucking kiss her.

Chapter Thirteen

JOSIE

Josie stared up into the face she knew better than her own. His hand was clasped around hers, sure and strong. His thumbs moved back and forth on her knuckles, and with each passing swipe, more of her defenses melted.

She bit her lip, not wanting to acknowledge the axis-tilting shift that was happening under their feet. She couldn't take her eyes off his mouth, the perfect bow-shaped perfection she'd thought so much about. A weight of anticipation settled on her chest, making her breathless.

He'd walked closer—or had she walked closer to him? And the light danced in his brown eyes. His head lowered to hers, hovering as it had done last time in the snow, coming so close.

She dared not breathe.

His hand still held hers, but she felt his other hand slide around her jaw, the weight of it burning into her. His thumb slowly came up to her chin, and each breath came out as a small prayer that he wouldn't stop.

Her heartbeat thundered in her ears as he pulled her closer and finally met her mouth with his.

Her breath caught in a climax of anticipation. He tasted

sweet and exactly like what she'd always imagined: a hint of maple, rum, and the scent that was just *Max.*

His lips parted hers, and she opened eagerly for him, bringing him closer. She'd wring every last drop out of this one perfect moment. The warmth of his hand cradled her head, and she melted into him. She traced her tongue against his lip, wanting more. Wanting to never let go.

He pulled away a fraction, and she gasped for air. His eyes met hers briefly before pulling her mouth back to his with a fiery urgency.

Yes.

Everything she'd ever dreamt of was right here. His hands climbed their way into her hair, cradling her head. Need shot straight into her core, wanting more, wanting everything from him.

She grabbed his shirt and pulled, kissing him harder. His arm wrapped around her, and she felt herself slide into his embrace so, so easily. His arms wrapped tight around her as if they were made for her to be there.

His tongue met hers in a surprise that shot electric threads straight into her core. *Fuck he was good at this.*

He licked her bottom lip, and a low moan escaped her control.

They both pulled back suddenly, dazed. She gasped for breath.

Josie seemed to be able to look everywhere except into Max's face. What was happening between them?

Just be normal. He's just your friend. Don't read into one kiss.

One mind-altering kiss.

She licked her lips, took a deep breath, and looked into Max's face. His arms were still wrapped tight around her, and her breath caught. She felt frozen in time. His eyes scanned her face with that scrutinized intensity from earlier in the day.

She dragged her gaze away from his eyes and bit her lower lip, trying to think what to say next. She pulled back, and his hands fell to her waist. Her wildest fantasy had just come true, but now what?

Josie was used to making things comfortable for other people, giving them an easy out so they didn't disappoint her. She laughed a little bit and took a step backward, her gaze going down to the floor.

"Jos," he said, his other hand grabbing her hip and keeping her in front of him. "We have to talk about this."

"I mean, this was a mistake, right? Just a one-time thing because you drank too much rum."

A smile threatened his lips. "I had one." His thumb stroked the side of her hip, and her breath hitched. She was gonna have a hard time concentrating if he kept that up. His hand came under her chin and forced her to look into his eyes. "Did you not like it when I kissed you?"

"Like it?" she said, staring at his lips. "I *like* felt tip pens. I *like* maple syrup. That was..." She paused, unable to find the words.

"Incredible," he finished. "You're incredible." His thumb traced her lower lip.

"I don't look like them," she said suddenly, her eyes in a panic.

His face was full of confusion. "Them?"

"Your ex-girlfriends. Mara: tall, thin, could fit in one leg of my jeans with room to spare."

"Josie, you're gorgeous," he said quietly. He brought her to him, her head resting against his shoulder, and leaned his head on hers.

He'd never been shy about calling her pretty, but she'd thought it was a "you're like my sister" kind of compliment.

"I don't have one type," he said. "Do you? Am I your type?"

Genuine worry crossed his face as he looked down at her, and Josie couldn't hold in a puff of laughter.

He was 6'2, had broad shoulders with thick, muscular arms, and was a romantic at heart... yeah, he was her type.

He was *the* type.

Her heart clenched. She didn't want to ruin what could be the one chance she had. He meant too much to her.

"You are obviously gorgeous, but I don't know," she said. "You're my best friend," she leaned back and ran her hands over his arms. She let herself squeeze them because, God, she'd always wanted to.

"You're my best friend, too," he squeezed back.

She sighed and knew what she had to do. "I don't want to lose you." She dropped her arms and stepped back. It was easier and safer to keep him in this box.

If she lost him, like she always, always screwed up any romantic relationship she'd ever had, she'd have no one. "I'm afraid." She realized she was mentally running away a million miles an hour. "I'm afraid that if we did anything, tried anything, I'd lose you forever, and you're my family. Well, you know what I mean."

He crossed his arms and chewed on the inside of his cheek. "You're sure?" he said, looking at her from his lowered head.

No, she thought traitorously. What she really wanted to do was shove him down onto the couch, straddle him, and finally fulfill all the fantasies she'd filed away over the last fifteen years.

"For now," she said, giving herself an out. Maybe there would be an apocalypse, and they'd be the only two people left. Even if she screwed up the entire relationship, then she wouldn't lose him forever. That could happen, right?

"I think you're just scared of what it could be," he said, shifting his feet and moving closer to her.

Chapter Fourteen

JOSIE

"Of course, I'm scared. I'm scared about everything. I'm scared about global warming, whether I paid my taxes correctly"—he huffed out a laugh at her—"scared that bears might get into my second-floor apartment because we live in Vermont, and those motherfuckers are crafty, so yeah. Of course, I'm scared of losing my closest person because I'm no good at relationships, and you mean a lot to me. If we did this, it would be..." She shook her head, caught in her emotions. Overwhelming tension clawed at her throat, and she fought back tears.

"Heavy," he said, stealing the words from her brain. He nodded and chewed on his lip. "All right. Just friends."

The rest of the evening, they kept their distance from each other. They were two tigers circling each other in a small cage, always within a ten-foot radius of one another but never getting closer than they had to.

After a few awkward hours, Max finally begged off to go to sleep. The power was still off and Josie had opted to stay on the couch again, given it was nearest to the fireplace. Max had a small fireplace in his bedroom that he stoked to heat the room so he wouldn't freeze. Maybe they'd be lucky, and the power would be back on before they woke up in the morning.

Josie fell into a fitful sleep of replaying their kiss again and again and again and again in her mind.

JOSIE BLINKED her eyes awake as a shiver woke her. She glanced at the fireplace and saw a dark, cold pile of ashes staring back at her. She looked outside; the sky was still black. A shiver retook her whole body, shaking it side to side. She'd fallen asleep in a sweatshirt, pants, and a blanket, but it wasn't enough.

She buried her nose underneath the blanket and closed her eyes, willing herself to sleep, but it just wasn't warm enough. She grabbed her phone and shone the flashlight over at the old-fashioned temperature gauge on the wall: thirty-five degrees.

Another shiver racked her body. She could re-light the fire, but she didn't know where the extra dry firewood was. She'd been too busy replaying the kiss in her mind to restoke the fire before she went to sleep.

Okay, I can sit here and freeze for another four hours, pray the power goes on, stumble around and try to get some blankets, or...

Her eyes traveled up to the loft overlooking the living room where Max's bedroom was.

No. Don't bother him; that would be weird. You kissed. Just grab more blankets.

She stumbled over to the hall closet where she knew extra bedding was kept and found thin, threadbare extra blankets worn from decades of use.

Fuck. She'd be a hunk of frozen beef by the morning if she didn't find something more substantial to cover her. She could try to build a fire at three fucking am in the morning, or... she sighed. Max had made a fire before he went to bed, the door was closed, and he was in a real bed. It was probably warmer.

Any embarrassment she might feel was shoved to the back of her head as she craved warmth.

She gently opened the door, and as she turned the handle and let herself into the darkened bedroom, a wave of warmth rushed over her, and she involuntarily shuddered at how delicious fifty degrees felt.

There was still a low light from the fireplace; warm embers were dying in the fireplace. It cast a glow over the plaid tartan comforter and four-poster king-size bed that somehow made Max look small. Max opened one eye and then propped his arm up. "Josie, you okay?" he asked with a gravelly, sleep-worn voice. His hair was rumpled to the side and she wanted to run her fingers through it.

"It's freezing downstairs. The fire went out. Can I sleep up here?" she whispered, even though it was just the two of them in the house.

"Of course." Max had fallen asleep on the other side of the bed, closest to the fireplace. Josie crept to the king bed, gently lifted the sheets, and perched on the edge of the bed far away from him. She was already starting to get feeling back in her fingers and toes.

She buried herself under the covers. The sheets were too far away from Max to be warm from his sleep, but she'd get warm eventually. An involuntary shudder shot through her one more time.

"You okay? You sure?" Max said, sleepy, and turned to face her.

She still faced away from him, not wanting to make this any more awkward than it already was. "Yeah, just cold," she said quietly. "I'll be fine." A few more seconds went by in trying to will herself to sleep when her body involuntarily shuddered, again, trying to warm itself up. The bed creaked, and she felt a strong hand grab her waist and yank her to the other side of the bed.

"Jos, you need to get warm," he said quietly in her ear.

The weight of his arm tucked around her middle, and heat emanating from his legs crooked into the back of her legs sent goosebumps of pleasure flooding through her system.

Max snuggled in, scooting her closer to him and settling onto his pillow, accidentally nuzzling the back of her neck with his stubble.

Feeling warmth seeping into her bones from Max, Josie closed her eyes with a smile, reminding herself this was temporary and decided to savor the moment.

A FEW HOURS LATER, Josie opened her eyes and realized she hadn't dreamed the last four hours. She was in bed with Max and his arm was still around her, but they'd shifted positions. She had cuddled up into the crook of his chest, and nuzzled her face against the soft muscle under her cheek. He was on his back with both arms wrapped around her and she almost squealed from happiness as she took in all the sensations of him.

She was plastered against his side and appreciated the warmth radiating off of him. She'd almost regained feeling back in her toes.

A gray, dim light peeked through the windows through the heavy flannel curtains. Josie's body had been on teacher's hours for almost a decade, and she guessed it was probably five-thirty or so, her usual wake-up time.

She glanced up at Max's face, and he was sound asleep. His chest rose and fell in large deep breaths, a small snore coming out every few seconds. She nuzzled her face against his chest, wallowing in his smell. She rarely got to be this close to him.

She closed her eyes, trying to memorize the feeling, the sense, what it felt like to have the weight of his arms around her.

Maybe she should get one of those weighted pillows because, damn, it felt nice to have something solid wrapped around her making her feel safe. No second-story bear would get to her with arms like these wrapped around her every night.

Max snored a little louder and shifted his weight, bringing her closer. He wrapped his arms tighter around her, and her body turned so one of her legs wrapped over his.

Maybe if she were lucky, they'd never get power back. She'd be snowed in forever and just have to live like this every day.

"Max." She whispered his name quietly. He didn't move; the gentle buzzing of his snoring continued.

Images flooded her head of what she'd imagined him doing to her in this bed, and she wanted him so badly. All the stars had aligned so she could be here, feeling his warmth and comfort right now. She'd probably never be here again and needed to savor it.

Josie reached up, pushing herself up closer to his cheek. She just wanted to feel the scruff of his cheek against her lips one more time. A simple, chaste, friendly kiss.

She brushed her lips against his cheek, and the gentle graze of his stubble against her lips shot straight to her pussy. She had to be honest just once; one time when it didn't matter. She had to tell him how she felt even though he was asleep.

"I want you," she whispered like a prayer.

As she pulled back, Max's arm tightened around her like a vise. She froze like a hunted animal, deciding whether to bolt.

"Did you mean that?" he said in his low, gravelly morning voice.

Josie's heart thundered underneath her, and she decided to

play dumb. So much for the honesty and bravery from a few seconds ago.

"Mean what?" she said quietly.

His head turned to meet her gaze, and his eyes looked like the stoked fires of hell, burning brightly. "You just said you wanted me, right?"

She licked her lips. Fuck, she couldn't lie to him, but her mind went blank. "I...I mean..."

As quick as lightning, he was over her, her hands pinned on either side of her head, his knees on either side of her hips. His eyes were bright and alert with hunger.

And holy. Shit. Was that his dick pressing into her as he straddled her?

"Josie, I am no saint. You've been in my arms all night and pressed against me so long I haven't been able to think straight. So I'll ask one more time: have your feelings changed?" he asked in a low voice.

Heat pooled in her middle, and she was gasping for air, she realized, trying to determine whether she was brave enough to answer with the truth. She'd thought of nothing else since he'd kissed her a few hours before.

Maybe it was because they'd slept entwined with each other all night. Maybe it's because his smell had completely enveloped her, and she didn't know where she ended and he began. Maybe it's just because she really, really, *really* wanted to have sex with him.

"Yes," she whispered. She stared up into his hulking frame above her.

His eyes glared into hers, serious and heated. She could get used to this new, sexy side of him.

He traced her cheekbone with his nose. "If we do this, you don't get scared. You don't run," he said, his low voice growling.

Her breath caught.

"I require a minimum of three dates, even if they're all shitty, even if it's weird, even if we decide to go back to being friends and never talk about it ever again. I'm not letting the possibility of you go without a fight. Three dates, Josie."

They stared at each other for a long beat.

Her bottom lip caught in her teeth.

Fuck it.

"Okay, three dates,"

"And one final thing," he paused, his hold on her hands tightening. "I prefer to be in charge."

Chapter Fifteen

JOSIE

She felt herself go wet at the feral hunger in his eyes. Where had this Max been hiding all along?

She nodded, not wanting to believe her luck. How could every one of her dreams come true at once?

"You have to tell me you want this, Josie." His tongue traced a circle on her neck as he buried his face in her nape. "I want to hear you say it, and I want you to tell me when you don't want it anymore."

"Yes…"

He pulled back and sent her an angled look, waiting. She trusted this man with everything she had and couldn't wait to see what he had in store for her.

"…sir."

A smile bloomed on his face. He leaned down and kissed behind her ear. "Good girl," he growled.

She arched against him, pressing her breasts closer to him. She fucking loved a man who took the lead.

His mouth was on hers in a flash. His tongue thrust into her mouth, and she met him with her own force. Each kiss was a punishing stroke, his stubble scraping against her cheek.

He thrust his hips against her, and the head of his cock hit the perfect place. She gasped, throwing her head back. God, she had been so horny for so long. She'd been in such close proximity to him for so many hours and wanted to sneak off to touch herself after feeling his muscles. Now he was here around her legs, and his mouth had made its way down to her breasts.

He yanked up her loose shirt and sweatshirt, exposing her nipples to the cool air. They puckered immediately, and his tongue licked each peak before he sat up, kneeling over her.

"Keep your hands above your head," he commanded.

She grabbed onto the headboard. "Yes, sir." She felt a drip of wetness run down her leg at her words. She bit her lip from the pleasure.

He sat up on his haunches, each hand cupping her breasts. "You are so fucking gorgeous it might actually kill me." Josie was very well endowed, and seeing herself spill out of his grasp as she felt so exposed had her squirming, trying to gain any friction she could between her legs.

He pinched her nipples lightly at first.

"Harder," she said, meeting his gaze.

"I am in charge." He leaned down and gave her a teasing, feather-light lick on each nipple.

She moaned in the delicious torture.

He leaned down to whisper in her ear. "I heard you moan for me Friday night." He nibbled her earlobe as she gasped in surprise. "I heard how wet you were as you wanted me to fuck you harder."

She met his eyes. "What did you do?"

He pulled his shirt off, and she gasped involuntarily. His muscles were thick, with a dusting of golden hair over them, but he was even bigger than she'd remembered from last summer. Each edge of his muscle was contoured, and his thick torso made her hands itch from wanting to run them over him.

He pulled out his cock, thick and dripping already.

God, of course, his cock was gorgeous.

He pumped himself into his hand, still kneeling over her, and a low groan came out of him. "I imagined fucking you as hard as you wanted," he grabbed her breast, "your tits bouncing from the force."

"Max, please." If she didn't have something on her clit soon, she would die. She writhed her legs together.

He dragged his cock against her breasts, and she couldn't take her eyes off it, of the sight of him over her. "Later that night, I imagined you were tied to this bed, and I ate your pussy until you screamed. Do you want that, Josie?"

"Yes, sir," she sobbed.

He moved like lightning and ripped away her pajama bottoms and panties. He kissed his way from her breasts, over her stomach, and down into her curls.

His tongue met her clit with a shocking tenderness, and he circled her with a slow, agonizing rhythm that had Josie in tears from pleasure.

"You taste so fucking good," he murmured, glancing up at her. "I knew you would." He grabbed her ass with both hands, lifted her up, and wrapped his arms around her. She was pinned down by his arms and made to take the pleasure he gave her. Wanting snaked its way up through her spine, her breasts, her lips.

"More," she cried again and again in a chant until he speared her with two fingers.

"Grab your tits," he ordered.

Fuck yes, finally.

He stroked himself as she pinched her nipples, his head still buried between her legs. She felt herself twist up until she was at a glorious cliff as he licked and licked and licked until she came with him on a shrieking cry.

Chapter Sixteen

The scent of hazelnut coffee woke Josie before she felt the mattress dip. Max waved the cup of coffee under her nose. She shot up, narrowly avoiding spilling the entire cup all over the bed.

"What time is it?" She rubbed her eyes, realized she was topless, and yanked the covers up. Her eyes shot to Max as he chuckled.

"I've seen it all, if you remember. Here," he said, giving her the cup of coffee. "The power turned back on a few hours ago, but you were dead asleep."

She grabbed the cup from him and bit the inside of her cheek. He leaned over and kissed her neck, and she felt the warm wave of goosebumps invade her body again. She leaned into the kiss and wished the moment would never end. He pulled away slowly.

"The snow's melting, so you can get out, but you should stay as long as you want." He squeezed her hand and stood up. "I have to go work, catch up from yesterday. The crew is here."

She took a sip of coffee and tried to get her brain to compute the last twenty-four hours. "Yeah, sure." She waved her hand. "Go do your thing."

She had promised him three dates, but he probably wanted to keep things casual, right?

He walked back to the bed and crawled over to her, where she lay in the middle, sheets and blankets tucked under her arms.

"Don't get weird. Don't think about it. Whatever you're thinking, stop," he said, already knowing her head was spinning into its own frenzy, putting up a wall between them.

Kneeling, he kissed her slowly. She leaned into it. His hand came up to grasp the back of her neck, and she felt the heat radiate around it as he pulled her closer. He pulled back suddenly.

"How about dinner tonight?" he said, his eyes searching hers. "Date number one?"

Josie took a deep breath. "Can we stay here? I don't want word getting out and everyone else knowing our business in case..."

He angled his head, sending her a stern look. "In case it all works out?"

"Sure," she said dryly, arching her eyebrow as she sipped her coffee.

"Stay as long as you like. I'll see you back here at seven."

A few seconds later, she heard him greet his crew. She snuggled under the covers, grasping the warm mug between her hands.

She let herself smile one hopeful smile as she replayed all that happened earlier that morning. They'd fallen asleep tangled up together, and Josie had never been happier. A nervous giggle escaped her as she threw a hand over her face. Visions of his head between her legs from last night flew back through her mind, and she needed to get out of bed before she got very distracted.

She took one more sip, and his words echoed like a reverent promise around her as she took in the cobblestone fireplace, the pillow that smelled like him, and her clothes in a pile beside the bed.

In case it all works out.

~

MAX

MAX POURED white wine all over the sizzling pan of bite-sized mushrooms. He knew approximately three recipes worth date-night status; his favorite one was chicken marsala. He glanced at the clock. Josie would be here in a few minutes.

Why did he feel so nervous? He'd already spent practically every second of the weekend with her and had known her for 20 years. She'd seen him at his lowest, including an ill-advised bachelor party trip to New Orleans, where he drank his weight in Goldschläger. He'd seen her at her worst, even though she was still pretty fucking cute.

A knock on the door sounded, and his heart thundered in his ears. What was wrong with him? Also, why was she knocking? She never knocked. And he was up to his elbows in ingredients.

Should he yell? No, that was weird. This was a date. He had to show her he was taking this seriously. He washed his hands and threw a towel over his shoulder as he jogged to the door. He threw it open, and his jaw dropped.

Josie was fresh-faced in a clinging sweater dress that high-lighted every single curve she had. Her cheeks were flushed from the cold, and her eyes were bright and shining if a little nervous. She clutched a bottle of Chardonnay as if her life depended on it.

"You knocked?" he said, sending her a warm smile, stepping back for her to come in.

"Well, this is a date, right?" she said, nervously looking down at the ground.

He closed the door, boxing her into the side of the entryway, and put his hands on either side of her head.

"This is definitely a date," he said in a low voice.

Her eyes went wide as he looked down at her. She'd fixed her hair so it fell in long flowing waves, much different than the floppy bun that usually lived on top of her head. She'd given herself some smoky eye makeup, and her lips were glossy. He was going to get that stuff all over his fucking face, but he didn't care.

"You look beautiful," he said quietly.

She stammered. "I like your shirt."

He loved this new dynamic between them. He could make *the girl who always had everything figured out* stammer just by looking at her with a wolfish grin. He slowly lowered his head and hovered above her mouth, knowing that he was torturing both of them but enjoying it all the same. "I like that dress."

Her voice was barely a whisper as her eyes stared at his mouth. "It's my date night dress."

He crushed his mouth to hers, unable to hold back.

All two decades of thinking about the possibility of what could be between them finally came out, and he wanted to taste every last drop of it.

His tongue stroked her lip, tasting the sweetness of her lip gloss and the musky heaven that was her scent. Her arms wrapped around his neck, and he stepped closer to her, deepening their kiss. His hands framed her waist, and his thumbs stroked her sides. His cock pulsed with wanting, remembering the goddess she'd been that morning under his hands.

No, be a gentleman. This is still a first date. He poured a bucket of mental ice water on himself and stepped back. Grabbing her hands from his neck and squeezing them. He needed to show her how it could be between them. How they could have the best of both worlds.

He pulled away, tasting her on his lips. "I might request you get a couple more of those date night sweater dresses," he said, his eyes running up and down her curves. He saw her cheeks go pink, and her smile took his breath away.

"Only if I get kissed like that on every date night," she said, still staring at his mouth. Her hand came up to wipe her lip gloss off his mouth, and he grabbed her wrist and kissed her palm.

Time to start their very first date.

Chapter Seventeen

MAX

"Something smells...done," she said, grimacing.

Oh shit.

He jogged back to the stove where the chicken marsala was now burned. "That's what happens when I get distracted." He turned off the burner and salvaged what he could.

She stood awkwardly in the kitchen, looking unsure.

"Josie, you're still my best friend. You can still do whatever you want in this house. Okay?" He smirked as he moved the sauce around, hopefully trying to rescue what was left of the unburned pieces.

She bit her lip and nodded. "I can open the wine?" She held up the bottle.

"I think we'll need it to get through this chicken."

They talked about their days, him trying to catch up on the farm and the haul of sap the crew brought in. She was catching up on assignments for the school week ahead. She had a busy week full of field trips and special activities for her class.

As they cut into their slightly burned chicken, he finally felt like they were back on a somewhat normal footing.

She took a bite, and he waited.

"This is interesting," she said, eyes wide. "How come you've never cooked before?"

"I've never taken you on a date before," he said as he speared a piece of broccoli.

"What do you normally talk about on dates?" she said, cradling the glass of wine between her hands.

"Crap. I forgot the candles." He hopped up, lowered the kitchen lights via the dimmer, and grabbed the box of matches. He didn't want her to feel like he was phoning it in.

"Ooh," she said, sending him a little wink. "Pulling out all the stops, huh?"

"I only get three chances to make this right," he said, striking a match and lighting a candle on the table between them and in the living room. "Want anything else while I'm up?"

"No, I'm stuffed." She still had half of her chicken on her plate, but maybe she was nervous. He sure as hell was.

He wouldn't even get close to the L-word tonight, but it hovered in the air between them. He knew he was a sappy romantic, fitting for his job, he guessed, but he loved love. He loved watching the possibility of two people finding each other against all odds.

So as he looked down into the perfect heart-shaped face that stared back at him as he filled her wine glass, he realized he'd been looking everywhere but right in front of him. Maybe on some level, he knew. He knew this was always the end game and was too scared to go for it.

The mood having officially been set, he sat back down. A quiet moment landed between them, and she toyed with a leftover mushroom on her plate. "I was thinking this morning about how I wanted to tell my best friend about this great guy I met last night."

Hope bloomed in his chest. "Yeah?"

She looked up at him with sultry eyes. He stood up, offered out his hand, and grabbed his glass. She stood, and they walked to the couch.

"What would you have told your best friend?" He flopped into the corner of the overstuffed couch and brought her down to sit beside him. He curled his arm around her and nestled her in close.

"I would have told my best friend," she said, looking down at her wine glass and thinking for a minute, "that he was very hot. Too hot."

Max choked as he swallowed a gulp of wine. "Too hot? Come on now."

She sent him a, *well, maybe* shrug.

'Too hot.' Well damn. "What else would you have told your best friend?"

She set her glass down and turned back toward him. He put his hand on her shoulder and pulled her down so her head rested against his chest.

"That he smelled amazing, he's thoughtful, and he's very, very," she dragged her hand up his chest, up to his neck, and onto his jaw, angling his head down to hers. "*Very* good in bed."

Well fuck me, he thought with derision. He wouldn't last another ten minutes with her next to him.

He claimed her mouth again. She was so tempting in his arms as he moved his hands up and down her curves. Slowly, heat built between them with each stroke. He let his hand linger at the top, swiping a thumb over her breast and at the bottom, giving her ass a territorial squeeze.

He was an idiot; he could have been doing this for the last ten years, getting everything he'd ever wanted in one perfect package.

He pulled back and looked at Josie. He loved seeing the low

flicker of candles in her eyes and thought his heart might break if it didn't work out between them.

"What would you tell your best friend about this date so far?" he asked, his thumb tracing her bottom lip.

"I'd say…" she thought for a minute, her eyes gazing up to the ceiling. *God, she was cute.* "…the chicken was terrible." He burst out laughing. "But the broccoli was nearly edible."

"Wait, hold on. My chicken is amazing. Everyone says so." He squeezed her, and she laughed.

"Do I need to remind my best friend that the man I made out with last night is *very* hot, and women are very cunning creatures? We'll do anything we can, including lying that the chicken marsala is delicious, for him to kiss us."

His jaw dropped open. "You said it was good."

"I said it was *interesting*," she said with a mischievous smile. "But, best friend, you didn't even let me finish."

"Okay." He settled himself back down, pride just a little bruised.

"It was all made up for because he's the cutest damn thing I've ever seen: he even made sure we had candles and a little red checkered tablecloth," She stared at his mouth with a delighted smile.

His willpower had been fully depleted, that fucking sweater dress under his hands, and he pulled her to him. She responded, drawing him even closer, winding her legs through his. He grazed his hands down to her bottom and lifted her, so she was straddling him.

Her hands framed his face as she kissed him; he hadn't felt this happy in so long. The taste of her wine-soaked lips coursed pure, golden happiness through his veins. He reveled in the feeling of her hair tickling his face as their tongues danced.

He noticed a consistent buzzing from the kitchen. It stopped and started again, stopped and started again. He pulled back. "You didn't bring a vibrator with you, did you?"

"What?" she said in a fog. "Oh, my phone."

She hustled over to her purse. "Brit. Hold on, slow down." She put a finger in her other ear as she listened intently to her phone. "Oh, um…" She sent him a nervous glance. "Yeah, of course, of course. I'll be there in ten."

She tapped the phone and set it back down into her purse. "Brittany's locked her keys in her car, which means she can't get into the apartment either."

He sighed. *The roommate giveth, and the roommate taketh away.*

"Want me to go with you?" Max offered.

"No." She glanced at the clock. It's already 9 p.m. and, you know, a school night." She sent him a cute little shrug and half smile. It was like a door had been unlocked, and he finally allowed himself to notice every single thing she did that made him want to haul her up to his bed.

He wanted to keep her here and make her coffee in bed again in the morning, but that was too much too soon.

"Right," he chuckled. "School night."

His hard-on had faded to a less embarrassing amount, so he stood up and walked her to the door, helping her put her coat on.

"I think I like this best-friend dating combo," she said as she shrugged into her coat. "I don't think you've ever helped me put my coat on before."

He turned her around and tugged her closer. He'd always felt a need to take care of her, and he finally let his hands and mouth do all the things he'd always wanted to do before. He gave her a brief kiss as his thumb swiped her cheek.

"Don't want Brit to freeze," he said as he pulled back. "Otherwise, I'd keep you here all night."

She let out a long sigh. "Despite being a terrible cook, you're very good at dating, Max." She put a hand to his jaw, and he leaned into it.

"Can I ask you for a second one?" he said, turning his head around and kissing her palm. She dropped her hand, and a smile burst onto her face.

"This week is crazy, but yes."

"How about Saturday afternoon? Hike at Bastion's Ridge?" They'd been on plenty of snowy hikes before throughout the rolling hillsides, but it would be fun to go as an official couple.

"You bring the coffee; I'll bring the sweater dress."

Chapter Eighteen

JOSIE

A week later, Josie hopped out of her beat-up Camry and tugged her dress down. She wore yoga pants and hiking boots, her long cute coat and sweater dress layered underneath it.

She checked her lipstick and hair in the side mirror of her car that was duct-taped together. Maybe someday she'd get a raise and could afford to buy something new, but until then, duct tape was her cure-all car fix.

"Creative engineering." She turned around and saw Max with a beanie pulled down around his ears, looking handsome. He was freshly shaved and in his regular hiking clothes, but he looked more put together than usual.

"If it's between fixing my mirror or buying school supplies, you know where my allegiances lie."

"Why didn't you ask me to fix it?" he said, walking towards her and bending down, kissing her cheek. His aftershave scent hadn't changed in fifteen years, and she closed her eyes, appreciating the familiar scent that always gave her a tingle.

He pulled back. "Hi," he said slowly.

She stared at his mouth. She got out a breathy "Hi," before she gave him a slow kiss. She adored his mouth, especially when it sent shocks of need straight down her, creating a molten pull in her core.

He pulled away and grabbed her hand. They'd done this hike a million times. It started as a way to sneak beers back in high school and eventually turned into their place, the place they would go when they needed each other's support.

"You look adorable," he said, tugging the hat that warmed her ears.

She had to agree that it looked pretty adorable. "Thanks. Finished it yesterday," she said, striking a pose with pride.

"Oh shoot." He turned around and jogged back to his SUV, pulling out two tall cups. "I promised you coffee."

"Doctored, I hope."

"Only the finest of Bailey's will do," he said, holding a tumbler to her. He grabbed her mittened hand firmly in his. "Ready?"

She looked into his face, and it felt like she was somehow living two lives at once. One Josie was on a date with a drop-dead sexy man who made her come harder than anyone else, and the other Josie was on a low-key hike with her Emergency Contact human.

"Why does this feel weird?" she said, quietly up at him.

"This feels weird?" he said, his brows pulling together.

"Well, you know, different. Good, but different. A good weird. You know, like me," she said, pointing to herself as she took a sip from her tumbler.

"I, for one, am a fan of good weird," he said, shrugging, smiling down at her.

They started up the crunchy, snow-covered trail. Dusk was imminent as the sun was already setting, and the purples and oranges reflected off the ice-covered branches. Josie snuggled her scarf around her neck and was grateful that she could knit a damn good cozy scarf.

They hadn't had a chance to talk the other night, their mouths being occupied with more important things, so when Josie spoke as Max said, "Are you—" they stopped and laughed. He squeezed her hand.

"I told you things might be awkward, but we're going to get through it." He pulled her closer, and she let her head rest on his arm as they walked up the winding sloping trail. She took a sip of her fortified coffee. "Go ahead," he said, elbowing her.

"When did you…" she started, not knowing if she could finish the sentence even though they'd already made it so obvious that they were into each other. "When did you start to see me as more than a friend?" She chanced a glance up at him.

"I don't know," he said, his rosy cheeks turning a little pinker. "When do you realize someone has become your favorite person? When you realize you want to see them every single day? When all the shared glances, all the laughs, all the support has accumulated into a mountain of possibility, and it's staring you in the face with perfectly pouting lips?"

Her heart thudded against her ribcage, and they stopped on the trail. The forest was quiet and glistening, sparkling amber refractions in the sunset. A gentle wind ruffled Josie's hair around her face, and he tucked it behind her ear and away from her sticky lip gloss.

"I don't think I realized it was happening until I was well and truly in it," he continued, with a quiet voice. "but I wouldn't change a second of it."

She chewed her lip so she wouldn't break into a completely dorky smile. He couldn't know how much she was completely and utterly in love with him. She had a solid fifteen years of pining for him under her belt, and she needed to put some distance between her and her feelings, or her mouth would betray her.

They'd stopped at a lookout point overlooking the forests below. He tugged her coat tighter around her, his hands lingering on her hips. She finally did what she wanted to do when they'd stopped at that spot so many times. She grabbed his scarf and brought his mouth down to hers in a brief, fierce kiss.

"You are such a sap," she said, her thumb wiping off lip gloss from his lips.

"One of us has to be the romantic in the relationship," he said, taking her hand and pulling her further up the trail.

"Hold on. You go ahead. I want to get a shot of you walking up the trail."

He gave her a silly look. "All right."

Sucker, she thought. *How many times would he fall for this trick?*

He got ten feet in front of her and stopped suddenly. "Wait a minute," he said, turning around. By that time, she had launched her first snowball.

She shrieked as he quickly rebounded a snowball at her. Packed balls of ice flew through the air until he charged her along the trail and rolled them into a mound of snow.

She loved any excuse to be near him, to finally touch him after all these years. He squeezed her waist against him and let his hands wander down her curves. She kissed him, sucking his firm, warm lip into her mouth and tasting him.

Maybe everything *could* all work out.

"I can't believe I fell for that," he said, wiggling her around on top of him; his eyes stared at her lips.

She giggled at the smile on his face. "That's why I'll always love you," she said without thinking.

Max's eyebrows shot up into his hairline. His eyes looked back and forth at hers in a silent question.

Oh.

Fuck.

Chapter Nineteen

JOSIE

Stupid, stupid mouth.

"I mean, I'm not *in* love with you," she said, panicking and pushing off of him, standing up and dusting snow off. "You know what I mean. We're friends–I mean, I love you like a friend and, um..." She started shaking her hands as if to try to explain. "Don't want to make it weird; just forget whatever I said. We should go." She spun on her heel and scurried back down the trail.

Shit, double-shit. The second date couldn't be the right time to tell somebody you've been in love with them for fifteen years.

Would he believe her white lie?

"Josie, wait!" he said in a commanding voice. "It's fine. I know what you meant," he said, catching up to her, but she noticed he didn't take her hand.

"Sure," she said, shrugging, her eyes focused on the trail in front of her, heading back along the snowy path to the car. The only thing that could make this moment worse would be if he also declared that he didn't love her.

This is what you do; you screw everything up. Even when you know the person better than yourself, you still screw it up. You ruin everything, Josie.

A chorus of *ruin, ruin, ruin* pounded into her head with each crunching step on the snow.

She glanced over him, and his hands were firmly tucked in his pockets, his eyes downcast. They finished the hike in silence as they walked toward their cars.

A few times, Max looked over and started to say something but thought better of it.

Think of something to say. He poured his heart out to you, and you acted like an absolute nutcase.

They stopped at her car door. "Hey, you know what? Just forget about what I said. Just pretend only the first half of the hike happened, then we were transported magically to where we're standing."

Max puffed out a laugh, took his hands out of his pockets, and grabbed her mittened hands. "It's fine, Josie." He tugged on her arms, bringing her closer. "It's fine, we're fine. We knew it could get weird. We're still on for date three, right?"

She licked her lips and nodded her head through her embarrassment.

"I've got to go," she said suddenly. "I'll text you about number three." She held in a sudden urge to panic and run.

She didn't want to hear that he didn't love her back.

It was only their second date, and she played it off like it was no big deal, but he had to know. He had to know she'd meant that she was in love with him.

He walked slowly to his car as she turned hers on. She looked in her rearview mirror and saw him hop in his car, looking at her with sad eyes.

Did she already screw up the best thing that could have ever happened to her?

. . .

A WEEK LATER, Josie wandered through the aisles of the Benning Falls bookstore. Max had a busy week with the weather warming up, and she'd been too embarrassed to bother him.

Her hands absentmindedly ran the length of the book spines in the warm, cozy bookstore.

"Hey, Josie!" Becca, the bookstore manager, sent her a friendly wave from across the store. Becca had taken over the bookstore a few months ago, and they'd hung out a few times as Becca settled in. She loved Becca's can-do, hell-or-high-water attitude as she adjusted to living in Benning Falls.

"Hey, Beccs," Josie said, waving with a half-hearted smile.

"Looking for something in particular?" Becca said, a stack of books on her hip and reshelving the ones that people had laid out along all the nooks she had created within the store.

"Eh." Josie shrugged. "Anything that will help me forget the last twenty-four hours."

"Oh my gosh, you should have texted immediately," Becca said, her eyes dancing. "Sounds very juicy."

"Don't want to talk about it yet." Josie gave her a small shrug.

"All right," Becca said, sending her an encouraging smile. "If you change your mind, you know I'm always down for some hot goss. Hey, I put aside a copy of that new sci-fi anthology for you."

"Oh, thanks," Josie said, smiling. It was nice to have a friend who appreciated her nerdy side. Who knew? Maybe Becca would be her only friend soon enough if she kept screwing things up with Max. Becca was flagged by a customer and sent Josie a small wave as she walked away.

Josie moseyed through the rest of the aisles; her head lost in repeating the events on the trail. *Hot kisses, the happy crunch of snow, and bam!* I love you *escaping my mouth as Max looks at me with horror.*

Might as well pick up some mind-altering sci-fi to escape the repeated slideshow of her failures. As she rounded the corner to the store checkout, she came face to face with none other than Max.

Damn small towns.

An unstated question hung in the space between them as she met his eyes.

"Um, hi," she said, her heart skipping a beat.

His eyes widened in surprise. "Uh, hey, Jos." His hands stayed in his pockets.

They were in the middle of the bookstore, which was busy for a Sunday evening. He bent down to kiss her on the cheek, but she stepped back with a head shake, indicating other people around. He dropped his and chewed his lip, unsure what to do next.

"In here buying a book?" he said after a moment of silence,

"Getting my vacuum serviced, actually," she said dryly, blinking up at him. He cracked a smile, and she did too.

"Always such a smart ass," he said as he held her gaze, sending her a smoldering smile.

He looked so good, even in his gigantic winter coat. His layered flannel shirt and Henley created a mouth-watering display that fulfilled all of her lumberjack fantasies.

"You?" she asked.

"Oh, sure," he said, nodding his head. "Came in to pick up my dry cleaning."

They both burst into laughter. His eyes held hers; there was heat and wanting behind them, but she still wasn't sure how to regain what they'd had before her slip.

"You remember our deal, right?" he said quietly. Anybody else looking at them would think it was just two friends running into each other and catching up. Not two people coming to terms with what could be the final puzzle piece or the nail in the coffin of their relationship.

"Yeah. Number three."

"Next Saturday?" he said. There was a weariness in his eyes that she didn't love.

"I'm free this week, early spring break," she said, shrugging. "So, I can meet on a school night."

"It isn't just a meeting, Josie," he said in a low voice, stepping closer to her.

Her hand itched with wanting to push his hair out of his face and grab his hand like she'd done only a few times before, but it had felt so normal and so right.

"How about tomorrow night?" she said suddenly. Maybe they could still salvage this. She could picture everything running out of her grasp if she didn't move fast enough.

He blinked in surprise. "Uh, sure. That sounds fine."

An awkward beat fell between them.

"Or if you don't want to..." she said suddenly.

"No, no. It's fine."

Manifest the destiny you want, Josie repeated to herself. That morning, she'd read a particularly inspiring quote on social media about deserving everything you want. Could she be worthy of deserving Max?

She squeezed her eyes and said, "Monday would be great," and blinked one eye open, looking back at him.

"You okay there, Jos?" he said slowly, smiling at her.

"Yep, never better. I'll see you tomorrow. Bye," she said, scooting around him and almost running out the door.

She had to get her head in the game for the third and maybe the final date ever with Max.

Chapter Twenty

MAX

Goddamnit. Max wanted to hurl his phone across the snow. That was the second guy to call off this morning.

The weather had warmed significantly over the last day, and he knew he'd need all hands on deck on his crew to harvest today's supply and get the trees ready for the next day.

They were starting their busiest season, but he couldn't blame the two guys for both being out with the flu that was going around. Better to keep everyone healthy, but it still meant everything would take longer today.

Shit, he might have to cancel on Josie. They were already in such a weird place.

MAX

Really looking forward to tonight, but a couple
guys called off sick, and it's a big day today.
Can we play it by ear?

The three dots of her text reply thought and thought and thought.

JOSIE

Yeah, sure

"Fuck," he muttered under his breath.

Why did they have to give in to temptation? Why did the power have to go out? Why did she have to feel so good in his arms?

He wiped a hand down his face in frustration. He didn't have time for mind games. He'd have to just take it at face value.

MAX

Okay, I'll let you know how today goes.

JOSIE

...

The three dots under Josie's name started and stopped, then started and stopped again. He let out a big breath and shoved the phone into his pocket.

She'd let him know if she needed something else.

Half an hour later, he was suited up for the chilly weather and headed out to the sugar shack. He needed to check his supply levels and gather buckets to change the taps in the southwest corner. He was about to head into the building when Josie's car pulled into the driveway.

He stopped short. He shielded his eyes from the sun, making sure he wasn't seeing things. Josie hopped out in her snowsuit, a tentative smile on her face. She'd braided her long hair into pigtails, and his heart clutched at how fucking adorable she looked. He'd wanted to make it less weird between them last night, but she had darted out like a deer on cocaine.

"Hey," she called as she crunched over on the snow to him.

"Hey. Did I miss a text?"

"You said you were two guys down," she said, smiling at him and shrugging. "We're still best friends."

Emotion clutched in his chest. *Still best friends.*

"Always." Their eyes locked, and she looked away, heat coloring her cheeks. "We're going to have to divide and conquer. Are you comfortable going with the guys?"

"Sure. Hey, Charles," she said, waving to the older crewman who had worked under Max's father.

"Well, hello, Miss Thornfield! My grandson giving you trouble this year?"

"Just the right amount," she called back, smiling at the grizzled old man. He nodded with a smile and a twinkle in his eye.

"Charles, Josie's with you today. She's filling in." He turned back to Josie, who had walked up next to him. "Thank you. I didn't expect this," he said, unable to take his eyes off her mouth. It was probably good that they'd be separated for most of today as he tried to get the day's haul in and bottled in time for their date.

"I brought my stuff in case we run late."

He blew out of breath. Maybe they were on more stable ground than he realized yesterday. "Good." He took a step closer to her and saw that his crew had started their trek through the sugar bush, walking from maple tree to maple tree, and were already several hundred feet away.

"I know you want to keep it quiet, but..." He chewed on the bottom of his lip. Her pouting mouth; it was just too tempting. "Can I kiss you in thanks?"

"Yeah," she said, looking up with a bright smile. He bent his head down and placed a gentle kiss on her lips. Just a reassurance, a payment of his interest, for later.

He tucked a loose strand of her hair behind her ear and stepped back so he wouldn't be tempted to do anything else.

"Just follow Charles and try to stay out of trouble," he said, sending her a wink.

"But I specialize in trouble." A sparkly smile lit up her face as she walked past. He enjoyed watching the sway of her ass as she walked through the snow drifts.

Yep, definitely good they'd be separated today.

For the next eight hours, Max did whatever came next: hauling in sap, putting it in his processing machinery, and bottling it up as fast as possible, so no mold or bacteria came into the syrup. He realized he'd forgotten to eat lunch as it was nearing six o'clock. They'd probably be able to finish up around six-thirty or seven. Thank God Josie had decided to come in and save him.

The crew had knocked off a few minutes before. Josie wandered into the building in her adorable snowsuit that hugged her curves. "Okay, if I take a shower?"

Max almost let a container boil over, the distraction of his thoughts of her naked in his shower and possibly joining her. "Sure," he called out, trying to keep his mind on the prize of perfect golden syrup. It wouldn't be worth destroying his day's haul after she came in and helped him out. "Thanks again," he said quietly to her.

"Just paying you back for your help in decorating my class-room the last seven months." She sent him a small smile. "Take your time. I love your shower." She sent him an eyebrow waggle.

He loved that she was already at home in his place. He wanted to see her there in six months, and six years, and six decades from now.

As he watched her trail up to the house, he realized with a thundering cloud of awareness that threatened to overwhelm him: *God, I am so in love with her.* He loved her soul, her body, every fucking part of her.

And two days ago, she'd said very specifically was not *in* love with him.

He licked his lips, thinking. It would be like losing a limb if they couldn't make this work, but he always liked a challenge.

Maybe he'd win her over yet.

Chapter Twenty-one

Josie stepped out of the glorious tiled shower and combed her long hair. She'd chosen cute but comfortable clothes to change into just in case Max wanted to do something bigger than just have an easy night in. Though she figured after a crazy day, he'd want to collapse onto the sofa and take it easy.

The concept of food delivery was foreign in Benning Falls. The population lived so far from each other that no restaurant offered the service, which meant they would have to cook for themselves tonight.

Josie hadn't thought to bring food, and she shuddered at the thought of going back into the cold now that she'd finally warmed up. Maybe she'd make them something.

The light was still on in the shop where Max was finishing up the latest batch of maple syrup. They had to bottle it immediately, and who knew how long that could take?

After the hellish day outside—how did he do this every day? —she decided some comfort food was in order. She poked through his cabinets and found remnants of potatoes, some meat, vegetables, and the ingredients for biscuits.

Josie liked to cook but hated making food for just herself. Leftovers only reminded her that she was single. God bless Susan Bard for keeping her son's kitchen well-stocked because she was sure Max didn't get all these staples for himself.

She absent-mindedly got out pots and pans, making herself at home in the large kitchen. The flagstones felt familiar under her feet, and she started a fire in the fireplace beside the kitchen to ward off the chill in the air.

Maybe Mara had stocked his freezer, she thought as she thawed all the ingredients. *No, they'd already been broken up by the time he was back.*

She thought back to the cryptic sentence that Mara had said to her. Josie hadn't told Max about the call because what would she tell him? "Hey, your ex-girlfriend was mad I was here, and she was totally bitchy about it?" Yeah, that would definitely win her a VIP pass to girlfriend-land.

A happy hour went by as Josie made buttery mashed potatoes, vegetables layered with the scents of garlic and onion, and braised beef; a whole comfort meal. The scents danced and tangled together in the air as she moved around the kitchen. She'd turned on the overhead cooking light and enjoyed the warm glow it cast over the bubbling stove.

She looked at the time, and it was almost nine o'clock. She considered bringing a plate over to Max just as the door flew open, and a cold burst of wind whipped in.

Max shut the door behind him, and his face flooded with relief as he spotted her in the kitchen. It looked like thirty pounds of anxiety had been lifted from his shoulders. "You're still here," he said, throwing off his shoes, hat, and mittens.

"Yeah, dinner's ready. I hope you don't mind that I made...." All the words fell out of her head as Max stalked toward her.

He stopped in front of Josie, both hands grabbing her, and

crushed his mouth down to hers in a fierce, claiming kiss that left no question unanswered between them.

Hope blossomed in her chest as she felt the graze of his stubble against her cheek. She kissed him back with everything she had, hoping that she could somehow communicate that she wanted him just as badly as she did a week and a half ago; she wanted to try to make it work between them. Her stupid mouth hadn't figured out a way to say that yet, or maybe she just wasn't brave enough.

He pulled away suddenly, and their eyes met.

"Sorry if you don't want—" he started.

"No," she interrupted him.

"No?"

"I mean, yes. I want. I want you. Oh my god, how are we so bad at this," she said, putting her head on his shoulder.

His arms came around her, and he rested his head on hers.

"I don't think *this* is so bad."

She chuckled. "I mean, this weird hokey-pokey that we do."

He burst out laughing.

She smiled at how much his chest shook under her. "What? You date second-grade teachers; you get second-grade references." She pulled back to look at him, a sparkle in her eye again.

"I know. You're just cute," he said, his hand coming to her cheek.

"For the record, though," She mustered up the courage to be honest, "I, like, really like it when you swarm in, march over to me, and take me." She squeezed her arms that had somehow found their way around his waist.

"And you said it was silly to watch all those romantic comedies." He raised his eyebrows playfully at her.

"I made food since I didn't want to go back outside," she said, sending him a pouting look.

"Absolutely perfect," he said, kissing her forehead. "Thank you. You're an actual lifesaver today. I'm gonna get cleaned up, but then we should talk when I get back."

She bit her lip. That had to be a good talk, right? He wouldn't storm in, claim her, and then say *JK, JK, just friends from here on out, you weirdo.*

"Sure." She put on a bright smile. He started peeling off his outer layers as he walked up the stairs, and she was reminded of just how hot he was. His broad shoulders strained under a thin shirt, tapering into a thick, muscular waist. The muscles banding his arms entranced her as he walked. Their relationship was worth fighting for so many reasons, but if nothing else, the man looked pretty damn good in tight clothes.

A short while later, Max bounded down the stairs in black joggers and a half-zipped long-sleeved polo, and Josie's heart melted a bit as she realized he'd even taken time to style his hair.

He looked stupidly, ridiculously handsome.

She'd just thrown her hair into French braids and was wearing a reasonably cute pair of yoga pants and the only other sweater dress she'd found. However, she had forgotten to pack makeup when she panicked this morning and tried to make her grand romantic best-friend gesture. *It's not like he hasn't seen me without makeup plenty of times before, but he did the little gel-flippy things with his hair.*

She could feel the strings of her heart actually being tugged.

"I planned to make the chicken marsala up to you with an early spring indoor picnic in front of the fireplace." He sent her a shy smile.

"I'm down for a picnic," she said, taking the biscuits out of the oven.

He sent her a nod and set up a flower-patterned tablecloth in front of the fireplace. It still felt a little awkward, but maybe a hopeful awkward. Josie plated their meals on the heavy ceramic plates, and the comfortable rhythm they so quickly fell into was not lost on her.

They ate in relative silence, with Max sounding like he was having an out-of-body experience every other bite.

He sent her a shocked look. "You've been able to cook like this the whole time I've known you?"

She sent him a very proud shrug. "We haven't dated before."

"Now I know I've been missing out on a lot of things." He leaned over and kissed her cheek. She pulled back and caught his eyes.

"I'm sorry," she said quietly. "For freaking out on Saturday and then at the bookstore, acting like I was possessed by the soul of a coked-up poodle."

"Seeing you leave the store without an arm full of books was weird. Becca asked if you were having some sort of stroke when you were leaving."

"You didn't—" she asked the unsaid question. Did he tell anyone?

"No one knows," he said, his hand coming over hers. He set his plate down. "But Jos, I want..." He paused. "This feels good, right?" he said, his eye searching hers. "I don't want you to feel like you have to run. I want to be honest with wherever this goes." His face looked at her with a tentative smile. "I want this to go really far, Josie. Farther than any fling, or any casual dating thing." He paused, licked his lips and met her eyes. "I'm only interested in forever with you."

How the fuck was he so brave? "You just put it all out there, don't you?" she said, impressed. "How do you do that?"

"Because I know you better than I know anyone else. If I came in and said I just robbed a bank, you'd grab your keys and ask, 'which way do we drive?' If I had really bad news, you would make me laugh, cry with me, and make a game plan because teachers always have a plan."

She felt an idiotic tear threatening at the corner of her eye and gulped it away.

"I know if something changed, we'd handle it because I want what's best for you, and you want what's best for me. The end," he said, slicing his hand through the air. "Full stop."

An emotional wave rolled through Josie that felt directly connected to her mouth.

"I lied to you a couple of weeks ago," she said quickly.

Why was she stone-cold sober for this confession? Her mouth had a mind of its own, though. "I've lied to you a lot, actually." Nerves tingled at the ends of her stomach and her shoulders tensed, even as his smile grew.

"This oughta be good." He moved their empty plates and grabbed one of the blankets from the couch. He threw it over their legs, snuggling beside her and leaning against one of the chairs. She settled herself in the crook of his arm.

She took a deep breath and met his eyes, her heart racing. "Remember that game of Never Have I Ever?"

Chapter Twenty-two

JOSIE

J osie took a deep breath and let the truth rush out. "I've never said *I love you* to anyone before."

Max's eyebrows raised. "But you dated that one guy for like a year. Cody?"

"Yeah."

"The worst," Max said, rolling his eyes.

"The absolute worst," she echoed.

"Not even to...who was that guy? The one who wanted to tattoo your name on his thigh?"

Josie laughed. "No, but..."

She paused, knowing this was it; she was on the precipice. Once she jumped, it was a free fall.

"It's because I was waiting to feel with them how...I felt with you because..." she paused.

Do it, Thornfield.

"I love you. I mean, I love you as a friend, and also, I'm *in* love with you," she rambled out quickly. She felt a small gasp in Max's chest next to her. "And I know this is our third date and, in theory, too soon, but I've been in love with you for a long time, and also, my god, I can't believe I'm still talking." Her hand came to her mouth. Maybe that would stop its chattering.

"Hey," he said, pulling her hand away from her face.

"It's just you were so brave, and then I thought maybe *I* could be brave, and, you know what? Maybe I was too brave." She sent him a dismissive wave and sat up to turn away.

"Hey," he grabbed her hand and brought it to his chest. "I also have a confession." His eyes locked with hers.

She felt she'd never breathe again until he either told her he loved her or to get the hell out.

"I also lied to you."

Oh no, no, no, no. This was her worst-case scenario.

"When you asked if you were the reason that Mara and I broke up."

"You said she didn't like you having friends who were women."

"Josie, she knew. She knew that I was in love with you even before I did. That you are my first phone call for anything, that you make me laugh the hardest, that my eyes linger on you too long when you aren't looking. She dared to tell me what I couldn't tell myself; I was in love with my best friend, and there was no turning back."

Josie gasped for air, not realizing she'd held her breath.

No turning back.

In love.

The words just kept running through her mind again and again.

"So..." she paused, her eyes searching his face. "...we're good here?"

A beat hung between them in the air, and he burst out laughing joyfully. She started laughing as delight bubbled up inside her. They belly laughed so hard they both had tears streaming down their face. One of his hands cradled her head against his chest as the other wrapped around her.

Every bit of stress that she'd been holding on to— that she might lose him, she might be forever by herself in the state of wanting more—evaporated with each peel of laughter.

She felt a kiss placed on her head. Just a sweet, simple gesture and her heart completely broke and shattered and glued itself back together at that moment.

Is this what it would feel like forever? Every day just handing her heart to this sweet man and knowing it would be okay?

His thumb moved against her side and grabbed her chin, angling it up to him. "I love you, Josie Thornfield. And yeah, we're good. Consider me your plus one for the whole foreseeable future."

"I just have one question," she said, a thought occurring. "When Mara called, she asked if you'd 'told me yet.' Did it have something to do with...this?" She gestured between them.

He bit his lip, smiling. "I guess I can tell you the whole truth. It's pretty embarrassing, though."

"Ooh, even better," Josie said, snuggling in.

"You remember that not-so-sexy bathroom?"

"The one with the spider cemetery that you had sex in? Uh-huh."

"Yeah." He repositioned her closer to him. "I was having a hard time... you know...." He gave her a grimace and waved a hand pointing to his crotch.

"Oh, yikes," she said.

"I mean, it was really gross, Josie."

"All right, all right. I'm not here to judge," she said, segueing back in, enjoying the story.

"Well, I needed to be able to do *something*, and as I was trying to get to the finish line,"—he angled an eyebrow—"I was having trouble, so I thought of you sunbathing by the pool last summer. And thinking of you turned into, um," he cleared his throat, "...accidentally saying your name out loud instead of hers."

Josie screamed, "Me?!" She would have been less surprised if a giant elk had opened the front door and sat down for dinner.

"Josie, it's always been you. And in particular, that one navy swimsuit with a deep v-neck cut. Unrelated question, do you still have it?"

"I have it, and I'll promise to wear it on our next date. I'm assuming we'll have one, you know, since you're *soooo* in love with me," she said, tickling his side. Her cheeks already hurt from her giant, goofy grin.

Josie thought she might expire from happiness.

MAX

"It's a date," Max said as he looked at his...girlfriend? He supposed?

Max knew the math he was doing in his head would terrify her. He was so in love with her, and he knew that he would propose in six months. He'd make himself wait—make them both wait—just to be sure they got all the worries out of their system.

Josie was excellent at inventing things to worry about.

It would be early fall in Vermont, and there was no better time to leap into new beginnings than the best season in the best place on earth.

He'd been lost in thought and hadn't realized that Josie had snaked her hand under his shirt, her fingers teasing at his side.

Her lips brushed back and forth against his neck, and he felt his cock go hard. He still hadn't *had* her and dreamed of nothing else since their first night together.

His hand came up to frame her jaw, his fingers sliding into her hair. "You have very good ideas," he said as she smiled a knowing, sexy smile.

His mouth caught hers, biting her lower lip. He kissed his way to her earlobe, and she moaned instantly. He tortured her, nipping and sucking while she squirmed beside him. "I want you on my lap."

She locked eyes with him and sat up, straddling his legs.

His hands grasped her hips as she leaned forward, bracing her hands on the couch behind him.

"Yes, sir," she whispered into his ear.

His cock twitched with want.

"Are you wet for me already?" His hands moved around her ass, stroking up and down, and she ground against him. He captured her mouth in a fierce kiss before she pulled away, gasping.

"Soaked."

His hand trailed up her thigh until it met her cleft and *fuck;* she was. His thumb found her clit with a hard press, and she threw her head back with a scream.

He kissed her neck and asked, between kisses, "How much do you love these leggings?"

She urged him on as he slid down her sweater dress until her tits almost popped out.

"I don't," she said, lost in the pleasure of his mouth.

Excellent.

His hands found her leggings, clutched the fabric around her pussy, and tore them with a sharp pull. The cheap cotton split in the middle, and he realized she wasn't wearing any panties.

His eyes met hers in an instant, a revelation, and she sent him a sultry smirk.

"Thought I might get lucky tonight," she said as she leaned down for a kiss. He hugged her tight to him, claiming her mouth.

He reached into his pocket and brought out a condom, tearing the package instantly. "Thought I would, too," he said, smiling at her.

Her sweater dress was pressed against her arms, and he gave it a final tug, releasing her breasts. He sheathed himself in the condom in one stroke.

"Fuck me, sir," she growled in his ears.

He almost came from those words but held himself back. He grabbed her hips and thrust into her. They stared at each other for that moment - the point where they were one, and there was no going back.

She started moving on top of him, biting her lip, and the sight of him fucking her through her leggings and her breasts bouncing was almost too much.

He looked up into her perfect face, full of such want and desire and love. He was the absolute luckiest man on earth.

They ground against each other, giving each other everything they felt, all the need and desire that had been waiting for so long. As they came together, he captured her mouth with a gasping need.

Josie rested her head on his shoulder, and he loved feeling her twitch with aftershocks around his cock.

"I don't want to know how you got so good at that, but all I can say is, thank you," she said and blew out a breath.

He laughed and moved her legs, so they were on the same side, snuggling up in his lap. He realized it was reminiscent of the fireman carry that he'd held her in only a few short weeks ago.

His thumb stroked her arm, and he nuzzled her against his chest. He felt so lucky he thought his heart might burst.

"You know what I'm thankful for," he asked as his head leaned against her.

"Cheap leggings?" she said, glancing up at him.

"I'm thankful you're such a klutz. Or you wouldn't have stayed the night, and then none of this would have happened."

She leaned back and smiled at him. "I'm thankful you're a worrywart and kept telling me to stay. Because otherwise, none of this would have happened." Her hand came up to his cheek, and he squeezed her tighter.

She sent him a transcendent smile. "I love you, best friend."

He kissed her soundly and brought her back to him, tucking her head under his. He closed his eyes, savoring the feeling of his best friend snuggling in his arms, finally, where she had always belonged.

"I love you back, best friend. Always."

Bonus Epilogue

Six Months Later

JOSIE

Josie combed a flyaway hair down as she stared at herself in the mirror, tamping down the panic radiating through her body.

Her new engagement ring glimmered in the bathroom lights.

Maybe this is a big mistake.

After Max had proposed last night, she'd had a spur-of-the-moment idea to get married at the courthouse the next day.

And here she was, about to get married after being engaged to Max for one, whole day.

She'd been riding the high of his proposal and just wanted to keep all the good feelings going—not worry about the cost and headache of planning a wedding in the middle of the school year.

And now on a September Monday afternoon, after taking

half of the day off work, she stood in a borrowed dress and felt all kinds of not good enough.

She desperately wanted to marry her best friend, her first and only love. But she couldn't let him down on their one big day as a couple.

Josie picked at the yellow lace dress she'd borrowed from her old roommate, Brittany. Luckily they were the same size and the dress was *just* fancy enough for the Benning Falls County Courthouse.

Max deserves better than this. He deserves a dream wedding and a dream bride.

A tear burned behind Josie's eyes when a tentative knock sounded at the bathroom door.

"Josie?" Max asked through the door, his voice soft and sweet. "You okay?"

Shit, shit, shit.

A sniffle escaped her. "Yeah," she said, her throat catching on the word.

"You're not having second thoughts are you?"

Goddamnit, it was so annoying having somebody who knew you so well. "Maybe," she muttered.

"Josie," he insisted, his tone nervous. "Open the door."

"But then you'll see me and it's bad luck."

"I'm going to see you when I drive us to the courthouse in ten minutes."

Josie reluctantly unlocked the door handle but held it still. "Okay, but you have to close your eyes."

"They're closed."

"Pinky promise?" She was stalling, she knew, but how could she get out of this mess? Produce a gorgeous size sixteen wedding dress out of nowhere by sheer will?

"Josie..." Max's voice edged toward frustration.

"Okay fine, fine, fine." She swung open the door and her eyes caught on Max dressed in his best three-piece suit.

Dark gray fabric flowed over his shoulders and nipped in at his waist. A vest underneath contrasted with his white shirt and dark tie. He looked so handsome she forgot to think for a minute. The suit fit every contour so perfectly it looked like he'd been sculpted into it, like a masterpiece. It was a relic from his former life in New York, walking up and down Fifth Avenue. She could picture him there, taking an important business call on the way to drinks. It was a far cry from the maple syrup farmer he'd turned into.

"Still there?" he asked, his eyes still closed.

"I'm here." Her voice was quiet and unsure. He looked like a model, and here she was in a second-hand dress.

He held out his hands to her. "Jos, we don't have to do this today. If you want a different wedding, just say the word. We won't do anything you're not comfortable with. I want you to be over the fucking moon when we get married."

"It's not that. I'm..." She paused, placing her hands in his. "I just think you deserve the best wedding."

His thumbs ran over her knuckles and warmth bloomed in her chest. "The best wedding is the one where I end up with you as my wife. That's all I need. Just my best friend by my side."

She worried at her lip. *Shit, probably have lipstick on my teeth now.* "But you deserve pictures and cake and people seeing how amazing you look. Your parents will be so sad when they find out they missed it, and maybe we *should* cancel but your sister is already on her way over from Boston, and now I've messed everything up." She rambled, her lip trembling near the end.

Max's family was a lot fancier than hers. They'd regularly gone on vacations to Orlando when he was a kid. They'd had big ski trips and big happy Christmases. It had been a far cry from the noisy, smokey trailer Josie had grown up in. Her family's idea of a big wedding was one with a fast food buffet. This wouldn't be good enough and his parents would never forgive her.

"If you want the perfect wedding," he said, eyes still closed as his hand slid up to her face to caress her jaw. "Then we'll wait for whenever you think the perfect day will be. We can get a big venue, invite everyone we know and put you in a big, poofy dress. Give you the wedding you've always dreamed of."

"But your parents—"

"—Are so excited we're together. Jos, we've never needed anything fancy. My favorite place in the world is up on our ridge together. My favorite moments are eating pizza in front of the fire, watching terrible movies. I'll wait as long as you want. If you want something fancy, I'll give you the wedding you always dreamed of."

Josie shook her head, leaning into his hand. "I never dreamed of weddings. I only dreamed of being loved."

"Well then that's settled." He gathered her up in his arms, eyes still closed. He kissed her, pressing her against him with a crush that turned her gooey. A melting sensation slinked down all the way to Josie's toes.

She pulled away. "But—"

"No more buts," he interrupted, "Unless it's yours over my knee. Now, can I *finally* open my eyes and see my bride?"

Josie pulled away and nervously fidgeted with her new engagement ring. She hadn't gotten used to the weight of it on her finger yet.

Max sighed. "Are you trying to kill me *before* we get married? 'Cause that's not how insurance fraud works."

She burst out laughing. "Okay, but remember this is a borrowed dress and maybe if we have a reception in a few months I'll look better."

"You'll look better when I strip you naked tonight." His husky voice and smile sent a thrill through her.

Josie sucked in a breath, eager for their wedding night. "Okay, you can open them."

Max fluttered his dark lashes open, and a light sparkled in his eyes as he took her in. An involuntary laugh of joy blew past his lips. "Wow," he whooshed out in a breath.

There was a sparkling moment as their eyes connected as they realized today could be the day.

He grabbed her hand and slowly spun her around. "I've got to take in the 360 degree view."

She'd curled her long blonde hair and could admit *that*, at least, looked pretty good. She'd inexpertly apply a coat of makeup. The heaviness of it felt weird on her skin, but it did make her eyes stand out more.

Max's delighted smile met his eyes as they reconnected with hers. "You look absolutely gorgeous. What's wrong?" He registered her nerves.

"No, nothing, I'm just—are you sure this is good enough for you?" Max deserved the world. He looked like a Ken doll come to life: muscular, handsome, sweet. He was the best person in her entire life, and she wanted to make it special for him. "We're doing this because of me, and I—"

"Don't you give it a second thought," he said, taking her hands in his. "I would marry you in the middle of a cow pasture, on a frozen tundra, or in a dingy county clerk's office. As long as there's a ring on your finger and you promise me you'll be mine, then you are the most perfect bride for me." He brought her knuckles to his mouth and placed a gentle kiss on them. "C'mon. Marry me today, Josie."

Tingles flooded down her arms. He could say that every day and she'd never get tired of hearing it. "Only if you say those exact words every day for the rest of our lives."

His eyes went wide, his smile growing, and in a flash he pulled her into his arms, swinging her in a circle. "Deal. No take backs."

A happy giggle escaped Josie's lips. This was really happening. She was marrying the man she'd loved her whole life. *Today.*

Max set her down, his mouth meeting her neck. "I still can't believe you're going to make me wait to go on our honeymoon," he murmured, leaving a trail of kisses on her skin. That slinking, lusty sensation cascaded through her again. This would never, ever get old.

"Do you know how hard it is to throw together a substitute plan with no notice?" Josie asked with a sigh as he nibbled on her earlobe. "Plus, the kids have their classroom spelling bee on Friday and I don't want to disappoint them by moving it."

Max rumbled out a laugh as he kissed her on the forehead. "Sometimes, Miss Thornfield, you should put your happiness before your students'." He pulled her hand, guiding them out of the bathroom.

She grinned and flipped off the lights, gathering her things to go to the courthouse. "Clearly you've never met a second grade teacher."

~

Josie nervously fidgeted at the counter of the county courthouse while Max finished his part of their license paperwork.

The rest of their wedding party was small; just three people. Max's friend Joe stood outside in the hallway with Josie's old roommate Brittany.

Josie checked her phone to see if Kelsey, Max's sister, had texted yet. She'd agreed to be the last-minute maid of honor and was driving like a bat out of hell to get there from Boston. None of Josie's family would be there. She wasn't even sure if her mom knew she was *dating* Max at this point.

Max handed their paperwork to the elderly lady at the counter who looked up at him with rounded, love-struck eyes. "You sure do look handsome today, Maxie," she croaked.

I feel you, sister.

"Thanks, Eunice," Max said with an indulgent smile. He checked his watch.

The office would only be open for another twenty minutes.

"You okay to wait for Kelsey?" Max asked.

"Of course," Josie said, giving him a nervous smile. She'd been good friends with his sister growing up, given they were neighbors. Kelsey was always the cool, older girl, teaching Josie how to apply eyeliner and use an eyelash curler. Josie had paid her back by taking care of her when Kelsey was super hungover after a college party and Josie was still in high school.

Kelsey had felt like family for a long time, so in a way, Josie would have family here.

"Number thirty-four," the secretary called out from the door to the clerk's office.

"That's us." Max looked down at Josie with excitement.

Josie debated. It was almost time for the courthouse to close for the day, but she didn't want to miss the one opportunity for Max's family to be there. "Maybe we should try again tomorr—"

The front door burst open, and Kelsey dashed through.

"I'm here, I'm here, I'm here! Did I miss it?" she said all at once, hair flying behind her as she dashed toward them. Max's sister was gorgeous, tall, and eyes followed her wherever she went, but her flailing arms caused even more of a ruckus.

"Just in time." Max grinned, pulling her in for a hug.

"Number thirty-four!" A monotonous, loud voice repeated from the end of the courthouse corridor.

"Want to see me get married?" Max asked Kelsey, his face lit with a smile and a mischievous glint in his eyes.

Kelsey huffed out a laugh as she bent over to catch her breath. "Mom and Dad are going to be so pissed they booked that month-long cruise and missed this. I can't wait."

"Hey, legs," Joe called from the corridor. He'd been standing outside of the small county clerk's office and had only just popped his head in. Kelsey's smile fell and a menacing glare replaced it as she stared him down.

"Joseph," Kelsey said with a curt tone.

"I'm feeling, like, some interesting vibes," Brittany, Josie's roommate, poked her head in. The tension between Joe and Kelsey was palpable.

What a motley crew to get married with.

"Come on," Max said, sticking his hand out for Josie to hold as they walked to the end of the hallway.

Josie bit her lip, still not feeling like things were right.

Something seemed off. It needed to be perfect when they got married, right?

As they got to the open doors leading into the civil ceremony room, Josie stopped and turned to him.

"Max, I want to marry you today, but not under fluorescent lighting with squeaky chairs and bad A/C." She squeezed his hand. "No offense," she said to the security officer standing guard at the door. He shrugged back at her.

Max shook his head and she saw his mind turning for an answer. "Maybe we could—"

"Well, if it ain't the two love birds," A gravelly, voice called. Josie turned toward the room and saw Charles, one of Max's seasonal workers, behind the Justice of the Peace podium. He had on his regular outfit of a shabby t-shirt, cargo shorts, and knee-high socks beneath strappy hiking sandals.

A smile bloomed on Max's face. "I didn't realize you were going to come to my wedding, Charles."

"I'm not just coming to your wedding. I'm *performing* it." Charles let out a chuckle. "My little side hustle is being a justice of the peace. Time's a tickin', though. There's a sunset with my name on it and I've got to be done here right at five o'clock."

Max turned to Josie. She saw the idea dawn on him the minute it occurred to her.

After a very minimal arm twisting and bribing Charles with three gallons of the season's best maple syrup, their motley crew gathered on Max and Josie's ridge as the sun set over the forest. Bright tangerine rays shone over the trees that were already beginning to change color. Splashes of buttery yellow birch leaves dotted the vibrant green of the forest, and Josie realized this was exactly where they were supposed to get married.

Charles smiled at them in front of the ridge's view. "Now, normally I keep this pretty brief because time is money, but in these beautiful surroundings, I'm feeling a little poetic this evening."

Josie clutched a small bouquet of wildflowers that Brittany had picked during the short hike up the trail. She looked around, taking a mental snapshot of her favorite people in her very favorite place, standing together with the best man she'd ever met.

If she died in the next ten minutes, she'd still have lived a happy life.

She'd found somebody to love her, and wasn't that all life really was? The search for somebody to see you? Someone to see all your cracks, all your nooks and crannies, and consider you beautiful still?

Josie knew that in fifty years, when she and Max were old and wrinkled, taking all day to get up to this part of the ridge, their love would be as strong as it was today. Hopefully stronger—they'll have witnessed each other's lives and said, *"Yes, I choose you every day."*

"Now, I'm probably the only Justice of the Peace you'll ever meet who's never been married," Charles continued, interrupting Josie's thoughts. "I've never found the *one* person who I want to wake up to every day. The *one* person to go on trails to nowhere with. The *one* person I'd take care of when they're sniveling with a cold, because I couldn't care less if that meant I got sick. Because, in my opinion, marriage isn't an agreement. It's not a contractual obligation, and you're *not* going to keep and obey one another."

A chuckle ran through the group at the idea of Max or Josie obeying one another. He caught her eye and winked at her, sharing the moment together.

Charles grinned as they turned back to him. "The marriage I wish for both of you is one where you want better for the other than you do for yourself. You want Josie to come out of this life better than you, Max. And Josie, you want Max to have a happier life than you ever thought possible for yourself. Marriage is an act of selflessness, and in that selflessness, we find love."

Charles' words echoed around Josie's mind, tugging at her heart. Warm, bright beams of the evening sun shifted, brightening Max's face as she looked up to him. Her love's face, who she'd do anything for.

Hurry up and make him mine, Charles.

"So, do you?" Charles said without additional preamble, turning to Max.

"I do," Max said quickly and firmly, without hesitation, looking directly into Josie's eyes.

"And Ms. Thornfield?" Charles said, turning with a mischievous smile. "Do you?"

An "I do," burst from of her, causing everyone to chuckle.

"Well then, by the power vested in me by the great state of Vermont, the county courthouse, and my own two cents, I now pronounce you husband and wife."

Three sets of whoops and hollers echoed behind Josie as Max grabbed her by the waist and hauled her up to him for their very first kiss as man and wife.

Josie whispered *husband, husband, husband* to herself all the way home. They'd gone out to dinner with Kelsey, Joe, and Brittany. Charles declined in favor of savoring the sunset. After many rounds of best wishes, they'd driven home in their SUV that had suspiciously been decorated with a Just Married sign and streamers while they were in the Burger Bar, Benning Fall's only restaurant.

Max's face had nearly split in two when he smiled at her as they'd gotten in the car, and had stayed that way the short drive to their home.

Home. It was really Josie's home now. Sure, she'd moved in a few months ago, but it had always felt slippery to her, as if something might go wrong and everything could change in a matter of minutes.

But now she had a husband.

And she intended to keep him.

"Is your brain done whirling yet, *wife*?" Max's hand covered hers as he pulled into their driveway.

"No. *Especially* not when you call me that." Josie turned to him, grinning. He leaned forward, unbuckling his seat belt as he kissed the side of her neck. She sighed into him. "I can't believe we did it. I mean, we're married. Just like that."

"Just like that," he murmured against the underside of her jaw. "It only took twenty years of friendship."

"Thank god for that snowstorm." Goosebumps bloomed across Josie's arms as Max nibbled on her earlobe. "So...what next?"

He chuckled against her. "Well, Josie, when two people love each other very much—"

She poked him in the ribs. Some things would never change and she was so, *so* happy about it. "I mean, how do you want to celebrate?"

"I was thinking a fire. But first"—he leaped out of the car—"don't move."

He jogged around to her side and flung the car door open. She eyed him, suspicions growing. "What are you doing?"

"Carrying you over the threshold." His hands were already sliding under her legs.

Josie looked at the long walkway to the front door and the four steps up to the porch. "Absolutely not. Max!" She screamed with laughter as he picked her up and closed the car door with his foot.

"That's it," he chuckled, doing his best to put on an orderly voice. "You'll be punished tonight for thinking I can't carry my hot-as-fuck wife to the house."

Josie hung onto his neck and held her breath as he walked up the stairs with relative ease. She fumbled around for her key in the awkward position and unlocked the door. He stepped across the threshold with her securely in his arms.

"And now we're officially man and wife," he smirked as he kicked the door closed.

"You are such a dork," she grinned, tightening her grip on

him. "And I love you." Josie thought she might combust from happiness the moment her feet touched the floor.

But Max hadn't put her down yet.

He walked to his kitchen island—no wait, *their* kitchen island now—and sat her down on top of it.

"You been upping your reps at the gym?" She joked as she slid her hands beneath the lapels of his suit jacket and under the bottom of his vest. She needed to feel him—had wanted to paw at him since seeing him earlier that afternoon.

"It helps that I regularly fuck you against the wall. I enjoy carrying you for practice."

Oh god, she did too. She'd been so nervous the first time they'd tried that, but she had to admit that being pinned to a wall by Max was unmatched.

He stepped back as he started unbuttoning his cuffs. *Yum.* "I thought I'd start a fire for us. First one of the season. And then I'll have my way with you until you tell me to go away."

"Or until 7 a.m. comes and I have to go to work," she said, giggling. "Whichever comes first." They'd take a proper honeymoon when the school had fall break in a few weeks.

He glanced at the wood pile. "Damn. It's low." Evening had started to fall already. He gave her a quick kiss on the cheek and started up the stairs. "Let me change and go chop some wood real fast."

"Do you want help?" She called with a smile, knowing what the answer would be.

"You'll just slow me down by ogling me," he shouted from their bedroom.

Max chopping wood ignited something primal in her. Something that wanted to have his babies and make soup and tend a fire.

And let him do whatever he wanted her to in bed.

As she started concocting a plan, he thundered down the

stairs in jeans and an open flannel shirt he was buttoning. "I'll be back in a few."

Josie hopped off the counter as her mouth watered. *That is my husband. Holy fuck.*

He swung the door closed as he walked out to the wood pile. It would *never* get old watching him chop wood, but she needed to strategize.

How can I make tonight special? She thought back to the lingerie she'd bought to surprise him yesterday. It sat, still dripping and tattered from their hot tub adventures last night after getting engaged. *This needs to be perfect. You can't have a hot-as-fuck husband and not seduce him on your wedding night.*

She mentally cataloged her wardrobe. She was a jeans and t-shirt girl, not a clingy dress or bondage lingerie girl.

But...she did have that one wrap dress. She ran upstairs for a quick change. *Did I wash it or is it still in the bottom of my hamper? Why am I not more prepared for my wedding night???* She had seven outfits for Star Trek day at school but a second set of sexy lingerie just for her wedding night? Of course not.

Josie started flinging clothes out of the hamper. She couldn't disappoint her new husband. Couldn't let him down on the one night that it really *super* mattered how sexy she was.

The wrap dress sat wrinkled and unwearable at the bottom of her hamper and she huffed in defeat. Her eye snagged to the view out the window—she could see Max at the wood pile from up here. It was a straight shot down from their bedroom.

Max picked up the ax and set up the first block of wood to split. With a massive swing, he split the large log into two smaller pieces, each flying in their own direction. He did it again, chopping the bigger piece into smaller ones.

A throb bloomed between Josie's thighs as she watched him, her lip between her teeth.

She thought back to the first night they'd spent together,

back when they were snowed in. Max had confessed to hearing her have a little *spicy* fun by herself, and though she was completely embarrassed, it had all worked out in her favor. He'd even said he even found it hot.

Maybe something similar could work this time. A sneaky smile broke onto Josie's face as she slipped out of her dress, bra, and panties.

Lingerie was great, but when your boyfriend—no, fiancé—no! *husband*—liked to see you naked, maybe that was the second best thing. Her eyes roamed the hard muscles of his arms as they hacked away at each block of wood.

Fuck, why was it so hot that he wanted to provide something nice for her tonight? He tossed down the ax and unbuttoned his shirt, his chest glistening with sweat.

Holy mother of hotness. Her own private stripe tease. The flaps of his flannel rippled in the wind as he continued to work. He liked to fill the basket before he came in, but based on how much he'd chopped already, she didn't have much time.

She cranked open the floor-to-ceiling window in front of her. A screen was the only thing between her and the cool evening air. Her nipples pebbled as the wind the air kissed her hot skin.

She ran a finger down into her pussy. It was already wet with wanting him.

Max hit another piece of wood, his arms flexing from the effort. The last of the light cast a glint on the sheen of his chest, sweaty from his efforts. Rippling muscles, full pecs flexing as the ax came down again, splitting the wood in two.

She tweaked her clit and let herself moan, enjoying being a display for Max. They owned the property as far as the eye could see back into the woods, so this show was for him and him alone.

His attention caught on her moan and he looked up, seeing

her behind the backlit screened window. A dark shimmer of need consumed his face. He ran his tongue along his bottom lip.

Josie grasped the top of the window frame and stretched lazily, giving him an excellent view of her tits. He locked eyes with her as she rubbed her pussy brazenly.

He bit his lip and shrugged off his shirt.

Yes. An even better show. Max was built. Hard work on the farm after years of personal training meant he could easily be a model. He had thick pecs that Josie loved to bite, a strong back with cords of muscles, and hard, flat abs that looked like he could break concrete against them.

She rubbed her clit, torturing herself, and threw her head back with a moan. Josie felt so fucking wicked being this naughty. Staring back up at her with sheer hunger, Max grabbed his ax once again and set another log of wood onto the splitter before slamming the ax down.

Josie perched her foot against the edge of the fireplace and lazily leaned against the wall, enjoying herself.

Those arms would wrap her up later. He'd make her come harder than she ever came alone, she knew that. She pictured his tongue swiping in and out, fucking her hard just like he hit the ax.

Crack. Another hit on the wood. It shattered into pieces. It reverberated into her core as her knees started to buckle.

"Max," she moaned, imagining exactly where his head would be later.

A curse came from outside. She looked directly down at him.

His eyes met hers in the waning twilight, hot and sharp with promise. He grabbed the bundle of wood in one hand, threw the ax with the other, and stalked toward the front door.

The front door opened before slamming shut, the wood

thrown with a clatter to the side in the kitchen. Every step Max took up the stairs boomed through the house.

He paused in the doorway of the bedroom, his bare chest heaving. His eyes drank her in as she leaned against the wall, arching her back with her arms above her head. Apparently being Max's wife made her want to be a siren, a sex kitten just for him.

He unbuckled his belt with a jerk, ripping it off in one smooth motion with a snap, and slowly unzipped his jeans so the head of his already hardened cock was visible.

"Fuck," Josie whispered, watching the bead of precum drip down his length.

The thread broke and Max charged into their bedroom like a wild animal. He crossed in two strides, and their mouths crashed against each other.

In a flash, his arms surrounded her. He invaded her, surrounded her, and she melted into him, his bare chest scraping against her tits in a way that now felt as familiar and necessary as breathing.

His mouth didn't leave hers for a moment as his hands moved under her ass. In one fluid motion, he picked her up and she wrapped her legs around him, knowing exactly where he was going, and he slowly, so *fucking* slowly, slid her down his body and onto his cock.

In the middle of their bedroom.

Josie gripped his shoulders, savoring her favorite sense of fullness, seating herself on Max's length. She clenched around him.

Max let out a long groan. "Fuck, you feel perfect on my cock."

Just the way he rasped out the words made Josie clench harder around him. Satisfaction crept over her as lust and need flashed across his face. He stumbled to their bed and fell onto it, keeping her seated on him.

His mouth found hers again as he thrust hard into her. Max trailed kisses along the column of her neck as if branding every inch of her as his. "You are so fucking sexy. And you are," he thrust into her, "my"—thrust—"*wife.*"

She could come right here, right now, just from being *claimed.*

He moved down to her breasts, his hands pushing them together, and buried his face into them with a moan. "And I'll be damned if anyone but me makes my wife come on our wedding night. Not even you." He stood, pulling out from her, and Josie blinked at the sudden loss of fullness.

A thrill ran straight down her spine and throbbed in her pussy when Max grabbed the belt that had fallen onto the floor.

"Hands above your head, wife."

Yes. She was in for a treat. Tingles flooded her skin. She threw her arms up over her head, more than happy to be back on this ride. "Yes..." *Do I call him husband? Sir?*

Her mind wandered as he walked to the other edge of the bed, jeans still flapped open with his hard cock hanging out covered in her wetness.

He arched an eyebrow at her as she paused, looking at him. "You still want to be a good girl?"

She bit her lip with a smile. He was letting her choose which they'd do tonight.

And she desperately wanted to be so bad while being his good girl.

"Yes, sir."

A satisfied glint flitted through his eyes as he wrapped his belt around her wrists and secured them around the bedpost.

Her heartbeat thrummed in her ears. What would he do to

her? She could always trust him, but the possibilities coursed through her mind like a raging rapid.

He leaned over and placed an upside-down long kiss on her lips, brushing back and forth against her. A promise of love and lust and all the best kinds of things. Josie darted her tongue out to taste him but he pulled away with a smirk.

Walking to the other side of the bed, he crawled between her legs, flushed pink with excitement.

"All the way open, love." He pulled her legs wider as he stared at her pussy with longing. "That's my good girl," he murmured.

He ran a finger along her sensitive seam, toying with her as he bit his lip. Pleasure clawed at her and she jerked against his hand, *needing* more.

"You looked gorgeous in that dress, wife. But this? Laid out at my mercy? Ready to come against my face? Perfection."

Her pussy throbbed at every word but her heart seized every time he called her wife. It still felt so foreign, new, unreal. But every touch, every glance from Max made it feel more real.

He settled his arms under her legs and wrapped his fingers around them, bracketing her in place.

Josie arched and pulled against the restraint as he blew a breath against her pussy, making it feel so good to be tied up. "Max, please," she moaned. She'd do anything for more. More of him anywhere against her.

"Arch that back for me, baby. I want to see your tits while I eat this pussy." His mouth slid against her clit and she arched her back in response to the curl of need winding through her.

She was desperate to move, thrust, but Max knew her, *really* fucking knew her, and he held her down in place. It would only make her orgasm that much better.

A moan ripped out of her and Max sucked and nipped even

harder, holding her hips in place as she writhed against him. "Fuck me, Max," Josie begged.

He lifted his head, lazily brushing his lips against the ridges of her pussy. "Be a good girl first," he drawled. "Scream my name when you come on my tongue." A slow lapping started along her entrance, darting in and out of her.

A freight train of desire urged Josie higher and higher. She wanted to ride his face so badly but he wouldn't let her, wouldn't let her move or do anything other than take the pleasure he ensured she had.

Fucking glorious.

She loved feeling exposed and sensitive and worshiped. His fingers dug into the fleshy parts of her thighs, claiming her.

Her hips bucked, seeking more friction as she clenched around nothing, craving him.

He slid a finger in as his tongue moved further up.

Yes, that's exactly what she wanted. She arched and strained, trying to take him deeper.

"More," she breathed.

"But you taste so good," he murmured, looking up at her, meeting her eyes. "I want all of you. Need to taste my wedding present and lap up every drop of it."

His tongue flicked against her clit, back and forth, as she cried out. Desire, lust, and filthy thoughts clouded her mind as she took what he gave her. She wanted to fuck every part of him, ride him, *anything* to give the release she ran toward.

She struggled against him, his hold just barely loosening so she could grind against his face as she spiraled higher and higher.

"That's it, come like my good girl," he rasped as he shoved two fingers into her and sucked hard on her clit.

Josie pulled against her restraint as a lightning ball of need arched her back and whipped her hips up. "Max," she screamed, higher and higher as she rode out her climax against his face, clenching around his fingers like a vise.

A blank fuzz sounded in Josie's ears as she fell back on the bed, wrung out and sweating from coming so hard her back cracked.

Well, I feel like a wife now.

Deep, heaving breaths wracked her body as she slowly came back to earth and Max kissed her stomach. "Next time, we can take a breather, but this time..." He leaned up and unclasped the belt from around her wrist, throwing it to the ground with a *clang.* Josie caught the fire in his eyes as he held himself over her with a wicked grin. "...I need to fuck my wife."

With a quick hand, Max flipped her on her stomach and yanked her hips back to meet his hard cock. His eyes connected with hers in the mirror across from their bed as he slid the tip into her. Josie loved the view of her ass in the air and Max's wide, rough hands on either side of her. His fingers dug into her hips as he slowly, slid home into her.

She clenched as he finally seated himself in her.

"Fuck. You feel so good."

Josie's breath had finally returned to normal after the hardest climax of her life. She smiled with promise in the mirror as she pushed up to all fours, knowing he'd love a view of her tits.

"Max," she moaned as one of her hands toyed with her nipple and she clenched around him, *hard.*

He cursed as he slumped over from the pleasure of it, grabbing one of the bedposts. "Christ, woman." He slid off the side of the bed, planting his feet firmly on the floor behind her, and drew her hips back as he plunged into her again. "C'mere," he murmured in a hoarse voice.

He drew her up against him, his hands on each breast as she arched her back. He still thrust inside of her as he buried his head into the side of her neck, eyes locked with hers in the mirror. His eyes branded her, claimed her. She was his and Josie had never felt sexier. He squeezed her as he thrust inside, her fingers wrapping around the back of his neck for leverage.

"Look at you. Look how fucking perfect you are. Taking this cock like such a good girl."

She shuddered with need at his words. Max had the best, *dirtiest* mouth.

Her tits bounced in his palms as he thrust harder and harder. "Give me another show," he ground out. "I want to see you again."

"Yes, sir," she breathed, her voice husky as the smack of him against her grew louder and louder. He growled in her ear at her words.

Her other hand went to her clit and toyed with herself, chasing her pleasure. She smiled, loving how wrapped around her finger he was. He might love to be in charge, but she knew what he craved more than anything: *her*.

The waves of need built and built as he pinched her nipples between his fingers, as he thrust again and again, getting faster, harder. His ragged breath sounded in her ear, full of lust and desperation. She rubbed her clit, lip caught between her teeth, eyes closed and lost in the pleasure of being thoroughly fucked by her husband.

"Eyes on me, wife." He said, voice husky with need. "I want you to see the moment I come inside you. Watch how well you take me."

Josie's eyes flew open and one of his hands moved to her pussy as his teeth scored her shoulder. She was being consumed, invaded by him.

And it was *perfect.*

His rough fingers flitted once, twice, three times against her clit before her climax rippled through her body and she screamed his name, writhing in his hands. His hand never stopped, pushing her past her breaking point, and she screamed higher and higher as her climax grew to burst. He thrust twice more into her, letting out a rough-edged curse before he curled around her, filling her with hot, wet spurts.

They paused, panting in the mirror, neither moving. They savored the stillness.

A shudder of Josie's climax rippled through her body and Max pulled her close, wrapping his arms around her. She felt so cherished in the heat of his arms. It felt like a welcome bath after a cold day, heating her from the inside out.

"I love you, wife," he whispered.

Josie turned to look at him over her shoulder. This man was kind, goofy, so sexy, and the perfect partner for her future.

And had just fucked her senseless.

"Love you back, husband."

A thousand sunbeams exploded in her chest as Josie realized this could be any night. Every night. *For as long as they both shall live.*

They'd have ups and downs like anybody else, but as Max gently laid her down and kissed her forehead before going downstairs to grab the firewood to build a fire in their room, Josie knew that her best friend would forever be her one true love.

THE END

BONUS-ER BONUS! Read four bonus newsletter-exclusive chapters, featuring Max's proposal to Josie (and a very creative use of a hot tub!). **To read, sign up for Elise's newsletter at <u>elisekbooks.com</u>**

ABOUT THE AUTHOR

Elise Kennedy is an author of cozy, spicy, heartfelt small-town romances. She lives in the midwest with her (very) patient husband and two perfect pups.

instagram.com/smalltown.romance
tiktok.com/@smalltown.romance